R

WHAT ONCE WAS LOST

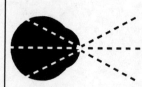

This Large Print Book carries the
Seal of Approval of N.A.V.H.

WHAT ONCE WAS LOST

KIM VOGEL SAWYER

THORNDIKE PRESS
A part of Gale, Cengage Learning

Detroit • New York • San Francisco • New Haven, Conn • Waterville, Maine • London

GALE
CENGAGE Learning®

LIBRARY OF CONGRESS CATALOGING-IN-PUBLICATION DATA

Sawyer, Kim Vogel.
    What once was lost / by Kim Vogel Sawyer.
        pages ; cm. — (Thorndike Press large print Christian historical fiction)
    ISBN 978-1-4104-6066-0 (hardcover) — ISBN 1-4104-6066-5 (hardcover)
    1. Large type books. I. Title.
    PS3619.A97W37 2013b
    813'.6—dc23   2013025239

Published in 2013 by arrangement with WaterBrook Press, an imprint of Crown Publishing Group, a division of Random House, Inc.

Printed in Mexico
1 2 3 4 5 6 7 17 16 15 14 13

For the posse —
We aren't "blood kin," but we are family.

A man's heart deviseth his way: but the LORD directeth his steps.

— PROVERBS 16:9

CHAPTER 1

Brambleville, Kansas
Mid-February 1890

"Amen." Her prayer complete, Christina Willems raised her head. Even after a full year of leading the residents of the poor farm in saying grace, she gave a little start as her gaze fell on Papa's empty chair at the far end of the table. Loneliness smote her, as familiar as the smooth maple tabletop beneath her folded hands. Would she ever adjust to her dear father's absence?

To cover the rush of melancholy, she reached for the closest serving bowl, which was heaped with snowy mashed potatoes, and forced a smile. "Herman, would you please carve the goose? Louisa did such a beautiful job roasting it. I'm eager to see if it tastes as good as it looks."

Louisa McLain, one of the two widowed sisters-in-law who had lived beneath the poor farm's roof for the past four years, tittered at Christina's compliment. "Now, Christina, you know roasting a goose is a simple task. But bringing one down so we can all enjoy such a treat? We owe Wes our thanks for his skill with a shotgun."

Wes Duncan's wide, boyish face blushed scarlet, and he ducked his head but not before he flashed Louisa a shy grin.

Herman Schwartz took the carving knife and fork and rose slowly, his arthritic joints unfolding by increments. Light from the brass gas lamp hanging above the table flashed on the knife's blade as he pressed it to the goose's crispy skin. While Herman carved, the others began passing around the bowls of potatoes, gravy, and home-canned vegetables grown in their own garden.

Young Francis Deaton watched Herman's progress with unblinking eyes, licking his lips in anticipation. He nudged his sister, Laura, with his elbow. "Lookit that, Laura. Finally get somethin' 'sides pork for supper! Ain't it gonna be good?"

His mother set down the bowl of boiled carrots and gave the back of Francis's head a light whack. Francis yelped and rubbed the spot as Alice shook her finger in her son's face. "Shame on you. We should be thankful for every bit of food the good Lord sees fit to give us, whether it be goose, pork, or gruel. Now apologize to Miss Willems for complaining."

Francis, his lips set in a pout, mumbled, "Sorry, Miss Willems."

Christina accepted the boy's apology with a nod and a smile. She well understood Francis's delight in the succulent goose. The poor farm residents consumed a steady diet of pork because pigs were the most economical animals to raise and butcher. They hadn't enjoyed a meal such as this in months — not since she'd evicted a ne'er-do-well named Hamilton Dresden for trying to sneak into Alice's room one night. The man had been lazy, shirking jobs rather than contributing to the poor farm's subsistence, but he'd been handy with a rifle, and their table had benefited from his good aim. Yet she didn't regret sending him packing. She'd rather eat beans and bacon seven days a week and feel that her charges were safe than enjoy wild game and have to worry about illicit shenanigans.

Their plates full, everyone picked up their forks and partook of the feast. While they ate, easy conversation floated around the table, covering the whine of a cold wind outside. It sounded as if a storm was brewing, but Christina had no concerns. The sturdy limestone construction of the towering three-story house could withstand Kansas wind, rain, hail, and snow. How she loved this house and the security it provided her and the needy individuals who resided beneath the roof of the Brambleville Asylum for the Poor. And what a unique group of needy now filled the chairs.

Louisa assisted Tommy Kilgore, the little blind boy who'd been deposited on the poor farm steps two years ago, and her sister-in-law, Rose, saw to the seven-year-old orphaned twins, Joe and Florie Alexander. Their newest arrival, a quiet young woman named Cora Jennings, who claimed her mother had cast her out, slipped from her chair and circled the table, refilling coffee cups.

On the opposite side of the long table, Wes helped himself to a second serving of corn and then ladled more gravy on Harriet Schwartz's plate. Observing the simple-minded man's solicitude for the elderly woman, Christina couldn't help but smile. Then she swallowed a chuckle when Francis stole a piece of meat from his sister's plate, earning a reprimand from his mother.

Christina held her fork idle beside her plate and simply basked in the feeling of family represented by this ragtag assortment of discarded humanity. Love swelled in her breast for every one of the people sharing her table, from chubby little Joe to gray-headed Herman. *Oh, Father . . .* A prayer formed effortlessly within her heart. *Thank You that even though Mama and Papa are with You now instead of with me, I am not alone. I will always have my residents who bring me such joy and fulfillment.*

"Miss Willems?" Wes's voice pulled Christina from her reflections. "Ain't there no bread? Need it to soak up my gravy."

Christina gave a rueful shake of her head. "No. We used the last of it at lunch. But don't worry. I mixed dough this afternoon, and before I retire this evening, I'll bake enough loaves to carry us through the coming week. We'll have bread with every meal tomorrow."

Rose turned her pert gaze in Christina's direction. "Would you like my help with the bread baking?"

The residents shared the operations of the poor farm to the extent their age and abilities allowed. Despite Rose's perky tone, her shoulders drooped with tiredness from dusting furniture and mopping the oak floors of the rambling house that afternoon. Christina squeezed the older woman's hand. "Bless you for your willingness, but I'll see to the bread making myself. And I'll see to the supper cleanup, as well." A soft mutter of protests rose, but Christina waved her hands and stilled the voices. "No, no, you've all done more than enough work today."

The others returned to eating with no further arguments. Satisfied, Christina pressed her fork into the mound of potatoes on her plate. Ultimately, the Brambleville Asylum for the Poor was her responsibility, just as it had once been her father's. She would honor his memory by meeting the needs of her charges as well as Papa had.

"Miss Willems. Miss Willems, wake up . . ."

The persistent voice cut through Christina's dreams, rousing her from a sound sleep. She blinked into the gray-shrouded room. A small shape in a white nightshirt, giving the appearance of an apparition, leaned over her bed. One of the children. Although weary, Christina chose a kind tone. "Yes, who is it?"

Hands pawed at the edge of the mattress. "It's me, ma'am."

Tommy . . . He no doubt needed someone to escort him to the outhouse. "Couldn't you rouse Francis?" Although Christina had assigned Francis the task of being Tommy's eyes, the nine-year-old often shirked his duty. Especially at night.

"No, ma'am. C'mon. We gotta hurry." Urgency underscored Tommy's tone.

Tossing aside her covers, she swung her bare feet over the edge of the mattress. The boy danced in place as she tugged on her robe over her nightgown and pushed her feet into her unbuttoned shoes. Regardless of Tommy's need, the February night was cold. Finally she took his arm. "All right, Tommy, let's go to the outhouse."

He pulled loose, stumbling sideways. "No! We gotta get everybody out!"

Fuzzy-headed from exhaustion — she'd plodded up the two flights of stairs to her attic room and tumbled into bed well after midnight — Christina caught hold of Tommy's shoulders and gave him an impatient shake. "Tommy, you aren't making sense. What —"

"I smell smoke! There's a fire." Hysteria raised the boy's pitch and volume. He clutched at her hands with icy fingers. "Please, ma'am, we gotta get everybody an' get out!"

Frowning, Christina sniffed the air. Only a slight hint of charred wood teased her nostrils. Tommy's sense of smell was heightened — certainly a result of his inability to see. She'd kept the stove burning late. In all likelihood the boy smelled the leftover coals and mistakenly believed a fire raged. She adopted a soothing tone. "Calm down, Tommy. I'm sure —"

"Miss Willems, please . . ." The boy began to sob, his body quivering. "We gotta get out, ma'am. We gotta get out *now*!"

As Christina began to offer more assurance, a screech rent the air, followed by a shout. "Fire! Fire!" The clatter of footsteps sounded on the stairs. Then Cora burst into the room and threw herself against Christina. "Kitchen's on fire!" she gasped.

Chills exploded across Christina's body. Curling one hand around Tommy's thin arm and the other around Cora's shoulder, she aimed both of them toward the gaping door. At the top of the narrow stairway leading to the second floor, she pressed Tommy into Cora's care. "Take him out and stay outside. I'll get the others." Trusting Cora to follow her directions, she hurried down the stairs. Papa's silver watch, which hung on a chain around her neck, bounced painfully against her chest, and she paused to tuck it beneath the neck of her gown before proceeding.

Her worn soles slid on the smooth wooden steps, but she kept her footing and charged through the upstairs hallway, banging on doors and hollering, "Fire! Grab whatever you can and get out! Everyone out!"

Doors popped open. Panicked voices filled the air. The pounding of feet on pine floorboards competed with cries of alarm. Assured that everyone was alerted and moving, Christina hurried to the ground floor. Smoke created a murky curtain, but she fought her way through it and flung the front door open. Frigid night air swept in, blessedly sweet, but a *whoosh* sounded from the opposite side of the house. Flames exploded behind the kitchen doorway, then attacked the wooden frame, taking on the appearance of dancing tongues. Would the floorboards catch fire and carry those hungry flames to the front door?

Her ears ringing with the fierce beating of her heart, Christina waved to the people on the stairs. "Hurry! Hurry!"

Louisa and Rose hastened past with clothing draped over their arms. Alice and her children followed, also carrying an assortment of pants, shirts, and dresses, the sleeves of which dangled toward the floor, threatening to trip them. Joe and Florie trailed Alice's family. Empty-handed, the pair wailed and clung to each other. Florie reached for Christina.

"Outside!" Christina commanded, giving the little girl a push toward the porch. She longed to comfort the distraught child, but comforting would have to wait — safety came first. Fear turned her mouth to cotton, but she continued to encourage her charges to hurry, hurry.

Cora, clothing draped over her shoulder, thumped down the stairs with Tommy hanging on to her arm. As the pair passed, Christina said, "Get buckets from the barn and start a bucket brigade. Alice, Louisa, and Rose will help you." Cora shot Christina a look of abject anguish, but she nodded as she stumbled out the door. Christina tried to count the number of people in the yard, but the darkness hindered her. Who hadn't yet escaped?

Heavy footsteps captured her attention, and she turned to spot Wes clopping down the stairs in his ungainly lope. He'd taken the time to dress, but his suspenders hung beside his knees, and his feet were bare. He reached the doorway and paused beside Christina, his wild-eyed gaze searching the yard. Then he grabbed the doorjamb with both hands. "Where's Herman? An' Harriet?"

Only two people slept on the main floor of the poor farm residence — Herman and Harriet Schwartz. Herman's advanced arthritis made climbing the stairs too difficult for him. Christina had been pleased to offer the elderly couple the small room, tucked beside the added-on kitchen as quarters for a maid.

She clapped her hands to her cheeks in horror. The kitchen was completely engulfed. She wouldn't be able to reach their room without running through the flames. "Oh, Lord, no . . . please, no," she moaned as helplessness sagged her shoulders.

Realization registered on Wes's square face. Although he was more than twenty years old, his simple mind gave him the reckless impulsivity of a child. With a strangled cry, he pushed off from the doorframe and scrambled in the direction of the kitchen. "Herman! Harriet!"

Christina raced after him and caught the back of his flannel shirt. "Wes! No!" He struggled against her grip, drawing her along with him. They tussled so close to the crackling flames that the heat scorched Christina's face and her body even through her heavy robe. Gasping for breath, she tried valiantly to pull Wes back, but he was too strong for her. He broke free and stumbled to the doorway with its dancing circle of fire.

CHAPTER 2

Wes stood illuminated by the bright flames, shoulders heaving and hands flying erratically as if swatting at bats, while ribbons of orange and yellow snaked their way up the varnished wood trim on either side of the door. His anguished wails carried over the crackle and snap of the flames. "Herman! Harriet!"

Choking on the smoke, Christina staggered after him. She wrapped both arms around his middle and tugged. Although he continued to cry in harsh, hiccuping sobs, he allowed her to draw him through the sitting room and into the yard, where they collapsed — Christina half on top of Wes's inert form — on the snow-dusted grass. Her lungs ached from breathing smoke, and her heart ached at the thought of dear Herman and Harriet trapped in their room, helpless against the onslaught. She squeezed her eyes shut and battled the desire to join Wes in wails of sorrow.

"M-Miss Willems? You will be all right?"

At the sound of the gravelly, weak voice, Christina lifted her head from Wes's shoulder. Herman stood a few feet away, his wrinkled face wreathed in worry. Harriet hovered near her husband, wringing her hands. Christina let out a gasp of relief and joy.

"Soon as we smell smoke, I push the missus out the window. Then I fall out behind her." He touched a bleeding scrape on his forehead, wincing. "I want to tell you the place, it is burning, but the stairs . . . All I could do just to walk 'round the house to the front."

Wes jolted upright, pushing Christina aside, and staggered across the grass. He threw his arms around Herman and buried his head in the curve of Herman's shoulder, sobbing. Christina crossed to Harriet and folded the woman in an embrace. *Thank You, Lord. Thank You . . .* Relief at finding the couple safe nearly buckled her knees. But she couldn't collapse. She had work to do.

She grabbed Wes's sleeve again and gave a mighty yank. "Come help with the buckets, Wes!"

Harriet and Herman took charge of the

children, and Christina and Wes raced behind the house. Cora, Louisa, Rose, and Alice had formed a line with Cora closest to the flames and Alice at the well. Wes took over dropping the empty buckets into the well's depths and hauling them up, and Christina joined Cora at the front of the line. Christina's arms ached, but she continued tossing bucketfuls of icy water onto the blazing walls until the roar died and only red-orange eyes of embers glowed from the charred shell of the kitchen.

With a heaving sigh, she let the last bucket fall from her numb hands and then sank onto the cold ground. Immediately the poor farm residents surrounded her. Florie and Joe dropped into her lap and clung. Hands patted her shoulders, and fingers clutched her arms. A chorus of voices — some crying, others comforting — filled her ears. In a huddled mass they held on to one another as the wintry wind chilled their frames.

Florie twisted around and cupped Christina's face in her small hands. "Miss Willems," — tears streaked the child's round cheeks — "where're we gonna live now?"

Christina drew in a ragged breath. She searched her mind for an answer but found nothing that would offer even a smidgen of consolation to the bereft souls shivering in the February air. She hung her head, closing her eyes against the sting of tears. *What should I do? Oh, Papa, how I wish God had answered my prayers to heal you from that respiratory illness. I need you now . . .*

"Miss Willems, I'm c-c-cold." Joe hugged himself and burrowed against Christina's side. "Can we go in?"

Christina glanced at the shivering bunch. Their nightclothes offered no protection from the cold. They needed shelter or they might all fall ill. The house's sturdy limestone walls had prevented the fire from consuming more than the wood-framed addition, but smoke would penetrate every room. They shouldn't go inside. There was only one other place of refuge.

She gently set the twins aside and struggled to her feet. "Let's go to the barn." She herded the group across the hard-packed, uneven yard to the large rock structure at the back corner of the property. When she and her father had moved into the house eighteen years ago, following Mama's death, Papa had bemoaned the distance between the house and the barn, stating how much smarter the Russian Mennonites were to build a barn attached to the house for ease in caring for the animals. Christina had agreed with Papa then, but now she thanked God the original owners hadn't followed the Russian Mennonite practice. If the barn had filled with smoke, too, they'd have nowhere to go.

The barn's interior, redolent of fragrant hay and musky animal scent, offered immediate comfort. Its walls of thick limestone blocks held the wind at bay, and Christina instantly felt warmer even though her breath hung in a little cloud before her face. She turned to Wes. "Can you light a lantern, please?"

At the spark from the flint, little Florie began to cry again and buried her face against Christina's middle. Christina understood — the tiny flicker on the lantern's wick now seemed sinister after witnessing the ravenous flames devouring the kitchen. But they'd need light to get settled, so she gave Florie a few consoling pats and told Wes, "Put the lantern on its hook there. Thank you. Now everyone gather near."

The others shuffled close. Their expectant faces looked at Christina, awaiting her directions. Tiredness — and responsibility — weighted her shoulders. They depended on her. She had to do something to assure them they'd all be fine. But where could she find assurance when only hopelessness crowded her troubled mind? Papa's voice crept through her memory. *"When in doubt, Christina, go to the Father. He alone has the answers to life's ponderings."*

She pulled in a shuddering breath — how her chest ached — and held her hands out to the two standing closest. Florie took one, Louisa the other. With out a word of instruction, they formed a circle and bowed their heads in readiness for Christina's petitions to the Lord.

"Heavenly Father . . . ," her voice rasped, the words scraping painfully against her dry throat. "Thank You for Your hand of protection and for allowing us to escape." A murmur swept through the small throng — thank-yous and soft sobs. "You brought us safely from the fire, and now we trust You to continue to shelter us, just as You have in the past." She injected confidence in her tone even as her insides trembled. They couldn't live in the barn! "Please guide us" — *Oh, Lord, please, please!* — "and meet our needs. I place Herman and Harriet, Alice, Laura and Francis, Louisa and Rose, Cora, Florie and Joe, Wes, and Tommy in Your capable, caring hands. In Your Son's precious name, I pray. Amen."

A chorus of *amen*s echoed. Then Florie tugged on Christina's hand. "Miss Willems,

25

you didn't say your name."

Puzzled, Christina frowned at the child.

The little girl pursed her lips. "You put all of us in God's hands, but you didn't put you in His hands."

The child's innocent statement raised a warmth in the center of Christina's chest. Peace flooded her, bringing a rush of grateful tears. She gave Florie a hug. "Honey, I'm always in God's hands." She swept a glance across the sad faces. "We all are." She straightened, drawing on the strength her father had taught her was always available. "Alice, I know you carried out some clothing. Can you dole out articles to everyone? We need to wear something warmer than nightclothes if we're to spend the night out here."

The thin-faced woman's eyes lit, seemingly relieved to have something to do. "Surely, Miss Willems." Alice bustled to the pile of garments lying on the barn floor. Her children and the Alexander twins scampered after her, their bare feet scuffing up bits of hay.

Louisa McLain leaned close to Christina and whispered, "Rose and I carted out clothes, too, and we can share with Harriet, of course, if need be. But I got a look at the things Alice brought, and they're mostly for

26

youngsters. None of us thought to grab shoes, and we don't have anything at all for the menfolk, I'm afraid."

Christina nibbled her lip. Wes had pulled on britches and a shirt over his long johns before leaving his room, but his bare toes had a bluish hue. Herman and Harriet huddled together in striped nightshirts, thick stockings covering their feet. The men would need britches and shirts, and everyone needed shoes quickly. They couldn't enter the house and scavenge for belongings — it wasn't safe — so the only place to find what she needed was in town.

Although she hated to leave the security of the barn and take the others out into the cold, she had little choice. Needs had to be met, and she couldn't see to them here on the farm.

Christina touched Louisa's arm. "As soon as we've dressed as warmly as possible, I'll have Wes hitch the team. We'll go into town. I'm sure people will offer us refuge until the house can be rebuilt."

Louisa's brow pinched. "I've heard some of the folks in Brambleville weren't too pleased about this fine house being made into a home for the destitute. They might turn us away, just as the innkeeper did to Mary and Joseph in Bethlehem."

27

Indignation raised Christina's chin. Let the townspeople try to leave her charges out in the cold! "I assure you, Louisa, we'll be taken in." She flung her arm around the older woman's shoulders and offered an assuring squeeze. "The good Lord provides a nest for the sparrow, and He won't leave His children in need of shelter."

Worry tried to eat a hole through Christina's stomach as she aimed the wagon north out of town. The *clop, clop* of horses' hoofs on frozen ground echoed across the lonely countryside. Only one poor farm inhabitant huddled in the back in the mound of hay — Tommy. Scarred, blind Tommy. Frustration rolled through her chest. He was just a little boy in need of care. Why did people find it so easy to turn him away?

She flicked the reins, urging the horses to pick up their pace. Dawn would break soon. Already the sky's velvety black was changing to a steel gray in the east. She'd promised the boardinghouse owner that she and Cora would prepare meals for her boarders — starting with today's breakfast — in exchange for a tiny sleeping room. So finding a place for Tommy *soon* was imperative. Lifting her face to the bright moon hovering just above the treetops, she whispered a fervent prayer. "Lord, the mill owner is our last hope. Please soften his heart."

"Ma'am?" Tommy's quavering voice carried on the icy wind.

Without turning around, Christina answered. "What do you need, Tommy?"

"I'm scared."

So was she. But she couldn't let Tommy know. Clutching the reins with one hand, she reached behind her with the other and found Tommy's head. She gave his tousled hair a gentle stroke. "It'll be all right. You wait and see." *Lord, let me be telling this boy the truth. He's already suffered so much loss.*

The lane leading to Jonnson Millworks curved to the right, illuminated by the moon shimmering blue on the wisps of remaining snow. With a firm tug on the reins, she guided the horses to take the turn. Minutes later she brought the team to a halt outside a long, nearly flat-pitched house with a railed porch running its full length. Wide, whitewashed boards ran up and down with narrow strips of wood nailed over each seam. Glass windows reflected the muted predawn light. Although far from pretentious, the house looked sturdy and welcoming.

Christina set the brake and held her borrowed skirt above her ankles as she climbed down. She then tapped Tommy's shoulder. "Come on out."

The boy cringed. "You sure I oughta? Might be better if they don't know who's wantin' to stay with 'em."

Pain seared Christina's heart. She resented the way people recoiled from Tommy. The boy couldn't see their reaction, but his acute hearing couldn't miss the startled gasps or dismissive snorts. If Mr. Jonnson also turned him away, what would she do? Tommy had already suffered the loss of his sight, been cast aside by his own family, and been rejected by half the town. How much must a mere boy be forced to bear? Although Mr. Jonnson might very well refuse to harbor the boy when faced with Tommy's limitations, she couldn't try to hide them. It wouldn't be honest.

Very kindly she said, "Come on now."

She led Tommy across a pathway formed of flat gray rocks to the porch. "Step up." The boards, cold and damp from the recent snow, creaked beneath their feet. Even before she raised her fist to knock on the wood door, a voice boomed from inside the house.

"Who's out there?"

At the deep timbre and stern tone, Tommy shrank against Christina. She coiled an arm around the boy's shoulders before answering. "Miss Christina Willems from the Brambleville Asylum for the Poor, Mr. Jonnson. Would you please open the door?"

"What for?"

Christina clenched her teeth. She was cold, tired, heartsore, and swiftly running out of patience. Sending up one more silent prayer for strength — at least the fifteenth since Tommy had awakened her a few hours ago — she gathered her remaining shreds of courage and said, "So I might speak to you without the need to holler."

Silence reigned.

Tommy shivered uncontrollably.

Christina's patience was whisked away on an icy blast of wind. She gave the door a solid thump with her fist. "Sir, will you kindly open this door and allow us entrance? It is cold out here!"

CHAPTER 3

Levi Jonnson set the lamp on the table near the door, tugged his suspenders into place, and finally gave the doorknob a twist. The handle of his pistol stuck out of the waistband of his trousers so he could easily grab it should the people on the porch prove untrustworthy. But when he opened the door and squinted against the early morning shadows, all he found was a disheveled-looking woman and a scrawny, barefoot boy dressed in britches and a plaid shirt at least two sizes too small.

Cold wind whisked through the door, making the flame on the kerosene lamp flicker. His fingers twitching on the pistol handle, he tipped sideways and peered beyond the pair. "Are you two alone?"

"Yes." The woman took hold of the boy's shoulders and urged him over the threshold, forcing Levi to step back or be run down. She caught the door and clicked it into place behind her. A shudder shook her frame, making the wild strands of hair escaping her shabby braid quiver. She drew in a ragged breath, swallowed, then turned a tired gaze on Levi.

"Thank you for allowing us entrance."

He'd hardly *allowed* it. She'd taken liberties. Before he could correct her, she went on.

"Mr. Jonnson, earlier this evening the poor farm residence caught fire, displacing thirteen souls. I've arranged temporary shelter in town for all but Tommy Kilgore." She put her arm around the boy's shoulders. A softness crept across her features as she gazed for a moment at the boy, who stood with his head hanging low. "I would be most appreciative if you could open your home to Tommy until I can make arrangements for our house to be rebuilt." Her pale blue eyes bored into his as she awaited a response.

He searched her face. Dark smudges marred her cheeks. The scent of smoke clung to both the woman and the boy. Her claim about a fire seemed true, and he didn't glory in their loss. But keep some strange boy in his house for who knows how long? Levi slipped his fingertips into his trouser pockets. "I can't house him, ma'am."

Her gaze narrowed. "Mr. Jonnson, I assure you I wouldn't be here were it not of grave importance. I was told in town you live alone." She gestured to his sizable sitting room, one eyebrow rising delicately. "You can't claim you lack the space to accommodate one small boy."

The boy in question seemed to shrink into himself as the woman talked. Levi experienced a pang of remorse. He didn't hold anything against the boy personally, but he lived alone for a reason. He didn't need the intrusion in his life. The sooner he could get the two of them out of here, the better.

He shifted his weight onto one hip. "Listen, lady —"

"My name is Miss Willems."

Levi scowled. "Listen, Miss Willems, I'm sorry about the fire. But I can't take in some boy —"

"His name is Tommy."

Levi sucked a slow breath and blew it out. Mercy, she was one irritating female. "I can't take in Tommy."

Miss Willems fixed him with a penetrating stare. "Are you rejecting him because of his blindness?"

Levi jolted. Blind? He looked at the boy, who slowly raised his chin. The boy's thick-

34

lashed, deep blue eyes stared ahead, un-blinking. Unseeing. Levi's heart rolled over.

"It would be particularly heartless to cast him aside because of something over which he has no control."

The woman's strident tone chased away the remnants of sympathy. "It has nothing to do with him being blind and everything to do with me single-handedly running a business. I don't have time to look after a boy. And I especially don't have time to make sure a boy who can't see doesn't get hurt out here."

"Tommy has a very keen sense of hearing. And he's extremely intelligent." Miss Willems's voice lost its sharp edge. Levi detected a hint of pleading in her tone and expression although she held her chin at a proud angle. "If you'll allow him to stay, he won't —"

"He can't stay." Levi reached for the doorknob, and his arm brushed the boy's shoulder. With a squawk of alarm, Tommy jerked toward Miss Willems, his hands paw-ing the air. She caught them and drew them down, murmuring softly to him. Levi stared at a patch of rippled skin on the boy's jaw. The pink, puckered flesh flowed down his neck and disappeared beneath the collar of his shirt. Levi's chest went tight. "What happened to this child?"

Sympathy played across her features. "He was injured in a boiler explosion." Still holding the boy's hands, Miss Willems peered at Levi over the boy's head. A steely resolve brightened her eyes. "Mr. Jonnson, I must find a place for Tommy. Every other family in town has turned him away. He's a boy — only a boy — in need of shelter. Won't you please offer a small corner of your home to Tommy?"

"Won't you please find a place here for my husband?" Ma's plea from long ago crept out of the recesses of Levi's mind. He recognized in Miss Willems's entreaty the same weary defeat wrapped in a thread of hope that had colored Ma's words. Levi shook his head. He said, "All right."

The woman's face lit.

He pointed at her. "But only until you can find someplace else for him to go. I've got a business to run, and I can't play nursemaid."

"You won't need to nursemaid Tommy." Miss Willems took hold of the boy's shoulders, guided him farther into the room, and eased him onto Levi's sofa. "Isn't that right, Tommy?" The boy stared straight ahead, his fingers clutching the edge of the sofa cushion and his mouth set in a sullen line. Miss

Willems gave his shoulder a pat, then scurried back to the door. "We escaped with only a handful of clothing, none of which belonged to Tommy. As soon as the shops open this morning, I'll make purchases and bring out adequate items for him. You needn't worry about providing anything more than shelter."

"And food," Levi said.

She nodded, seemingly unaware of the sarcasm in his tone. "But as I said earlier, only until I can find the means of rebuilding."

Levi scowled. "Remember, I told you to keep looking for someplace else for him to go. This can't be a long-term arrangement."

"Of course not." Despite the tiredness rimming her eyes, she spoke cheerily. Her skirts swirling, she crossed to the sofa and leaned forward to place a kiss on the scarred side of Tommy's face. She whispered something Levi couldn't hear, and the boy hunched into himself. Then she returned to the door. "Thank you again, Mr. Jonnson." She pulled open the door and hurried out as if she feared Levi might change his mind. Smart lady.

Levi latched the door and then turned to look at the boy. He sat stiff as a statue on the edge of the sofa where Miss Willems had put him. As Levi stared at him, the boy slowly turned his head, his unblinking eyes seeming to search for something.

"Mr. Jonnson?"

"What is it, boy?"

"I'm Tommy."

Levi ground his teeth. If this boy turned out to be like Miss Willems, they might not get along so well. "What do you need, Tommy?"

"To use the outhouse."

Levi swallowed a snort. No trouble, huh? He thumped across the floor and took hold of the boy's skinny arm. "All right then. I'll take you."

Tommy twisted his face around, aiming his unseeing gaze in Levi's direction. "Thank you, sir."

A lump filled Levi's throat. "Let's go, huh, and then you can stretch out on the sofa and get some sleep."

Chapter 4

Cora stayed next to the dry sink on the other side of the kitchen and listened to Miss Willems gently argue with the boardinghouse owner.

"I know what we agreed to do in exchange for our room, Mrs. Beasley, but I'm asking you to please understand. I have other responsibilities and many other people depending on me."

Mrs. Beasley's beady eyes snapped beneath her thick gray brows. "You can be seein' to your other responsibilities when you've finished up here. Them dishes won't wash themselves. An' your shoppin' an' such won't pay your keep. So you decide what you oughta do." She whirled and marched through the hallway leading to the dining room.

Miss Willems looked after Mrs. Beasley, released a heavy sigh, then hung her head.

Cora folded her arms over her chest and

huffed. "That Miz Beasley . . . She might've given us a room to share, but she didn't do it out of kindness. She just wanted somebody to take over all her work."

Miss Willems sent a mildly disapproving look in Cora's direction. "Now, now, we mustn't complain. We did agree to kitchen duties in exchange for the room. We should be grateful her former housekeeper chose to leave last week, providing us with a room and means to pay for it."

How could Miss Willems stay polite when Mrs. Beasley was so fractious? Cora had never met anyone as even-tempered as Miss Willems. Cora sniffed. After only a few hours in the Beasley Boardinghouse, she suspected she knew why the former housekeeper had left. That Mrs. Beasley was persnickety and bossy. But if Miss Willems wouldn't complain, neither would she. Cora eased up beside the other woman and touched her arm. "If you need to go an' see to the others, I can clean up in here on my own." It was the least she could do, considering all Miss Willems had done for her, treating her kindly and taking her in after Ma told her to git.

Even though dark circles rimmed her eyes, Miss Willems still offered Cora a warm smile of thanks. Cora couldn't help wondering why a pretty lady like Christina Willems wanted to spend her days caring for a bunch of misfits.

Miss Willems's gaze drifted over the pile of dishes, mugs, pots, and silverware. "I can't leave all this to you. You need to rest. You're pale and unsteady on your feet after your bout of sickness this morning."

Cora looked away, shame igniting within her. Miss Willems had heard her retching into the bushes?

Miss Willems slipped her arm through Cora's and led her back to the dry sink. "With two of us working together, we'll finish these in no time, and then you can lie down until we need to start lunch. Our short night and all the excitement must have worn you out. So you wash and I'll dry, hmm?"

"Yes, ma'am." Cora busied herself ladling water from the stove's reservoir into the wash pan. Apparently Miss Willems didn't understand the reason for Cora's sickness. Relief made her knees weak. She had to keep this secret as long as she could, because when she was found out, she'd be set loose again. And then what would she do?

Steam rose from the dishwater, carrying the scent of lye soap. Nausea rolled through Cora's middle, but she braced herself

41

against it. She wouldn't get sick again. She wouldn't! She couldn't let anybody guess the truth.

Tommy awakened to the sound of metal clanking against a tin plate and the smell of ham and beans. They'd eaten lots of beans at the poor farm. Beans with ham. Beans with pork fat. Beans without ham or pork fat. He liked them best with ham. For a minute the smell made him think he was home, but the stiff fabric beneath his cheek and the unfamiliar woven blanket covering his body reminded him he wasn't.

Opening his eyes — although why he bothered, he couldn't explain, since the darkness was the same whether his eyes were open or closed — he pushed the blanket aside and sat up.

A deep voice came from somewhere behind him. "You awake, boy?"

Tommy hugged himself. He wished Mr. Jonnson wouldn't call him "boy." Before his accident Pa called him "Son." After his accident Pa called him "boy" in a voice that always sounded angry. *Get outta my way, boy." "What'd you do now, boy?" "You're so blamed clumsy, boy!"* Tommy didn't want to think about Pa, and he didn't want to be called "boy." So he sat with his lips clamped tight and didn't answer.

"Need the outhouse?"

Tommy wished he could say no. He didn't want anything from this man who took care of him only because he had to. But need overcame stubbornness. He nodded.

Feet clomped on the floor, growing louder as the man neared, then a hand grabbed his arm. Mr. Jonnson's fingers held tight as he guided Tommy through the house and out the door. After the warmth of the blanket, the cold air seemed even colder than it had last night. Tommy shivered, the chill from the ground making the bottoms of his feet sting.

"Should've had you put on some of my old boots," Mr. Jonnson said. "They'd be way too big but still better than nothing."

Although the man's voice was gruff, Tommy appreciated him thinking of boots. He might trip in too-big boots, but as Mr. Jonnson had said, it'd be better than nothing. The hinges on the outhouse door creaked, and Mr. Jonnson gave Tommy a little push.

"There you go. I'll wait right outside." The hinges creaked again.

Tommy felt his way to the single hole and took care of business. Then he called, "I'm done." Hinges creaked, firm fingers clasped his arm, and once again he plodded over cold, rough ground, guided by a man he knew only by the sound of his voice and the hard calluses of his work-roughened hands.

Blessed warmth surrounded him when they entered the house, and Tommy couldn't hold back a sigh of relief to be out of the cold. He hoped Miss Willems could afford to buy him a coat. The walk to Mr. Jonnson's outhouse was seventeen paces farther than the one at the poor farm.

"Sit down here." Mr. Jonnson pressed Tommy into a chair. Wooden. Spindle-backed. Tommy inched his hands forward, and his fingertips encountered a tabletop. A cool, smooth plate sat directly in front of him. He fingered the plate's rim, searching for warm spots that would indicate whether it had been filled yet. A hand grabbed his wrist.

"Stop that. You can't eat with your fingers. Those beans are hot. You'll burn yourself." Tommy knew what he'd been doing, and he considered saying so, but what good would it do? Nobody thought a blind boy had any sense. Mr. Jonnson pushed a slim utensil into Tommy's hand. "Use this."

He ran his thumb up the length of the utensil and found a smooth bowl instead of tines. A spoon. Good. He had mastered a

44

spoon. He leaned forward, sniffing. Yes, the plate held beans. Gripping the spoon in his fist, he dipped, scraping the plate until he connected with something soft. He scooped and lifted the bite.

Hot! With a startled gasp he spat out the beans and fumbled in search of something to drink to cool his tongue. The backs of his fingers collided with a mug, and he heard a clatter, followed by Mr. Jonnson's sharp intake of breath. Chair legs screeched across the floor. Boots thundered. Tommy sat, listening, knowing what had happened, and waited for the scolding to begin. *"Clumsy! You're so clumsy, boy! Can't you do nothin' right?"* The angry words rang through his mind.

He let his burning tongue hang from his mouth while he hunkered against the back of his chair, his fists tight against his chest, ready for the blows to fall from the darkness. He yelped when fingers grasped his wrist, but then something cool and smooth was pressed against his hand. A glass. He groped for it. Liquid sloshed over its rim and splashed across his fingers. He gripped the glass with both hands and raised it to his lips, slurping eagerly.

Tommy drank every drop of the water, then lowered the glass, panting. He bobbed his head in every direction, his ears tuned for a scrape or a bump that would tell him where Mr. Jonnson now stood. Finally the sound of Mr. Jonnson clearing his throat came from nearby. Hands plucked the glass from his grip, and a soft *thunk* let him know it had been placed on the table. Chair legs scratched the floor, muffled *whisks* indicated trousers meeting the seat of a chair, and then a wry voice spoke from across the table.

"Before you put the next bite in your mouth, blow on it. Like I said before, those beans are hot."

Tommy stared straight ahead, his heart bumpity-bumping in amazement. Mr. Jonnson hadn't hollered at him. Hadn't whopped him. And he hadn't called him "boy" this time.

Midafternoon, Christina guided the horses up Mr. Jonnson's lane. A trail of gray smoke rose from the rock chimney, flavoring the air. It was such a relief to know Tommy was safe and warm. And the clothes in the bag behind the seat would add to his comfort. The new mercantile owner, Jay Creeger, had carted in a good supply of ready-made clothing in all sizes when he and his wife, Mary Ann, had moved to Brambleville from

46

the Outer Banks of North Carolina. After Christina told the friendly pair about the fire, Mrs. Creeger insisted on extending Christina credit. Thanks to the Creegers' benevolence, all her charges now owned two pairs of underclothes, stockings, one complete outfit, shoes, and a coat. She hoped the mission board sent funds quickly so she could repay the mercantile owners without delay.

She drew the team to a halt, set the brake, and grabbed the bag containing Tommy's clothes. Holding the collar of her new wool coat closed beneath her chin, she stepped onto the porch.

Mr. Jonnson opened the door even before she knocked and gestured her in. "Tommy heard the horses. I figured it was you."

Christina crossed directly to Tommy, who was perched on the sofa in the same spot she'd left him hours ago. He looked so small and alone. Sympathy twined through her middle. She smoothed his hair with her fingers as she sank down beside him. "Hello, Tommy." She placed the bag of clothes in his lap. "I have a treat for you — new clothes! I've been delivering clothing to the other poor farm residents, and all of them asked me to tell you hello when I saw you."

Tommy's somber expression didn't

change. As hard as she'd tried, she'd never managed to coax a smile from the boy. It seemed the accident had stolen more than his sight. She'd never met such a joyless child, and the desire to put him at ease and to assure him that he was loved filled her with such intensity she struggled to breathe.

Pulling the sullen boy into a snug embrace, she whispered, "We'll be together again soon." How she prayed her words proved true. She and Wes had ridden out to the poor farm that morning so he could care for the chickens, goats, pigs, and cow. In the full sun of morning, the charred shell that had once been their kitchen seemed even sadder than it had in moonlight. She leaned back and spoke brightly. "For now, let's get you changed, and I'll take the pants and shirt you're wearing back to Francis."

Tommy didn't protest, so Christina reached for the buttons on his shirt. From his spot by the door, Mr. Jonnson emitted a grunt. He charged to the sofa and snatched the bag from Christina's lap. She reared back, startled by his behavior and his furrowed brow.

"Come here, Tommy." The man took hold of Tommy's arm and tugged him upright. With the bag swinging from his fist, he propelled Tommy across the floor and past an elaborately carved fireplace mantel and a drop-leaf wood table with two spindled chairs before stopping in front of a raised panel door with a carved medallion gracing its center. He released the boy long enough to open the door, then gave Tommy a little push into the room. Dropping the bag on the floor, he said, "Get yourself changed and then come out. Miss Willems and I will be waiting."

Christina leaped up and darted for the room. But Mr. Jonnson closed the door and stepped into her pathway. Arms folded over his chest and feet widespread, he shook his head. "Let him be."

She reached for the brass doorknob, her heart banging against her ribs. "But he can't see. How can you expect —"

"He has fingers, doesn't he? And he's smart enough to figure out how to push a button through a buttonhole. He's what — nine, ten years old?"

"Eleven," Christina said. "But —"

"Then he's old enough to dress himself. So let him do it." He stood guard in front of the door, his eyes daring her to try to get past him.

She balled her hands on her hips. "Mr. Jonnson, I will not allow you to mistreat Tommy. He's —"

49

The man took a wide step forward and caught her arm. He aimed her toward the sofa, and she had no choice but to scuttle along beside him, her face flaming at his high-handed treatment. When he gestured to the sofa, she sat, but she glowered at him.

Mr. Jonnson perched on an oak rocking chair across from her and rested his elbows on his knees. As he brought his face near hers, the crackling flames in the fireplace brightened his features and brought out the strands of honey in his thick blond hair. The stubbornness she'd glimpsed when he'd yanked Tommy away from her disappeared, and she found herself mesmerized by the fervency in his gaze.

"Miss Willems, that boy's far too old to have you tucking in his shirt and buttoning his britches."

Not a sound could be heard from the room behind her. Was Tommy sitting on the floor in the dark, waiting for someone to help him? She swallowed. "That may be, but Tommy isn't like most eleven-year-old boys. He has a handicap. That makes him special."

"But it doesn't make him helpless."

Irritation tightened her chest and sharpened her tongue. "Tommy has been in my care for nearly two years now. After only a few hours with him, you think you know what's best?"

"I can safely say mollycoddling isn't best."

Her jaw dropped. "M-mollycoddling? That's what you call giving him protection and care?"

"When it cripples him, yes."

Christina gasped.

"Listen . . ." He tipped his head, his blond brows pulling inward. "Don't you think it might embarrass him to have to ask for help with everything? Sure, it makes you feel good to help him, but thanks to you, that boy can't even walk to the outhouse on his own."

"Well, of course he can't! He can't see where to go!"

"But he can feel. And you said yourself, he can hear. Why not let him use the senses he's got to guide him?"

Christina shook her head, frustrated. "How on earth is he supposed to *hear* his way to the outhouse?"

Mr. Jonnson chuckled. "Well, his nose works just fine, so . . ."

Was she really discussing outhouse usage with a man? And a stranger at that! She started to rise, but he reached out a hand to stop her. His palm and the pads of his fingers all wore calluses. For a moment

Christina stared at his hand, amazed by what she perceived of Mr. Jonnson based on that wide, rough, work-marked hand.

"Miss Willems?"

She lifted her gaze to his face. Determination squared his jaw, but the flames from the fireplace made his green-blue irises sparkle, softening his appearance. Why hadn't she noticed before how handsome he was? She gulped.

"I have a business to run here. I can't spend my day taking Tommy back and forth to the outhouse, buttoning his shirt, or combing his hair. He'll have to do those things for himself." He pressed his palms to his thighs and rose to peer down at her. "So if you think that's too much for the boy, then you might want to hasten finding someplace else for him to go. I won't baby him."

An uneasy thought wriggled through Christina's mind. Was he contrary enough to manipulate her? Perhaps he was being rough on Tommy so she would take him with her now. The idea rankled. "Mr. Jonnson —"

At that moment hinges squeaked, and shuffling steps sounded behind her. Christina turned in her seat and spotted Tommy inching toward the sofa, hands outstretched, chin bobbing in his awkward way of gaining a sense of placement. His shirt was buttoned unevenly, and one side of his collar was under his ear at an odd angle. He'd managed to jam the tails of his shirt into his pants, but wads of fabric clumped in front. His boot strings resembled snarls of yarn left over from a kitten's wild play. Oh, such a sight! She jumped up and met him halfway across the floor, determined to put everything to rights.

Tommy clutched at her. The first smile she'd ever seen from him lit his thin face. "I did it, Miss Willems. Do you see? I did it."

Christina blinked twice, amazed by the pride in the boy's voice. "Y-yes. I . . . I see."

A low-throated chuckle sounded from the other side of the room. Christina turned slowly and fixed her gaze on Mr. Jonnson. He stood, feet spread wide, arms folded over his chest, and a grin that communicated *I told you so* twitching at his cheeks. Heat flooded her face. She whirled back to Tommy.

"You did very well, Tommy." She spoke briskly, trembling with embarrassment. "And since you're all . . . all dressed," — another rumble of amusement reached her ears and propelled her toward the door — "I should return to town." She scurried to her waiting wagon before Levi Jonnson had another chance to laugh at her.

CHAPTER 5

Levi crossed the floor and fastened the door latch. Miss Willems had skedaddled in such a hurry she'd left the door yawning wide open behind her. Not too kind of her, allowing in the cold February air. But he supposed he wouldn't hold it against her. Laughter threatened. She didn't seem to like being proved wrong. But he'd sure done it. Or, maybe more accurately, Tommy had.

He turned and spotted the boy, rooted in place right where Miss Willems had left him. "Are you going to stand there all day?"

Tommy's chin jerked, his head shifting to locate Levi. "N-no, sir."

Levi rubbed his finger under his nose. The kid had dressed himself, but his stuttered speech and the way his fingers fidgeted against his pant legs screamed uncertainty. Without warning, an image from two decades ago paraded to the forefront of Levi's mind — his father slumped in a chair, his blank stare boring a hole in the wall while Ma combed his lank strands of gray hair into place. Levi gave himself a shake, sending the memory into hiding again.

He crossed the wood-planked floor, retrieving his comb from the shaving table as he went, grabbed Tommy by the wrist, and pressed the comb into his palm. "Here. Use it. You've got a rooster tail tall enough to brush the rafters."

Tommy jolted, but then a wobbly grin broke across his face. "You made a joke, Mr. Jonnson."

Had he? Levi drew back, his pulse tripping into double beats. When was the last time he'd drawn on humor? Not since —

Tommy raised the comb and made an awkward sweep from his forehead to the base of his skull. Levi watched, battling the urge to guide the boy's hand. But he knew all too well how treating someone like an invalid made him an invalid. He aimed his feet for the back door.

"When you're done there, just drop the comb on the table. I'm going to rig up a rope from the door to the outhouse so you can find your way without my help. A boy who can dress himself and comb his own hair can take himself to the outhouse." Levi grabbed his coat from the hook beside the door and headed outside.

Christina brought the horses to a stop at the livery stable and handed the poor farm's wagon and team over to the livery owner with a polite thank-you. Icy wind turned the powdery snow into writhing snakes that danced across the boardwalk beneath her feet. Gusts tore strands of hair from the heavy twist on the back of her head and tossed them across her face as she made her way to the boardinghouse. She hugged herself as a shiver shook her frame, but not even the chilly blasts could erase the flush from her face.

Oh, how foolish — and even worse, how fastidious — she'd felt, standing before Tommy with Levi Jonnson's low-pitched laughter rumbling in her ears. Hadn't the man seen the ill-tucked shirt and mismatched buttons? If Tommy were to appear in town dressed in such a manner, he'd become a laughing-stock. Yet somehow the man had made her feel as though she were in the wrong for wanting to help the boy!

She entered the boardinghouse through the kitchen door. "Only payin' guests use the front entrance," Mrs. Beasley had snapped when she and Cora had arrived early this morning. Christina looked around the room, seeking either Cora or their benefactor, but the room was empty except for a patchwork cat snoozing on the rag rug in front of the stove. Christina creaked open the door to the little room she and Cora had been instructed to share. Cora lay crosswise on the bed, a faded quilt wrapped around her body, sleeping soundly. Holding her breath, Christina backed out and closed the door with a muffled *click*.

Tiredness assailed her as she sank into a painted bentwood chair and rested her elbows on the worn surface of the kitchen worktable. She wished she could stretch out and take a nap. But she had too much to do. Although each of her charges was sheltered for the moment, she needed to arrange for permanent placement as quickly as possible. First thing that morning she'd sent a telegram to the mission board, informing them of the calamity, but she should pen a long letter detailing the fire's damage and making a formal request for the funds to rebuild.

The cat mewed and crept from its dozing spot, stretching each orange, white, and black splotched leg as it came. With a lithe leap, it claimed her lap and curled into a ball. Although Christina needed to locate pen and paper, she took a moment to run her fingers through the cat's soft nape. A rumbling purr rose from the contented feline, and Christina relaxed against the back of the chair, some of the morning's tension draining away.

"Feels good, doesn't it, kitty?" she crooned in a singsong whisper. "You enjoy me petting you, and I enjoy it, too. I always feel better when I'm ministering to someone else, even if the someone else is a cat." A bemused laugh left her lips, but as quickly as it rose, it faded. Mr. Jonnson's comment concerning Tommy, *"Sure, it makes you feel good to help him,"* played through her mind, stinging her with its conjecture that she only reached out to Tommy to please herself.

Heavy footsteps sounded in the hallway. The cat dove off Christina's lap, snagging her skirt with its back claws. The animal claimed a hiding spot beneath the stove, and Christina jumped up as Mrs. Beasley stormed into the kitchen.

" 'Bout time you was back." The boarding-house owner plunked her thick hands on her hips and glowered at Christina.

"Yes, I realize I was gone a bit longer than I'd anticipated, but —"

"Don't wanna hear no excuses." The woman's brows formed a stern V. "That lazy friend o' yours put herself to bed right after you left an' ain't done a lick o' work all afternoon. She gonna be takin' an hourlong nap every day?"

Christina stifled a sigh and prayed for patience. Her father had always proclaimed a soft answer turned away wrath, but he might not have been so quick to quote the proverb if he'd been forced to deal with Mrs. Beasley. "Cora is far from lazy, ma'am. We had a trying night, and —"

Mrs. Beasley waved her hand, shooing away Christina's words. "Gonna be supper-time in less'n two hours, an' I promised the boarders chicken an' dumplings. So you'd best get to wringing a chicken's neck."

A sick feeling overcame Christina. She'd never killed a chicken. Before Father died, he'd handled such unpalatable tasks, and afterward Wes had done any needed butch-ering. "Oh, Mrs. Beasley, I —"

A loud snort left the woman's lips. "Don't tell me you're squeamish." She made it sound akin to being a bank robber.

"Well, I —"

"I'll do it." Cora entered the kitchen. Her eyes appeared bloodshot and her dirt-brown hair stood out in disarray, but she held her shoulders square. She snagged an apron from a hook on the wall and turned a resentful look on Mrs. Beasley. "I reckon

I'm not too lazy to kill a dumb cluck."

Mrs. Beasley's gaze narrowed. "An eavesdropper, are you?"

"I don't consider it eavesdroppin' when you're overhearing things about your own self."

The older woman pointed a finger at Cora's face and opened her mouth as if preparing to unleash a torrent of words, but Christina stepped forward. "If we're to have chicken and dumplings ready by the supper hour, we'd better get to work. Cora, head out to the chicken coop and . . . do what you must." She watched Cora scurry out the back door, then she moved to the stove and began ladling water from the reservoir into a pot. They'd need to scald the chicken before it could be plucked, and time was of the essence. "Mrs. Beasley, will buttered carrots be an acceptable accompaniment to chicken and dumplings?"

Mrs. Beasley's thick brows crunched together. "You makin' fun o' me?"

Christina blinked in surprise. "Fun?"

She folded her arms over her chest. "The way you talk. 'Acceptable accompaniment.' You tryin' to make me look foolish?"

"Of course not, ma'am!" Christina's parents had valued education, and her mother — raised and educated in the East

— had tutored Christina. After Mama died, Papa sent Christina to the same boarding school Mama had attended, and she'd remained there for four years, developing the skills she needed to teach any children who resided at the poor farm. Her cultured speech made her feel close to her well-bred mother. She gulped and said, "I apologize if I've offended you."

Mrs. Beasley sniffed twice, her chin high. "Buttered carrots'll be fine. An' bake up a gingerbread cake for dessert. Recipe's in my little box on the shelf." Nose in the air and skirts swishing, she stomped out of the kitchen. The moment she disappeared around the corner, the cat came out of hiding and preened against Christina's leg. She scooped up the animal and gave it a nuzzle.

"I'm glad you're more agreeable than your owner," she whispered into the pointed black ear. After giving the cat a quick squeeze, she put it down and stoked the stove with an armload of wood to hasten heating the pot of water. Not until steam rose and little bubbles burbled along the pot's edges did the back door open and Cora step through with a red-speckled hen dangling from her hand.

Christina stared at the limp bird, her stomach churning, then raised a sympathetic glance to Cora. "Oh, you did it."

"I did it." Her white face bore mute testimony to her displeasure in the task. She plopped the dead chicken on the table, then shuddered. "Probably wouldn't have had the courage if she" — a belligerent toss of her head toward the doorway indicated Mrs. Beasley — "hadn't got my dander up, callin' me lazy." Then her expression softened. "Thanks for defendin' me, Miss Willems. I promise I won't be sleepin' any more afternoons away like I did today."

Christina gave Cora a quick hug. "Don't worry about needing a nap. Truth be told, I could have used one myself after our short night." She lifted the chicken by one prickly foot and dunked it up and down in the pot. Steam seared her hand, but she gritted her teeth and continued to dip and lift until the feathers clung like a second skin to the bird's carcass and the smell of scalded down singed her nose. Holding the dripping bird well in front of her, she carried it to the table and stretched it out for plucking.

"Want my help?" Cora asked, her white face puckering as she gazed at the sorry-looking hen.

Christina grabbed a handful of feathers and yanked. "Mrs. Beasley wants gingerbread cake for dessert. Why don't you retrieve the recipe from the little box over there and start baking. The ginger smell should make things more pleasant." She wrinkled her nose as she yanked out a few more feathers, revealing pink mottled skin beneath.

"Yes, ma'am." Cora wiped her hands on her apron and moved to the possum belly cupboard in the corner, where she began scooping flour from the biggest drawer. "Tell you what, Miss Willems. You just plan on turnin' in right after supper, and let me do all the cleaning. That nap freshened me right up."

As lovely as a long night of sleep sounded, Christina dismissed the idea. "I have other work to do after supper. I must locate pen and paper and get a letter posted to the mission board. They'll expect a full report about the damage to the poor farm and information on where each resident has been housed."

Cora angled a glance over her shoulder. "Everybody got a place to stay?"

Christina shook wet feathers from her fingers. "Florie and Joe are with the banker, Mr. Tatum, and his wife. Reverend Huntley arranged for Herman and Harriet to board with the church organist, Widow Dwyer. The butcher and his wife offered their back room to Louisa and Rose. Alice, Laura, and Francis have moved in with the seamstress, Tina Claussen. Wes insisted on staying near the horses, so he's bedding down in the tack room of the livery stable. And Tommy . . ."

Once again Levi Jonnson's smug grin and amused chuckle rose to torment Christina. She fell silent as embarrassment heated her face.

Cora turned, worry marring her brow. "Tommy's all right, isn't he? You found a good place for him, too?"

How Christina prayed that Tommy's placement would prove to be good rather than harmful. But she shouldn't concern Cora — the young woman had been very kind to Tommy, more than most. She forced a smile. "Tommy is fine. He's with the mill owner, Mr. Jonnson."

Cora's face took on a dreamy expression. "Mr. Jonnson . . . I recall seeing him in the mercantile one time. He's a handsome man." Her hands stilled in measuring ginger into a blue-striped bowl.

As Christina recalled his sturdy build, thick blond hair, and callus-dotted hands, heat filled her cheeks. "Yes. Well." She pinched off stubborn pieces of down from the chicken's flesh. "Handsome he might be, but he's also quite cantankerous."

As Cora pushed a wooden spoon through the cake batter, a wonderful aroma drifted from the bowl. "But he took in Tommy, you said. So he must not be too cantankerous."

Cora had no idea how the man had balked. Or the way he'd treated her. And Christina wasn't about to share those things with the young woman. She reached for a knife to gut the clean-plucked bird. "As I said, Tommy is fine. But . . ."

If only Papa were still alive, she could share her concerns with him. Despite Tommy's rare smile of success this afternoon, she held real misgivings about the care he would receive from Mr. Jonnson. But she didn't dare voice her worries to Cora or to any of the poor farm residents. They looked to her for guidance. She couldn't lean on them.

Cora tipped her head. "But . . ."

Christina shrugged, offering another smile, which she hoped passed as untroubled. "Oh, it doesn't matter. In no time at all, the mission board will provide funds to rebuild, and we'll all be together under one roof again." *Please, Lord. Soon . . .*

CHAPTER 6

Tommy clung to the rope with one hand and held his other hand in front of him as he counted his steps to the outhouse. *Fifty-three, fifty-four . . .* The rope's rough fibers pricked his palm, but he wouldn't let go. His heart pounded. Although he'd already made this trek by himself three days in a row, he still battled dizziness when he was outdoors on his own. Fear made him break out in a sweat despite the cold wind that stung his bare cheeks, pulled at his jacket, and tousled his hair. If the wind tore him loose from the rope, how would he find his way back to the house?

"If you get into trouble, give a holler. I'll come running." The promise Mr. Jonnson had made the first time he'd sent Tommy to the outhouse alone trailed through his head. His fear eased. He'd be all right. Mr. Jonnson was in the house, fixing breakfast. Only seventy-eight paces in all. He could

holler loud enough to be heard from seventy-eight paces.

Seventy-six, seventy-seven . . . His palm smacked the outhouse wall. Batting at the damp wood, he located the door and creaked it open. With the door's edge firmly in his grasp, he finally released the security of the rope and stumbled inside. The walls blocked the wind, and he sighed, his warm breath whisking around his nose.

He giggled, remembering Mr. Jonnson saying that once spring arrived, he might not need the rope to find his way to the outhouse — his nose could probably guide him. That Mr. Jonnson . . . Even though he was mostly serious, every now and then he said something funny. Tommy liked those moments. When Mr. Jonnson joked with Tommy, he felt normal. Normal, not a help- less blind boy who had to be tiptoed around and treated all careful-like the way most people did. Even Miss Willems.

His business finished, Tommy fastened his britches and pushed the door open. His nostrils filled with the crisp scent of late winter as he caught hold of the rope again. He sniffed the air as he counted his way back to the house. Another aroma — rich, musky, leaving a tang on the back of his tongue — reached his nose. He'd never smelled anything like it before Miss Willems brought him here, so the scent had to come from Mr. Jonnson's mill.

The man spent most of the day away from the house, working in his mill. What did he do out there? The sounds were interesting — scrapes and *thud*s and rhythmic *whish-whish*es. And the smell . . . Tommy breathed deeply, savoring the essence. Curiosity tied his insides into knots. What made those sounds and interesting smells?

Before the accident had stolen his sight, he'd asked lots of questions, and Pa had always shown him the answers. But afterward when he asked, "What're you doin', Pa?" Pa got mad and told him to get his groping hands back before he ruined something. So Tommy didn't ask. But he couldn't help pondering and wishing he knew.

He stepped into the house, and the savory smell of bacon chased the unknown scent from his nostrils. His stomach rumbled. He licked his lips and shuffled in the direction of the table with his hands outstretched, eager to sit and have breakfast. Just as his fingers encountered the back of his chair, Mr. Jonnson spoke.

"Huh-uh. You haven't washed up yet."

Tommy stood with his hands outstretched,

waiting for a dripping cloth to drop into his hands.

"Well, now, don't just stand there." Mr. Jonnson's voice came from the kitchen area. "You know where the washbowl is. The water's warm, and soap's in the dish to the right of the bowl, like always. Wash your face while you're at it."

Heels dragging, Tommy angled his body to the left and counted eight steps. On the final one his hip bumped the stand where Mr. Jonnson kept a washbowl, soap, and a length of toweling ready. Warm water splashed his front, and he grunted.

"Just water." Mr. Jonnson's calm voice came from behind Tommy. "It'll dry. Dip your hands and soap up. The eggs and bacon are getting cold."

Again Tommy paused. The man was close — so close he felt his breath on the back of his head. Would he push up Tommy's sleeves? put the soap in his hands? He waited, but the *thump* of boot heels on the floorboards told him Mr. Jonnson was walking away. Tommy drew in a breath. Part of him appreciated Mr. Jonnson treating him like any other boy, but part of him was afraid. If he made a mess, he couldn't clean it up. A person had to see a mess before he could clean it up. And he didn't want to make messes for someone else.

He tipped his head, listening. Soft clanks and clatters carried from the kitchen — Mr. Jonnson serving up the breakfast. Tommy was on his own. His hands shaking, he shoved his sleeves to his elbows and carefully felt around on the stand for the soap. His fingers found the smooth lump. He lifted it and dipped it in the water, then rubbed it between his palms. The scent of lye stung his nose, and his hands became slick. He plopped the wet soap back into its dish, returned his hands to the water, and wrung them together until all the slickness washed away. Then he leaned forward and rubbed his wet hands over his face. Droplets dribbled down his chin, and he gingerly felt around for the towel. The rough cloth in hand, he rubbed his face first, then wadded the fabric around his hands until they felt dry.

"You done over there?"

"Yes, sir."

"Well, come on, then. Let's eat."

Tommy dropped the towel on the edge of the stand and felt his way to the table. He slid into his chair, his fingers eagerly searching for the edge of his plate. Good smells rose from the plate. At the poor farm they'd always used eggs for baking instead of plain old eating. Tommy licked his lips, eager to taste them.

Chair legs scraped on the floor, so Tommy knew Mr. Jonnson was sitting. Miss Willems always prayed before they ate, but Mr. Jonnson didn't bother. So Tommy slid his fingers along the plate's rim and found a fork. He picked it up, poked it around on his plate 'til he'd stabbed a bite, then filled his mouth with a chunk of fried egg. He couldn't resist releasing a low "Mmm . . ."

Mr. Jonnson chuckled. "A real treat, isn't it? Since it's Sunday, I thought we'd have something special."

Tommy lifted another bite. "We goin' to church since it's Sunday?"

"No."

Something in the man's tone changed. Just a little, but enough to make the fine hairs on the back of Tommy's neck prickle. He swallowed the bite of flavorful eggs. Even though he tried not to ask questions, one spilled out anyway. "How come?"

Mr. Jonnson harrumphed. "I have no use for hypocrites."

Tommy scowled. Although hunger made him want to dig in, he braved another question. "What's a . . . a hypocrite?"

"Somebody who says one thing but does another."

The man's voice lost its usual musical quality and held a hard edge. He sounded more like Pa than like himself. Tommy shivered, his pleasure in the fine breakfast slipping away.

"If you ask me, churchgoers are the worst kind of hypocrites." Mr. Jonnson's fork scraped on his plate again and again, as if he was chasing the food around. "So I keep my distance."

Tommy'd been a churchgoer before his accident. He'd gone with Ma and his brothers and sisters. After his accident, after Pa took him to the poor farm, he sat in on Bible reading, singing, and prayer with Miss Willems. She called what they did "church." That meant, in Mr. Jonnson's eyes, he was a hypocrite. Someone to be avoided.

A sharp *clank* — the fork smacking the plate — made Tommy jump. "Eat up, boy. When you're done, I'll show you how to wash dishes. It's time you started earning your keep." Chair legs screeched. Boot heels thudded away.

Tommy ate every bit of food he could find on his plate, but the eggs and bacon had lost their appeal. An ugly thought filled his head. The more things he could do for himself, the less time Mr. Jonnson needed to spend with him. Maybe Mr. Jonnson wasn't helping him learn because he liked him but because he wanted to avoid him.

Maybe Mr. Jonnson wasn't so different from Pa after all.

Cora slipped into the church pew beside Miss Willems, her face flaming. Since they'd come in late, thanks to Mrs. Beasley insisting they clean up the breakfast mess before leaving, the only open pews were way in the front. How she'd hated parading past all those well-dressed parishioners who cradled Bibles in their arms the way Ma used to hold a jug of spirits. Ma had never taken Cora to church — she said church folk were uppity. Cora wrinkled her brow, puzzling over Ma's comments. Miss Willems sure was different from the way Ma described church folk. Maybe Ma wasn't so all-fired right about everything. Maybe — her heart fluttered as a tiny root of hope tried to take hold — Ma wasn't even right about Cora.

While the preacher read from his big black Bible and then talked, Cora fiddled with a torn cuticle on her thumb and sent a quick glance over her shoulder. Her heart lifted when she spotted the familiar faces of the poor farm residents scattered among the congregation. Florie and Joe, Louisa, Rose, Alice and her youngsters . . . Wes was there, too, way in the back, sitting between Herman and Harriet. She waggled two fingers at him in a little wave, and he offered his great big, face-splitting grin in reply.

Miss Willems cleared her throat, and Cora zipped her attention forward. But she didn't listen. The preacher's deep voice might put her to sleep if she wasn't careful. Tiredness wore at her bones. Part of it was the work. Resentment pricked. Mrs. Beasley kept both her and Miss Willems so busy they hardly had time to sit. But part of it was — She shut out the thought. She shouldn't allow such disgraceful reflections while sitting on a church bench!

She wouldn't have come to church at all if Miss Willems hadn't insisted. She hadn't minded the services Miss Willems led at the poor farm on Sunday mornings. Just Miss Willems reading some scriptures, talking a little bit, and then all of them singing a song or two together. Coming to church, though, meant being with a slew of people she didn't know. Being gawked at. Judged maybe. But how could she say no to the woman who treated her so good? Besides, she'd have a chance to see the others and catch up with them. Not even Miss Willems had managed to get away and check on everybody in the last couple of days. Mrs. Beasley flew into an ugly dither anytime Miss Willems mentioned needing to see to her other responsibilities. So Cora could sit through a sermon if it meant getting to talk a bit with the people she considered her only friends.

The moment the service ended, the poor farm residents rushed at Miss Willems as if she were a stream and they were dying of thirst. Cora watched the woman hug each resident in turn, laughing even while tears filled her eyes. Longing flooded Cora's frame. Ma had never hugged her, not even when she was little. The one time Cora had let somebody hug her, it had felt so good she'd done things she shouldn't have. So as much as she wanted to hug — to *be* hugged — she hung back until they were all done.

"Miss Willems, Miss Willems!" Florie danced in place, her yellow braids flopping. "Miz Tatum says you an' Cora an' all the others" — she swept her arm to indicate the group — "can come to her place for lunch so's we can spend the day together."

Joe pressed forward, his hands clasped beneath his chin. "You'll come, won'tcha, Miss Willems?"

Miss Willems smoothed Joe's cowlick into place. "Of course we'll come."

The others murmured happily, and Cora couldn't resist a little crow of exultation.

Mrs. Beasley didn't serve a noon meal on Sunday, so she'd told them as they'd hustled out the door that they wouldn't be needed back until four to get supper started. Hours away from the boardinghouse and its dictatorial owner! Hours with the poor farm residents! Cora couldn't think of anything better. Except not being in a family way without the benefit of a husband.

Little Florie tucked her hand in Cora's and beamed upward. "Let's go, Cora!"

Tears stung Cora's eyes. The child was so young. So innocent. So welcoming. But soon — sooner than she wanted to consider — this little girl would be encouraged to stay away from her. Because once Miss Willems and the others learned about her shame, they'd want nothing to do with her, just like Ma.

Louisa stepped to Cora's other side and slipped her arm around her waist. "While we walk to the banker's place, you tell me how you and Miss Willems've been getting along over at the Beasley Boardinghouse. I hear tell that woman's got a parlor with furniture nice as anything the town's ever seen."

Truth be told, the one time Cora had set foot in the parlor, Mrs. Beasley had screeched, "Out! Out! For payin' guests only!" But she could tell Louisa plenty about the boardinghouse's cantankerous owner. She opened her mouth to launch a list of complaints, but a proverb Miss Willems quoted when Cora complained about Mrs. Beasley — *"He that is void of wisdom despiseth his neighbour: but a man of understanding holdeth his peace"* — stilled her tongue. Soon enough these people she admired would learn how void of wisdom she truly was, but until then she could hold her peace.

She sent Louisa a bright smile. "You heard rightly. That parlor's just about the prettiest room I ever did see."

CHAPTER 7

Christina squeezed Mrs. Tatum's hand as they paused beside the door leading to the porch. "Thank you so much for your kind hospitality. We all enjoyed ourselves."

Afternoon sunlight bounced off the edges of the door's oval beveled glass and created a halo above the woman's crown of pure white braids. She and her husband had both been angels to the poor farm residents today, allowing them a time to visit and relax. And the dinner they'd been served — roasted meat, boiled potatoes, stewed okra and tomatoes, both tart and sweet pickles, thick slices of homemade bread slathered with butter and jam — as much as they wanted. Such a treat for people accustomed to eating simple meals.

The woman waved her hand as if shooing away Christina's words. "Nonsense. It's the least we can do, considering the tragedy that befell all of you." She tipped her head and lowered her voice. "Have you determined the cause of the fire?"

Christina's stomach wrenched at the question. No matter where she went in town — the café, the telegraph office, the mercantile — someone was sure to ask how the fire started. She gave the only answer she knew. "It began in the kitchen, but beyond that I don't know."

Mrs. Tatum gave Christina's hand a sympathetic pat. "Such a sad thing, displacing so many people." She clicked her tongue. "I'm certain it was an accident, no matter what peop—" Her eyes widened, and red streaked her cheeks. She released Christina's hand with a jerk and stepped back. "But you said you needed to return to the boardinghouse, and here I'm blathering on." An unnatural laugh spilled from her lips. "You and Cora feel free to stop by anytime to see the children. Joe and Florie miss you, you know."

When the banker's wife mentioned their names, the blond-headed pair bounced up from their spot on the parlor rug where they'd been constructing a wooden puzzle and dashed to Christina. Their enthusiastic hugs couldn't quite erase the unease tiptoeing up her spine.

"We do miss you, Miss Willems — a whole

lot," Florie declared, her rosy lips curving into a pout.

"An' Francis an' Laura an' Tommy, too," Joe added.

Mrs. Tatum curved her arm around Joe's shoulders and fitted the child against her ribs. "Francis and Laura have come by after school a time or two to play, but I know the twins would dearly love some time with their friend Tommy."

Joe bounced on his toes, his face alight. "Yes! Can Tommy come visit? Huh, can he?"

Florie took up the cry as well until their combined voices were a cacophony of excitement. Christina started to calm them, but Mrs. Tatum leaned in first, capturing each child by the chin and tipping their faces upward. "Shh, now, you mustn't bombard Miss Willems. She has enough to manage without arranging visits between you and your friend. Mr. Tatum and I will do our best to let you spend some time with Tommy." She straightened and offered a smile to each crestfallen face. "Now, tell Miss Willems and Cora good-bye, and go finish your puzzle."

The pair offered halfhearted farewells and trudged across the floor to Cora. Christina battled a wave of . . . what? Hurt? Jealousy? Or maybe it was resentment. How quickly

Mrs. Tatum had usurped Christina's place in the twins' lives. Father would no doubt encourage her to be grateful the twins were responding so well to their new caretaker, but despite her best efforts, Christina couldn't summon gratitude. Her heart felt bruised.

Even so, she forced a smile. "I appreciate your making an effort to bring the twins and Tommy together. At least Joe and Florie have each other, and Francis and Laura are nearby, but poor Tommy is all by himself at the Jonnson mill with no other children to entertain him." And Mr. Jonnson had made it quite clear he had no interest in providing the boy with company.

Mrs. Tatum shook her head, her brow puckering. "Oh, you placed Tommy at the mill?" Her tone held an element of dismay. "That explains why the boy wasn't with the others at service today. Mr. Jonnson isn't" — she cleared her throat delicately as if seeking the appropriate words — "a believer. My Harold is a deacon, and he said Reverend Huntley has visited and invited the mill owner to attend services on numerous occasions, but . . ." Another light *ahem* replaced any final thought.

For reasons beyond Christina's understanding, protectiveness tightened her chest.

"Mr. Jonnson is the only one who was willing to take in Tommy, so there must be good in him." She clung to her bold statement, praying it was true.

The woman's eyes widened. "Why, certainly I never meant to intimate . . ." She ducked her head, the halo from the beam of sunshine disappearing with the motion. After several tense seconds she met Christina's gaze once more. "Perhaps, Miss Willems, Harold and I could make room for Tommy here. Then he'd be with Joe and Florie rather than so far from town with a man who is . . . who is quite busy."

Mr. Jonnson had given the same excuse — he was too busy to take proper care of Tommy. So why had she spoken in defense of the man? And why didn't she immediately accept Mrs. Tatum's offer?

Cora bustled up behind Christina, her new coat from the Creeger Mercantile across her arm. The sight of the coat reminded Christina of the many people who'd reached out in kindness to the displaced residents. What would they have done had the town refused to harbor them? Cora touched Christina's arm, her expression hopeful. "You gonna fetch Tommy here, Miss Willems? Be nice, I think, to have him closer."

Christina gave Cora a thoughtful look. "You're right." Mrs. Tatum's willingness to offer shelter to Tommy was an answer to prayer. She turned to the banker's wife, ready to ask when it would be convenient to bring the boy to her home. "I appreciate your willingness to make room for him here. But I think" — Christina drew in a breath, conflicting emotions suddenly tumbling through her chest — "we'll leave Tommy where he is for now."

Cora gave a start. "You sure, Miss Willems?"

Christina searched her heart. Was she declining Mrs. Tatum's offer out of jealousy? Seeing Joe and Florie respond so readily to the woman's admonition had pained her. *Lord, I want to do the right thing for Tommy.* An image of his beaming face appeared in her memory, his triumphant voice ringing in her ears: *"I did it, Miss Willems. Do you see? I did it."* Peace settled around her as gently as new-fallen snow. She smiled. "Yes, I'm sure."

"Well, if you change your mind, let me know." Mrs. Tatum spoke sweetly, but a hint of disapproval glimmered in her eyes.

Christina slipped on her coat and bade the others farewell along with a promise to check on each of them during the week.

Then she and Cora headed through the crisp air for the boardinghouse. Cora lagged, her head low, as they passed houses with picket fences and leafless bushes in the yards. She sent sidelong glances in Christina's direction but remained silent until they turned the final corner. Then she came to a sudden halt. "Miss Willems, I don't reckon I oughta question you. Rose and Louisa, they told me how your pa sent you to a school for young ladies after your ma died. You — you've had a lot more learnin' than me, an' I probably don't have any more sense than some old goose, but —"

Christina put her hand on the young woman's shoulder. "Cora, you are much smarter than a goose, old or otherwise. Please do not disparage yourself."

Pink stole across Cora's cheeks. Whether from pleasure or embarrassment, Christina didn't know, but she intended to praise Cora as often as she could. The poor girl seemed weighted by boulders of unworthiness. Cora's shoulders trembled briefly as she sucked in a mighty breath. She raised her chin and looked squarely into Christina's face.

"Are you leavin' Tommy outside of town because of what folks're sayin' about him?"

Christina's hand fell from Cora's shoulder.

She took a stumbling step backward, confusion and concern smiting her. "What are folks saying?"

Cora grimaced. "Now, I don't take much stock in gossip, but Louisa and Rose are plain irate at the rumors flyin' around town. I told 'em they needed to let you know, an' I hoped maybe they'd already talked to you, but . . ."

Christina caught Cora's arm and gave it a shake. "Cora, please, tell me what is being said."

Cora's furtive glances flicked left and right, her brown eyes becoming slits of secrecy. "They said folks're blaming Tommy for the fire. Sayin' those scars on his cheek show he's been burned once, which means he can't be trusted around stoves an' such, an' that he probably did somethin' foolish that sent the poor farm up in flames."

Christina gawked at Cora. Mrs. Tatum's evasive comment returned to taunt her. Could people really be so unkind as to hold a defenseless boy accountable for the destructive fire?

Cora's eyes pooled with tears. "Louisa and Rose, they've been trying to set people straight on it — sayin' no, sir, it couldn't've been Tommy — but folks always wanna blame somebody." For a moment Cora's face twisted in despair, but she shook her head, replacing the pained look with a fierce scowl. "But they hadn't oughta talk that way about Tommy. Ain't right."

No, it wasn't right. But how should Christina handle the situation? When she was a child and wrote home from school, heartbroken over something one of the other girls had said about her, her father had sent a letter advising in his tender way, "Christina, people will talk. You cannot change this. But what you can do is live in such a way that those who hear the ill comments will not believe them." At the time she'd wished her father had advised something more stringent or had offered to visit the school and tell the spiteful girl she needed to hush. Thinking of people saying such hurtful things about Tommy raised her hackles again, and she longed for someone — someone big and strong and forceful — to bring an end to the gossip.

But she shouldn't harbor vengeful thoughts. Father had taught her to turn the other cheek, just as Jesus instructed. She only wished it weren't so hard.

Linking arms with Cora, she aimed their feet toward the back of the boardinghouse. "Thank you for telling me."

Cora hunkered forward, squeezing Christina's elbow against her ribs. "What're you gonna do?"

Christina raised her chin. "I'm going to ignore the senseless chatter. After all, we know that Tommy isn't to blame. Next week two representatives from the mission board are coming by train to inspect the property." She eagerly anticipated the men's arrival. The sooner the mission board provided the funds to rebuild, the sooner she and the poor farm residents could gather under one roof again. Although her days were busy working for Mrs. Beasley, she missed the camaraderie and feeling of satisfaction her ministry at the poor farm offered. "When they discover the source of the fire, the gossip will burn out just as the coals at the house did."

Cora followed Christina through the back door into the kitchen. While Christina removed her coat, Cora lingered near the door, toying with the buttons on her coat. "So you gonna leave Tommy out there at the mill or bring him in to the Tatums? Seems like if the banker an' his wife took him in, it'd show folks they aren't worried about Tommy doing something dangerous in their house."

Christina nibbled her lower lip, considering Cora's question. Mrs. Tatum had indicated Tommy would be welcome if Christina changed her mind about his placement. Harold Tatum was well respected, and surely the townsfolk would see his acceptance of the boy as proof there was no reason to fear him. If bringing him into town would end the speculation about the boy, then it would be worth it.

Once more the image of Tommy's bright smile, pride radiating from his face, intruded. She scrunched her eyes closed, sending the memory away. Mr. Jonnson had asked her to find another place for Tommy as quickly as possible, and she'd agreed to do so. She should keep her word.

Christina hung her coat on a peg beside the door, defeat bowing her shoulders. "I'll take the poor farm's wagon to the Jonnson mill one day this week and fetch Tommy. You're right. He needs to be here in town with the rest of us."

Cora beamed.

Christina tried, but for reasons she little understood, she couldn't conjure a smile in reply. "Let's get supper started before Mrs. Beasley scolds us, shall we?"

CHAPTER 8

Levi stepped out into a bright, clear morning. He paused at the edge of the porch, taking in the expanse of blue overhead. For weeks gray clouds had masked the Kansas sky. Even though the wind stung his cheeks and made the inside of his nose burn, he let his gaze drift from horizon to horizon. Such a big sky. And blue. Everywhere blue. Much like *Mor* had described the sky over the ocean when she and *Far* had crossed from Sweden before Levi was born.

If his parents had stayed in Sweden, would Far still be alive, healthy in mind and body?

Thoughts of his father tarnished his pleasure in the crystal-bright sky. He set his feet in the direction of his mill. His boot heels thudded on the hard-packed earth as he made his way to the slope-roofed, sturdy plank building waiting at the edge of his property. As he closed the distance between his house and the mill, anticipation built in his chest. Another day of labor. Easier labor, he admitted, than what he performed in spring and summer, when the river ran free and turned the waterwheel to power his saw, but such rewarding labor. He would savor these final days before the layer of ice on the river melted, which would mean setting aside his planer, adz, chisels, and awls.

Regret pricked. Such pleasure he found in those tools. Tools with wooden handles worn smooth by his grandfather's hands, first used in a country far away from these rolling Kansas plains. Using them to craft beautifully detailed pieces of furniture, fireplace mantels, and jewelry boxes filled him with a satisfaction unlike anything else. If only —

He gave himself a little shake as the past threatened to encroach on his present. There was honor in his warm-weather work, too. He only made boards in the warmer months, but boards were important. Boards from his mill became houses and stores and barns. He made straight cuts, true cuts, so whatever was built would be square and strong. As long as people had the good sense to put the building on a firm foundation and protect the wood with a coat of paint, he wagered his thick-cut boards could withstand a century of Kansas's erratic seasons.

The hinges creaked on the wide door when he swung it open — a familiar sound. Comforting as a lullaby. Here in the sanctuary of his mill, the place that allowed him to make an honest living with his two hands, he spent his most peaceful moments. Always busy in here. Which meant no time to think.

Although the walls blocked the wind, the mill was frigid, its windows and even the exposed square heads of the iron nails pounded into the rafters holding a coat of frost. With a hurried step he crossed to the bricked corner where a black potbelly stove hunkered. Kindling filled a basket, and split wood waited in a neat pile beside the stove. He reached for the kindling first, earning a spark with two quick strikes of his flint.

Within minutes a tiny fire crackled. With practiced ease, he layered wood over the blaze, blowing gently to encourage the fire to grow. He watched the flames lick upward, darkening the creamy white wood, and although he welcomed the warmth, he couldn't deny a sense of regret at what must be sacrificed in order to stave off the cold. How it pained his craftsman's heart to see wood that could become carved medallions or turned legs or delicate spindles turned to char. He slammed the iron door shut with a solid clank.

A startled intake of breath sounded behind him, and he whirled around. "You!" Hands clenched into fists, he stomped across the sawdust-strewn floor and took Tommy by the upper arm. Everything within him wanted to shake the boy senseless, but he kept a rein on his anger. At least where his hands were concerned. He grated out harshly, "What are you doing here?"

"I-I followed you." Tommy's teeth chattered. His eyes, blue as the cloudless sky, seemed to stare at Levi's chest. "Wanted to know what you do out here. It . . . it smells good."

The boy's comment took the edge off Levi's fury. Was there any sweeter smell than fresh-cut wood? He couldn't fault the boy for following his nose to the source of the aroma. But he shouldn't have come on his own. Levi loosened his grip but didn't release the skinny arm.

"Listen to me. You can't come traipsing out here. The mill is next to the river. What if you'd missed the building and stepped on the ice instead?" A shudder rattled Levi's frame as he considered the possibilities. He gave Tommy's arm a shake. "It was foolish to leave the house."

The boy jutted his jaw. "It's lonely in there all day by myself. Why can't I be with you?"

Levi closed his eyes, stifling a groan. The empty black behind his eyelids brought a rush of empathy he didn't want to feel. He snapped his eyes open. Tommy stood sullen before him. Helpless as a lamb being led to slaughter. What must it be like, sitting day after day in a dark world with nothing to do? Of course the boy wanted companionship. Needed companionship. But Levi didn't.

He turned the boy toward the doorway. "You can't be out here, Tommy. A mill is a dangerous place for a boy who can't —" He swallowed. "For a boy. You have to go back to the house."

Tommy dug in his heels. "Lemme stay. I'll sit still, an' I won't touch nothin'. I promise. I just don't wanna be all alone again. The days are so long when I'm by myself."

Levi sucked in a big breath and held it. He liked working alone. Liked his solitude. And he had real concerns about the boy stumbling around in the mill, running into things the way he did in the house sometimes. He huffed out his breath. "Won't be much fun just sitting."

"That's all I do in the house — just sit." The boy's voice held an edge.

"And it's colder out here than inside."

"I can keep my jacket buttoned."

"I'll be working. I won't be paying you any mind."

"Don't care." For a moment Tommy's chin quivered. When he spoke, he'd lost the hint of beligerence. "It smells good out here . . ."

Levi shook his head. He must be losing his senses to give in so easily. He marched Tommy to a nail keg near the stove where he'd catch some warmth. "Sit."

The boy eased onto the keg's lid.

"And stay there."

"Yes, sir." A triumphant grin tipped up the corners of Tommy's lips.

Grinding his teeth together, Levi stomped to his workbench. He uncranked a wooden vise. "You'll be hearing funny noises, but don't you get up to explore. You just stay right on that keg."

"What'cha doin'?"

"Never mind that. Just do as I say."

The boy's shoulders lifted and sagged. "Yes, sir."

Levi turned his back on Tommy and set to work clamping a square of wood between the vise's jaws. When the wood piece was secure, he picked up a chisel and positioned it to begin a rosette in the square's center.

But something made him pause and peek over his shoulder.

Tommy sat, hands pressed between his knees, chin raised and eyes closed. His nostrils flared as he sucked in air, and a smile — one of pure satisfaction — formed on his face.

Something seemed to roll over within Levi's chest. He jerked his gaze back to his workbench and bent over the piece of wood. Miss Willems needed to get the kid out of here. And soon.

Tommy listened to *scritch-scritch*es and rasping scrapes and rattling *clank-clank-clank*s. He sniffed his fill of the rich, almost sweet smell that permeated the building. Just as he'd promised Mr. Jonnson, he neither moved nor said another word. But as the minutes turned into hours, his back-side became so numb he could no longer feel the wooden keg beneath him. He needed to get up.

Cocking his head, he focused on the *whisper-whish* coming from somewhere across the room. Each *whish* sent a fresh essence to his nose. If he shifted to sit on the floor, maybe he'd be closer to whatever made the funny sound and good smell. Mr. Jonnson had told him to sit. Sitting on the floor wouldn't be disobeying.

His legs reluctant to unbend, he slowly pushed himself upright and stood for a moment, stretching his back. Warmth from a stove touched his left side, so he inched right before easing himself to the floor. His palms encountered bits of grit. He brushed them together, and the scent increased. He lifted his hands to his nose and sniffed. Something was sucked into his nose, and he fought off a sneeze.

Cross-legged on the floor, he brushed his palms on his pant legs and then reached out again to pat the floor in search of something new to explore. His fingertips encountered a hardened, curled strip. He lifted it. Sniffed it. The curl carried the same aroma as everything else. But it didn't make him sneeze. Pleased, he stretched his hands as far as he could reach and gathered more of the curled strips. He filled his lap with as many of the pieces as he could find. Then, eyes closed and tongue poked out in concentration, he began fitting the curls together.

His fingers gently flattened the curls, layering them this way and that. He tried to picture them in his mind, drawing on his memories of when his eyes could see color and form. Somewhere along the line, his brain had forgotten how things appeared, but he continued to toy with the curls until he'd formed a chain of sorts. Pleased, he let out a little chortle.

"What're you doing?"

At Mr. Jonnson's question, Tommy dropped the chain. He planted his hands on the gritty ground and pushed himself upright. What had he been doing? He couldn't find a description. He patted the air, seeking the makeshift seat.

Scuffs warned of Mr. Jonnson's approach. Tommy shrank back, uncertain how the man might react. Too often Pa's anger had exploded out of nowhere. Mr. Jonnson hadn't hurt Tommy before, but that didn't mean he wouldn't.

"Who taught you to weave?"

Tommy frowned. Weave? He remembered his ma weaving reeds into baskets. But she hadn't taught him to do it. He'd just watched. "N-nobody."

"Then how'd you learn?"

"Learn what?"

A snort — amused or disgusted, Tommy couldn't be sure — left the man's lips. "To weave."

Tommy hunched his shoulders. Although heat still eased along his side, he shivered. "I . . . I don't know how to weave."

For long seconds silence reigned in the mill. Then a chuckle rumbled. Not a mean chuckle intended to make fun, but one that held a note of humor. Tommy's stiff shoulders relaxed.

"Yes you do."

Tommy tipped his head. "I do?"

"Well, you must. Feel what you did here."

Mr. Jonnson's palm cupped the underside of Tommy's hand and lifted it. The smooth curls he'd played with dropped into his waiting grasp. His fingers trembling, he gently pinched the curls. To his surprise they held together. "I weaved?"

Another chuckle. "Well, kind of. Come here." Mr. Jonnson's hand gripped Tommy's elbow. Tommy scuffed alongside the man for several paces. Then Mr. Jonnson took his hand and pressed it flat against something smooth. "Feel that."

Tommy gingerly ran his fingers across a flat yet somewhat bumpy surface. Curious, he curled all but one finger back and explored slowly, thoughtfully, tracing the line of the bumps with his fingertip. In the back of his mind, a memory teased — sliding his fingers along the slick reeds of one of his ma's homemade baskets.

"You're feeling the seat of a chair." Mr. Jonnson spoke with great patience, but

Tommy detected a thread of excitement in the man's tone. "It's woven from strips of reed, but it isn't called weaving. It's called caning."

Tommy dropped to his knees and slipped one hand beneath the seat. With curious fingers he explored the top and bottom of the seat's intricate pattern. "Why's it called caning?"

"I'm not sure. Maybe people originally used strips from cane to make the seats."

Tommy nodded. The pattern intrigued him, the narrow strips going side to side and crosswise, over and under. Automatically, his eyes closed as his fingers traced up, back, up again. "I like the way it feels."

"You think you could do it?"

Tommy jerked, settling his backside on his heels. "Wh-what?"

"Could you do it? Weave strips together that way?"

Tommy swung his head this way and that, trying to get his bearings. Was Mr. Jonnson making fun of him? He didn't sound like he was teasing, but still . . . Pa's voice taunted from the past: *What'samatter, boy? Can't you do it? If you can't even milk a cow without missin' the bucket, what good are you?* Tommy's mouth went dry.

"C'mere."

Once more a hand grasped his elbow and guided him to another place in the mill. Mr. Jonnson took hold of his wrists and slid his hands onto something slender and hard. As tall as Tommy's chest. With flat slats leading up and down. Another chair. With gentle pressure Mr. Jonnson pushed Tommy's hands to where the seat should be, then let go. His hands plunged through an opening.

"A mouse chewed the cane on this chair." There was a long pause, almost as if the man was trying to decide whether to say anything more. Then his words rushed out. "Do you want to fix it?"

Tommy ran his hand over the seat, feeling the edges of chewed cane. Prickly. Tattered. So different from the completed seat on the first chair, which had felt smooth and orderly. He wanted to fix it, but apprehension coiled his insides into knots. Sliding a few discarded curls together didn't mean he could cane a chair. A lump of longing filled Tommy's throat — a longing to be useful. The desire nearly choked him.

"I'd like you to try."

He wanted to try, too. He swallowed and dared to share his worry. "I might mess it up."

That chuckle came again. Soft. Gentle. Soothing. "You can't make it any worse than it is right now."

Tommy's finger scraped the chewed-away edges of cane. He snickered.

"So you gonna try?"

Tommy drew in a breath and released it slowly, gathering courage. "Yes, sir. I'll try."

CHAPTER 9

Brisk wind raced across the smoke-smudged limestone wall of the beautiful Victorian and sent a chill straight through Christina's wool coat. She'd waited more than a week for the mission board to send representatives to examine the fire-damaged house, and during that time she'd anticipated their commitment to rebuild. How could they allow such a lovely place — a house with leaded-glass windows, a spindled and gingerbread-bedecked wraparound porch, and fish-scaled turrets — to languish? Even more significant than its proud appearance, the Brambleville Asylum for the Poor provided a needed ministry, one she and her father had committed themselves to filling. The men's somber, negative reaction to her desire to reopen the house chilled her even more deeply than the relentless Kansas wind.

"But I can't just walk away. This is my

home." Christina hugged herself, battling tears.

Wes, standing behind Christina's shoulder, leaned in. "House itself ain't ruined. Place just needs new walls an' a new roof on the back where the kitchen used to be."

The older of the two men who'd been sent to examine the property cleared his throat and pushed his round-lensed spectacles higher on his bulbous nose. "Do you have experience in construction, young man?"

Wes crunched his lips to the side. "You mean, have I done any buildin'?"

"That's precisely what I mean."

Wes's broad shoulders hunched into a sheepish shrug. "Chicken coops an' fences."

The two mission board men exchanged a look. The older one spoke again. "Although I'm certainly no expert in carpentry, I admit it appears the main body of the house is unscathed. Smoke damage, of course, but nothing structural. Even the roof — with the exception of the area above the kitchen add-on, obviously the place where the fire originated — seems to have been spared damage."

Christina's hopes rose.

"But I still can't recommend approving the necessary funds for the project."

Her toes were starting to feel numb.

Christina shifted from foot to foot on the brittle grass to keep the blood flowing. "Mr. Regehr, please help me understand. If the house is salvageable, why not approve rebuilding the kitchen?"

Mr. Regehr clamped his lips together, and his thick gray eyebrows descended into a scowl. For several seconds he glared at her, the way a schoolmaster might try to intimidate a misbehaving student. Christina fidgeted beneath his stern look, but she wouldn't be cowed. Bringing the poor farm residents back together was too important to allow one man's negativity to deter her. Finally he harrumphed and flung a disgruntled look at the other man.

The second man, tall and thin with gray-blue eyes so pale they almost seemed colorless, aimed his gaze somewhere beyond Christina's shoulder. "If I might be frank, Miss Willems, the board isn't certain the asylum should continue . . . at this location."

A strand of hair, pulled free from the figure-eight twist on her head by a gust of wind, tickled her cheek as trepidation teased her soul. When Father had taken the position as the poor farm's manager, he'd been instructed to prepare for full occupancy since the county had no other suitable place

105

for the area's destitute. "Does the board intend to open a poor farm elsewhere in Shawnee County?"

"No, but —"

"Miss Willems?" Wes danced in place, his long arms wrapped across his middle. "Can we finish our talkin' in the barn? The wind's fixin' to freeze my nose off."

Apparently the two visitors agreed, because without a word they turned and strode toward the solid rock barn. Wes bounded ahead, and Christina scurried alongside the black-suited men. Wes held the door open while everyone stepped inside. Then he closed the double doors and dropped the crossbar into place. He released a shuddering breath, a relieved smile creasing his square face. Gesturing to a low bench along one stall, he said, "Miss Willems, set yourself down. I'll fetch some barrels an' such for the fellas."

"No need." The older man's gruff voice stopped Wes in his trek across the barn. With a resigned lift of his shoulders, Wes leaned against the closest support beam and traced designs in the dirt with the toe of his boot. Mr. Regehr planted his feet wide and folded his arms across his chest. "We won't be here long enough to warrant sitting."

Christina had started to lower herself onto

the bench, but Mr. Regehr's blunt statement brought her upright again.

"Breneman, finish your explanation, and then we must return to town."

Mr. Breneman gave a solemn nod. "Miss Willems, when the Brambleville Asylum for the Poor opened, it was under your father's direction. While it's no fault of yours that he's no longer overseeing the operation, the board has some concerns about leaving it in your hands."

Christina's jaw dropped. Shortly after her father's death, she'd received a visit from the head of the mission board, and she assumed the board was confident in her ability to serve as manager. After all, her parents had been involved in mission work from the time she was born. She'd grown up learning to serve. She knew no other means of living.

Her entire frame began to tremble. She eased onto the bench lest her quivering legs chose to collapse. "Not once in the past year when I've communicated with the board via letters and monthly reports has anyone expressed concern."

Mr. Breneman grimaced. "We aren't making accusations, Miss Willems. But you certainly understand it is . . . er . . ."

"Unseemly," Mr. Regehr mumbled.

"Unconventional," Mr. Breneman said loudly, "to place a single lady, such as yourself, in a position of leadership."

Christina held her hands outward, confusion creating an ache in her stomach. "Then why didn't the board replace me when Father passed away? Why wait until now?"

"The board agreed it would be less than Christian to remove you from your home when you were in the midst of mourning your father's death." Mr. Breneman's tone, although businesslike, held a note of apology. "We voted to wait a year before approaching you about assigning a new director. It's only coincidence that the fire occurred when the year of mourning had reached its end."

Across the barn Wes pushed off from the upright beam and stomped toward the men, his hands balled into fists. Christina jumped up and tried to waylay him, but he charged past her. "You ain't sendin' Miss Willems away!"

"Now see here." Mr. Regehr held up both palms, his eyes narrowing into slits. "This doesn't concern you."

Wes raised his chin, defiance glittering in his eyes. "Does too. Miss Willems, she's like . . . like a ma to me. Her an' her pa took me in. She taught me to read an' write when teachers said I was too dumb to learn. Her pa showed me how to care for critters — cows an' chickens an' pigs — and to put seeds in the ground an' make 'em grow. Don't know where I'd be or what I'd be doin' if Miss Willems an' her pa hadn't said, 'Yes, sir, Wes, you're welcome here.' I . . . *we* — me an' all the others — need her. An' you can't send her away!"

"Wes, hush now." Christina put her hand on his arm, touched beyond words by his fervent pleas on her behalf. But the expressions on the board members' faces communicated defensiveness. She couldn't alienate them now — she needed them to be willing to listen. Her fingers applying gentle pressure to Wes's forearm, she faced the men. "I suppose having a woman in charge of the poor farm is a bit unconventional. To some people's minds, even unseemly."

She wasn't sure, but she thought Mr. Regehr humphed. She resisted flicking a glance at the man. "But I assure you, nothing of an unseemly nature has occurred beneath the poor farm roof either before or after my father's death."

Mr. Regehr arched one brow. "That's not what Mr. Hamilton Dresden indicated."

Wes jerked, and Christina's hand fell away

from his arm. Her heart skipped into double beats of anxiety. Unpleasant memories flooded her mind. "When have you spoken to Ham Dresden?"

Mr. Breneman dropped his gaze to the barn floor. A red flush rose from beneath the badger fur collar of his coat and crept toward his ears. "Two months ago."

Heat seared Christina's face. She could well imagine what the man had told them. The evening she'd cast him out of the farm, he'd spouted every kind of vile threat imaginable. "I see." She tipped her chin. "I assume the board believes his account over the report I sent to explain why I'd asked him to find another place to live?"

"Now, Miss Willems, of course we don't question your honesty." Mr. Breneman's gaze landed briefly on Christina, then flittered downward again. His smooth-shaven cheeks glowed red. "But we can't simply discount the man's complaint. After all —"

Wes growled, "That man's a lazy, no-good scoundrel. A liar, too."

Mr. Regehr stepped forward. "He might be. But the fact remains that if he came to us with his accusations, he's shared them in other places as well. Even if they aren't true, it casts aspersions on the mission as a whole."

Mr. Breneman added, his tone pleading, "Don't you see, Miss Willems? If we'd had a man in charge of the poor farm, Mr. Dresden wouldn't have been able to make accusations of impropriety."

Indignation tightened Christina's chest. "The only person behaving with impropriety was Hamilton Dresden himself."

"And, presuming Dresden did behave inappropriately, would he have had the courage to do so if a *man* had been leading the asylum?"

Mr. Regehr's question stabbed Christina's soul. She feared he was right. Defenseless against the accusation, she fixed the men with a worried frown. "So you're willing to permanently displace thirteen innocent souls" — she deliberately counted herself in the number — "because of one man's deplorable choice."

"Of course not." Mr. Regehr employed his impatient schoolteacher tone again. "The mission board is currently seeking placements for each needy person who's been calling the Brambleville Asylum home. As a matter of fact, we're prepared to take the Schwartzes with us today and settle them in an asylum near Hillsboro, where a ground-floor room is available."

Wes clawed at her arm, his eyes wide with

alarm. Christina took his hand and started to protest the decision to take Herman and Harriet away, but Mr. Regehr went on.

"We've long held apprehensions about the asylum's location so far from town or helpful neighbors. Had your father not been such a capable leader, we probably wouldn't have purchased the property in the first place. A larger city — Lawrence, for example — might be a more appropriate location."

Arguments formed in Christina's head, but she bit her tongue and remained silent. She sensed Mr. Breneman might be willing to listen to reason if Mr. Regehr weren't standing guard like a snarling dog chained to a mansion's porch column. She'd address the situation again — soon — but in a letter to the entire mission board. She'd already spent more than an hour at the poor farm property, and she still needed to drive to the Jonnson mill and retrieve Tommy before starting supper at the boardinghouse.

She forced a congenial tone. "Very well, gentlemen."

Wes gawked at her. "Miss Willems, you ain't gonna let 'em —"

Patting Wes on the arm, she aimed a steady, unblinking look at the pair of board

112

representatives. "Shall we return to town now?"

Wes sniffled as he followed Christina to the four-seat buggy they'd borrowed from the liveryman. Although Wes gave her a look of betrayal, he helped her onto the front seat while the visiting men climbed into the back. Her heart ached at the firm set of Wes's jaw and the tears welling in his eyes, but she couldn't offer assurances. Not with Mr. Regehr and Mr. Breneman so close they'd hear every word. And not until she'd had a chance to petition the entire board about reopening the poor farm under her direction. She wouldn't offer Wes false hope.

In town the mission representatives shook Christina's hand in farewell. Mr. Breneman offered a meek apology for being the bearer of bad news, but Mr. Regehr marched off toward the hotel without a backward glance. Mr. Breneman trotted after him, his smooth cheeks bearing bright banners of embarrassment.

As soon as the two men were gone, Christina slipped Papa's watch from beneath her coat and peeked at its round face. She had an hour before she'd need to help prepare supper at the boardinghouse, which offered sufficient time for another errand. She turned to Wes. "Would you please hitch the poor farm horse to our wagon?"

Wes folded his arms tightly across his chest and presented his back to her. "Why?"

In spite of his belligerence, Christina answered kindly. "Because I need to drive to the Jonnson mill."

Wes spun around so fast he nearly lost his balance. "The sawmill? You gonna ask Mr. Jonnson about rebuildin' the house?"

His hopeful expression tore at Christina. "I need to retrieve Tommy. The banker and his wife said they'd take him in."

His mouth formed a grim line, and he drew back. "So you're gonna dump Tommy on somebody else? Not even gonna try to take care of him your own self? Not gonna try to keep Herman an' Harriet here or take care o' any of us anymore?" Although he sounded more befuddled than angry, his questions flayed her.

Christina held a hand toward him in supplication. "Wes, please listen to me. I —"

He shook his head and scurried toward the horses, which shuffled within their traces. He grabbed a bridle, sending a hurt look over his shoulder. "Don't wanna talk right now." He gave the bridle a yank, and the horses obediently stepped forward.

Christina started after him, intending to ask him to be patient and to give her a chance to work things out, but his stiff shoulders and the firm clomp of his boots against the hay-strewn ground dissuaded her. When Wes was upset, he couldn't reason — she'd learned that from working with him over the past years. She should give him an opportunity to calm down. Time with the horses always soothed him. She'd come back later when he'd be more cooperative.

In the meantime she had an important errand. Tugging the collar of her coat more snugly around her chin, she half walked, half trotted across the street to Creeger Mercantile. The brass cowbell hanging above the screen door clanged a raucous greeting as she entered the store, and Mrs. Creeger bustled from behind the counter, hands outstretched.

"Good afternoon, Miss Willems! Come over by the stove — warm yourself. You look chilled clear through despite that nice new coat."

Christina allowed the gregarious woman to escort her to the stove in the center of the store. She held her palms to the heat, offering Mrs. Creeger a smile. "This feels wonderful. The air is so cold. It makes me eager for spring."

Mrs. Creeger laughed, her eyes crinkling

with merriment. "Jay says we're sure to have another snow before we bid good-bye to winter. In case he's right, we should find you a scarf and some gloves. We can't have you freezing your nose or fingers!"

Christina clapped her hands to her cheeks, abashed. "Oh, Mrs. Creeger, I am so sorry. I met with representatives from the mission board today, but we only discussed the house. I forgot to ask when to expect funds to cover the bill here at the mercantile."

"Now, don't you worry about that." Mrs. Creeger dismissed Christina's concerns with a flippant shrug and bright smile. "We won't send out notices until the end of the month, so you've got a good week and a half yet to get things settled with the mission board. Besides, Jay and me admire how you're trying so hard to take care of everybody, and you with not even a roof to call your own. We've been praying for you."

Christina blinked, tears stinging. "You . . . you have?"

"We surely have." Mrs. Creeger slung her arm around Christina's shoulders and squeezed. "And we'll keep on praying, every day, for you and all those folks who've been scattered to the winds because of that awful fire."

"That's so kind of you, Mrs. Creeger.

Thank you."

The woman gave Christina another squeeze, then dropped her arm. "You're welcome. But please call me Mary Ann. Jay and me, being new in town, haven't made many friends yet. It'd be nice if a woman close to my age called me by my given name."

Mary Ann Creeger radiated as much warmth as her wood stove. Christina couldn't help but smile. Had she ever had a friend? Not someone dependent on her, not someone looking to her to lead and guide, but a friend with whom to chat and laugh and even pray? No, never — not even during her boarding school years, when her serious nature held her aloof from the other girls. She'd just been offered a precious gift. "I'd like that, too. And you may call me Christina."

Mary Ann's face lit up. "What a lovely name! Well," — she looped her arm through Christina's — "Christina, you come right over here and choose a scarf and a pair of gloves."

"Oh, but —"

"No arguing! Jay will tell you there's no sense arguing with me because you'll never win."

Christina laughed at her new friend's

mock scowl. "Very well. Thank you. And while I'm choosing things, might I add writing paper and envelopes to my account? I need to send some missives as quickly as possible."

"Why, of course. I'll get those for you while you choose your gloves." Mary Ann scurried off, her floral skirts swinging.

Christina lifted a pair of dark-green knitted gloves from the box and cradled them between her palms. Papa had always liked green — he called it the color of new growth. She hugged the gloves to her chest and closed her eyes, sending up a silent prayer. *Lord, the poor farm needs new growth. Help me find the words to convince the mission board to rebuild. And please . . . please . . .* One tear slipped from beneath her closed lid and formed a warm trail to her chin. *Please let me continue to serve.*

CHAPTER 10

"Mr. Jonnson. There's a wagon comin'."

Levi set aside his chisel at Tommy's announcement and crossed to the window. His breath steamed the pane, and he swept it clean with the cuff of his flannel shirt, then peered out. Sure enough, the same horse and wagon that had deposited Tommy on his doorstep nine days ago was rumbling up the lane. On the driver's seat, with a green scarf knotted beneath her chin, perched Miss Willems.

A grin tugged at Levi's cheeks. Even from this distance and with a sheen of steam hindering his view, he recognized the determined tilt of the woman's chin. His mother would have called her *modig* — plucky. And Mor would've been right.

He flicked a baffled glance at Tommy. "I don't know how you heard it already — it's not quite halfway up the lane — but you were right. Miss Willems is coming." Tommy's face broke into a wide smile, but he didn't leap to his feet. Levi headed toward the little enclosure of sawhorses he'd erected to keep Tommy from stumbling into any of the mill's equipment. "Want to go greet her? You can follow the rope from the mill to the house and take yourself."

Tommy shook his head, the motion awkward. "Wanna stay right here. Want her to see how I'm workin'."

The pride emanating from the boy put a lump in Levi's throat. Without a word of complaint, Tommy had spent the bulk of the day twisting together pieces of hemp rope that Levi had sliced into four-foot lengths and nailed to a board. Although the ropes didn't yet form an intricate pattern, they held together. With practice and time, the boy would figure it out.

Earlier, Levi had laid aside his tools and watched Tommy work, entranced not only by the fingers, as busy as a spider spinning a web, but by the boy's intense concentration. But after only a minute or two of Levi's observation, Tommy's hands had paused, his gaze bouncing erratically around the mill. "M-Mr. Jonnson?"

"Right here, Tommy. What's wrong?"

The boy sagged in obvious relief. "Didn't hear nothin'. Thought you'd left me."

Levi had assured Tommy he wouldn't leave without telling him, then had returned to his work. He'd made sure to keep his hands as busy as Tommy's so the boy wouldn't have cause to worry. Amazing how much the boy perceived by using his ears.

The grind of wooden wheels against hard-packed earth now reached Levi's ears. Miss Willems had stopped the wagon at the edge of the porch. Before she could alight, Levi swung the mill door open and called, "We're in here."

Without a word she released the brake, gave the reins a flick, and drew the horse to a halt near the mill doors. He stepped to the edge of the wagon and held out his hands, a silent offer to help her down. Why he'd decided to be gentlemanly, he couldn't say — she'd never needed his assistance before. But somehow it seemed the right thing to do. Her gaze lit on his waiting hands, and she drew back for a moment, her brow puckering as if uncertain. But then she placed her gloved hands in his and allowed him to assist her.

The moment the soles of her scuffed black boots reached the ground, she pulled free of his light grasp and gave him a disapproving frown. "Did you say 'we' are in the mill, meaning Tommy, too?"

Levi slipped his fingertips into his trouser pockets. He allowed a wry grin to climb his cheek. "Good afternoon, Miss Willems. How are you today?"

Her cold-reddened cheeks blazed to a deeper hue, and she pursed her rosy lips as if she'd tasted something sour. The bodice of her wool coat expanded with a deep breath. As she released the air in a steamy little cloud, her expression softened, and a weak curve replaced the stern line of her lips. "Please forgive me. I've had a rather trying afternoon, and I'm afraid my manners are lacking." She clutched her elbows, a slight shiver shuddering her frame. "Did you say Tommy is inside the mill?"

"That's what I said." Levi ambled toward the wide-open door, aware of the patter of feet behind him. "We've spent the whole day out here." He gestured for her to come in, then gave the door a yank, sealing them inside. He watched her release the buttons on her coat one by one while searching the dimly lit room. Her eyes seemed to take in every minute detail. When her gaze landed on Tommy's corner, those blue eyes flew wide open, and she slapped one hand over her mouth.

Tommy shifted to one knee, his face

crunching in concern. "Miss Willems, is that you?"

The woman flung a brief, venomous look at Levi, which took him so by surprise he staggered backward two steps. Then she darted to the corner, pushed aside one of the sawhorses, and threw her arms around Tommy. She cradled the boy's head against her shoulder and pressed her cheek to his hair while she murmured to him.

Tommy remained stiff within her arms, his eyes blinking so slowly Levi could count the blinks. Then she bolted upright. One hand remained on Tommy's shoulder, but the other balled into a fist and landed on her hip. Her eyes blazed fire as she glowered at Levi. "*Misssster* Jonnson, would you kindly explain yourself?"

He stifled a chuckle. Yep, modig. With her narrowed eyes and the way she hissed his name, she reminded him of a cornered snake. Except he'd never seen a snake so pretty. He shuffled forward a few steps but kept a good distance between them. A cornered snake might strike. "Sure. If you'll tell me what you need explained."

"You've placed Tommy in a — in a cage!" She gestured at the circle of sawhorses. "He's a boy, not an animal or a criminal in need of confinement! Is this your idea of proper treatment?"

Levi's amusement fled, and his hackles rose. "Ma'am, I —"

"And look at him!" She caught Tommy by the elbow and hefted him to his feet. A man's silver watch, suspended on a chain, swung back and forth across her chest with her jerky movements. "Sawdust in his hair." She fluffed the strands. A shower of tiny wood bits flew around her hand. "And on his clothes!" She smacked at the boy's knees, dispelling more bits. "Fingertips raw and bleeding . . ." Holding the boy's hands aloft, she cringed.

Levi did, too. He hadn't realized how much the bristly hemp had cut into Tommy's flesh. He should've chosen something else for the boy to use for practice. Before he could offer an apology, she rushed on.

"And don't think all the ropes strung from building to building out there escaped my notice. Why, it's a veritable maze! Placed, no doubt, to save you the trouble of escorting Tommy."

Tommy patted the air near Miss Willems's shoulder. "Miss Willems? Miss Willems?"

She ignored the boy and stomped toward Levi, fists on her hips and eyes sparking. "Have you simply confined him and gone about your business as if a boy in need of care was never placed in your keeping?"

Levi growled under his breath. Maybe she was a little too modig. He aimed his finger at her face and matched her scowl with one of his own. "I told you I wouldn't mollycoddle him. I told you I've got a business to run and I don't have time to play nursemaid. And you still left him here, so don't turn all high and mighty and act like I've done something wrong. I've done exactly what I said I'd do — I let that boy fend for himself."

She stared at him in open-mouthed amazement. While she was quiet, for once, he took advantage.

"And let me tell you something else, Miss Willems." Levi lowered his hand and gentled his voice. "He's done just fine." Levi tipped sideways slightly to look at Tommy, who stood, arms rigid at his sides, right where Miss Willems had left him. "He takes himself to the outhouse, thanks to the guiding rope. He dresses himself and feeds himself and washes his face. Even combs his own hair." Behind Miss Willems, Tommy's tense stance relaxed. Levi decided to tease a little, hoping to earn a smile from the boy. "Of course, he can't get his cowlick to lie down." He aimed a smirk at Miss Willems. "But then, I'd wager you couldn't either."

Tommy snickered, but Miss Willems's stern expression remained the same. She yanked her scarf from her head, mussing her hair. Light brown strands — the color of stained oak — framed her flushed cheeks. "But confining him. Placing him in what amounts to a cage . . ."

Levi resisted rolling his eyes. "Miss Willems, I didn't do that out of meanness. I've got dangerous equipment out here. As you've pointed out, Tommy can't see. I didn't want him getting hurt. So I built the barrier to protect him."

She shifted slightly and peered over her shoulder at Tommy. The anger seemed to slowly drain from her stiff frame. "Oh . . ." She swallowed. "Well, he does look as though he's been well fed. And except for the sawdust, he's clean."

Levi bit his tongue to hold back a snide remark.

Then she spun on him again. "But his poor fingers, all torn and bleeding. Why were you forcing him to tie knots?"

Levi opened his mouth to instruct her to address Tommy. The boy had a tongue, and she should encourage him to use it. But before he could form the words, Tommy interrupted.

"He wasn't makin' me do it." Tommy

inched in their direction, his hands outstretched. Miss Willems met him halfway.
The boy clung to her, his expression pleading. "I wanted to. It wasn't Mr. Jonnson's
doing at all."

"You *wanted* to tangle together pieces of
rough rope?"

Levi grimaced. Did the woman know how
disparaging she sounded? He cleared his
throat. "He's not tangling ropes, ma'am.
He's weaving. Trying to learn how to cane."

Miss Willems crinkled her nose. The
gesture carved years from her appearance.
"Trying to learn to . . . what?"

"Cane," Tommy said. Excitement made
the boy's voice shoot high like a saw blade
humming at full throttle. "So I can fix Mr.
Jonnson's chair. A mouse chewed the seat,
an' —"

"Tommy, slow down." Miss Willems shook
her head. "I don't understand what you're
saying."

Levi strode to the wall, removed the damaged chair from the pegs, and plopped it on
the floor in front of Miss Willems. "See
here? A mouse chewed a hole in the middle
of the seat, so the caning came undone."
He explained how Tommy had inadvertently
formed a loosely woven pattern with some
discarded wood curls. "I figured, if he can

weave strips of wood, maybe he can weave reeds or sisal. He wanted to try."

Miss Willems slipped her arm around the boy's shoulders. "I apologize for accusing you falsely, Mr. Jonnson." Considering she was delivering an apology, she certainly chose a tart tone. "Well-meaning you might be, but it's clear you lack the awareness of what is an appropriate activity for Tommy." She looked again at the boy's fingertips, and pain creased her brow. "His fingers require attention — some salve and bandages."

Levi gestured in the direction of his house. "I've got some —"

"No need. I'll see to his injuries when we reach town. I know Mrs. Beasley keeps medicinal supplies in a cabinet." Miss Willems began herding Tommy toward the door. "Let's gather your things, Tommy, and before long I'll have you all bandaged up and ready to go to Mr. and Mrs. Tatum's house."

Levi reared back. What?

Tommy halted, jerking free of Miss Willems's hold. "What?"

"Mr. and Mrs. Tatum's house, where Joe and Florie are staying." Miss Willems caught Tommy's wrist and gave a gentle pull. "They said you could stay there, too. So let's go."

Dumbfounded, Levi remained rooted in place and watched the woman try to draw Tommy to the yard. The boy turned stiff and uncooperative. He wrenched his hand from her grip.

"Tommy . . ." She sent a pink-cheeked glance in Levi's direction. A hint of pleading shone in her eyes.

Levi chewed the inside of his cheek. He should help Miss Willems — encourage the boy to go. But his tongue refused to form words.

Miss Willems cupped her hands on Tommy's shoulders. "Tommy, when I brought you here, it was only because I couldn't find someplace else. Do you remember? Mr. Jonnson told me this wasn't a safe place for you to stay and asked me to find another place for you quickly."

Levi's chest tightened. He'd been heartless that night. Honest, but heartless.

"I've done that. So now it's time to go." She lifted her gaze to Levi, her expression firm. "Mr. Jonnson, if you'd be so kind as to collect Tommy's things and put them in the wagon, we'll be on our way."

Tommy knocked Miss Willems's hands from his shoulders and turned in a circle, his arms reaching toward Levi. He took two steps, and his toe caught on a rock. With a cry of alarm, he plummeted toward the ground. Levi bolted forward and caught him before he fell. Tommy gripped Levi's jacket with both fists.

"Mr. Jonnson, I wanna stay here. I wanna learn to cane." The boy held Levi's jacket so tightly his knuckles turned white. "I want . . . I want to *do* something."

Levi's pulse tripped hard and fast. His mother's voice drifted in from long ago: *"If you'd only get up and* do *something, Axel, how much better you would feel. Please — get out of your chair and do something."* Far hadn't heeded Mor's words, and they'd all been forced to watch him drift deeper and deeper into himself until he'd finally gone to sleep and didn't wake again. Did such a fate await Tommy if forced to simply sit and do nothing?

But why should he feel responsible for this boy? Hadn't he decided long ago his life would be easier if he kept to himself? He knew all too well that some people deceived you. Some people abandoned you. If you let them get close, some people broke your heart. A pain — like a fist squeezed tight — gripped his chest. He wouldn't let himself be hurt like that again.

He took hold of Tommy's upper arms and set him aside. "Go with Miss Willems. You can learn caning at the banker's house. They'll have string or rope, too. You don't need to be here to do something." His dry throat turned his words harsh.

Tommy blinked up at him, confusion evident in his pinched brow. "But what about your chair?"

Levi gritted his teeth. "Never mind the chair, boy. Just go."

Defeat slumped Tommy's shoulders. His hands fell from Levi's jacket. "M-Miss Willems? Take me to the wagon."

"I'll get his things," Levi said and headed past them to the house. It wouldn't take long — the boy owned next to nothing. Levi snatched up the few belongings, wadded them into a ball, and returned to the wagon. Miss Willems had already helped Tommy onto the high seat, and she stood poised beside it, watching for him. He pressed the bundle under the seat.

"Thank you for allowing Tommy to stay with you." She sounded prim. Proper.

He responded in kind. "You're welcome." He offered his hand, and she allowed him to assist her into the wagon. He stepped back. "Bye, Miss Willems. Bye, Tommy."

The woman smiled in reply as she picked up the reins, but Tommy stared straight ahead, unmoving, as if he hadn't heard the farewell. But Levi knew better. And, to his surprise, it hurt to be ignored.

CHAPTER 11

Cora hunched over the slop bucket with a plump potato and a paring knife in her hand. Long coils of brown peel fell from the blade and landed with a *plop* in the smelly bucket. She glanced at the Regulator clock tick-ticking on the kitchen wall. Miss Willems had said she'd be back in time to help with supper preparations, but Mrs. Beasley wanted supper on the table precisely at six. The hands had already moved toward five o'clock. It wasn't like Miss Willems to go back on her word. Had something happened to her?

She reached for the final potato in the bowl on the table. Before she picked it up, though, the scuff of feet on the back stoop captured Cora's attention. Finally! She dropped the knife next to the bowl and bounded to the door. But instead of Miss Willems, Wes stood outside the door, shivering.

Cold wind wheezed through the door opening. She caught Wes's coat sleeve and drew him over the threshold, then snapped the door shut with a firm *click.* "What're you doing here? Have you seen Miss Willems?"

A frown marred Wes's normally placid face. "I seen her. Drove her an' them mission men to the house. I wanted to talk to her again. She here?"

Cora shook her head and scuttled to the stove — that wind chilled a person clear through in no time. When would the cold leave and spring arrive? "Huh-uh. I was hopin' you were her. She should've been back an hour or so ago."

Wes dragged his boot heels across the floor as he approached the stove, hands extended. His frown didn't melt when he reached the heat. "I'm mad at her, Cora. Don't like to be mad, but . . ." He raised his shoulders and held them there, like a turtle trying to shrink into its shell. "Gotta talk to her. Can't let her give up."

A chill of foreboding wiggled its way down Cora's spine. "Whaddaya mean 'give up'?"

"Them mission men, they said they didn't wanna build the house up again. Said if they were gonna have another poor farm, it'd be someplace else. Like Lawrence."

Cora staggered to the table and collapsed in the chair. She stared at Wes, her pulse galloping faster than a runaway horse. She needed a home, but she couldn't go back to Lawrence! "But why?"

" 'Cause they don't want Miss Willems runnin' the poor farm anymore. Said it was . . ." He scrunched up his face, his eyeballs rolling back and forth as if seeking something hidden. Then he huffed out a breath. "Unseemly."

Goose flesh broke out on Cora's arms. She snatched up the potato and knife and set to flicking bits of peel into the bucket. "They say why?"

Wes yanked out the second chair and folded himself into it. Elbows on the table edge, he leaned close. "You know Ham Dresden?"

Cora searched her memory. She'd heard the name, but she didn't know the man. "Huh-uh."

"Oh, that's right. He was gone before you came." Wes snorted. "Good riddance, too. Never met such a lazy man in my whole life. If Miss Willems sent him to the garden to chop weeds, he'd stretch out under a tree an' take a nap. If she sent him to the barn to feed the animals, he'd climb into the loft an' hunker down in a pile of straw. He was

135

a fine one for sleepin'. For eatin', too. Only time I saw him set himself to doin' something with any ginger, it was liftin' a fork."

Relief shuddered through Cora's frame. They weren't blaming the unseemly behavior on her. At least not yet. She'd finished peeling the potatoes, so she fetched a cooking pot. "Were the mission men upset that Miss Willems let Ham Dresden stay at the poor farm?"

Wes scratched his head, uncertainty pinching his features. "Don't think it was the stayin' that bothered 'em so much as . . . somethin' else. But I don't know what the somethin' else is."

Cora cut potatoes into chunks and dropped them into the pot. A troubling thought formed in the back of her mind. Miss Willems was old. Lots older than Cora. Probably twenty-eight. Maybe even twenty-nine. And she wasn't married. She must be getting desperate for a husband. Had she let this man — this Ham Dresden — stay at the poor farm without working for his keep because she was sweet on him? Had there been some indecent goings-on? Cora didn't want to think such things about Miss Willems, but she'd known too many women who gave precious parts of themselves to win men, only to be cast aside in the end.

She gulped. "Sure is troublesome, isn't it? Maybe —"

"So I *did* hear a man's voice."

Cora jerked, slicing her thumb with the knife. Wes leaped to his feet and clutched his chest, shock on his face.

Mrs. Beasley stormed to the table, anger mottling her jowled cheeks. "I thought I made it clear I don't allow male callers. You think I want every tongue in town waggin' how Miz Beasley's got a sparkin' house?"

Wes inched away, his eyes so wide they appeared ready to pop from his head. Even though he towered over Mrs. Beasley and was a man to boot, he hurried out the door like a hawk chased off by a sparrow's ferocity. And left Cora all alone to fend off the disgruntled sparrow.

"Wes didn't come here to spark."

"Well, you two sure seemed mighty cozy there at my table."

Heat ignited in Cora's middle. Ma's sneering face appeared in her memory. *"What you doin' cozyin' up to some man? You're no better'n them gals who live in the bawdyhouses!"* Cora blurted, "He wasn't here for me. He was lookin' for Miss Willems."

Mrs. Beasley's scowl deepened as she scanned the kitchen. "She's not back yet?"

Cora inwardly groaned. Now Miss Willems would get the sharp side of Mrs. Beasley's tongue for sure. Couldn't she ever do things right? "Meetin' with them board fellas must've gone longer than she thought." She squared her shoulders. "She's gotta get things settled. Get the rebuildin' started." Even though Wes had said the mission men didn't intend to rebuild, Cora had to hang on to hope. Where would she go, what would she do, if they closed the Brambleville Asylum for good?

Mrs. Beasley huffed impatiently. "She's turned out to be more trouble than she's worth with all the runnin' around she does. Checkin' on this person, checkin' on that person, meetin' with people . . ." She pointed her finger at Cora. "I hope you're gonna be able to get supper on the table on time all by yourself. Else the two o' you are gonna have to find some other place to take you in. I'm not runnin' a charity here, you know."

There couldn't be a charitable bone in Mrs. Beasley's body. Cora wanted to say so, too, but Miss Willems's instruction to repay evil with good helped her hold the words inside. "I'll have supper ready."

"You'd better. An' it better taste good, too." Her nose in the air, she departed.

Cora wilted into the chair and pressed both palms to her stomach. Did she only imagine it, or was a small bulge starting to form? She jolted upright and finished chopping the potatoes. As she layered slices of salt pork in a skillet, she looked again at the clock. Five twenty-five. Her pulse stuttered. She could get supper on the table on time without Miss Willems's help. But smiling and being pleasant while she served, the way Mrs. Beasley expected? Impossible. Too many troublesome questions plagued her mind. She feared she wouldn't be able to hide her worries any better than she would soon be able to hide her swollen belly.

Levi slid his tin plate onto the table, then scooted up his chair. His fork lay on the edge of the plate, waiting to be used to stab bites of steaming corned beef hash. Levi grabbed the fork, but instead of plunging it into the mound of hash, he held it in his fist like a spear and stared at the empty chair across from him.

Nine days. Only nine days of sharing this table with someone. How could he have gotten used to having someone in the house — how could he have gotten *attached* to someone — so quickly? When dishing up his supper, he'd come close to pouring a glass of milk. And he didn't drink milk. Nine days, and he'd set a pattern for himself.

"Narr . . ." He flayed himself with the word his father had often muttered to himself, feeling every bit the fool for getting entangled in that boy's life. Now the boy was gone. Time to forget him. To forget the past. To focus on what waited around the bend.

He jammed the fork into the hash and lifted a bite. He chewed, his thoughts rolling onward. Only one more week and March would arrive. He swallowed. Took another bite. That meant spring. The river would thaw, the water would flow, and the mill would run again. So it was a good thing Miss Willems had fetched Tommy. Once the mill was running, he couldn't have a blind boy wandering around, maybe getting hurt. He tried to swallow, but the food stuck in his gullet. He slapped the fork down so hard his plate jumped.

No longer hungry, he snatched up the plate, marched to the kitchen, and dumped the contents back in the pan. Maybe he'd eat it later. But for now . . . With a determined stride he returned to the table, hooked Tommy's chair, and carted it to the corner. Plopped it down the way a frustrated mother might disgrace a naughty child.

There! No empty chair gawking from across the table, no reminder of a sightless boy who'd somehow ignited a spark in the center of Levi's chest. Now he could forget.

Christina glanced at her watch as she bustled in the back door of the boarding-house. Six fifteen! So late . . . Two battered tin plates holding chunks of buttered pota-toes, thin slices of fried pork, and a pile of greens dotted with onions sat on the little kitchen worktable. The food smelled won-derful, and Christina's stomach lurched in desire to sit down and partake. But they needed to serve the boarders first as Mrs. Beasley had instructed.

She whipped off her hat, scarf, and gloves, tossed them on the bed, then clattered back to the kitchen in time to see Cora step from the dining room doorway. Christina offered her most apologetic look. "I had a dreadful time with Tommy at the Tatums. He didn't want me to go, so I had to stay until he calmed down. What can I do now that I'm here?"

"Just sit down an' eat before the food gets cold." Cora moved past her to the stove and lifted the green speckled coffeepot. "Food's on the dinin' room table, an' folks are eatin'. I'm gonna take the pot in there an' serve 'em all a second cup, then —"

"I'll do it." It was the least she could do after leaving the entire supper preparation to Cora. "You look peaked. I shouldn't allow you to work so hard."

"Not sure Miz Beasley would approve of me slackin' off."

Christina grimaced. "Has she been fussing again?"

Cora shrugged, a feeble attempt to appear unconcerned, but hurt glittered in her eyes. "No worse'n usual." She flapped her hands toward the dining room. "Best get that coffee in there. I noticed Ol' Miz Perkins had already drained her first cup."

Bracing herself for a verbal barrage the moment she entered, Christina carried the pot through the short hallway leading to the dining room. Mrs. Beasley shot her a sour look as she circled the long walnut table refilling cups with the steaming black liquid, but the woman kept her lips clamped together.

With everyone's china cup filled to the brim, she placed the pot on an iron trivet in the middle of the table and scurried back to the kitchen. Cora stood at the stove, ladling hot water from the reservoir into a washbowl. She caught Cora by the waist and pushed her gently aside. "These pots and pans will keep. Let's sit together and eat."

For a moment it seemed Cora would argue, but then she released a little sigh. "I am hungry." She sank into one chair, her shoulders slumping. A wide yawn stretched her mouth. "And tired, too."

"Well, I'll do all the cleanup tonight so you can turn in early. Bow your head." Christina spoke a brief blessing for the meal, then said, "Amen." She examined Cora while she ate, noting the dark circles beneath her eyes and the pallor of her skin. She set her fork aside. "Cora, are you ill?"

Cora jolted. The potato she'd stabbed fell from the tines. "Wh-why do you ask?" She cupped her stomach with one hand, and her fingers trembled.

Christina's concern heightened. "You look pale, and you're so tired all the time. I know you've had" — she lowered her head for a moment, not wishing to embarrass Cora — "some difficulty holding down your food."

Pink splashed Cora's cheeks, and she fiddled with her fork. "I'm not sick, Miss Willems. Honest."

"Are you sure? We could take you to the doctor. Ask about a tonic . . ."

A strange smile quirked up one side of Cora's mouth. "Ain't no tonic that'll do me any good."

Fingers of trepidation stole across Christina's scalp. "Cora, you don't . . . You aren't —"

"Miss Willems!"

Mrs. Beasley's screech startled Christina so badly she nearly upset her chair. She bounced up and scurried to the dining room. "Yes, ma'am?" she gasped out between breaths.

"We're ready for our dessert. And we need more coffee."

Given the stridency of the woman's tone in summoning her, Christina had at least expected to find a spider descending from the ceiling. She clamped her hands over her pounding heart to keep it from escaping her chest. "Did you say . . . dessert?"

Mrs. Beasley huffed. Christina had never met anyone as adept at expelling mighty breaths of air as this woman. "Yes, dessert. Didn't you bake pies this mornin' like I told you?"

Christina moaned. Just as she was setting out the ingredients to roll the crusts after lunch, the boy from the telegrapher's office had summoned her to the train station to meet the mission board representatives. "I'm so sorry, Mrs. Beasley. I was called away, and —"

"An' you neglected your duties here."

Eight pairs of eyes stared at Christina — one furious glare and seven gazes ranging from disappointed to embarrassed. She squirmed, as uncomfortable as she'd been when Mr. Regehr had mentioned Ham Dresden's accusations. She couldn't easily change Mr. Regehr's opinion of her, but perhaps she could mollify the sweet-toothed boarders and their irascible hostess. "What if I whip some cream and put it over sliced peaches? Would that suffice?"

One of the women boarders licked her lips, but Mrs. Beasley blew out another noisy breath and flapped a hand in dismissal. "I suppose."

Christina turned to go.

"But we're gonna have us a talk this evenin'."

CHAPTER 12

"Miss Willems, can I talk to you . . . about somethin' important?" Caught in that hazy place between dream and sleep, Christina snuffled. "Did you say something, Cora?"

"Yes, ma'am." The bedsprings creaked as Cora repositioned herself. "Can we talk?"

Truthfully, Christina had no desire for another chat. Her meeting with the mission board representatives hadn't gone well, she'd had a distressing back-and-forth exchange with Levi Jonnson, followed by Tommy's heartrending pleas for her to stay — something she couldn't possibly do — and then the day had ended with her listening to Mrs. Beasley's diatribe and veiled threats of expulsion. Could she take one more piece of bad news without falling apart? Probably not. But how could she refuse Cora? Obviously the young woman held a grave concern.

Christina forced her bleary eyes open and

rolled in the bed to face Cora. A scant amount of moonlight slanted through the lace-draped window, creating shadows in every corner of the small room. Christina focused on Cora's pale face, only inches from hers. "What is it?"

"Wes came by this afternoon, an' . . ."

Christina stifled a groan. Another failed conversation.

"He said the mission men aren't gonna give you money to build the house back. He said the mission men want somebody else to run the poor farm." Icy fingers found Christina's arm and dug in, the grip desperate. "Miss Willems, what'll we all do if the poor farm doesn't get built again? We can't stay here for . . . forever."

According to Mrs. Beasley, they might not even be able to stay until Christina located a large enough house to accommodate all her charges. Assuming she could secure funds to purchase another house. Worries attacked, tempting her to dissolve into tears. But Christina couldn't allow emotion to buckle her. She drew a fortifying breath.

"I never intended for us to stay here forever. Just until we get our house back." Wherever that house may be. "I don't want you to worry, Cora. God will take care of us." The words slipped effortlessly from

147

Christina's lips. How many times had she heard her father say the same thing? Papa's faith was so strong. He'd expected Christina to be strong, too. She wouldn't disappoint him.

"You keep sayin' that, but Wes said . . ." From the other side of the mattress, Cora paused, her eyes wide. "He said the mission men wouldn't let you be in charge anymore because there was some man at the poor farm before I came. Some man who . . . who . . ." She gulped, the sound loud in the nighttime silence. "Did he woo you?"

Christina raised up on one elbow. The bedsprings twanged in protest. "Absolutely not!"

"N-no?"

If Christina hadn't known better, she would have thought Cora sounded disappointed. "Of course not! Why, I would never . . . *never* . . . engage in anything less than an acceptable relationship with a man. And certainly not with someone who resided beneath my roof!"

"I . . . I see."

Recalling Cora's odd statement at the supper table, Christina touched her shoulder. "Cora, was there something else you wanted to tell me?"

"About what?" Defensiveness colored

Cora's voice.

Christina pinched her brow, worry striking anew. Oh, how she hoped Cora wasn't seriously ill. Years ago, even before Mama died, a man had come to her parents' house to spend his final days in order to spare his family the painful task of watching him succumb to an incurable sickness. Perhaps Cora faced a similar fate. Using her gentlest tone, Christina asked, "About why you've been so tired and wan of late?"

Cora rolled the opposite direction, pulling the pile of covers up to her ear. "No, ma'am."

"Are you sure? You can talk to me, Cora. About anything. Anything at all."

Very slowly Cora turned her head and peeked at Christina with one brown eye. A tear glistened. Tousled brown hair fell across her lashes, flicking with each blink. "You say that, but . . ."

Christina grazed Cora's shoulder with her fingertips. "I say it because I mean it. I'm here to help you. I want to understand."

Cora's eye squeezed shut. The tear slipped free, leaving a silvery trail down Cora's pale cheek. "No way you can understand. Not somebody like you, who . . ." She released a shuddering breath. Flopping fully on her side again, she faced the wall. "I'm tired,

Miss Willems. Good night."

"Good night, Cora." Christina lay back down and pulled the covers to her chin. Warm and snug, tired and in need of rest, she waited for sleep to claim her. But blessed rest eluded her. Cora certainly carried a heavy burden, yet she refused to share it. All the day's failures washed over her.

Papa would have convinced the mission board men to provide funding.

Papa would have spoken firmly yet kindly with Mr. Jonnson.

Papa would have reassured Wes and helped Tommy understand why the Tatums' house was the best temporary shelter for him.

Papa would have managed to lead Cora to a place of peace and comfort.

The tears she tried valiantly to hold at bay filled her eyes. She wanted so much to emulate her dear, steadfast father. *Dear Lord, why must I always fall short?*

After cleaning up the breakfast mess, Christina instructed Cora to rest, slipped paper and the stub of a pencil into her coat pocket, and then set off for the livery. Wes always drove out to the poor farm mid-morning to see to their animals, but she hoped she'd catch him before he left. She wanted to ride along today. The ride would give her and Wes a chance to talk, but she'd also be able to examine the house at her leisure, perhaps make some sketches of the damage to share with the mission board. And she intended to visit Papa's grave. How she longed for her father's sage counsel.

By the time she reached the livery, her nose felt frozen. Snowflakes danced in the air. Apparently Jay Creeger's prediction of another snowfall prior to spring had been accurate. Christina raised the collar of her coat around her jaw and hurried the final few yards to the livery's wide opening. As she stepped inside, she called, "Hello? Is anyone here?"

From a shadowy stall at the back, Wes emerged. One of the things Christina had always liked about Wes was his ready smile. Although learning didn't come easily and people sometimes tormented him, the young man had always possessed a cheerful outlook. It pierced her to see him frowning as he trudged across the floor to meet her.

Christina forced her quivering lips into a smile. "Wes, I'm glad you haven't left for the poor farm yet. I'd like to ride out with you today."

"Why?"

His blunt response was a knife in Christina's breast. The fire had damaged much more than the house — it was eating away at the once easy, comfortable relationships she'd shared with the residents. "So we can talk. I'm sorry I missed you at the boarding-house yesterday."

Wes dropped his gaze and drew arches in the dirt with the toe of his boot. "Me, too. I won't bother you there again." He sent a brief look in her direction before examining the ground again. "That lady, she's real noisy."

Christina took a forward step and placed her hand on Wes's forearm. "I'm sorry if she hurt your feelings."

He shook his head, shrugging. "Didn't hurt my feelings. Just scared me. I didn't like her." He looked Christina full in the face. "Cora doesn't like her either. She wants to leave that place." A hint of accusation colored his tone.

Christina sighed. "Wes, will you believe me if I say I'm doing everything I can to bring us all together again?"

He offered another slow shrug, his gaze angling to the left.

Christina squeezed his arm. "Have I ever lied to you before?"

"I dunno."

His response hurt. Yes, the fire had certainly stolen something precious — Wes's trust. She injected as much confidence in her voice as her tight throat would allow.

"I can't make promises about what will happen, because I don't know for sure what the mission board will choose to do. But I promise to try to convince them to rebuild or, at the very least, to allow me to purchase another property where you, Tommy, Herman and Harriet, Alice and her youngsters, Joe and Florie, Cora, Rose, and Louisa can all live together again." She tugged at his arm until he met her gaze. "Do you believe me?"

Wes turned his head slowly, almost imperceptibly, until his puzzled gaze landed on Christina's face. "What about you?"

"Me?"

"You gonna live there, too?"

Oh, how Christina wanted to remain with the others! They were her family — without them, she was as useless as a boat without oars. But the men had been adamant about not putting a woman in charge of the poor farm. "I-I don't know, Wes. I'll try, all right?"

He heaved a giant-sized sigh. "All right, Miss Willems." A sad smile quivered at the corners of his lips. "Your pa told me enough times when I was thinkin' I was too dumb to do something, 'All a fella can do is pray an' try.' I reckon that's all you can do, too."

"Pray and try." She'd heard the advice so many times. She could still see her father's tender expression as he'd uttered the words. "Thank you for the reminder, Wes."

"Well, you ready to go on out?" Wes's face crunched into a look of abject sympathy. "That cow's prob'ly ready to burst by now."

Christina laughed. "Yes, let's go."

They rode in silence, but to Christina's relief it was a companionable silence, yesterday's animosity dissolved. Snowflakes, dry and light, wisped from the white-smudged sky and dusted the brown landscape. Despite the cold temperatures, she noted the white maples were beginning to bud — a hopeful sign that winter would soon come to an end.

Wes parked the wagon outside the barn and hopped down. He trotted to the barn without offering Christina a helping hand, but she didn't mind. The cow needed his attention more than she did. Holding her skirts to the side, she used the wagon wheel as a ladder and then crossed the hard ground to the back of the house.

Each time she glimpsed the blackened walls and sagging roof above what had once been a warm, functional kitchen, her heart ached with regret. The mission representa-

154

tives had agreed the fire had started in this room, but how? Alone and without distractions, Christina gingerly stepped into the charred shell. She thought back on the last night in the house — the final day. She'd turned in long after the others, determined to bake a sufficient number of loaves of bread to last for a week.

She toed what remained of the firebox, now a splintery pile of ash and blackened slats, recalling how she'd filled the box twice to fuel the stove's belly. She stared at the iron Majestic stove, at its door hanging from one hinge, and tried to remember if she'd dampened the stove when she'd finally finished the baking. She'd been so tired. What if she'd left the flue open? Or neglected to extinguish every coal before turning in? Her pulse began to pound, her head throbbing as she forced herself to think, think . . . She was the last one in the kitchen. Had she done something foolish and caused the fire?

She'd intended to draw rough images of the damage and to formulate a plan for rebuilding to prove to the mission board she possessed the ability to bring the poor farm back into operation. But if she was to blame for the fire, how could anyone —

including herself — see her as capable of handling such a large responsibility?

CHAPTER 13

Tommy held tight to Joe's hand and allowed the younger boy to lead him to church for Sunday morning service. The Tatums' house was close to the church building — only eighty-seven paces. Tommy counted each one, trying to lift his feet rather than scuff, the way Mr. Jonnson had said a man walked.

Tommy's toe bumped against something solid, and he started to pitch forward.

Joe grabbed his arm with both hands. "Careful! You almost pulled me over."

"Sorry."

"It's all right. Reckon you couldn't see the steps." Taking Tommy's elbow, Joe said, "Gotta go up. Up. Up. One more . . ."

Eyes closed, hand outstretched, Tommy took five steps across what seemed to be a porch. He paused while a knob turned and hinges moaned. Then two more forward steps, after which a door clicked closed, and the wind wasn't pushing against his back anymore. They were inside.

"We're s'posed to sit down front," Joe said. He took Tommy's hand and started moving.

Their footsteps on the wooden floorboards echoed in the building. Tommy shivered even though the room was toasty warm. How he hated not knowing if people were sitting on the benches, watching him being herded along like a dog on a leash. He whispered, "Is anybody else in here?"

"Not yet." Joe spoke out loud, his voice bouncing off the walls and returning. "Just you an' me. Mrs. Tatum wanted us to get settled before people started comin' in. Not sure why."

Tommy knew why. The woman was shamed by him. She hadn't come right out and said, "Tommy, I'm ashamed to be seen with you," but her actions let him know. If people came to the door, she shuffled him out of the room before letting them in. He had to eat in the kitchen instead of at the dining room table with the others. He didn't even have a bed — just a pile of blankets on the floor in the room Joe and Florie shared. Oh, she talked nice to him. Real nice. Too nice. The way people did when they pretended to like you. But he knew. Tommy hated it at the Tatums' house.

"Here you go." Joe's hands grabbed Tommy's shoulders and gave a little push. Tommy flopped backward, and his bottom connected with a hard bench. The bench squeaked — Joe settling in beside him — and then silence except for a *tick, tick, tick* from over his head, somewhere on the right.

Tick, tick, tick counting off the minutes.

Tick, tick, tick counting off the useless days of Tommy's life.

Since the day the boiler had exploded in his face and he woke up in a world of darkness, the only time he'd felt useful was those few days at Mr. Jonnson's. Out there he'd wiped his own nose. Buttoned his own clothes. Washed his own dishes. And he would've learned to cane, too, if Miss Willems had left him there. He asked Mrs. Tatum every day for rope or string so he could practice, but she always said no. He'd never learn it if he couldn't go back to Mr. Jonnson's.

Tick, tick, tick . . .

Hinges squeaked. Cold air blew into the room. Footsteps sounded. Joe bumped Tommy's arm. "People's comin' in. Service'll be startin' soon, I guess."

Tommy stared ahead into the nothing world and set his jaw in a stubborn jut. When the service was over, he'd have Joe take him to Miss Willems. He'd tell her straight out how he wanted to go to Mr. Jonnson's again. And if she wouldn't listen, he'd find a way to get there himself.

Christina glanced at the pendulum clock. Ten 'til noon. The service was nearing its end. Lying in bed last night, unable to sleep, she'd decided she must unburden herself to someone. The reverend seemed the logical choice. Although she didn't know Reverend Huntley well — Father had always conducted their own services at the poor farm, and she'd taken over the task when he passed away — she felt certain a minister would be willing to listen, counsel, and hold in confidence anything she shared.

Just as they had at the close of last week's service, each of the poor farm residents made their way to her bench and greeted her the moment the final prayer ended. Joe pressed Tommy to the center of the group, and Christina cupped his cheeks and gave him a quick perusal. Neatly combed hair, clean clothes with his shirt tucked into his britches, shoestrings tied into perfect bows. Oh yes, the Tatums were taking excellent care of Tommy.

She leaned forward and planted a kiss on his forehead. "I'm so glad you're here with all of us today."

He curled his hands around her wrists. "Miss Willems, I gotta talk to you about —"

Christina spotted Reverend Huntley striding down the aisle. She gently extracted herself from Tommy's grasp. "Just a moment, Tommy." But the man moved past her before she could capture his attention. She sighed.

He pawed at her arm. "Miss Willems, I —"

Florie darted forward and threw her arms around Christina's waist. "Miz Tatum says she can't have ever'body over today 'cause she invited the Huntleys an' the Spencers. She says she'll ask you all to come some other time."

Disappointed murmurs circled the group, and Christina bit back her own expression of dismay. If the reverend and his wife were supping with the Tatums, he wouldn't have time to meet with her today. But perhaps he'd make time for her tomorrow, were she to ask.

"Miss Willems?" Tommy sounded fretful.

She gave his shoulder a soothing pat. "I need to speak to someone, Tommy. Please excuse me." She passed Florie to Rose and scurried after the minister. "Reverend Huntley? Reverend, wait, please."

The man stopped at the base of the steps. The wind ruffled his hair and lifted the collar on his coat. He gave the wool fabric a quick flick, then ran his hand over his head. "Yes, Miss Willems?"

She clattered down the steps and stood beside him. The sun sent a shaft of light into her eyes, forcing her to squint, but the yellow orb did little to warm the day. She gestured toward the church. "Could we step inside? I'd like to speak with you."

Reverend Huntley grimaced. "I apologize, Miss Willems, but my wife gave me strict instructions not to dally today. We're joining the Tatums to welcome the newest family to town, and she said if I delay, the chicken Mrs. Tatum is roasting might be shriveled to an inedible crisp."

Christina wrung her hands together. "Then I won't keep you." She backed up onto the first step. "I'll try to speak with you another time."

The reverend inched toward the house next to the church. "I could meet you this afternoon. Four o'clock?"

Christina fingered Papa's watch, thinking. If she started supper preparations early, she should be able to meet at that time. "I'll come back then. Thank you."

As he hurried off, Mrs. Tatum stepped to

Christina's side. "Miss Willems, I hate to intrude on your time with the children, but we have guests coming. Would you please send them on to the house? I would appreciate Florie's help setting the table."

"Of course." Christina returned to the church, where the poor farm residents were donning their coats. She helped Tommy with his buttons, then said, "You children hurry on home now. Mrs. Tatum is waiting for you."

Joe took Tommy's hand and pulled, but Tommy yanked free. "Miss Willems, I gotta talk to you about something!"

Christina hated to ignore the boy, but Mrs. Tatum had specifically asked her to send the youngsters immediately. She gave Tommy a gentle nudge toward Joe. "You go on now. Don't keep Mrs. Tatum waiting."

"C'mon, Tommy!" Joe grabbed Tommy's hand again, and this time he allowed Joe to lead him out. However, he scuffed along, his head low. The boy's dejected pose pricked Christina's conscience. Perhaps she should go after him and see what he needed.

Cora handed Christina her coat. "Think maybe Miz Beasley'll let us slice that leftover beef tongue for sandwiches? There's not enough of it left to do much else."

Christina jolted. She needed to hurry to

the boardinghouse and get as much done as possible for the boarders' evening meal if she wanted to carve out time to meet with Reverend Huntley at four o'clock. Slipping into her coat, she decided she could go see Tommy after she spoke with the minister. Surely whatever the boy needed could wait that long.

She smiled at Cora. "We can ask. Let's go."

Reverend Huntley escorted Christina into a small, cramped room lined with overflowing bookshelves in the back corner of his house. Only one window looked out over the side yard, and the tall church building blocked sunshine from entering the room, but a pair of iron wall sconces held oil lamps. Their warm glow brightened the tiny space. He gestured to an armless, diminutive parlor chair on one side of a desk, which filled the center of the room, and he slid into a massive wooden chair on the other side.

"Now then." He aimed a smile in her direction. "How are plans to rebuild progressing?"

Christina crossed her ankles and offered a weak smile. "Not well, I'm afraid. The mission board is reluctant to spend the funds to repair the damage."

The reverend's eyebrows rose. "I assumed they'd want to get started as quickly as possible so you folks could get settled again."

Although he'd used the term *you folks,* setting the poor farm residents apart from others in the community, Christina sensed no animosity. A man of God would be compassionate rather than having the mindset that being destitute equated with being lazy. The only lazy person she'd encountered in all her years serving with her parents was Ham Dresden. But she didn't want to think about Ham.

Folding her hands in her lap, she said, "That is still my goal, of course. But . . ." She'd come fully intending to share her concerns about how the fire started, but she found herself tongue-tied. How could she admit she might be responsible for upsetting so many lives? Even the reverend, a man trained to offer support and encouragement, would view her as a failure if he knew.

She stood. "I'm sorry, Reverend Huntley. I shouldn't have troubled you." She turned toward the door.

He rose and extended his hand across the desk. "Miss Willems, please don't go."

She hesitated, two desires — to escape and to unburden herself — warring within her soul.

"You must have a reason for asking to see me." He spoke gently. Much the way Papa used to speak to her when she was frightened or upset. "Won't you trust me with whatever is bothering you?"

The kindness in his voice, the warmth in his eyes drew Christina to the chair. She sat, and he slipped back into his chair. She sighed, and the concern that had weighted her since her meeting with the mission board representatives spilled from her lips. "Reverend Huntley, do you find it . . . unreasonable for a woman to be the director of a poor farm?"

The minister leaned back, propping up his chin with one hand. "What's required?"

"Organizing residents into work groups, interviewing possible new residents, preparing food, keeping the books . . ."

"And you feel inadequate in those tasks?"

"Absolutely not." Frustration welled. Christina held her hands outward. "I grew up assisting my parents in their ministries, which have always been positions of service. Between my upbringing and the schooling I received, I believe I am more than capable of performing the necessary tasks. But I've been told that, given my gender, it isn't proper for me to be in a position of leadership."

The minister plucked a book from one of the shelves behind him and flopped it open on his desk. He flicked several pages, scanning the text. Then he turned the book so it faced Christina. "Read this."

She leaned foward and recited the lines indicated by his square-tipped finger. " 'Let your women keep silence in the churches: for it is not permitted unto them to speak; but they are commanded to be under obedience, as also saith the law. And if they will learn any thing, let them ask their husbands at home: for it is a shame for women to speak in the church.' " The words seem to spear her with accusation. She swallowed. "So you agree . . . a woman has no place in a ministry position?"

"On the contrary."

Christina shot the minister a puzzled look. "But that says —"

"I imagine this is the scripture used as evidence by whoever has discouraged you. I've heard it used in like manner before." A soft smile played on the man's face. "Many Bible scholars believe that when Paul wrote this warning to the Corinthians, some women were trying to take over the church, creating conflict. They needed to be reprimanded. But I don't believe every woman has been ordered to silence. If God has placed in your heart a burning desire to serve, then He intends for you to serve."

A burning desire . . . She considered his choice of words. Did she possess a burning desire to serve? She gave herself a little shake. Of course she did. She found fulfillment and happiness in serving. From her earliest memories she'd been taught to reach out to the poor and downtrodden, just as Jesus had. Apparently Reverend Huntley saw no reason why her status as a woman should prevent her from continuing in service. But he didn't know everything yet.

She yearned for release from the heavy burden of guilt. Had she started the fire? She filled her lungs, gathering courage. "Reverend Huntley, there's something else."

He tipped his head. "Yes?"

"You see, I —"

The door flew open, banging the back of Christina's chair. Mrs. Huntley dashed to the edge of the desk. "Willard, I'm sorry to disturb you, but you must come at once."

A frown creasing his face, the minister rose and rounded the desk. "What is it, Abigail?"

She glanced at Christina, her eyes wild, then turned to her husband. Although she spoke in a rasping whisper, Christina heard every word. "Mrs. Tatum is here, quite distraught. It's the boys. She can't find them anywhere."

CHAPTER 14

A fear so intense it threatened to smother Christina propelled her from her chair. "What do you mean she can't find them? They've got to be there somewhere!"

Mrs. Tatum stepped into the doorway and began to blubber. "I've looked everywhere — every room, every closet, the outbuildings . . ." She turned a pitiful look on Christina. "Oh, Miss Willems, we had such a delightful lunch. Joe and Florie charmed the Spencers, and we lingered at the table for nearly an hour. Neither Joe nor Tommy seemed unhappy. I don't understand why they would leave." She covered her face with her hands and sobbed.

Reverend Huntley patted the woman's back. "When did you last see them?"

"After the Spencers left, I sent the boys to their room while Florie and I saw to the cleanup. Later when Florie went to the room, she found it empty."

Christina scrambled into her coat. Her shaking hands struggled with the buttons. "We need to organize a search party. I'll go to the livery and fetch Wes with our wagon. Reverend, will some of the men from the church help look?"

"Of course, Miss Willems. I'll have everyone meet at the livery so we can each choose a direction to search." He placed his hand on Christina's shoulder and offered an assuring smile. "Don't fret now. Two small boys — one of whom can't see — surely couldn't go far. We'll find them."

Christina bit her lower lip to keep from crying. What if Tommy had run off because she'd ignored his plea to talk? Perhaps if she'd taken the time to listen to him, he and Joe would be safe, snug, and warm at the Tatums' house right now. Guilt ate away at the fringes of her confidence. No matter what Reverend Huntley had said about God wanting her to serve, she feared Mr. Regehr might be right. She wasn't fit to be in leadership.

"How m-much farther, T-T-Tommy?" Joe's teeth clacking together sounded like the tips of tree branches tapping together in the wind.

Tommy hugged himself. "Not sure. When

171

I went before, I rode in a wagon."

Joe's hand gripped Tommy's elbow so hard it hurt. He kept them moving forward, their feet stumbling over tree roots and rocks and their clothes catching on prickly branches. "How long a r-ride?"

In constant darkness Tommy couldn't always determine the passing of time. He shrugged. "Maybe fifteen, twenty minutes."

"We been walkin' a l-lot longer'n th-that."

Although Tommy couldn't determine how long they'd been trying to make their way to the Jonnson mill, he knew it'd been a while. The wind was a lot colder than when he and Joe had sneaked out the front door, so the sun must be going down. "I know. But horses can walk faster'n people."

"Wish we h-had a h-horse right now. My feet're tired."

"Wanna rest a minute?"

"Uh-huh."

Joe's hand tugged on Tommy's arm, and Tommy dropped onto the ground. Now that they weren't thrashing through brush, something — a gentle sound — reached his ears. His heart leaped in anticipation. He felt the area around him with both hands. The soil was damp and covered by thick grasses. The dry blades pricked his palms, but he didn't care.

"Joe, are we by the river?"

"If you stick your feet out too far, they'll be on ice. Water's all froze along the bank."

Elation filled Tommy's chest. They'd done it! They'd reached the river! The mill was on the river — Mr. Jonnson had worried Tommy might fall into the water, so he'd put up ropes. If they'd found the river, they'd find the mill.

He pressed his hands between his knees and rocked in place, excitement coursing through him. "Look up an' down the river, Joe. Do you see a building with a water-wheel on its side?" When he was little, his pa had taken him to a gristmill on the river. Tommy had watched the half-submerged wheel go round and round, mesmerized. He wished he could see it in his head now, but the images were all erased.

Scuffling sounds let Tommy know Joe was standing up, looking. Then a disgruntled *huff* sounded next to Tommy's ear. "I don't see no such thing. River winds around. All I see is bushes an' trees an' water." Joe snugged up to Tommy, his head bumping against Tommy's shoulder. "We ain't gonna be able to get there by ourselves, Tommy. Let's go back to the Tatums', huh? I'm cold an' hungry."

Hurt tightened Tommy's chest as he

thought about sitting in the kitchen by himself while laughter and happy chatter carried from the dining room. Mrs. Tatum had been real nice while she scooted him up to the table at noon, telling him to enjoy his dinner and even putting the spoon in his hand. But then she'd said to stay put because *"the Spencers are new in town, Tommy dear. Mr. Tatum and I must make a good impression. As soon as they've left, I'll have Joe come fetch you."*

"Fetch you." Like a dog.

Tommy clenched his fists. "You go on if you want to, but I'm not goin' back to the Tatums' place."

"It's gettin' close to dark, Tommy. You can't stay out here!"

Tommy clawed at Joe and caught hold of his jacket. He held tight even though the younger boy squirmed. "You said you'd help me. We found the river, an' the mill's on the river. We gotta be close."

Joe pried Tommy's hand loose. "If it gets dark, I won't be able to see it any better'n you can."

Desperation welled, turning his voice into a whine. "Please, Joe. If we follow the river, we'll find it. I know we will."

"Which way, Tommy? Which way do we go?"

Tommy nibbled his lower lip. He tasted blood. The wind must've dried his lips out good. "I . . . I ain't sure, but —"

"Then I'm goin' back to town."

A memory clubbed Tommy. "Wait!" He reached out and captured Joe's arm. Joe grunted, but he plopped down beside Tommy. "The mill . . . it'll be built where the river flows *at* it. So if we follow the river against the flow, we'll find the mill!"

"You sure?" Joe sounded doubtful.

Tommy nodded his head so hard his ears rang. "I'm sure. C'mon, Joe. You can get us there. I know you can."

"B-but it's cold, Tommy. An' I'm real hungry."

"Mr. Jonnson's house'll be warm. An' he'll give us somethin' to eat." He'd let both boys sit at the table with him, too. Tommy shook Joe's arm. "Let's go. If we get movin', we'll warm up some."

Joe grumbled, but he rose and pulled Tommy up with him.

"Thank you, Joe."

"Let's just hurry, huh? It's gettin' dark."

"Won't be long before it'll be too dark to see anything."

Christina acknowledged Wes's somber statement with a worried nod. She sat on the edge of the wagon seat, one hand curled over the front board and one holding tight to Papa's watch like a talisman. For hours they'd been searching with no sign of either boy. She'd called Tommy's and Joe's names so many times her throat ached, and she sounded hoarse. But she ignored the discomfort and called again, "Tommy? Joe? Tommy!" No answer.

Wes kept the horse moving at a slow, steady *clop, clop, clop.* Everything within her wanted to rush the russet-colored mare, to force it into a thunderous run that would bring her quickly to the boys. But a snail's pace allowed time to scan both sides of the road. She and Wes had covered perhaps a mile and a half — a great distance for two little boys on foot in the cold.

Reverend Huntley had gathered a dozen men, who spread out in every direction. The minister had instructed them to return to the church and ring the bell if they found the children. While squinting through the gloaming for a glimpse of Tommy's blond head or Joe's blue jacket, she listened for the clang of the steeple bell. But so far only the clop of the horse's hoofs, the occasional chatter of a squirrel, and the whistle of the gusting wind through the trees had greeted her ears. Her chest constricted in fear, hindering her breathing. Where could those boys be?

"Oh, Wes . . ." Christina gulped back tears. "If we don't find them, if something horrible happens to them, it will be all my fault."

Wes flicked a frown in her direction. "You didn't send them young uns out the door. They did that on their own."

"I know, but . . ." She clamped her lips closed and continued to scan the roadsides in silence. Would it absolve her conscience to tell Wes she'd failed to listen to Tommy when he'd needed her? No. And it wouldn't do Wes any good either, to know how thoughtless she'd been. She kept her worries to herself as the horse continued its steady progression northeast.

The moon slipped above the leafless treetops, its face smudged by the presence of clouds. Not a single star winked against the gray backdrop. So dark. And so cold. The boys must be terrified. *Please, please* . . . Her heart tried to pray, but guilt and self-recrimination kept a petition from forming. God must be as disgusted with her as she was with herself.

Wes tilted his chin toward the sky. "Nightfall, Miss Willems. An' it's gettin' c-colder by the minute. We oughta t-turn around an' go back." His lips were blue, his cheeks and ears bold red, and he shook so badly the entire seat quivered.

As much as Christina hated to concede defeat, it made no sense to continue in full darkness. Several of the searchers had set off on foot, lanterns in hand. They'd have a better chance of spotting the boys than she and Wes would. Although it pained her to leave the responsibility to others, she needed to see to Wes's needs, too.

"Yes, I suppose we —" Ahead, two squares of soft yellow pierced the deep shadows. Christina pointed. "That's the Jonnson place. Let's stop there and warm up a bit before returning to town."

Wes snapped the reins on the horse's back, and it broke into a trot. As the wagon rolled into the yard, the door to the house opened, and Mr. Jonnson stepped onto the porch. Lamplight flowed through the open doorway, throwing the shadow of his wide-legged stance across the porch boards. Suspenders dangled by his knees, and his feet wore thick gray socks in place of boots. How rugged he appeared — solid, masculine, able. Deep within her the desire to melt against his strong chest rose up and sent her heart to fluttering. From where had this longing come? She took hold of Wes's arm, ready to tell him to turn the wagon back to the road, but a convulsive shudder shook the man's entire frame. He needed warmth.

"Miss Willems, is that you?" A puzzled scowl marred Mr. Jonnson's face.

"Yes." Christina waited until Wes set the brake. Then she scrambled over the wagon's edge, talking all the while to cover her erratic emotions. "I saw your lights and hoped you might allow us to come in and warm up a bit. Wes and I have been out searching for two lost boys, and we're chilled clear through."

He met her at the edge of the porch. "Who's lost?"

"Tommy. And another of my young charges, Joe."

Mr. Jonnson's brow pinched into lines of worry. "They in the habit of running off?"

Christina shook her head, battling tears. "No. But since the fire, things have been so unsettled. Especially for Tommy, being moved from place to place. I suspect he's the one who masterminded the escapade and brought Joe along to be his eyes." Her voice broke. She hugged herself to keep from leaping into his arms. "I'm dreadfully worried and want to keep looking, but . . ." Wes shuffled up behind her, his clamped hands beneath his chin and his shoulders hunched. He trembled from head to toe. "Wes must get warm. May we come in?"

Mr. Jonnson ushered them over the threshold without a word. Wes scuttled directly to the blazing fireplace and extended his hands. Standing side by side with the tall mill owner, her restiveness heightened. Their last exchange played through her mind. She'd been accusatory, even unfair. She'd angered him, yet he'd remained controlled. This man both irritated her and yet inexplicably intrigued her. A rush of warmth filled her cold cheeks. She lowered her head to hide the evidence of her discomfiture. She hoped the fire chased away Wes's chill quickly so they could be on their way.

Mr. Jonnson gestured toward the fire. "Do you want to warm up, too?"

Christina fiddled with a loose piece of yarn on one glove. "I'm fine. I have a heavy coat and my scarf and gloves. Poor Wes has only a jacket." She should have insisted he borrow at least a hat and some gloves before setting out. Another regret. She kept her gaze aimed at the toes of Mr. Jonnson's socks. "Had he been adequately clothed for the brisk wind, we wouldn't have troubled you."

"It's no trouble." He turned and strode

away, removing his feet from Christina's line of vision. He moved to a chair in the corner, sat, and began to tug on his boots. "I'll bundle up and set out while you two get warm."

His meaning penetrated the fog muddling Christina's brain. "Y-you're going to look for them?"

He gave her a dumbfounded look that most likely matched hers. "Those boys have to be found, Miss Willems. Cold as it is, they won't last a night out there. Especially if we get the snow my knee's been telling me is coming." He rose, slipping his suspenders into place. A scowl created deep furrows across his forehead. "You think I'd just sit here and toast my toes while Tommy and some other boy are out there, cold and lost?"

"Well, I suppose I —"

The scowl turned into a grimace of remorse. "Especially since it's my fault Tommy's out there."

"Yours?" Christina shook her head, confused. "Why?"

"I shouldn't have let you take him the other day. He didn't want to go."

Recalling the way Tommy had clung to the man brought on another wave of guilt. She pressed it back with a show of defensiveness. "He's a child. He doesn't know what he wants."

"Doesn't he?"

Christina fidgeted beneath his calm, steady look.

"He's trying to get here, you know."

Until that moment Christina hadn't allowed herself to acknowledge what her instincts had told her. She'd chosen this route over all the other directions she could have gone because deep down she knew Tommy would try to return to Mr. Jonnson. "Yes, I know."

For one long moment they gazed into each other's eyes, unspoken communication crossing the three-feet-wide expanse of wood-planked floor between them. The tenderness in his eyes sang notes of awakening in Christina's heart and chased away every vestige of animosity she'd held toward this man.

He gave a jolt and walked over to a cupboard where an unlit lantern stood ready. He lifted the globe, ignited the wick with the flick of a match, then settled the globe in place. Finally he looked at her again, and his face wore the familiar closed expression she'd witnessed on earlier visits. A chill wound its way down her spine despite the warm house and heavy wool coat.

"I'll go on foot, so you just take your wagon on back to town when you're warm again."

Christina snatched his coat from a hook beside the door and held it out to him. "I'm going with you."

His lips formed a grim line.

"I'm going with you," she repeated. Before he could speak a word, she turned to Wes. "Wait for me here, Wes. If" — *when* — "we find the children, you'll be able to transport all of us to town."

"All right, Miss Willems." He sank down on his haunches before the crackling flames. "Be careful."

"I will." She faced Mr. Jonnson, lifting her chin in a challenge. "Let's go."

CHAPTER 15

Levi did his best to keep his gaze forward, where the beam of his lantern lit the pathway, but it wasn't easy. He was too keenly aware of the woman trudging along beside him.

Wind whipped the tails of her scarf over her shoulders. Little strands of hair — darker in the scant moonlight — wisped around her cold-reddened cheeks. Her skirt tangled around her ankles, threatening to trip her. But she uttered not one word of complaint. Even as heavy snowflakes began to fall from the dark sky, covering her scarf and shoulders with lace, she kept putting one foot in front of the other. Kept calling the boys' names again and again with a voice raw and croaky. His admiration for her determination grew greater with every step they took.

Back in his house when they'd fallen silent and stood like two pillars on opposite sides of a porch, staring into each other's eyes, he'd experienced a tug unlike anything he'd felt before. Everything inside of him had strained to cross the expanse of floor between them and gather her into his arms. To offer her protection. To reassure her. Only the presence of the big, rawboned man at the fireplace had kept him from following through on the temptation.

Now as they trudged across the rough landscape with nothing but a faded half moon and a hoot owl as witnesses, he was glad his hands were busy — one holding the lantern aloft, the other holding the collar of his coat closed against the wind and increasingly heavy snow. If they were free, Miss Willems would be caught in an embrace. And he sensed she wouldn't be averse to it. He needed to be careful.

They'd covered perhaps a mile and a half, moving over an ever-thickening blanket of snow, when a gust of wind tore the scarf from Miss Willems's head. She lunged to catch it, but it flew out of her reach, somersaulted across the ground, and landed at the edge of the river. One fringed tail snaked across the ice and dipped into the frigid flow.

Levi couldn't step out on the ice and collect it for her — too dangerous. And with it wet, she wouldn't be able to wear it anyway. He glanced at the sky, its whitish cast promising even more snow, and made a suggestion he knew she'd resist. "We should turn back."

As expected, she drew herself upright and gave him a stubborn look. "Absolutely not!"

Levi hid a smile. Although her response was foolhardy, he would've been disappointed if she'd said anything else. But someone had to be reasonable. "You'll catch your death with your head uncovered. And besides, how do we know someone hasn't already located the boys? We could be wandering around out here for no good reason."

She tugged the collar of her coat around her ears. The snowflakes that had gathered on the heavy gray wool dropped down her neck, and she shivered. "They haven't been found yet. The church bell hasn't rung." Then her brow puckered with worry. "We'd hear the church bell out here, wouldn't we?"

On a clear Sunday — the one day he didn't close himself in his mill — he could hear the bell pealing across the miles. With them closer to town, they'd surely hear it despite the wind. "Yes. Is that the signal?"

She nodded, hunkering even deeper into her collar. Lantern light fell on her form and turned the snowflakes on her hair into glittering diamonds. A woman as refined and lovely as Miss Willems shouldn't be out in the middle of the night, freezing her nose off, yelling until her throat turned raw. He would continue searching if that was what she wanted, but she needed to go back.

He took her by the elbow and turned her toward his house. "Let's get you back, and then I'll set out again."

She jerked loose. "No! Mr. Jonnson, please, I must keep looking for the boys. They are *my* responsibility." Tears glistened in the corner of her eyes. "*I* must find them."

Even though she spoke the words in a rasping whisper, her tone held an intense fervency. Levi frowned. "What does it matter who finds them as long as they're found?"

"It matters." She turned her gaze away, her chin trembling. "You want to blame yourself for Tommy's running away, but you aren't to blame. I am. I . . . I failed him today." She brought her head around and fixed him with a pleading look. "I can't fail him now. I must find him. And Joe." That stubborn jut returned to her jaw. "If you don't want to keep looking, I understand. But I would appreciate the use of your lantern while I continue the search."

Levi shook his head. Headstrong female! She'd probably catch pneumonia. He might, too. With a muffled growl he set the lantern on the ground, yanked off his hat, and plunked it on her head. She looked ridiculous with it settled around her ears, and the wind was more chilly with his head uncovered, but what else could he do? He'd never met a more modig woman. Despite the grim situation, a grin twitched at his cheeks. Mor would like Miss Christina Willems.

He snatched up the lantern. "All right. Let's go."

For the next half mile, the only words they uttered were calls to the missing boys. Her voice was becoming more and more hoarse, so he took up the call. "Tommy! Joe! Answer if you hear me!" And, finally, when the snow fell so thickly it hindered his vision even with the bright glow of the lantern, he heard a faint reply.

"Mr. J-Jonnson? W-we're here."

Miss Willems grabbed his arm with both hands. "Did you hear —"

"Shh!" He tipped his head, straining to determine the direction of the voice. "Call again, Tommy!"

"Here! We're here!"

A second voice — younger and higher — joined in. "We're here! We're here!"

Levi, with Miss Willems clinging to his arm, stumbled up the bank. Halfway to the top of the rise, the lantern's yellow beam fell on two small, shivering forms huddled together beneath an overhang of scraggly brush. Snow clung to the thickly woven branches, creating a canopy of sorts. They'd found a makeshift shelter, and they appeared to be fine. Relief turned Levi's bones into rubber, and he nearly lost his footing.

Beside him Miss Willems choked out, "Oh, thank You, dear Lord." Levi echoed the words in his heart, startled by the sincerity underscoring the silent prayer.

The smaller boy bounded upright and half walked, half crawled across the snow-covered ground to Miss Willems, sobbing. She hugged him, murmuring assurances to him.

Levi set down the lantern and reached out to catch Tommy's hands. "Come on out of there."

Tommy stood, his sightless eyes blinking rapidly. A smile stretched across his chapped face. "You found us. I knew you would. Thank you, Mr. Jonnson."

Now that the boy stood before him, repeatedly shuddering with chills but safe, anger replaced the relief of moments ago. He took hold of Tommy by the upper arms and gave him a firm shake. "What were you thinking to take off like that? As cold as it is, you could've froze! And if you had, you'd be accountable for your little friend over there, as well. You were irresponsible, Tommy, and I'm disappointed in you."

Miss Willems hurried up beside them, the younger boy hanging on to her coat. "This isn't the time for scolding. We need to get the boys someplace warm, and we need to alert the others that they've been found."

Levi tamped down his frustration and nodded. "You're right." He drew Tommy tight against his side. "But we're going to have a talk about making good decisions."

To his surprise the boy beamed. "A-all right, Mr. Jonnson. If y-you don't mind, I'd l-like to have s-some supper, get w-warmed up, and maybe s-s-sleep a little. But then . . . then we'll have us th-that talk."

Christina sat on the edge of the narrow bed in Mr. and Mrs. Tatum's back bedroom and watched Tommy and Joe as they slept. The boys lay snug together on the mattress, their tousled blond heads — one with strands as thick and straight as straw, one with soft coils — tipped toward each other. Tiredness slouched her forward. How good it would feel to stretch out and sleep, too, but she couldn't. Not yet. Squinting against a fierce pounding in her temples, she shifted her gaze from one flushed face to the other and listened to their deep, even breathing, as the doctor had instructed.

"Keep them warm and force lots of liquids," Dr. Lang had cautioned with a worried frown. "They're both strong, healthy boys, but they could take a turn, given the length of time they spent in the cold and the soaking they received from the snow. So keep a watch."

So Christina ignored her aching throat and throbbing head and kept watch as the hands on the clock moved toward noon. She should be at the boardinghouse, assisting Cora, but Louisa and Rose had promised to lend a hand. She'd stay right here until she knew both Tommy and Joe were fine.

Outside the door the banker and his wife were engaged in a whispered conversation. Although Christina couldn't hear their words, she sensed it involved the children. Mrs. Tatum sounded particularly distressed, and Christina's sympathy stirred. The children were certainly suffering from their foolishness — frostbit fingers, toes, and ears as well as a fever — but their caregivers had been given quite a fright, too.

A single pair of footsteps sounded in the

hallway, and then the bedroom door inched open. Christina glanced over her shoulder, clutching the edge of the mattress to keep herself from toppling when dizziness struck. The banker peered through the opening, and she gestured him in.

He tiptoed up behind her and looked down at the sleeping pair. A hint of compassion lingered in his eyes, but she also glimpsed something else — a dogged resolve that raised her apprehension.

"Miss Willems, we must talk." Although he spoke barely above a whisper, Joe stirred.

"Shh," Christina crooned, stroking Joe's curly hair.

The boy murmured, squirmed a bit, and then snuggled his head on Tommy's shoulder. Tommy made a face, but his eyes remained closed. She waited for a moment to be certain the boys wouldn't rouse. Then she rose and pointed to the hallway. Mr. Tatum followed her out.

After clicking the door shut, Christina leaned against it and raised her gaze to the grim-looking man. "Yes?" She winced. Speaking hurt, and she sounded as croaky as a decades-old bullfrog.

He locked his hands behind his back as if keeping a grip on his control. "Miss Willems, we think it best if you find another location for the children."

Christina's heart sank. "But they're sick. You heard what the doctor said. They need rest and to stay warm."

The man flinched. "Of course they're welcome to stay while they recover. But as soon as they are well enough to be moved, they must go." He glanced up the hallway as the clank of pots and pans carried from below — his wife apparently beginning lunch preparations. Then he turned back and pinned Christina with a grave look. "Please understand, we aren't cold hearted. But my wife . . . she has a delicate disposition. She struggled even when our youngsters were still living at home, constantly worrying some ill would befall them. The boys' slipping away has shaken her confidence. Caring for three children, one of whom is handicapped, has proven more of a burden than she can bear." He shook his head. "I'm sorry, but it was a mistake for us to invite the children to reside with us. You must find other arrangements."

Other arrangements? She'd battled so hard to make these arrangements. What other options did she have? If only she had resources beyond what the mission board provided, she'd purchase property on her own and open its doors. But her parents had never saved a penny. Whatever extra they possessed they gave away to those in need. She had nothing on which to draw now.

Christina's head swam. She grabbed the doorknob and clung to keep herself upright. "I . . . I . . ." Oh, how her head throbbed. She touched the back of her hand to her forehead. "Oh my. I believe I may be ill."

Mr. Tatum darted forward and took her arm. He guided her back into the bedroom and helped her sit on the second bed in the room, the one they'd indicated Florie used. "Stay here," he said, "and I'll fetch the doctor to take a look at you." He strode out of the room.

Christina had no desire to suffer another bout of dizziness. Palms pressed to the patchwork quilt, she sat as still as possible and drew deep breaths into her aching chest. Very slowly she turned her head to look at the still-sleeping boys. Such a tight fit on that little bed together. She should shift one of them to this second bed as soon as the wave of weakness passed.

Two beds . . .

She scowled. The Tatums had indicated all three children shared this room, which meant there should be three beds. Had the two boys been sharing that narrow bed?

How uncomfortable for them. Then her gaze dropped to the corner, where a pallet of some sort was rolled against the wall. An ugly picture formed in her head, painted not only by the rolled bedding but also by the curious comment Tommy had made early that morning as Mr. Jonnson placed him on the mattress. She pressed her memory, seeking the boy's exact words, and they returned in a rush. "A bed . . . Oh, a bed . . . It feels so good."

She'd passed several well-furnished bedrooms when she and Mr. Jonnson had carried the boys through the long hallway to this room last night. Why hadn't the Tatums allowed Tommy the use of one of those beds? If the boy had been denied appropriate sleeping accommodations, what else might he have lacked while under their care? She didn't want to think ill of the banker and his wife — they were, after all, leaders in the community — but what else could that rolled-up stack of quilts mean? If her suppositions were right, no doubt this was why Tommy had asked to speak with her. And she'd put him off, which told him his concerns weren't important to her.

A sudden worry struck — were her other charges living in less-than-acceptable situations, too? The throb in her temples increased. She groaned, closing her eyes and pressing her hands to her head. So many things to fix, and she didn't know where to begin. *Father, help me . . .*

The squeak of the door handle turning drew her attention. She forced her head upward as Mrs. Tatum, escorted by Florie, slipped into the room. Florie scampered to Christina and climbed up beside her. Christina knew she should push the child away — if she was ill, she might inflict the sickness on Florie — but the little girl's presence was comforting. At least Florie seemed happy and well cared for.

"Harold asked me to let you know the doctor is seeing to another patient right now, but as soon as he's free, he'll come here." Mrs. Tatum stood stiffly beside the door, her hands clamped against her ribs. "It shouldn't be long."

Christina slipped her arm around Florie's waist and looked up at the woman. "That's fine. While we're waiting," — each word was a knife slicing her throat — "will you please tell me where the children have been sleeping?"

Mrs. Tatum's brows came down in a sharp V. "Why, in this room, of course."

Slowly — oh, how her head pounded! — Christina glanced around the space. "There are three children and two beds. Have the boys been sharing that bed, or . . ." She looked pointedly at the rolled bedding, then turned again to Mrs. Tatum.

The woman's lips pursed. "As you can see, there's scarcely room in here for two beds, let alone three. So I laid out a pallet on the floor."

"For Tommy," Florie supplied.

"Of course." Mrs. Tatum spoke briskly. "Joe and Florie were already settled. It seemed unkind to force one of them to give up their bed for a —" Her teeth clacked as she closed her jaw.

A chill zinged from Christina's scalp all the way down her spine. "For a . . ."

For several seconds Mrs. Tatum stood with her jaw tightly clenched. Then she threw her hands outward and raised her chin, defiance on her face. "It isn't as if he'd know the difference. After all, he can't see where he's sleeping."

"A bed . . . Oh, a bed . . . It feels so good." The relief in Tommy's voice as he'd muttered the words had pierced Christina.

Florie tugged at Christina's arm. "Tommy had to eat in the kitchen instead of eating with all of us. Mrs. Tatum said he'd drop food on her pretty rug." The child wrinkled her nose. "She doesn't like him much, I don't think."

Mrs. Tatum snapped, "That's quite enough, Florie. Go out to the parlor. You shouldn't be in a sickroom."

Florie leaned against Christina, but Christina gave her a little nudge. "Go on now. Mind Mrs. Tatum." With a sigh the little girl scuffed out of the room. The moment she departed, Christina pushed herself to her feet. With the backs of her knees locked against the bed's frame, she gripped Papa's watch for strength and faced Mrs. Tatum. "If you were concerned Tommy would be a burden, why did you offer to take him in?"

The woman sniffed. "You'd left him with that Jonnson man, who never attends services and keeps to himself like a hermit. It was our Christian duty to be certain Tommy was placed in a God-fearing home. So we took him in." Her gaze narrowed. "And despite your insinuations, we have not mistreated him. He's been fed, clothed, and sheltered."

To Christina's shame she'd looked at Tommy's clean clothes and combed hair and thought him well cared for. But true care went deeper than the surface. Her entire body trembled, less from the fever than from indignation. It pained her throat to speak, but she would have her say. "Fed,

198

clothed, and sheltered — yes. But treated differently than the two sighted children in your care. Did you stop to think how it would make him feel?"

Again Mrs. Tatum released a derisive sniff. "How would he know if the other two children slept in a bed or sat at a different table? For all he can see, everyone in this household sleeps on the floor and eats at the kitchen table."

Christina gawked at the woman. She'd encountered this mind-set before — that somehow a person with a handicap was of less value than a whole, healthy person — but she would never have expected it from a woman with such apparent intelligence. If only her throat would allow her to rail in fury. But she could merely rasp, "Just because he can't see doesn't mean he can't feel — he knows there are beds in this room. Or hear. I'm sure he listened to every word and every clink of a fork in the dining room. Of course he knows the difference."

Stumbling forward two steps, she released the watch and aimed a quivering finger at Mrs. Tatum's face. "The Bible I have read my entire life instructs us to treat others as we would like to be treated. *Others*, Mrs. Tatum, which implies everyone we encounter. Would you like to sleep on a mat on the floor or be forced to sit alone in the dark?"

"Well, I —"

"Of course you wouldn't!" She pressed a palm to her aching throat, irritation at the woman's insensitivity giving her the strength to continue. "You claim Mr. Jonnson is not God fearing, and you intimate he is less than acceptable because he keeps to himself, but guess where Tommy was going. To Mr. Jonnson. Because apparently he felt more valued by a godless, reclusive man than by a well-to-do, supposedly Christian man and wife! That, in my opinion, Mrs. Tatum, is reprehensible."

The woman's face flamed red. She drew back, her eyes shooting darts. "You are certainly welcome to your opinion, Miss Willems, but as of this minute you are no longer welcome in my home. I shall ask the doctor to transport you to the boarding-house when he arrives. And as soon as he deems the boys well enough, I expect all three of the children to be removed from beneath my roof as well." She whirled and stormed out of the room.

Christina's knees gave way. She staggered to the mattress and sat. Defeated, she let her head droop low. Papa's watch swung like a pendulum, its silver face glinting in the soft lantern light.

A soft, frightened voice reached her ears. "Miss Willems?"

She turned her head and looked at her young charges.

Tommy and Joe sat up in the bed, their fever-flushed faces aimed in her direction although Tommy's eyes seemed locked on her shoulder while Joe squarely met her gaze. Joe spoke again. "Miss Willems, where are we gonna go?"

Christina had no answer.

CHAPTER 16

Doctor Lang, at Mrs. Tatum's insistence, bundled Christina in his buggy and drove her to the boardinghouse immediately upon completing his examination. The night's snowfall had left behind a thick coating of white. The sunshine reflecting on the snow was so dazzling it hurt her eyes. But the wind had blown itself out, and she enjoyed the cool air against her feverish cheeks. The doctor helped her into the house, using the front door — although Mrs. Beasley fussed about the snow they tracked in — and insisted she go straight to bed. He left a bottle of foul-tasting medicine with which she was to gargle twice a day and informed her to rest until the fever broke.

Cora stood in the doorway with Louisa and Rose peering over her shoulders. All three women seemed to absorb the doctor's directives, and the moment he departed, Cora dashed to the wardrobe and removed

Christina's nightgown from its hook. "Here you are, Miss Willems. Get yourself under those covers now. Me an' the sisters" — Cora had chosen the nickname for the widowed sisters-in-law, who'd been together so long they had begun to resemble each other — "will see to the cookin' an' such 'til you're on your feet again."

Christina shook her head weakly in protest. "Oh, but —"

"Not one word," Louisa stated. The elderly pair stepped into the room, hands on hips, and glared down at Christina. "Rose did some nursing when she was younger, so she'll look after you while I assist Cora in the kitchen. You just turn your attention to getting well."

Christina took the cotton gown but crushed it in her lap rather than donning it. She shifted her gaze from Louisa to Rose. "As much as I appreciate your kindness, I can't expect you to disrupt your routines to take over my responsibilities here."

"Humph. Disrupt our routines, she says." Rose rolled her eyes. "Ever since the fire, the two of us have been sitting in a little room from morning to night, darning socks and tatting doilies to keep ourselves occupied. Coming over here and helping will be a treat." She shook her finger in Christina's face, her eyes twinkling. "I intend to be certain you follow each one of that handsome doctor's orders. So" — she shooed the other two out of the room — "you go see to dinner. I'll get our Miss Willems settled."

Christina allowed Rose to assist her into her nightgown, and then she slipped beneath the quilt. So lazy to be in bed in the middle of the day, but once she'd stretched out on the soft mattress, she lost all will to rise. Rose fluffed Christina's pillow before placing it gently beneath her head. After pulling the covers to Christina's chin, the dear woman bent forward and deposited a brief kiss on her forehead.

Rose straightened and offered a sweet smile. "I'll go fetch a glass of cool water and put it here on the stand for when you feel thirsty."

Not since she was a child of ten — before Mama died — had someone tucked her into bed with such tenderness. Tears stung Christina's eyes. Before she could form a thank-you, the woman exited the room with a swirl of dark gray skirts.

Although she appreciated Rose's kind ministrations, she couldn't deny a fierce sense of guilt. She was supposed to be taking care of the others, not having them take care of her. She rolled to her side, tugging the quilt to her ear, and allowed her eyes to close. She must do exactly as the doctor directed so she could get well as quickly as possible. Rose and Louisa could help Cora with kitchen duties, but many other, more pressing responsibilities awaited Christina. And she couldn't allow anyone else to assume those.

In the days following his midnight trek along the riverbank with Miss Willems, Levi worked morning to night preparing his mill for spring's busyness. Outside, he cleared the ground where he'd store the logs awaiting the saw's blade, and he prepared pallets to hold the cut lumber so it wouldn't sit on the damp ground. Inside, he oiled the gears, sharpened the blades, tightened all the nuts, checked the thick leather belts for signs of rot and the metal fittings for rust. He worked carefully. Steadfastly. Meticulously. The way his great-uncle had taught him.

He paused, oilcan in hand, and allowed himself a moment of reflection. He hadn't seen Uncle Hans in a dozen years. Was he still alive? He'd be fairly old by now — late seventies, for sure. A chuckle formed in Levi's chest. If he knew his great-uncle, the man was as spry as a man half his age. Levi had never seen a harder worker than Hans Jonnson — and positive, to boot. When things went awry, Uncle Hans would smile and say to his son, *"Väl, if this is the worst thing that ever happens to me, I think I will end my life in good stead."* If Far had adopted such an attitude, he might be alive today.

Levi shook off thoughts of Far. The man was dead and buried, and it was best to leave him in his lonely grave. He put the oilcan to work again, his thoughts moving ahead to April, when the first load of logs he'd ordered from the timber company in Arkansas would be transported by tugboat up the Missouri River to the mouth of the Kansas River. There, he would retrieve them and make use of the waterway to bring them all the way home. He'd spend most of the month carting logs to his mill. Then in May he'd begin sawing those logs into usable lumber.

Thanks to Uncle Hans's patient tutelage — treating Levi like a son rather than a great-nephew — Levi had learned a trade that served him well. Still, in the back of his heart, he harbored the desire to use his cut boards for himself rather than sell them to be turned into sheds and crates and houses. Not that there was anything wrong with sheds, but how could a shed compare to a fine cupboard or a delicately spindled cradle? His earliest memories were laden with the scent of wood and resin and turpentine. When he carved an intricate rosette or a leafy design, the image of his father's hands always formed in his mind.

Such a fine craftsman Far had been. But working on his own, he hadn't been able to build enough furniture to provide for his family. So he'd taken on a partner. And thus began his descent into a deep melancholy that crippled first his mind and then his body.

With a grunt of aggravation, Levi thumped the oilcan on the workbench. He sat and lowered his head to his hands. Why all these thoughts of Far and Uncle Hans today? Hadn't he left Wisconsin behind? Of course he had. He'd set off for Kansas and the opportunity for a new life. A life free of his father's never-ending sadness and the pitying whispers of his neighbors. He earned a good wage with his cut lumber — enough even to set money aside so he could use the winter months to craft furniture for his pleasure.

He straightened, determined to turn his attention to the present. He had the best life here on the rolling Kansas plains —

making money with his sawmill and finding satisfaction in practicing his craft. And by keeping his operation small, he could depend only on himself. He might use the skills he'd learned from Far, but he would never, never become his father.

Saturday morning Levi hitched his team to the wagon and headed for town. He had two purposes for this trip — to purchase his weekly supplies and to have the promised talk with Tommy. When he'd carried the boy into the banker's house last Sunday — well, early Monday by the time he and Miss Willems had made it back to his house, awakened Wes, and then driven the poor farm wagon to town — both of the little runaways were exhausted, chilled to the point of constant shivering, and suffering from frostbite. Talking to Tommy then would have been as pointless as talking to a chunk of wood.

So he'd returned to Brambleville Tuesday morning, his speech all prepared, but Mrs. Tatum's cleaning lady had sent him away, saying Tommy was sick and needed to rest. But Tommy would be better by now, for sure, and they'd have that talk. Man to man. Where the boy was concerned, Miss Willems surely didn't have enough starch to reprimand him. She treated him like an invalid even though she said he was bright. He *was* bright. Too bright to be allowed to get by with such shenanigans as sneaking out. And in the middle of a snowstorm, to boot.

As the horses clopped toward town, Levi couldn't help comparing today's weather to that of a few days ago. The final days of February had been the coldest of the month, carrying snow on frigid blasts of wind. Although wind still coursed across the landscape, not even a small patch of snow remained. Instead, clumps of green were beginning to appear, the sky was clear, and the morning air — brisk but not biting — held a sweet scent. On this first day of March, it seemed as though Sunday's foul storm had been a dream. If he lived in Kansas for a hundred years, he'd never stop marveling at the rapidly changing weather.

He reached Brambleville's main street, where the white painted Community Church with its tall bell tower sat on a corner. The banker's home — a two-story, red-brick Georgian with round fluted columns supporting an arched porch roof — towered next to the church building. Levi bounced his gaze across the trio of gabled windows breaking up the stern line of the deep pitched roof. If the house were his, he'd soften those gables by inserting a lacy pediment. Would Mr. Tatum purchase such trims from Levi if he presented his idea to the man?

"Whoa," he called, pulling back on the reins. The horses obediently stopped. Levi set the brake and hopped down, removing his hat as he strode toward the door. He gave the raised panel oak door a solid *bump, bump, bump* with his knuckles, then waited.

Moments later the door opened, and the banker's wife stood framed in the opening. She gave him a puzzled look. "Mr. Jonnson . . . yes?"

He nodded. "That's right."

"How may I help you?"

This woman spoke primly, the way Miss Willems did, but somehow Miss Willems fell short of sounding haughty. Mrs. Tatum might learn a thing or two from the poor farm director. He tapped one foot against the painted floor, eager to get this errand completed. "I've come for Tommy."

Her eyes grew wide. "You have?"

"I came last Tuesday, but he was still sick. Is he better?"

She stepped back, ushering him in with a wave of her hand. "Both he and Joe are fully recovered. They complain of some discomfort where they were frostbitten, but I suppose that's to be expected." She closed the door behind him, then headed up the wide, spindled staircase, still talking. Although she hadn't instructed him to do so, he followed her. "I sincerely hope the scare they received from their time of wandering will be enough to keep them from ever attempting such a foolish pursuit again. Of course" — she paused and shot a sour look over her shoulder — "if Tommy hadn't been here, Joe never would have gone. He was perfectly content with Harold and me." A weary sigh left her lips. "But I needn't worry about that anymore since you're here."

The woman was putting a lot of faith in his being able to talk sense into Tommy. For the boy's sake, he hoped it wasn't ill placed. She turned a corner, and the staircase emptied into a broad landing with hallways stretching on both sides. Levi trailed behind her down the right-hand hallway, passing several white painted doors before stopping at the hallway's end.

She held her hand out toward the last door. "He's in there, just where you deposited him earlier this week. The only difference is the latch at the top of the door. I had Harold install it so I could be certain Tommy would do no more wandering. His thoughtless behavior took a good ten years from my life span, I'm sure. His belongings are in there, too. I trust you know what is his since he stayed with you previously."

"His belongings?"

"Well, certainly." Her tone turned tart. "You'll want to take the few things he owns with him."

Levi shook his head, furrowing his brow in confusion. "Mrs. Tatum, I just want to talk to Tommy."

She drew back. "But you said you had come for him."

"I came to talk. Not to take him."

A mighty huff exploded, and she rolled her gaze toward the ceiling. "I should have known that woman wasn't making any effort to find another location for Tommy."

"That woman . . ." He frowned. "You mean Miss Willems?"

"Yes, Miss Willems! I've tried to be patient with her. She was, after all, quite ill, thanks to gallivanting all over the countryside in search of those two reckless boys."

Levi's heart lurched. She'd been ill? How ill?

Mrs. Tatum continued in a grating tone. "But even though the Spencer family took Joe and Florie two days ago, which indicated she'd been well enough to make arrangements for the twins, she's sent no one for

Tommy. I suspect Miss Willems is trying to teach me some sort of lesson by forcing me to care for the boy." Her chin quivered, and plump tears appeared in the corners of her eyes. "She all but accused me of being cruel to him."

Mrs. Tatum had locked him in a room by himself. That didn't seem kind to Levi. But he could understand the woman's reasoning. After having the boy escape, she probably felt extra responsibility for keeping him safe. He scratched his chin. "I wouldn't know anything about that, ma'am. I'd just like to speak to Tommy if you don't mind."

She reached up and unhooked the silver clasp, then pinched her skirts between her fingertips and flounced up the hallway.

Levi opened the door and peeked into the room. The window shades were pulled, and no lamp lit the space. With the room cloaked in shadows, it took a minute for his eyes to make out the two beds covered with patchwork quilts, a tall bureau, . . . and Tommy, seated on the floor in the corner with his forehead on his knees and his arms wrapped around his legs. Despite Levi's intention to dive into a stern lecture, sympathy twined around his heart. The boy looked plenty dejected. And his morose pose raised memories of another time, another place, another person . . . Levi swallowed.

"Tommy?"

Tommy's head bounced up, and his palms landed flat on the floor. "Mr. Jonnson?"

The joy in the boy's voice sent a shaft of unexpected emotion through Levi. Affection. He genuinely liked this boy. "It's me." He covered the short distance between them, took Tommy by the arm, and hoisted him to his feet. "We have some talking to do, yes?"

Tommy's bright expression faded.

Levi drew in a deep breath, ready to give the boy his promised talking-to, but then he expelled the air in one big *whoosh.* "Let me gather up your things first. I'm taking you out of here."

CHAPTER 17

Christina dipped her pen and recorded, *A new family in town, the Spencers, are now providing shelter for Joe and Florie. This is the children's second placement. I am gravely concerned the children's security has been shaken. Different homes mean different structure, which makes it difficult for children to adjust, especially children at the impressionable ages of Joe and Florie.* She paused and blew on the ink to dry it. Leaning forward tightened the thick wool sock wrapped around her neck, and she reached to remove it.

Across the table Cora gave a squawk. "No, ma'am! Rose said I was to make sure you kept that on all day! Said it's sure to make your throat better."

Although Christina's fever was completely gone and she'd regained her strength, she still spoke with a raspy voice. Earlier that morning Rose had arrived with a gray sock soaked in some kind of potent mixture. Christina had nearly gagged from the smell, but Rose had insisted the mixture of herbs, garlic, and camphor would have Christina's throat better in no time. She'd been wearing it for more than an hour, and, thankfully, her nose had adjusted to the unpleasant aroma, but she still sounded as if someone had run sandpaper over her vocal cords. So rather than replying to Cora's reprimand, she merely nodded and turned her attention back to the letter on the table.

While Cora shelled peas and the calico cat dozed under the table between Christina's feet, she read back through her entire missive to the mission board. She'd filled two pages, updating the board on her charges' situations. Alice, Laura, and Francis all shared one small room, which was dreadfully uncomfortable for them. Wes continued to reside in a stable. After living in Brambleville for a half-dozen years, surely Herman and Harriet were pining away from loneliness in their new location. Cora always looked wan and tired — the work at the boardinghouse was too hard for her. Tommy was without a place to stay. Louisa and Rose had no complaints about their present location, but they missed having a home for which to care and a garden to tend.

The garden! Before long they'd need to plant vegetables and put in their corn and hay crop for animal feed. She'd always been proud of how much money she saved by canning vegetables and gathering berries and nuts to feed the poor farm residents. Would the board delay repairing the house until it was too late for Wes and her to plant seeds for a good harvest? She picked up the pen once more and added a reminder about the importance of being settled in time to put in the garden. She supposed Mr. Regehr might find her request impertinent since he'd been adamant about not leaving her in charge. But even if she was forced to step aside — oh, how her heart ached at the thought! — the others would still need to be fed, so a garden was imperative.

Just as she prepared to sign her name, someone tapped on the back door. Cora set aside her bowl and crossed the floor to answer the knock. Mr. Jonnson, with Tommy in tow, stepped over the threshold. Christina's heart fluttered at the sight of the tall, blond-haired man. Although she'd never been given to girlish infatuation, she recognized stirrings toward the mill owner. She gave herself a shake. Those kinds of thoughts had to be quashed. She had too many responsibilities to allow herself to become

217

enamored with a man, no matter how strong and handsome.

She shifted her attention to Tommy. The boy remained just inside the door, his hands clasped before him and his head bobbing about in his typical manner of trying to gain an understanding of his surroundings. As she moved toward him, hands outstretched to deliver a hug, his face pursed into a horrible scowl.

"Something stinks!" He pinched his nose.

Christina came to an abrupt halt. Heat flooded her cheeks, and she touched the sock at her neck. "You can smell that?"

Mr. Jonnson burst out laughing. "Miss Willems, a skunk would be less noticeable." He wrinkled his nose, his green-blue eyes dancing with merriment. She wished he'd stop looking so young and attractive. His appearance was doing funny things to her middle. He angled his head away from her. "What is it you've got there?"

Christina cringed. "A concoction one of the poor farm residents stirred up to help my throat."

He nodded but kept his distance. "I can tell you need something. You sound like rusted gears. But that smell . . . phew!"

Tommy inched backward until he collided with the closed door. "Miss Willems, you smell terrible."

Christina shot the boy a disgruntled look, which was silly since he couldn't see it.

"Now don't get all ruffled up, ma'am," Mr. Jonnson said, his eyes twinkling despite his stiff stance. "Usually you smell very nice."

She did? She blinked at him, startled.

Pink streaks crept from his collar toward his clean-shaven jaw. He rubbed his finger under his nose, an embarrassed chuckle rumbling. "This just isn't one of those days."

Behind him Cora snickered. Then she giggled. And then a full-blown laugh — the first Christina had ever heard from the young woman — poured from her. Laughter doubled her over. Mr. Jonnson shot Cora a grin before joining in, and then Tommy began to laugh, too — the three of them creating a joyful trio of merriment. In spite of herself, Christina found herself unable to squelch her own laughter. She did stink. And in that moment it *was* funny.

Laughter rang for several seconds, and for a moment Christina's troubles seemed to melt away. How good the unfettered laughter felt. How long had it been since she'd allowed herself such an expression? Too long . . .

Mrs. Beasley stormed into the kitchen

from the hallway. The cat darted beneath Christina's skirt, and Christina, Cora, and Mr. Jonnson fell silent. Tommy's chortling gurgle rang loudly on its own for a few more seconds before he sucked in a big breath and stifled it.

Hands on hips, the boardinghouse owner glowered at the now-silent circle. "What is the meaning of this ruckus?" She fixed a squint-eyed glare on Mr. Jonnson. "And what is he doing in my kitchen?"

Christina turned toward the aggravated woman. "I apologize for the noise, Mrs. Beasley. We —"

The woman backed away, her face crunching into an expression of horror. "You reek! It turns my stomach!" Waving both hands at Christina, she backed up. "Get rid of that before you stink up the whole house. We'll discuss this later." She escaped down the hallway.

Someone sniggered. Christina whirled around to see Cora covering her mouth with both hands. An apologetic look crept across her face. "I'm sorry, Miss Willems, but I've been trying to find a way to keep her from comin' in here an' hollerin' at us. Reckon we just found one."

Christina knew she shouldn't, but she couldn't hold back a chuckle. "Well, from now on I'll allow you to wear the sock. I believe I've had quite enough of this aroma for one day." She removed the offensive length of gray wool and tossed it into their sleeping room. Then she pulled Tommy into a hug, kissing his wind-tousled hair. He smelled of springtime — a delightful scent — and she filled her senses with it. Her arm around Tommy, she looked at Mr. Jonnson. "As Mrs. Beasley asked, what are you doing here?"

The twinkle faded from his eyes, replaced by a deep concern. "I'm here about Tommy. I guess you could say I just kidnapped him."

"You what?"

Mr. Jonnson turned to Cora. "Could you take Tommy somewhere for a few minutes? Maybe to that room" — he tilted his head toward the bedroom — "or to Mrs. Beasley's parlor?"

Cora scowled. "We ain't allowed in the parlor, an' with that stinky sock in our room, I'm not goin' in there." She took Tommy's hand and drew him away from Christina's protective arm. "C'mon, Tommy. I ain't seen the outside since last Sunday. Let's go get us some sunshine." She escorted the boy out the back door.

As soon as the pair departed, Mr. Jonnson gestured to the small worktable. "Could we sit for a minute? I need to talk to you."

Each time over the past few weeks when she'd been invited to talk, the bearer had brought bad news. Christina's stomach knotted. Instinctively, she reached for Papa's watch and curled her fingers around the cool disk. Fortified, she gave a nod and preceded him to the table. The cat trotted along beside her and leaped into her lap the moment she sat.

A lopsided grin formed briefly on Mr. Jonnson's face before he slid into the opposite chair. He pointed to the furry creature. "Found yourself a friend, huh?"

"Yes. She's a sweet girl." Christina ran her hands through the cat's soft fur, finding comfort in the animal's presence. "I'll miss her when Cora and I return to the poor farm."

"When do you think that'll be?"

Christina frowned. "I wish I knew . . ."

"It needs to be soon."

His somber tone chilled her. "Why?"

Mr. Jonnson rested his joined hands on the table's worn top and leaned forward slightly. Sunlight streamed through the window and fell on his face, bringing out the lighter strands of honey in his hair and emphasizing the green flecks in his eyes. "Because you have to get Tommy back to his home. You should've seen him in the room at the Tatums' house. I couldn't leave him there." The man blanched. "It's not a good place for him."

She ducked her head, guilt weighing her down.

"The sooner you get the poor farm house repaired, the sooner he'll feel secure again."

He wasn't telling her anything she didn't already know, but how could she do it on her own? She glanced at the letter she'd written, hoping the words would be enough to persuade the mission board to act swiftly.

"It's been what now . . . nearly three weeks?"

Miserably, Christina nodded. Long, weary, sadness-laden weeks.

Mr. Jonnson continued, his gloomy tone becoming matter-of-fact. "The weather's nicer now. Spring is a good time for building, if the house can be rebuilt."

"It can be," she injected.

He tipped his head, genuine concern glimmering in his eyes. "Then why haven't you started?"

His insinuation that she had made no effort to repair the house or to see to the needs of the residents stung. "Mr. Jonnson, I cannot manufacture the funds required to take on a project of such magnitude. I rely on the mission board for financial support, and they are —" In her mind's eye the disdainful faces of Mr. Regehr and Mr. Breneman chastised her anew. She couldn't bear to tell Mr. Jonnson the mission board was unwilling to support her place of ministry. Somehow she would convince the members otherwise. She would!

Mr. Jonnson sat silently for several seconds before clearing his throat. "Are they lacking funds?"

Christina knew the board struggled to keep all its projects in operation. She nodded.

"What if I . . ." He leaned back and closed his eyes for a moment, as if arguing with himself. Then he gave a little jolt and fixed his unsmiling gaze on her once more. "What if I donated the lumber. Would it help?"

Christina clapped her hands to her face. Had she heard him correctly? Had he just offered to provide the lumber needed to repair her home — her place of service?

"I haven't seen the house. I don't know how much damage was done. But I could ride out today, take a look around, get an idea."

Christina's ears rang, but Mr. Jonnson's steady voice somehow managed to penetrate the high-pitched whine inside her head.

"I've got some of last season's lumber left over — knotty pine, all flitch cut, so there are different widths, but the depth is all the same. It would do for rebuilding the outside walls."

Excitement created a flurry in Christina's stomach. "Y-you'd give it to me?"

He offered a slow nod.

She searched his somber face, her desire to understand this man overriding every other emotion. "But why?"

His lips twisted into a wry grimace. "I . . . have my reasons." And then he fell silent.

Christina fiddled with the letter she'd penned. If she added yet another paragraph, sharing Mr. Jonnson's wonderful contribution with the mission board, would it be enough to convince them to reestablish the poor farm at its present location? Might they even credit her with acquiring such a generous donation and rethink their stance on her ability to lead? Her breath came in little spurts as she considered the mill owner's offer. She couldn't refuse. She didn't dare refuse.

But before she accepted his offer, she needed him to know exactly how much lumber would be required. She set the letter aside. "Before you commit to this donation, Mr. Jonnson, it's best you examine the house. Noon is still three hours away. If we hurry, we can be there and back before it's time for Cora and me to serve lunch. Would that be acceptable to you?"

CHAPTER 18

Cora, one arm around Tommy and the other holding the quilt closed around them, jounced back and forth as Mr. Jonnson's wagon rattled along the road on the way to the poor farm. Tommy was pressed so tightly against her side they moved as one in the wagon's bed. She smiled down at him even though he couldn't see it. It felt good — *right* — to have him nearby.

She'd been drawn to Tommy from her first moments at the poor farm. Any fool could tell he was hurting. Hurting from being shucked away, same as she'd been. Maybe he'd been able to sense her deep pain — he possessed an odd way of seeing with his heart since his eyes didn't work anymore — because he'd seemed to attach himself to her. Seemed to like her more than the others at the poor farm. She chuckled, marveling. What a pair they were, him with his broken eyes and her with her broken spirit.

And no hope for either of them to regain what they'd lost.

The wagon hit a rut, jarring the wagon. Tommy released a little yelp and flailed his arms. Cora gripped him tighter and turned to glance at the seat, where Mr. Jonnson and Miss Willems sat side by side in silence. "We almost there?"

Miss Willems stayed facing ahead, all hunkered in her coat with a lap robe pulled clear up to her hips, but she nodded. "I can see it now."

Mr. Jonnson lifted his chin as if peering ahead. "From the front you wouldn't know there'd even been a fire."

"The kitchen was added on the back, along with a bedroom that was originally used by the maid," Miss Willems explained. "The bedroom was badly damaged, but the kitchen is nearly destroyed."

"So the fire started there?"

"Yes."

Beside Cora, Tommy began to quiver. His face had turned white. She jostled his shoulder. "Tommy?"

He bit his lower lip and buried his face in the quilt.

Concerned, Cora started to tell Miss Willems that something was wrong with the boy, but before she could, Mr. Jonnson turned in at the poor farm's lane, and Miss Willems pointed ahead.

"Wes is here tending the animals. Do you want to park near the barn? Perhaps Tommy and Cora would like to visit with Wes while you and I go to the house."

Mr. Jonnson drew up alongside the poor farm's wagon, and his pair of horses greeted the poor farm's mare with some snuffling noises.

Cora threw aside the quilt and helped Tommy to the side of the bed. Mr. Jonnson caught him under the arms and lifted him out. Then the man reached for her. For a moment she froze, another picture replacing the one of Mr. Jonnson. Hands extended to her, a wide grin and knowing eyes offering an invitation. That day she'd taken those hands, let them pull her into a clutching embrace. And now nothing was the same. She scrunched her eyes tight, willing the memory away, then opened them to look into Mr. Jonnson's face. His friendly, honest face. She shivered. She wouldn't allow any man to touch her. Not again. She shook her head, and he backed away.

Mr. Jonnson offered his help to Miss Willems instead, and she accepted without a moment's pause. Jealousy coursed through Cora. If only she could turn back time. Not go to that hayfield with Emmet Wade. Then maybe she'd feel worthy of attention from a nice man like Mr. Jonnson. But then again, maybe not.

Gaze downcast, she clambered out of the wagon bed, careful to keep her skirts tucked tightly to her legs. When Miss Willems alighted, she and Mr. Jonnson headed for the house. Part of Cora wanted to follow them — to hear Mr. Jonnson say whether or not he had enough leftover boards to repair all that needed fixing. But most of her wanted to escape the uncomfortable feelings caused by looking at his hands extended to her.

She caught Tommy's elbow. "C'mon. Let's go check on Wes an' all our critters, huh?"

Tommy nodded. He still looked a little pale, and he crunched his lips together as if something pained him. Maybe the cold air and bouncing around had been hard on him — he had been awful sick after all. Cora hurried him into the barn, where it was warmer.

Wes came at them, pitchfork in hand and a huge smile splitting his face. "Hey!" He caught Tommy in a bear hug, then grabbed Cora the same way before she had a chance to think. "What you doin' out here?" He bumped Tommy's shoulder with his massive fist, still grinning. "You come to help muck stalls?"

"Miss Willems an' Mr. Jonnson're lookin' at the house, checking out the damage," Cora said. Tommy rocked in place and bobbed his head around, sniffing the air. Remembering how he'd smelled the fire first, she wondered if he was reliving their last night in the poor farm house. If so, they weren't good memories. Cora went on, hoping her next words would cheer the boy. "Mr. Jonnson says he's willing to give us the wood to fix it. Leastways, the outside. An' Miss Willems said if we can get the outside done, we can live in it until we have enough money to fix the inside."

Wes let out a whoop, and Tommy jumped at the sound. Cora threw her arm around the boy's shoulders and squeezed, trying to give some comfort. Tommy sure seemed rattled. Or spooked.

Holding on to Tommy, she spoke to Wes. "I wouldn't complain about leavin' the boardinghouse. That Mrs. Beasley, she's a real bearcat."

Wes ambled toward a back stall, the pitchfork over his shoulder. "Least you got a decent place to stay." He jammed the fork's tines into a pile of hay and tossed the clump of yellow straw over the stall's wall for the cow. "Me? I been sleepin' with the animals." He paused, leaning on the pitchfork handle, and sighed. "Been warm enough and dry. Even so, sure will be glad to get in a bed again." He returned to forking up hay.

Cora looped her arm through Tommy's and followed Wes. "You know anything about buildin', Wes?"

Wes paused and puffed out his chest. "I know . . . some."

"How long, you reckon, before those walls are all fixed again?"

He worked his lips back and forth, his forehead wrinkling in deep thought. "Well . . . if just one man's seein' to it, it'll take a while. But if there's a whole crowd . . ." His eyes flew open wide. "Hey! You ever heard of a barn raisin'?"

Cora shook her head.

"I seen 'em. Lots of 'em where I used to live." Wes shivered. Cora suspected they were excitement shivers instead of cold ones. "Whole lotta folks get together. The women, they bring food to keep everybody satisfied, an' the men all work an' get a barn up in one day."

Cora crinkled her nose. "A day? You sure? That don't seem likely."

"I'm tellin' you, I've seen it." Wes poked

232

straw over the stall where the two goats resided, and they bleated in appreciation. "If a whole bunch o' folks from town would come together, we could get that house built — outside an' inside — an' all move back in again, like it oughta be."

Cora chewed the inside of her lip. "Dunno, Wes. Seems like we'd need more'n just hands to get all that work done. Takes a heap of money, too. An' money ain't somethin' we've got."

Wes headed for the toolroom at the back of the barn. Cora took Tommy's hand and trailed after him. He hung the pitchfork on its hooks, then stood staring at the implement, his hands in his pockets. "When Mr. Willems ran things, there was always money. Never any extra, but the mission board, they sent what he needed. Didn't seem like it took all that much to get help." He turned toward Cora and frowned. "Don't wanna sound mean or anything, 'cause you know I'm right fond of Miss Willems, but I can't figure why them mission men ain't wantin' to give her the money. They don't even wanna keep her in charge."

Tommy's mouth dropped open. "They — they're sendin' her away?"

Cora shook her head hard, giving Wes a fierce look to hush up. But the big man kept on talking.

"They said a man oughta be runnin' the place." Wes scratched his head. "I'm wonderin' if they've got a man all picked out to run the place. They talked about Ham Dresden. Sure hope they ain't gonna put that lazy coot in charge."

Tommy's entire frame began to tremble. Cora huffed in aggravation at Wes's thoughtlessness and turned Tommy toward the wide doorway. They'd only taken a couple of steps when Miss Willems entered the barn. Tommy must have heard her skirts swishing or smelled the lilac water she wore, because he broke loose from Cora's grip and stumbled forward, his hands reaching out.

Miss Willems dashed forward and caught him. He fell against her, shaking. Miss Willems looked at Cora, all befuddled. "What's wrong with him?"

Cora chewed her lip. "It's — We was just —"

Wes stomped up behind her. "It's my fault, Miss Willems. I was tellin' Cora an' Tommy about what the mission men said — about them thinkin' it'd be better if somebody else ran the poor farm." His face changed to a rueful scowl. "I didn't mean to upset Tommy." He stretched out one hand and gave the boy a few awkward pats on the back. "I'm sorry, Tommy. I shoulda kept quiet."

Cora gave the talkative man a blistering look. He should've kept quiet, for sure! She turned to Miss Willems. "But don't you worry, Miss Willems. We — all of us — we wouldn't want anybody but you to take care of things. If those mission men ask us, we'll all say we want you. Won't we, Wes?"

Sheepishly, Wes scuffed his boot toe on the ground. " 'Course we will."

"So see?" Cora forced as much cheeriness into her tone as she could muster. "You don't got to worry for one minute, Miss Willems. Like you're always sayin', God'll take care of it." Was the God Miss Willems prayed to listening? "You ain't gonna be goin' anywhere."

Miss Willems set Tommy aside. "Did you hear what Cora said, Tommy? There's no reason to worry, is there?"

Tommy couldn't see the fear in Miss Willems's eyes, but Cora sure could. She held her breath while Tommy gave a hesitant nod.

Miss Willems took Tommy's hand. "We're finished here, and we need to get back. Are you ready to go, Cora?"

The women said good-bye to Wes and then hurried out to the wagon, where Mr.

Jonnson stood waiting for them. He boosted Tommy in first, then helped Miss Willems onto the seat. Cora used the wagon wheel as a ladder and climbed in with Tommy. As soon as they were settled, Mr. Jonnson pulled himself up next to Miss Willems and released the brake.

Mr. Jonnson and Miss Willems talked quietly together on the seat, but the grind of the wheels on the hard ground kept Cora from hearing their words. She wondered if Tommy could hear them. His ears seemed to pick up things easier than hers did. She started to ask him, but when she glimpsed his worried face, she decided to leave him be. Instead, she stared at the poor farm buildings slowly disappearing behind the gentle rise in the road. Her heart twisted in her chest. The poor farm was the best home she'd ever had. And Miss Willems was so nice, taking in people nobody else wanted, like Tommy with his blind eyes and Wes with his simple brain. When Cora finally found the courage to tell Miss Willems her secret, surely the lady wouldn't make her go away. But if some man came along to be in charge, he'd send her scooting for sure.

She pulled Tommy tight against her side, seeking comfort. He rested his head on her shoulder. "It'll be all right," she murmured.

" 'Course it will." She hoped Tommy found more peace in her assurances than she did.

Levi drew the team to a halt outside the boardinghouse. He watched the young woman named Cora plant a kiss on Tommy's cheek and whisper something in his ear before scrambling over the edge of the wagon and dashing for the house. Tommy sat right where she'd left him, in the middle of the hay-strewn bed, hands limp in his lap and his shoulders slumped.

Frustration stabbed, carried on a wave of anger. In his short time with the Tatums, the boy had lost the fragile confidence Levi worked so hard to instill in him. He wouldn't take Tommy back to that house no matter what Miss Willems said.

Aware of Tommy's very sharp hearing, Levi dropped his voice to a whisper. "Mrs. Tatum told me a family named Spencer took in the other two youngsters from the poor farm. Do you suppose they'd be willing to let Tommy stay there, too?"

Miss Willems sent a quick, sympathetic look to the back of the wagon. Moisture brightened her eyes, and she shook her head. "I asked. Although they aren't terribly young — late twenties or early thirties — they've only been married a couple of years.

They said three children would be over-whelming."

Despite the seriousness of their conversation, Levi battled a grin. Miss Willems's gravelly voice didn't fit the sweet curve of her jaw or the soft upturn of her lips. Full sunlight brightened her face, bringing every small feature into view. Levi found himself examining her by increments, and he found the inspection pleasing.

Up close, her eyes were a clear blue lined with thick, curling lashes. Three very faint freckles decorated the bridge of her nose, and one more resided on her left cheekbone — the perfect spot for a man to place a kiss. A few gentle lines creased the corners of her eyes, and her lips were full and a soft rose color. She was as she described the Spencers — not terribly young — but she appeared as fresh and unspoiled as a new oak leaf freshly unfurled.

His stomach twinged, and he turned his gaze forward before his thoughts took him in directions he had no business going. "Then what will you do with him?"

Shifting her body sideways, she angled her gaze toward the boy. "I . . . I suppose I'll keep him with me."

Levi had gotten a peek into her room when she'd tossed that stinky sock away. A bed, a washstand, and a wardrobe filled the entire space. She and Cora probably tripped over each other in there. "There's room for Tommy?"

"Well . . ." She nibbled her thumbnail, still staring at the back of Tommy's head. "It will be a tight fit, but . . ." She looked at him, a desperation in her eyes coupled with a hesitant expectation. "It won't be for long. You said you had enough lumber to repair the walls and the roof of the house. And the weather is clearing, so work can be done. So it won't be for long. Isn't that right?"

With her whispering and the rasp in her voice, he wasn't sure he'd heard her correctly. It sounded as if she expected him not only to donate the lumber but also to do the work. He hadn't intended to put the boards up, just provide them for someone else to use. He had his own work to do. At the end of the month, logs would be coming, and he had an oak buffet he wanted to finish before then. To take on repairing the poor farm's house would mean setting aside his own project. It would also mean working with Miss Willems and possibly the mission board. Maybe even bringing on a couple of other men to help. A sour taste filled his mouth.

"Miss Willems, if you can find three strong

men with a little know-how, those outer walls could be up and the roof repaired in less than a week."

Her face fell, the hint of expectation fading so quickly it stung Levi to the center of his soul. Should he offer to do the work himself? He had the know-how, and if he worked late into the evening at home, he might still be able to finish his buffet.

"Mr. Jonnson . . ." She held one hand toward him. Encased in a glove of green yarn, it looked impossibly small and delicate. He took it very carefully and looked into her face, which seemed both stalwart and subdued at the same time. "I thank you for your wonderful contribution." She withdrew her hand so slowly he didn't realize it was moving until he held air. "I pray God will bless you for your generosity." Turning her gaze to the back of the wagon again, she raised her voice. "All right, Tommy, let's go in."

Levi remained frozen on the seat as she climbed down and then moved to the back of the wagon to assist Tommy. Hand in hand, the woman and boy walked behind the boardinghouse. Even then he sat, staring at the spot where they had disappeared, with an aching emptiness in his chest. An emptiness so large it seemed to consume him. But he couldn't identify its source.

CHAPTER 19

Wagons crowded the street outside the Creeger Mercantile. Saturday was come-to-town day for the area farmers, but even so, Levi had never seen this many wagons here. He glanced up and down the street, puzzled. Was something special happening in town? He drove around the block and parked beside the bank on the opposite corner of the street. Hopefully, he'd be able to pull closer when it came time to cart out his supplies. With his lengthy list it would take several trips to load his wagon, and he didn't look forward to trekking up and down the boardwalk, arms laden with crates.

The cowbell jangled as Levi entered the store. Its merry clang barely carried over the cackle and chatter of no less than a dozen female shoppers who clustered around a large table in the center of the room. Mrs. Creeger waved from her spot behind the sea of sunbonnets, a beaming smile lighting her face. "Good morning, Mr. Jonnson! Jay's in the storeroom, but he'll be right out to take care of you."

Levi nodded in reply, then ducked between aisles to get out of the way of other customers. He listened to the mercantile owner's wife chat with shoppers, calling each by name and inquiring after children, horses, and husbands. How the woman already knew everyone in town after only a few months in Brambleville, when Levi couldn't call half a dozen residents by name after his years in the small town, confounded him.

People stepped around him, choosing items from the shelves. A few glanced in his direction — a couple of them even offered a brief, impersonal smile. But none attempted to engage him in conversation. Not like they did with each other or with Mr. and Mrs. Creeger. He was in their midst but somehow set apart. The same empty feeling that had captured him as he watched Miss Willems and Tommy walk hand in hand to the boardinghouse swooped in again. What ailed him?

"Ah, Jonnson, there you are." Jay Creeger marched up the aisle, brushing his palms over the bib of his starched white cobbler apron. He laughed, jabbing his thumb at the activity behind him. "Lost you in the throng. Running a special on dress goods today. I reckon every woman in town'll be sportin' a new dress by the end of the month!"

That explained it. He recalled his mother hurrying to the local mercantile when a shipment of calicoes and ginghams arrived, eager to choose a length for herself. A new dress, Mor always said, was a ritual of spring. Did Miss Willems have the funds to purchase a length of dress goods? He doubted it. For some reason the thought made him sad.

He dug his list out of his pocket and handed it to the mercantile owner. "Do you have time to fill this?"

"Oh, sure. Mary Ann's seeing to the ladies, and they're all so busy yakking I can take care of your order with nobody missing me." Jay perused Levi's lengthy list. He tapped the paper with one finger. "Got everything but this," he said with a mild frown. "We stock coal oil, corn oil, an' cottonseed oil but not linseed oil. I can check the catalog and order some for you, though, if you don't mind waiting for it."

Levi shrugged. "They probably have it at the Feed and Seed." It meant another stop, but he'd need that oil to finish his buffet.

"If you want, you can head over to the Feed and Seed while I'm packing your things. You got quite a list here. Probably take me fifteen, maybe even twenty minutes to fill it."

"That suits me. I'll be back soon." Levi sidestepped around the chattering throng and walked out onto the boardwalk. The happy voices of the shoppers faded behind him as he made his way to his wagon. Atop the seat, he heard only the crunch of wagon wheels and the steady *clop, clop* of the horses' hoofs. In the past the familiar sounds had never seemed melancholy, but in the few minutes it took him to reach the Feed and Seed on the far edge of town, loneliness descended with a heaviness that threatened to smother him.

For years he'd lived and worked alone with only his horses and his tools for companionship. And he'd been content. Alone had meant peaceful. Secluded. Secure. But now the cloak of solitude weighed on him like a rain-soaked wool blanket. In that mercantile, surrounded by people from the community he'd called home for a dozen years, he'd been out of place. A stranger.

He drew the team to a halt outside the Feed and Seed, hopped down, and entered the barnlike structure. A few men loitered in the corner around a barrel holding a checkerboard. The owner glanced over at Levi when he strolled past, but he didn't offer a word of greeting. Levi made his way to the back wall where shelves held various jugs and tins. On the second shelf he found a gallon-sized tin of linseed oil. Not until he set it on the counter did the owner separate himself from the small group of men and join Levi.

The man squinted at a little paper square tied to the handle with a piece of string. "That'll be thirty-two cents."

Levi nearly snorted. No "Howdy." No "How's your day going?" Just a price. But why should he expect anything different? In all his times of visiting this store, had he ever started a conversation with the owner? Of course not. In fact, the few times someone had tried to draw him into their discussion, he'd made it clear he wanted to keep his distance. He deserved the aloof treatment he now received. But even so, it rankled.

He dug a quarter, nickel, and two pennies from his pocket and slid them across the counter. The owner plopped the coins into a wooden box and headed for the game without offering a word of thanks.

Levi stared at the man's broad back.

Something odd — something he couldn't define — built inside his chest. He sucked in a breath and blurted, "Have a good day."

In unison, each man at the checkerboard lifted his head and gawked at Levi. The owner gave a little jolt, stopped, and sent a puzzled frown over his shoulder. Several seconds ticked by before the owner cleared his throat. "Yep. Thanks. You, too, Jonnson."

Levi nodded, letting his gaze scan the checkers players and observers. Partly pleased with himself, partly embarrassed, Levi trotted out to his wagon. The short drive to the mercantile gave his erratic pulse time to calm. What had gotten into him, hollering out that way? Yet he couldn't deny it had pleased him to speak and be spoken to in return.

No wagons had vacated their spots in front of the store, so he parked at the end of the block in front of the bank again. When he entered the mercantile, Mrs. Creeger offered a smile and then cupped her hands beside her mouth. "Jay! Mr. Jonnson is here!"

Mr. Creeger bustled from the storeroom, bending backward against the weight of a large crate in his arms. He smacked the crate onto the counter, wiped his brow, and shot a smile in Levi's direction. "That's the last of it. Lemme get you tallied up here, an' then I'll help you carry everything out."

Levi leaned against the counter and observed the womenfolk while Mr. Creeger added up his bill. The ladies handled bolts of cloth the way he handled a piece of oak. They stroked the fabric as if checking for splinters. Traced their fingers along the fibers the way he followed the lines of grain. One flipped a bolt over several times and snapped the fabric across the table, peering down its length much the way Levi looked down a plank to be sure it was straight. The fabric was even light brown, like a piece of stained wood, but unlike wood it bore tiny clusters of blue flowers tied with pink ribbon.

The blue flowers matched the color of Miss Willems's eyes, and the pink reminded him of the color that flooded her cheeks when she looked at him. Wouldn't she be pretty as a picture in a dress sprigged all over with blue flowers? He waited to see if the woman admiring the fabric would ask Mrs. Creeger to cut a length. After several seconds of perusal, the woman shook her head, rewrapped the bolt, and slid it beneath some others on the table.

Levi quirked his finger at Mrs. Creeger.

She bustled over, her friendly face

wreathed with a smile. "What can I do for you, Mr. Jonnson?"

He pointed at the tip of the bolt sticking out from the pile of colorful fabrics. "How much is that brown with the blue flowers?"

"All our calicoes are three cents a yard today. That's only a half penny over whole-sale."

He'd overheard three other women request nine yards each, so he assumed Miss Willems would need a similar amount. He added quickly in his head — nine yards would cost twenty-seven cents. For Miss Willems, twenty-seven cents was probably a small fortune. But she needed another dress. She'd worn the same one — a plain, trim-fitting dress, solid green, the color of pine needles — every time he'd seen her for the past three weeks. But he couldn't buy that fabric for her. Could he?

Mrs. Creeger said, "Did you want me to cut a length of that for you, Mr. Jonnson? It would make very nice curtains."

"Well, actually . . ."

Two of the women at the table peeked over their shoulders at him, their heads tipped in his direction. They reminded him of a pair of robins listening for worms. He chewed the inside of his cheek. He couldn't ask for that fabric now. As soon as they saw

Miss Willems sporting a dress in the brown fabric with blue flowers, they'd surely put two and two together. And then add their own speculations and come up with five.

He shook his head. "Never mind."

With a smile Mrs. Creeger returned to her other customers.

Levi turned his back on the table of fabrics, but an image of the soft brown cloth with blue flowers danced before his mind's eye. He blinked twice, dispelling the vision, and focused on Mr. Creeger's pencil scratching an amount at the end of a column of numbers. He had more than enough to buy without adding twenty-seven cents worth of dress goods to the list.

After paying his bill, Levi accepted Mr. Creeger's offer to help carry everything to his wagon. Even with two pairs of hands, they made three trips before they finished loading the crates of canned goods and sacks of flour and cornmeal. When they'd set down the last items, Levi lifted the back hatch into place.

Mr. Creeger offered a broad grin as Levi secured the hatch. "Anything else I can do for you, Mr. Jonnson?"

Levi started to tell him no, but a memory stopped him — Miss Willems's hopeful expression as she'd questioned how long it would take to rebuild the kitchen walls at the poor farm. And Levi heard himself say, "As a matter of fact, Mr. Creeger, maybe there is something you can do."

CHAPTER 20

"I'm tellin' you, he can't stay here."

If Miss Willems hadn't put her hand on his shoulder, Tommy would've jumped out of the chair and tried to escape. The boardinghouse lady's voice — the same angry voice that had told Miss Willems she reeked — was high pitched and hateful. And she was talking about him.

"Mrs. Beasley . . ." Miss Willems sounded kind most of the time, but compared to the other lady, she sounded extra nice right then. Her fingers were warm and comforting on his shoulder. "I apologize for not asking permission to bring Tommy here, but I had little choice."

Tommy ducked his head. Just once couldn't someone say, "I want Tommy," instead of "I have to take Tommy"? How would it feel to be wanted by somebody?

Miss Willems went on. "And it won't be for long. Mr. Levi Jonnson is donating the lumber to rebuild the damaged walls at the poor farm. In no time at all, I'll —"

"He ain't stayin' here." Mrs. Beasley must've come closer, because she sounded even louder. "I only got the one room for hired help. You can't put a boy his age in there with you two women. 'Specially a boy who ain't even kin. It's not proper!"

"It ain't like he can see anything." Cora sounded almost as angry as Mrs. Beasley. Tommy knew she meant to defend him, but her words pained him. Pained him bad. He covered his ears with his hands to try to block their words, but the voices still came through.

"Besides that, it takes more food to feed an extra mouth. That's an expense. Anybody who stays here either has to pay or has to earn his keep." A mighty huff exploded — Mrs. Beasley, Tommy was sure, because he'd never heard either Miss Willems or Cora make a noise like that. "Just what's that boy gonna do to pay his way around here?"

The hand on Tommy's shoulder began to tremble. The fingers held on tight, the way he'd held to those ropes Mr. Jonnson had strung to guide him around his property. "I . . . I shall request funds from the mission board to cover Tommy's expenses

253

here." Miss Willems sounded croaky from her sore throat. And maybe from trying not to cry.

Another mighty snort. "You been writing letters to that mission board pret' near every day, an' no money's come through the mail yet, now has it?"

"Well, no, but —"

"I'm startin' to think that mission board's just a bunch of hooey an' you're playin' everybody in this town for fools!"

Tommy's breath came hard and fast. Miss Willems would never convince the boarding-house lady to let him stay. Would he have to go back to the Tatums' and sit in that room all by himself day after day for the rest of his life? Maybe he deserved to sit all alone, because if he'd told Miss Willems that he'd smelled Hamilton Dresden's cigars, the poor farm house never would've gotten burned in the first place. Dresden's warning rang through Tommy's head: *"Tell anybody I was here, boy, an' I'll come back an' lay into you like nobody's ever done before. You an' me got us a secret now, an' you'd best keep it. You hear me, Tommy-boy?"* Fear overwhelmed him, and he whimpered.

Arms wrapped around him, and Cora's scent filled his nostrils. Her voice blared next to his ear. "Mrs. Beasley, you just hush now. You're scarin' Tommy."

"Yes, please," Miss Willems added. "There's no sense in upsetting him."

"He ain't the only one upset."

The boardinghouse lady still talked real mad-like. She wasn't a nice person at all, and he didn't want to stay here. He opened his mouth to say so, but a knock on the back door stopped him. The boardinghouse lady let out another loud huff, and then feet pounded on the floor. Hinges squeaked, and Mrs. Beasley said, "What do *you* want?"

"I need to speak with Miss Willems. May I come in?"

Tommy gave a little gasp of recognition. He wriggled free of Cora's embrace and pushed himself to his feet, reaching for the man. Callused hands caught his, and Tommy clung, smiling so big his cheeks hurt. "Mr. Jonnson . . . Mr. Jonnson . . ." He couldn't find any other words to say.

Christina wanted to take hold of Tommy and pull him away from the mill owner. The boy's expression — rapturous, as if he'd been delivered — raised a wave of envy. At one time the poor farm residents had looked to her the same way Tommy now looked to Mr. Jonnson. They'd trusted her, depended on her, giving her a sense of purpose. But not since they'd been scattered to the winds. Now uncertainty and an element of betrayal lingered on their faces when she spoke to them. And she couldn't blame them. She'd failed them — all of them. Her sense of self was fading as surely as smoke dissipated from a fire.

She cupped both hands over the watch resting against her bodice and turned to Mrs. Beasley. "Ma'am, if Cora and I are to have lunch ready for the boarders, we need to get started. Can we continue this discussion later?"

Mrs. Beasley rolled her eyes and lifted her hands in a gesture of futility. Without a word she stomped out of the kitchen. Christina waited until the woman's footsteps faded away before facing Mr. Jonnson. She angled her gaze away from Tommy's firm grip on the man's hands.

"About what did you need to speak to me, Mr. Jonnson?" She moved to the worktable and picked up an apple and a paring knife. On the other side of the kitchen, Cora began slicing carrots into a soup kettle.

Mr. Jonnson followed Christina to the table, Tommy moving beside him like a shadow. "I wanted to let you know Mr. Creeger posted a notice in the mercantile, asking men to help put up the walls and roof at the poor farm."

Her hands stilled, a coil of red peel dangling from the apple. "He did? Why?"

Mr. Jonnson shrugged — a sheepish gesture. "I asked him to."

She should appreciate Mr. Jonnson's kindness, yet instead of gratitude, resentment filled her. She wanted — no, she *needed* — to be the one who set things to rights at the poor farm. The mission board would never view her as capable if someone else took charge. "But why?" Christina heard herself, recognized the recalcitrance in her tone, but couldn't quite squelch it.

"Because you needed help." Confusion colored his voice. He cocked his head. "You didn't intend to put up those walls yourself, did you?"

She lowered the half-peeled apple to her lap. Of course she couldn't put up the walls herself. But she could certainly make arrangements with those who could. She sought an explanation that wouldn't make her seem churlish. "I planned to ask for volunteers after church services tomorrow."

"That might not be necessary. I saw several women reading the notice as soon as Mr. Creeger tacked it to the doorjamb. It's likely they'll go home and tell their men about it. So the men will probably approach you about helping."

Mercy sakes, he had the whole town taking care of her. Christina hung her head. Earlier that day she'd blessed him for his generosity. Now she wanted to tell him to stop interfering. She sat in silence, battling her raging emotions.

He stepped close to the table. "Miss Willems?" When she lifted her head, he smiled down at her. A soft smile. A sweet smile. A smile that could melt the hardest heart. She steeled herself against it. "You don't have to thank me. It's the least I can do to help you get settled again."

He'd misinterpreted the reason for her speechlessness, but Christina couldn't find the strength to correct his assumption. She sat, tongue-tied and unmoving, and gazed into his green-blue eyes. His intentions were honorable even if he had usurped her position. Papa would thank him. Papa would praise him. Papa would —

She shook her head, clearing her thoughts. She wasn't Papa. If she were — if she were at the very least a man — she would already have the funds she needed to reestablish the poor farm and get everyone settled. But she wasn't a man, and somehow she had to prove to the mission board that she, a mere female, could operate the poor farm as well as any man. Even as well as her own father. Her future depended on it.

Drawing in a deep breath, Christina set the apple aside and rose. She looked squarely into Mr. Jonnson's face. "I appreciate all you've done. Truly I do. But now I must ask that you cease any further assistance and allow me to proceed as I see fit."

The warmth in his eyes faded.

"You see, Mr. Jonnson, the poor farm is my responsibility." She squared her shoulders and raised her chin. "Please allow me the privilege of making reparations."

The muscles in his jaw clenched and unclenched. His Adam's apple bobbed in a swallow. Very slowly he folded his arms across his chest. "All right, Miss Willems. If that's the way you want it. But before I go, I'd like to make sure you're handling one very important responsibility." He glanced at Tommy, who stood nearby with his sightless gaze aimed in Mr. Jonnson's direction. "What about him?"

She didn't care for the challenge in his tone. "He's staying here with me."

"Not according to your landlady, he's not."

Christina narrowed her gaze. "Were you listening at the door?"

"I didn't need to. I could hear her hollering before I came up the walk."

Heat flooded Christina's face. Who else might have heard Mrs. Beasley's verbal barrage? She cleared her throat and spoke with more confidence than she felt. "Despite Mrs. Beasley's claims to the contrary, Tommy will stay here with me until we can move back into the house at the poor farm."

"Are you sure?" He angled his head, his expression stern. "Because I don't want that boy returned to the Tatums."

How dare he dictate to her! "Mr. Jonnson, I fail to understand why you find it your concern that —"

"You made it my concern when you brought him to my doorstep. He made it my concern on a snowy day when he got lost trying to return to my place. It's my concern because he ran away *to me.*" Although spoken softly, the emphasis on his final two words didn't escape her notice. "And I want to be assured he won't go traipsing across the countryside again."

"He won't!"

"Are you sure?"

Christina took Tommy by the arm. "Tommy, I know you've heard everything Mr. Jonnson and I have said. Promise him you'll not run off again."

Tommy clamped his lips together.

Christina gave his arm a little shake. "Tommy?"

Cora settled the lid on the pot of soup and crossed to Tommy. She wrung her hands, her brow furrowing into lines of worry. "You're upsettin' Miss Willems, Tommy. Promise her you won't run off again."

Tommy turned his face toward the floor.

Mr. Jonnson cupped his hands on Tommy's shoulders, forcing Christina to relinquish her hold on his arm. "Tommy." The single word carried authority. Tommy lifted his head. "What you did last Sunday, taking off without telling anybody where you were going, was dangerous. It caused a lot of people heartache, most especially Miss Willems. You were reckless and irresponsible, and we . . ."

He paused and glanced at Christina. Although she'd told him to allow her to proceed unaided, suddenly she welcomed his intrusion. Welcomed his use of the word *we*. Not since Papa's death had she shared her burdens with a partner, and for a few brief seconds, a glorious feeling raced through her frame. She liked being part of a *we,* and the recognition both elated and frightened her.

261

Mr. Jonnson went on. "We expect better of you. I know you're an honest boy, so when you promise not to do anything so foolhardy again, we can believe you." He turned Tommy toward Christina. "Now make that promise to Miss Willems."

A sullen expression crept across Tommy's face.

Mr. Jonnson nudged the boy's upper arm. "Go ahead. We're waiting."

The soup began to boil, rattling the cover. Tommy jerked at the sudden noise, but he remained stubbornly silent.

Mr. Jonnson let out an exasperated breath. "Tommy, if I were your father, I'd haul you to the woodshed right about now."

The boy's face lifted. Panic shone in his expression. "Don't be mad at me!"

Mr. Jonnson met Christina's gaze. The earlier frustration she'd glimpsed melted in light of Tommy's distress. "I'm not mad, Tommy. I'm disappointed."

Tommy's chin quivered. "But I can't make that promise, Mr. Jonnson, 'cause it'd be a lie. No matter where she puts me, I won't stay. I won't stay anywhere except with you." He flung his arms around Mr. Jonnson's middle and buried his face against the man's shirt.

Christina's wonderful feeling of kinship

with Mr. Jonnson washed away on a wave of hurt. Looking at Tommy in the man's embrace — Mr. Jonnson's embrace rather than her own — she felt as though her heart had shattered. She'd done nothing but love the boy from the moment she'd helped him over the poor farm's threshold. Why did he reject her now?

CHAPTER 21

Levi stood, arms at his side, chest aching. The boy's skinny shoulders heaved with sobs. He should hug the boy — offer comfort. But something in Miss Willems's expression froze him in place. Not anger. Not even disappointment. It went deeper than disappointment. Her face reflected anguish. An anguish that pierced him to the center of his soul. He battled a mighty urge to put one arm around the boy and the other around the woman. But he did neither.

Taking Tommy by the shoulders again, he set the boy aside. Deliberately positioned him so his arm brushed against Miss Willems. He expected her to immediately embrace the still-sobbing boy, but she didn't. Instead, Cora bustled over and pulled Tommy into her arms. She rested her cheek on his hair and murmured to him. Miss Willems watched the pair, bright tears quivering on her thick lashes, but she made no move to take over the task of reassuring Tommy.

Levi touched Miss Willems's arm with his fingertips. He waited until she shifted her gaze to meet his. "You know he'll try it again — try to get to my place."

She nodded slowly. "Yes. Yes, I have no doubt . . ."

Levi pulled in a breath and blew it out in a noisy rush. He had to be as much a lunatic as folks said his father was, but he couldn't risk Tommy getting lost again. Maybe falling into the river or encountering a wild creature. He forced the words past gritted teeth. "So let me just take him."

Within the circle of Cora's arms, Tommy's sobs came to a shuddering halt. Miss Willems stared at the boy for several seconds, indecision playing across her pale face. While she stood in silent uncertainty, Levi went on.

"As you said, it won't be for long." It'd better not be. He couldn't afford to get himself too firmly attached to the boy. "And it'll help you keep peace between yourself and Mrs. Beasley." If peace was possible with the irascible woman. "And if he's with me, he won't be running off anywhere. I'll keep him safe." He ran out of reasons for her to entrust the boy to his keeping. So he closed his mouth and let her think.

The multicolored cat sauntered from under the stove and bumped against Miss Willems's legs. She leaned down and gave the animal a few idle strokes, almost as if she was unaware of the action. Then she straightened abruptly. The cat zipped back to its hiding spot, and Miss Willems turned a stern frown in his direction.

"Since I seem to have no other alternatives, I accept your offer to provide sanctuary to Tommy until we can return to the poor farm."

A relieved grin formed on Tommy's tear-stained face.

"But . . ." Her brows descended, an attempt to appear fierce that fell far short. A face as pretty as Miss Willems's just didn't have the ability to look harsh. "If you take him, I shall expect you to see to all his needs, including spiritual. I want him in Sunday worship services."

Levi stifled a snort. She had no idea what she was asking of him. He hadn't set foot in a church for more than thirteen years. Not since Far's death. He'd made a vow to himself at his father's grave that he'd never darken a church door again, and he expected to honor it until his own dying day.

All those pews filled with self-righteous busybodies spouting "God is love" but turning their backs on his family when they needed help the most . . . He'd never join them.

"I don't go to church."

She frowned. "I understand that's been your practice. Mrs. Tatum informed me of your lack of faith." The frown changed from disapproving to disheartened. A hint of sympathy glowed in her blue eyes. "I won't say I approve of your choice to refrain from worship, but I shan't judge you for it. Each of us is responsible for our own decisions concerning faith. But Tommy is still a boy who needs guidance. The Bible — God's holy Word — is the best source of guidance. He should be in services."

"And if I refuse, what then?"

She released a delicate sigh, turning her gaze on the boy. "I'll keep him with me."

Tommy opened his mouth, and Levi staved off the impending protest with a hand on the boy's shoulder. "Even though he's pretty much promised to run off the first chance he gets?"

She continued gazing at Tommy. "Yes."

Levi couldn't imagine why attending worship was so important to her. In his experience all the lovely words flowing from the mouth of a preacher were just that — lovely words with no real meaning behind them. It seemed foolish, maybe even cruel, to force that drivel into the boy's head. Someday he'd learn the truth and feel as betrayed as Levi had when his walls of faith had crumbled. But if that's what it took to keep the boy safe with him, he'd take Tommy to church.

"All right." He forced the concession through gritted teeth. "I'll bring him in."

Christina stood with the other parishioners as the minister delivered a closing prayer. Worshiping with fellow believers had always provided peace and joy in the past, but on this Sunday morning she fought an element of discouragement. Even though several men had approached her before the service started and had offered to help rebuild the fire-damaged walls, even though Tommy was in attendance, even though Reverend Huntley presented a beautiful sermon on maintaining one's faith in the midst of conflict, she felt unsettled.

While Reverend Huntley prayed, she offered a private, internal prayer. *God, bring us all back together quickly so I can resume my ministry. I miss my family desperately, and I feel so lost . . .* Tears stung, and she blinked rapidly to clear them as the minister said, "Amen."

She took Tommy's hand and followed the others into the yard where the March sun beamed bright and cheerful in a clear blue sky. A brisk breeze carried scents of springtime — aromas that had always given her heart a lift. She breathed deeply, but the sweet potpourri of new growth failed to raise her spirits. Only reconstructing the poor farm walls would rebuild her contentment. When she took Tommy to meet Mr. Jonnson — the man had indicated he would wait at the livery stable — she would ask when he intended to deliver the lumber to the poor farm. She hoped it would be soon. Already nearly three weeks had slipped by, with her charges spread from hither to yon. Oh, how she longed to be under one roof again.

"Miss Willems?" Rose's voice cut through Christina's thoughts. "Did you hear what Alice said?"

Christina shook her head.

Alice's daughter, Laura, stepped forward, her face beaming. "Miss Claussen says we should all come to her place today for Sunday dinner. She fixed a big pot of lamb stew, and I helped her make biscuits last night. She says we can use her parlor and visit all afternoon if we want."

The spinster seamstress had a very small house, and extending such an invitation had to be a sacrifice. Christina owed so many people a debt of gratitude. She forced a smile to her face. "That's very kind of her. Is everyone going?"

Laura said, "All but Joe an' Florie."

Her brother, Francis, made a sour face. "I was wantin' to play some with Joe. But the Spencers already left."

Christina hadn't even had a chance to greet the twins and inquire after them. She swallowed her disappointment and put her hand on Francis's shoulder. "Perhaps Mr. Jonnson will approve Tommy staying with us for lunch and the two of you can spend some time together."

"Not the same," Francis mumbled, and his mother gave him a hard nudge. The boy blushed crimson. "I mean, spendin' time with Tommy'll be just fine."

"You children take the others to Miss Claussen's house now," Alice said to Laura and Francis. "I'll walk with Miss Willems to the livery." She sent Christina a hesitant look. "I need to talk with you."

Christina's stomach rolled over in apprehension, but she merely nodded.

"C'mon!" Francis headed off with Laura,

Wes, Rose, and Louisa trailing behind.

Alice fell in step with Christina as they walked toward the livery. "Miss Willems, as kind as Miss Claussen has been, that room I'm sharing with the children is getting smaller and smaller."

Christina cringed. "I know. But it shouldn't be much longer. Perhaps by this time next week, we'll —"

"We won't be here by next week."

Christina stopped, forcing both Alice and Tommy to come to a halt. She gawked at the woman, her heart pounding. "Where will you be?"

"In Detroit. My husband's sister-in-law lives there. She wrote last week and told me that since her youngest got married and left home, she's got room now for the children and me. She said there's a lantern factory that hires both men and women, and I could probably get a job. She even offered to send train fare — it arrived yesterday."

An expression of wonder crossed the woman's face. "Why, when Oscar died, I thought I'd be beholden to others for the rest of my life. But now . . ." — she sighed, a smile toying with the corners of her lips — "now I'll be able to provide for myself and my youngsters. Laura's really taken to cooking and cleaning since we've been with

Miss Claussen, so I know she'll be a big help to me. Maybe, if the job pays enough, I'll even be able to get us a small house of our own so we won't need to share with my sister-in-law."

"Oh, Alice . . ." Christina embraced the woman, happiness at Alice's prospect of beginning a new life in Detroit warring with a sadness she knew was selfish. But how she would miss Alice, Laura, and Francis. For three years they'd called the poor farm home.

Alice pulled loose and linked arms with Christina, urging her to move forward. "We'll leave on Tuesday's train, and we hope you'll come say good-bye before we go. You and your father were angels on earth to my youngsters and me. We'll never forget you."

Christina didn't answer. Her throat ached too badly to form words. They reached the livery, and Mr. Jonnson sat on a bench just inside the barn's double doors, which were rolled back to allow in a breeze. He rose and met them on the boardwalk.

Tommy blurted, "Miz Deaton, Laura, an' Francis are movin' away. To Detroit."

Mr. Jonnson offered a polite nod. "Is that so?"

"Yes," Alice said, her cheerful voice a direct contradiction to the sorrow weighting

Christina's heart. "We'll be leaving on Tues-day."

"I wish you well," Mr. Jonnson said. He turned to Tommy. "You ready to go?"

Tommy didn't release Christina's hand. "Can I stay an' eat lunch with Miss Willems an' the others? It'll give me a chance to say good-bye to Francis an' Laura."

Mr. Jonnson scratched his chin. "I hadn't intended to stay in town all day."

"Perhaps you'd like to join us for lunch, too." Alice issued the invitation. "We made plenty, and I'm sure Miss Claussen wouldn't mind one more around the table."

"Or," Christina cut in, fearful the man might agree to join them but uncertain why the idea bothered her, "if you need to return to your mill, I could have Wes drive Tommy out to your place early this evening."

The man nodded, flooding Christina with alternating waves of relief and disappoint-ment. "That sounds fine. And while you've got Tommy, I'll load up that lumber and haul it out to the poor farm so it'll be ready whenever the men have time to get the walls put up."

"Aren'tcha gonna help with the buildin'?" Tommy asked.

Mr. Jonnson aimed a smirk at Christina. "I think Miss Willems has things well in hand. No need for me to oversee the project."

Christina's face became a raging furnace. He'd only reiterated what she'd said yesterday. Why did it sound so petty and childish when uttered by him? She gave Tommy's hand a little tug. "Come now. The stew will be cold if we don't hurry to Miss Claussen's." She scurried off before the mill owner could make her feel any smaller than she already did.

CHAPTER 22

"Are you going to wear an apron to the train station to say farewell to Alice and her children?"

Cora, caught in the middle of loosening the strings on one of Mrs. Beasley's voluminous aprons, turned slowly to face Miss Willems. The woman wore her familiar dark green muslin dress, but she'd donned a straw bonnet with tiny pink silk roses and green leaves sewn all along the brim. She looked trim and perky. Cora felt frumpy by comparison in her oversize, stained apron with strands of lank hair hanging along her jaw.

Miss Willems held out a second bonnet — dyed blue straw with a cluster of snow white ribbons hanging down the back. "Why not wear this instead? Miss Claussen was so kind to share some of her millinery with us."

"I, um . . ." Cora gulped. She wanted to

see the Deatons off, to wish them well on their journey and new place to live. But how could she remove the apron? She'd missed five of her monthlies, and the little bulge was becoming a big bulge. Her dresses were so tight she could barely button them. Now that the weather was mild, she couldn't hide beneath a coat. The apron, especially since it was cut to fit a larger woman, concealed her growing belly. She didn't dare leave it off.

She tangled her hands in the apron skirt's folds. "You just go an' tell 'em so long for me. I'll stay here an' get lunch started."

Miss Willems offered a puzzled look. "But we just put away the breakfast dishes." She lifted her watch and checked it. "We have sufficient time to go to the station, give Alice, Laura, and Francis a proper send-off, and then return to prepare lunch."

Something within Cora's middle shifted — a little foot? Lately she'd been feeling more movements. After seeing her ma lose three babies in a row, she knew she should be grateful this babe thrived. But Cora's heart pounded. What would she do when her belly grew so large an apron wouldn't hide it? What would she do when the babe emerged from her womb? Fear made her mouth dry. She turned her back on Miss

Willems and started fussing with the clean mixing bowls on the sideboard.

"I thought to bake some egg pies. We'll need 'em cool before we serve 'em, so . . ."

Miss Willems moved up behind Cora and touched her shoulder. Cora braced herself for the question she knew would come one day soon. Miss Willems said in a tender voice, "Is it too hard for you to tell them good-bye, Cora?"

Cora's stiff shoulders slumped. Saying good-bye was hard, so she didn't need to fib. She nodded.

"Well then, you stay here. I'll be sure to give each of them a hug from you. Will that be all right?"

Guilt smote her. She should go — should tell Alice, Laura, and Francis good-bye herself. They were her friends, and hiding away might be hurtful to them. But not hiding away might reveal things she wasn't ready to confront. Still facing the sideboard, Cora whispered, "Thank you, ma'am."

Miss Willems gave her shoulder a pat and then stepped away. "I shouldn't be gone long. Alice said the train leaves at nine." A sad sigh reached Cora's ears, and Cora looked over her shoulder. Tears had welled in Miss Willems's eyes. "How strange it will

277

be to return to the poor farm without them."

Cora swallowed. She sought a means of comforting Miss Willems. "But me an' Wes an' Tommy an' Rose an' Louisa an' the twins — we'll be there. An' maybe there'll even be somebody else who needs a place to stay."

Miss Willems smiled and whisked her fingertips beneath her eyes. The tears disappeared. "Of course you're right, Cora. My father would say this is God's way of making room for someone else in need." She turned the knob on the door. "I'd better go before I miss them." With another quick smile she left.

Cora stood at the window and watched Miss Willems scurry across the stepping-stones that led to the front walk. The woman held her head high, her slim figure moving with grace. Pressing her hands to the mound beneath the apron skirt, Cora pondered how much longer until the bulk made her clumsy and slow.

Miss Willems disappeared from Cora's view, and she turned her attention to mixing a crust for pies. As she rolled the dough into an ever-widening circle, she envisioned her belly growing bigger, bigger. With a little cry she sank into a chair and buried her face in her elbow. "Make it go away, God," she moaned, soaking her sleeve with hot tears. "Make it go away . . ."

The train chugged around the bend, carrying Alice, Laura, and Francis away. Christina remained on the depot platform, watching and waving, until the smoke from the stack floated over the treetops, and the bright red caboose was swallowed up by brush along the track. Then she turned to the others who'd gathered to tell Alice good-bye. Wes, Rose, and Louisa all wore sad faces. Christina forced a smile, determined to cheer them.

"What a wonderful opportunity Alice and the children have waiting. God has certainly blessed them."

Wes rocked on his heels, his mouth forming a deep frown. "Almost feels like we had a buryin'. We won't never see Alice an' the young uns again."

"We will miss them for sure. But it's better for them to be with family," Rose said staunchly, giving Wes's arm a brisk pat.

Wes hung his head and scuffed his toe against the wide, weathered planks. "I thought they was with family, bein' with us."

Christina's heart lurched. She well understood Wes's sadness. Over their years together she and the poor farm residents had become a family of sorts. With both Papa and Mama gone, she had no one else to call kin. Partly to comfort Wes, but mostly to comfort herself, she said, "But we still have each other, Wes. And very soon" — to her great relief the men intended to meet at the poor farm this coming Saturday to erect the walls — "we'll be back in our home again." Surely the mission board wouldn't send away the one responsible for rebuilding the walls.

Wes sighed, his large shoulders rising and falling. "That'll be nice, Miss Willems. That'll be right nice."

The group turned and ambled toward the center of town. Wes walked ahead, and Rose and Louisa flanked Christina. As they passed the schoolhouse, Rose pointed to the wild game of tag taking place in the schoolyard. "Listen to those youngsters."

Christina peeked at her watch. "Hmm, it's rather early in the morning for a recess."

Rose chuckled. "Don't reckon the time matters much to the students. The teacher's probably giving them some extra breaks with spring arriving. This nice weather's got them all wound up."

Louisa clicked her tongue on her teeth. "It's too bad Joe and Florie didn't get to come to the depot and say good-bye to Laura and Francis. They probably don't even know their friends have gone."

"Maybe we should go over to the school and tell them," Rose suggested.

Since she hadn't gotten to talk to the children on Sunday, Christina liked Rose's idea. She turned to Wes. "We're going to see Joe and Florie. Do you want to come along?"

"Nah." Wes waved his hand toward the livery. "Gonna go out to the poor farm. Time for me to see to the critters out there."

Christina bade Wes farewell, and then she and the two sisters-in-law made their way to the schoolyard. Children darted everywhere, loud and happy, but she didn't spot a pair of matching curly-blond heads in the throng.

"Maybe they're inside doing an assignment," Louisa mused. "Should we go in and check?"

Christina hated to disturb them if they were working, but she also wanted to let the two know the Deatons had left. "Louisa, would you like to go in? Rose and I will stay out here so it's less of an intrusion."

Louisa nodded and hurried up the stairs. Christina and Rose waited beside the porch, staying out of the way of the rambunctious youngsters. Moments later Louisa emerged with a puzzled scowl on her face. She caught Christina's elbow and drew her toward the road. "The teacher says the Spencers came this morning and told her the children wouldn't be in school anymore."

With the children's shouts filling her ears, she wasn't certain she'd heard correctly. She sped her steps, Rose and Louisa scurrying along beside her, until they'd put some distance between themselves and the schoolyard. She stopped and took Louisa's hand. "Did you say the Spencers withdrew the children from school?"

"That's what the teacher said." Louisa's lined face pinched with concern. "Do you suppose the youngsters are ill?"

"I don't know," Christina said, "but I intend to find out." She set off for the residential area of town with Rose and Louisa dogging her heels. They reached the Spencers' pleasant clapboard house, but no one answered her knock on the door. Her worry mounting, Christina stepped off the porch and walked to the backyard. There, Mrs. Spencer was pinning shirts and britches to a wire strung between the house and a small shed. She paused with a wet shirt in her hands when she spotted Christina and the sisters-in-law approaching.

"Good morning, Miss Willems." The woman greeted her cheerily. If something was amiss, she didn't indicate it. "How are you today?"

Christina clasped her hands around her watch, willing her jumping stomach to settle down. "I'm fine, thank you. I wondered if I could speak to you about Joe and Florie."

A sad smile appeared on Mrs. Spencer's face. "Oh yes, it was awfully hard for us to tell them good-bye yesterday. We got rather attached to them in our short time together. We even considered adopting them. But we've been married such a short time, and" — a pretty blush stole across her cheeks — "of course, we plan to have our own youngsters someday. But we hope Joe and Florie'll be happy in their new home."

Christina shook her head, thoroughly confused. "Their new home? What new home?"

Mrs. Spencer dropped the shirt into a basket near her feet and stepped away from the line. "The Kansas Children's Home, of course."

Both Louisa and Rose gasped. Christina pressed the watch to her chest. "You . . . you sent them away?"

"Not me." The woman edged even closer,

confusion marring her brow. "A man came by here yesterday. He said he was to take the twins to the children's home."

Christina's knees went weak. She staggered to the edge of the yard where a painted bench sat beneath a tall elm tree. As she sank onto the bench, Rose and Louisa scurried over and began patting her shoulders. Pressing her hands to her pounding temples, Christina stared at Mrs. Spencer, who slowly followed. "Did he say anything about Tommy?"

"The little blind boy? No." Mrs. Spencer frowned. "But I can't imagine an orphanage taking in a child who can't see. With all the children in their care, they wouldn't have time for one who needed extra attention." Mrs. Spencer perched on the bench beside Christina. "I assumed you'd arranged it. He made it seem as though you wanted the twins in a different place — a place with other children. I'm so sorry. I thought you knew."

The children . . . gone? Christina's head spun. "The man who came . . . did he tell you his name?"

"Yes. He introduced himself as Mr. Silas Regehr."

Mr. Regehr had indicated the mission board would arrange placements for the poor farm residents, but she hadn't imagined him taking the children without her knowledge. And to an orphanage, where they would be lost among a veritable sea of other needy children? Joe and Florie wouldn't receive the care and attention to which they'd grown accustomed during their year with Christina. Rose, especially, had doted on the pair.

Christina leaped up and charged across the yard toward the street, her watch bouncing. Mrs. Spencer called after her, but she ignored the woman and aimed herself for the train station. She pumped her arms, her skirts swirling around her ankles. Her pulse pounded in her temples.

Louisa and Rose puffed up beside her. "What are you going to do?" Rose asked.

Christina barely flicked a glance at the woman. "I'm going to get those children back."

Rose clapped her hands together. "Praise be! An orphanage is no place for our Joe and Florie."

"But how will you get them back?" Louisa's fretful tone pierced Christina's ears. "You don't have money for a train ticket, do you?"

Rose added her concerns. "Three tickets . . . That will cost dear."

Christina stopped as abruptly as if she'd encountered a stone wall. What was she thinking? She didn't have travel money, not for herself or the twins. Even if she did, she might need to complete some sort of paperwork and receive approval before the children's home director allowed her to take them. That could require days. Which would mean paying for meals and a hotel room.

She drew in deep breaths, bringing her galloping pulse under control, and forced herself to think rationally. Mr. Regehr had taken them away. She'd simply insist he bring them back. By next week the poor farm house would be repaired so she and the others could move in again. He'd have no reason to keep the children away from her once she could put a solid roof over their heads. It would be hard to wait — everything within her wanted to demand their immediate return — but the mission board would be more likely to heed her request if her house was ready for occupation.

"You're right." Christina reached out, and Rose and Louisa each took one of her hands. She clung hard, seeking comfort from their firm grips. "I can't go chasing after them. But" — she gave each woman a determined look — "next week, when we're all in our house again, those children will come back to us. You'll see."

CHAPTER 23

Levi smiled as he observed Tommy rubbing a rag over the breakfast dishes and then fingering the plate to be certain every bit of cornmeal mush was washed away. The boy groped for the drying towel, wiped the plate with it, then inched his way to the cupboard and clanked the plate into place.

Tommy's face broke into a grin. "All done! Let's get to work."

No one would be able to deny the pride in his tone and in his erectly held shoulders. In the past week Levi had seen confidence bloom in the boy. And most of it came from the progress he was making in learning to cane. He wasn't adept enough yet to tackle a chair seat or any other project, but his nimble fingers could form discernible patterns with canvas strips that Levi had cut to emulate cane. The canvas didn't cut his fingers the way hemp had, but the boy had shown Levi his callused fingertips before bed last night and crowed, "Look! I've got working hands, just like you." Something warm and welcome had flooded Levi's chest at the comment, and the good feeling was with him still this morning.

He slapped an arm around Tommy's shoulders. "Let's go."

They stepped from the porch to the yard and headed in the direction of the mill. They'd taken only a few strides before Tommy stopped and sniffed the air. "Smells like rain's comin'."

Levi searched the sky. Overhead it was mostly clear — just a few wispy streaks of white way up high — but in the north it appeared a thunderstorm was building. He shook his head in wonder. How had Tommy detected rain clouds from miles away? "I think you're right, Tommy, but I bet it won't hit until this evening."

The boy scowled. "Miss Willems, she's countin' on gettin' the house done so we can all move in again. If it starts rainin', will the men be able to build those walls at the poor farm?"

Levi nudged Tommy's elbow to get him moving again. A rainstorm could delay the rebuilding. Miss Willems had come out twice during the week to check on Tommy, and each time she'd assured him they'd be back in their own home soon. She seemed to need the assurance even more than Tommy did — the boy was content with Levi. And Levi had to admit he had come to enjoy having the boy around. But he didn't mind Miss Willems showing up on his porch now and again either. What man wouldn't enjoy looking at her comely face?

He choked out a startled cough, sending away the thoughts of Miss Willems. "Kansas storms blow through pretty quick. If it lets up by morning, they can probably still work. It'll just be messy."

Tommy offered a slow nod, but he didn't smile. "Oh."

Levi paused, stopping Tommy with a hand on his arm. "What's the matter?"

"Once the house is fixed, I . . . I'll have to leave."

Levi's chest tightened, but he forced a cheery tone. "Well, sure. But that's a good thing, right? Don't you miss Miss Willems and the others?"

"I guess so." The boy's thick lashes swept up and down a few times. "Miss Willems took good care of me. Cora an' Wes an' the others — they *all* took care of me." A hard edge crept into his voice.

Levi put his hand on the boy's shoulder and squeezed gently. "They love you,

Tommy." He knew it was true. He'd seen the way Miss Willems, Cora, and even the older residents from the poor farm looked at Tommy. Miss Willems's tenderness toward the boy was motherly, protective. Maybe too protective, but he supposed that's why God gave children both a mother and a father — a mother to be tender and a father to make the youngsters toe the mark. Leastwise, that's how it had been in his house. Until Far stopped being a father. He cleared his throat. "Nothing wrong with that, is there?"

Tommy lowered his head. "I reckon not. Except . . ."

Levi cupped Tommy's chin and lifted his head. "Don't hang your head when you're speaking, Tommy. Keep your head up and talk plain. Now, what's troubling you?"

Tommy aimed his face at Levi's. His eyes seemed to gaze right through him. "They take care of me like I'm a baby. But I'm not a baby." His voice grew stronger. He angled his chin high. "I'm a man."

Levi stifled the chuckle that threatened. Tommy might not be a baby, but he wasn't a man. Not anywhere close yet. However, he wouldn't squelch the boy. "I know you aren't a baby, Tommy, and you do a fine job of taking care of yourself. I'm proud of all the things you're learning. As you grow older, you'll learn even more things. But you know something?"

"What?"

"Even a man needs to show appreciation to those who care for him." Levi's throat tried to close. For years he'd harbored resentment toward his mother for doing everything for his father. An equal measure of fury resided inside him for his father's refusal to try to get better. The burden wore him down. He'd carry his grudges to the grave — after so many years they were a permanent part of him — but he'd do whatever he could to keep Tommy from picking up a similar burden. "Remember, they're only doing what they think is best for you. Even if you can't appreciate what they do, you can appreciate why they do it. Do you understand?"

Tommy's lips pursed as if he'd tasted something unpleasant. "I think so, Mr. Jonnson."

"All right then. Let's get some work done before that storm blows in, huh?"

The boy cast off his frown. "Yes, sir!"

"Oh no . . ." Christina rested her fingers on the windowsill and looked at the dark clouds rolling in from the north.

Cora turned from the pie safe. "What's wrong?" The weariness in her voice matched the defeated slump of her shoulders.

"A storm." Christina closed her eyes, blocking views of the coming storm and Cora's sad countenance. *Why now, Lord?* She supposed the area farmers were pleased to see rain clouds. A bountiful harvest relied upon adequate moisture. Thus far no spring rains had fallen. But couldn't nature have waited one more week to bring its first storm of the season?

Cora carried two jars to the table and set them down. The *thud* of thick glass connecting with wood joined with the distant roll of thunder. "Never knew you to be scared of a storm, ma'am." Cora removed the top from the closest jar and dumped the contents — pickled okra — into a bowl. She lifted one crisp pod and nibbled it.

Christina sent an impatient glance in the young woman's direction. "The storm doesn't frighten me." Hurt crept across Cora's features. Christina pushed aside her frustration and spoke more kindly. "If it rains, the men might not be able to work on the poor farm walls as they'd planned."

"Didn't think about that." She made a face and tossed the half-eaten okra into the slop bucket. "That means we'd hafta stay here even longer. Sure was lookin' forward to bein' back in our own place."

"So was I . . ." Christina chewed her thumbnail and gazed at the darkening sky. She'd promised Tommy, Wes, and the McLain sisters-in-law they wouldn't have to wait much longer to return to their home. The area men had arranged to work on Saturday since their own jobs kept them busy the rest of the week. The lumber was already in the barn, delivered by Mr. Jonnson for the men's use. But unless the storm passed quickly, they'd likely postpone putting up the walls.

From behind her, Cora's timid voice quavered. "You reckon if we prayed, God'd send the storm scootin' around us?"

"I don't know, Cora." Her indecisiveness startled her. When had she stopped trusting in the power of prayer? Hadn't she always told the residents God listened when they prayed and responded in the best possible way for them? Her fingers groped for Papa's watch and closed around it. Over the past few weeks, facing the loss of her house and the loss of contact with the people she loved like family, her faith had somehow drifted out of reach. She looked at the sky again, seeking a ray of sunshine — a glimmer of hope — but all she saw was roiling clouds against a murky gray expanse.

She slapped the windowsill in aggravation and turned away from the unwelcome sight. Apparently God had decided to ignore her pleas for assistance. Was it because she'd brought this turmoil on herself and her charges by foolishly causing the fire? Her father taught her that God is not a God of harsh judgment yet each person has to face the consequences of his actions. If she was being punished for thoughtlessness, it didn't seem fair that the other poor farm residents must suffer as well.

Plates and cutlery for lunch waited on the sideboard — a shorter stack than what was needed for the evening meal since some of Mrs. Beasley's boarders chose to eat at the local café or took sandwiches for their lunch. Christina carried the items to the dining room and set them on the blue-checked cloth — white napkins and silverware placed just so on either side of blue willowware plates. She performed the task by rote, grateful for a few moments when she didn't need to think.

She and Cora carried in platters and bowls containing ham sandwiches, cucumbers swimming in buttermilk, pickled okra and beets, and spiced peaches. As she returned to the kitchen to fetch the coffeepot, someone knocked on the back door. She scurried over, wiping her hands on her apron, and swung the door open wide. Rain-scented air gusted through the opening and pushed her skirt against her legs. She let out a little gasp of surprise.

A man stood on the stoop. He swept his hat from his head and met Christina's gaze, earning a second gasp — this one of trepidation. He stepped over the threshold and grinned. "Howdy, Miss Willems. The new mercantile owners told me where I could find you. Workin' as a maid an' cook now, huh?" He chuckled. "Must be a real comedown for you."

"Hamilton Dresden . . ." Christina pressed her palm to her fluttering heart. "I thought you'd left Brambleville."

"Oh, I did." He swung his hat against his pant leg, creating a *whish, whish, whish* that matched the pitch of the wind. "But as you can see, I'm back."

Thunder rumbled. Tommy's stomach clenched. He was hungry — lunch had been quite a while ago — but the twinge in his midsection wasn't because of hunger. He hated the sound of thunder. Especially close thunder. The rumble and crash reminded him too much of another sound on the day his life had changed forever.

His hands started to shake. He'd mess up his weaving if he wasn't careful. Eyes closed, tongue tucked in the corner of his lips, he formed a loose slipknot at the end of the strips, just as Mr. Jonnson had taught him. Not too tight, or he'd ruin the weaving above it, but tight enough to keep everything from unraveling. He ran his fingers over the knot. It felt fine. Real fine. He sat back on his haunches and let out a sigh.

Tap, tap, tap . . . Raindrops pattered on the mill's tin roof. Tommy didn't mind the sound of rain. Like fingertips drumming on a desktop. Pa used to drum his fingers when he was deep in thought. Ma would say, "You're gonna poke a hole through that wood if you're not careful." And Pa would grin. Tommy missed those days.

"We'd better get to the house." Mr. Jonnson's voice came from close by, startling Tommy out of his woolgathering. "Good, you've got that tied off. Let's head in before the hard rain hits, or we'll get soaked."

A hand curled around Tommy's upper arm, drawing him to his feet, and the hand tugged. Tommy trotted alongside Mr. Jonnson, his feet slipping on the wet ground. He didn't bother counting the steps. Mr.

Jonnson would tell him when they reached the porch.

"Up," came the man's voice, and Tommy lifted his foot. The porch boards felt solid beneath his soles. A door squeaked, and Mr. Jonnson's palm on his back urged him inside. Tommy moved to the side to allow Mr. Jonnson to enter. Then he felt his way to the sofa. He stood with his hand on the sofa's back, his skin tingling.

"The air is funny," Tommy said.

"What do you mean?"

He shrugged. He couldn't define what seemed different, but something made him feel as though pins pricked his scalp.

A soft chuckle carried across the room. "I think the storm's just got you spooked. From the looks of things, we're in for a real gullywasher."

Tommy tipped his head, listening to the sound of the storm. The raindrops picked up their tempo, their *tap-tap*s plinking hard and fast on the windows. The wind howled, and a clap of thunder rattled the panes. Tommy jumped.

"I'll get us a fire going," Mr. Jonnson said. *Thud*s and *thump*s let Tommy know Mr. Jonnson had dropped wood into the fireplace. "Once we take the chill off the room, it won't feel so funny to you."

Tommy eased onto the sofa cushion and pressed his palms between his knees. He hoped Mr. Jonnson was right because he couldn't shake the feeling that something bad was coming.

CHAPTER 24

Raindrops fell in a soft, steady patter. Gray shadows bathed every corner of the room. Midnight had passed, according to the chimes from the clock in the parlor, and tiredness plagued her, but worry — a more intense disquiet than she'd ever experienced before — held Christina's eyelids open.

She didn't want to be ensnared in fretfulness. Her father had often preached on the futility of worry. "Worry," he'd said, "is telling God you don't trust Him." Christina examined her heart, seeking the faith she'd claimed as a young child and had staunchly defended her entire life. But her feeling of unease deepened because for the first time in her twenty-eight years, she found herself questioning whether or not God was truly there.

"Oh, Papa, I need your wisdom . . ." She whispered the plea to the gray-shrouded ceiling. But Papa couldn't answer. And God had steadfastly ignored every prayer she'd uttered since the night of the fire. How else could she explain the mission board's refusal to help rebuild, the delay of her own plans to repair the house, and the one-by-one removal of the people she'd grown to love? If she cried out to God now, would He listen? Unwilling to be rejected once again by her heavenly Father, she held her anguish inside, where it churned painfully through her stomach.

Thunder rumbled, and Cora stirred. She sat up, glancing around in apparent confusion until her gaze fell on Christina. She squinted for several seconds, as if trying to determine if she was awake or dreaming, and then she yawned. "Rain botherin' you?"

Christina offered a mute nod that rustled the starched pillowcase beneath her head.

Cora sighed and lay back down, folding her hands over her stomach on the outside of the covers. "If it don't stop soon, those men'll put off rebuildin' our walls for sure." She peeked sideways at Christina. "But if it rains itself out by mornin', think maybe it'll be dry enough on Sunday for the men to do that buildin'?"

Christina grimaced. "Sunday's a day of rest."

Cora snorted. "For men maybe but not

for womenfolk. We still hafta cook and clean up." She yawned again, her stomach rising and falling. "Mrs. Beasley didn't rent a room to that man who showed up tonight, did she?"

Christina's pulse sped into double beats at the mention of Hamilton Dresden. Of all the people who'd entered the poor farm's doors, he was the only one who'd made her feel uncomfortable. The day she'd informed him he could no longer stay at the poor farm since he had broken the stringent "no visiting rooms of residents of the opposite sex" rule, he'd turned menacing, vowing no woman would order him about. In her mind's eye she could still see his snapping eyes and sneering lips. Had Wes not stepped up beside her in a show of support, Ham might not have left. Today he'd been congenial, chatting as if they'd never had an unpleasant word between them, but he still made her uneasy.

"No." Great relief underscored Christina's simple answer.

"Good," Cora said on a sigh. "He looked like the type who would eat a body out of house an' home. Didn't look forward to cooking for him. It'd be a heap o' work, I reckon."

Recalling the large amounts of food the

man had consumed while at the poor farm, Christina agreed. "Well, we needn't worry about it. He won't be staying here." She didn't bother to explain that Ham Dresden hadn't been able to pay for a week in advance, one of Mrs. Beasley's requirements. Christina had expected him to rant or to promise to have the money soon, but he'd merely tipped his hat — an amazingly nice hat, considering his presumably penniless state — and departed with a grin on his face. Yet she suspected they hadn't seen the last of him.

"I suppose we can hold out one more week here." Cora's tone turned musing. Almost melancholy. "One week won't make much difference. Sure it won't."

Christina wanted to scream that one week made a tremendous difference. Another week before she could insist Florie and Joe be returned to her care. Another week with Wes living in a stable. Another week away from Tommy. Another week of Herman and Harriet languishing far from their familiar home and of Louisa and Rose grating on each other's nerves in their tiny shared room. Another week of feeling helpless and useless and aimless. Why couldn't Cora understand she needed the poor farm house finished so she could regain her sense of self? But screaming would only wake the entire house and would solve nothing. She bit her lower lip and kept her thoughts inside.

After a few moments another yawn stretched Cora's mouth wide. Then she rolled to her side, bouncing the bed. She settled, and soon deep, even breaths let Christina know she'd fallen asleep again. Christina closed her eyes, willing sleep to claim her as well, but when dawn broke, gray and drizzly rather than rosy and bright, she was awake to witness it.

Saturday morning after the breakfast cleanup, Christina braved the rain with a folded week-old newspaper held over her head as a makeshift umbrella and set off for the mercantile. Although the walk was only three blocks, by the time she reached the Creegers' store, the paper lay in a soggy heap across her bonnet, and her dress was drenched. Mary Ann Creeger took one look at Christina and burst into laughter. But when Christina didn't join in, she stilled her laughter and hurried around the counter, hands outstretched.

"I'd say this rainy day has washed away your sunniness, Christina. We don't have a fire going in the stove to warm you, but I can offer a towel to blot some of that water."

Christina dropped the sodden newspaper onto the cold stove. "There's no sense in soiling one of your towels. I'll only be here a few minutes, and then I'll be out getting wet again. I came to speak with Mr. Creeger."

"He left to make a delivery to Old Mrs. Bronson. It's gotten too hard for her to get out, so we take her canned goods and such every week."

"I hope he wore a slicker." Christina scowled at the window, where raindrops danced in rivulets down the square panes. "I don't think it's ever going to stop."

Mary Ann slung her arm around Christina's wet shoulders and guided her to two carved rocking chairs tucked in the far corner of the store. "It's quiet right now — quietest Saturday we've had since we moved to Brambleville. The rain's got most everyone holed up, I reckon. I was bemoaning the lack of business to Jay earlier, but now I'm grateful. With nobody around needing my attention, I can take some time to chat." She seated herself in one of the chairs and gestured to the other. "Sit a spell."

Christina looked at the caned seat and finely formed spindles, then held out her soggy skirts. "I probably shouldn't."

Mary Ann waved her hand, wrinkling her nose. "If a wet skirt does it damage, then the chair isn't worth its six-dollar price." Christina still hesitated, and Mary Ann reached out to take her hand. "Please, Christina. Sit down and tell me what has you so heartsore. Can't be just the rain that's caused your sad face."

Christina sank into the chair. "It shows that badly, hmm?"

Mary Ann released a short, light laugh. "The sparkle's gone right out of your eyes. I know rainy days affect some people that way."

"I don't mind rain," Christina said, leaning her head against the rolled back of the rocking chair. The chair sat so comfortably. If she closed her eyes, she might drift off to sleep. "I'm just discouraged by the timing."

"Ahhh." Mary Ann nodded. "The rebuilding was supposed to happen today."

Christina sighed. "Yes." She turned her head slightly to stare at the steady rainfall. "I was so hoping to be back in my own home by this evening."

"Can't say I blame you. Even though Jay and me are happy here in Brambleville, there are times I miss our old home something fierce. We loved it so."

Christina didn't mean to be nosy, but an

underlying sadness in the woman's voice stirred curiosity. "Then why did you leave it?"

Mary Ann set her rocking chair in motion. "I suppose you could say we needed a fresh start. Away from bad memories."

Remorse stung Christina. She touched Mary Ann's hand. "I'm sorry if I reminded you of something unpleasant."

"Oh, now, don't apologize." A sad smile played at the corners of Mary Ann's mouth. "You see, Jay and me have lost three babies in our years of marriage. After the third one the doctor told me I wasn't meant to be a mother — my body just won't carry a baby. He quoted the verse from the first chapter of Job: 'The LORD gave, and the LORD hath taken away; blessed be the name of the LORD.' " A soft, mirthless laugh left her throat. "I confess, it took me a while to accept we'd never have children and still be able to bless the Lord's name, but after much prayer I'm at peace with it now. I have Jay, and he is content just to have me, so I am blessed."

Christina couldn't imagine the strength and faith it must have taken to overcome such a deep loss. She didn't know what to say to her friend, so she sat in silence.

After a few minutes Mary Ann spoke

again. "How'd you end up living on a poor farm, if you don't mind my asking?"

"I don't mind." Christina began to rock gently. "My parents were managing a poor farm in Iowa when I was born, so I grew up watching them minister to folks who weren't able to provide for themselves."

"Sounds rather dreary."

Christina shook her head. "Far from it. It's a blessing to reach out to others in need. I know you understand that. You reached out to me when I needed clothing and other articles for the residents after our fire."

Mary Ann shrugged. "But we've been repaid for those things. Someone from the mission board — Mr. Regehr, I think he said his name was — came in last week and took care of the bill."

"He did?" Why hadn't the man come to see her while he was in town? Instead, he'd sneaked around, paying off the debt and then removing Joe and Florie from her care. What else had the mission board done without her knowledge?

"Mm-hmm. Paid it in full. But" — Mary Ann frowned — "he said something curious. He said to close the poor farm account for good, to allow no more charging. They aren't shutting down the poor farm, are they?"

Fear turned Christina's mouth to cotton. It seemed that's exactly what the board intended to do. And if they did, where would she go? "I . . ." — Christina gulped — "I hope not. It's my home." She blinked back tears. Holding Papa's watch loosely in her hand, she shared, "My mother died when I was ten, and shortly after that the mission board asked my father if he'd be willing to establish a new poor farm in Kansas. Papa thought a change would be good for both of us, so he said yes, and he moved here to Brambleville while I attended a school for young women near Boston. When I'd finished my schooling, I came to help Papa by tutoring children who resided at the poor farm. I've been there ever since."

"So it's all you've ever known." Mary Ann sounded pensive.

"I suppose it is." Christina idly traced the etching on the watch's face with one finger. "And I'm eager to return to it before I lose any more of my residents."

"What do you mean?"

Christina explained the Schwartzes' and Deatons' departures, but she couldn't bring herself to tell Mary Ann about the twins. In part, she saw no point in mentioning it because she intended to get them back. But mostly she felt it would be cruel to talk about the temporary loss of the children after learning of the Creegers' permanent losses.

"So," Mary Ann said, "people who move into the poor farm don't necessarily stay there forever?"

Christina shook her head. "Not always. Sometimes — such as with elderly residents — they're with us until they pass away. We have a small cemetery behind the house where some of our former residents have been laid to rest." What would happen to the cemetery if the mission board closed the poor farm? Who would care for the graves? "Younger people sometimes just need a place to stay until they finish school or recover from an illness or find employment. We never know how long we'll minister to someone, but we try to be available for as long as we're needed."

The back door slammed, and moments later Jay Creeger stepped from the storage room at the back into the main part of the store. His hair was damp, and his boots dripped muddy water, but except for the bottom twelve inches of his trousers, his clothes were dry, proving the effectiveness of his slicker. He strode to the women and held out both hands to his wife. A smirk twitched on his bearded cheeks. "You see?

I'm not made of sugar after all. I didn't melt in the rain."

Mary Ann laughed and pushed herself up from the rocking chair to shake her finger beneath her husband's nose. "As if anyone would accuse you of being made of sugar. You're pure vinegar, and we all know it!"

The pair shared a laugh that left Christina feeling like an interloper. She rose. "Mr. Creeger?"

"Yes?" He slipped his arm around his wife's waist.

Heat flared in Christina's face, and she shifted her gaze slightly to the right of the couple. Why did evidence of the Creegers' loving relationship create such turmoil within her? "Since today's rain made it impossible for the men to work at the poor farm, I wondered if I might prevail upon you to put up a new placard about working next Saturday instead."

"Why, certainly! I'll get one penned and put it on the window before the end of the day. And any man who comes in, I'll be sure to point it out to him." The man's helpfulness knew no limits. How Christina appreciated this genial pair.

"Thank you so much." Her voice quavered.

The man grinned. "It's no trouble at all."

"We're glad to help you," Mary Ann added.

Christina smiled, warmed by their kindness. "If there's ever anything I can do for you, I trust you'll let me know."

The two glanced at each other as if communicating silently. Then Mr. Creeger turned a serious look on Christina. "Actually, there is something, if you'd give it some thought."

Christina waited, ready to agree, no matter what his request was.

"Mary Ann and me, we've stayed busier here than in our former town. Probably because there we were one of four mercantiles, and here in Brambleville ours is the only one." He scratched his chin. "Sometimes we're so worn out at the end of the day we hardly have the energy to eat our supper before we fall into bed."

Christina shook her head slightly, uncertain how she could help the Creegers get more sleep.

He drew in a big breath. "If you'd be kind enough to ask the ladies who've been living out at the poor farm if any of them would like to take on a job here, we'd be much obliged to have an extra pair of helping hands."

CHAPTER 25

As Levi hitched the horse to his wagon, he squinted against the bright Sunday morning sun. The clear sky overhead gave no evidence of the recent rain. If it weren't for the muddy ground beneath his feet, he might have thought yesterday's gray gloom was just a dream. By the time he finished securing the rigging, he carried a half inch of goo on his boots. He scraped them as clean as possible on the edge of the porch stairs, then tromped to the door and stuck his head inside the house.

"Tommy? You ready?"

"Comin'!" The boy moved across the floor from the bedroom to the front door, hands wavering in front of him and head bobbing but picking up his feet rather than shuffling. He'd slicked down his hair with water and tucked in his shirt, which was buttoned all the way to the top. He'd even managed to tie a black ribbon, albeit a little crookedly,

313

around his neck. He looked spit-shined and happy, and just seeing the cheerful expression on the boy's face gave Levi's heart a lift.

"Pretty muddy out here," Levi said as Tommy stepped over the threshold onto the porch. "All that muck is bound to muss your boots and maybe even the hem of your britches. So here . . ." He took Tommy's hand and placed it on his shoulder. "Let me piggyback you to the wagon."

Tommy drew back. "You sure? I ain't piggybacked on anybody since I was a kid."

Levi swallowed a chuckle. Over the past week Tommy had frequently referred to himself as grown-up or a man. Not being cosseted by womenfolk had turned his thoughts around. Levi wouldn't argue, but neither would he confirm Tommy's claims to having left his childhood behind. Levi bent forward slightly, bracing his hands on his knees. "We'd better keep your boots clean so you don't muddy up the church floor. Just give a hop."

With an embarrassed giggle Tommy caught hold of Levi's shoulders. He bounced on his heels a few times before giving a nimble leap and straddling Levi's hips. Levi looped his hands beneath the boy's knees and carted him to the wagon with

Tommy's laughter huffing in his ears. He grinned as he set the boy's behind on the wagon bed. Tommy scooted backward, using his heels to propel himself all the way to the front.

While Levi climbed aboard, Tommy scrambled over the seat's back and settled himself, hands in his lap, chin angled high with a grin splitting his face. "That was fun. My pa, he used to gimme rides around the yard sometimes before —" His grin faded.

Levi took up the reins and released the brake. "Before . . ." He flicked the reins, and the horse strained forward, pulling the wagon toward the road.

Tommy hung his head, his shoulders slumping like a deflating balloon. He jostled with the wagon's movement as though he lacked the strength to hold himself erect. "Before I got blind and burned. After that, Pa didn't seem to like me much." A huge sigh heaved from the boy's lungs. "Most people didn't like me much after that."

Levi's chest twisted painfully. He groped for something — anything — that might offer a whisper of comfort. "It seems to me you have quite a few friends: Cora and Wes and Miss Willems." Instantly an image of the woman's sweet face gazing tenderly at the boy filled his memory. Levi had scorned her for caring too much, but at least she hadn't rejected Tommy.

Tommy raised one shoulder as if warding off Levi's words. "Miss Willems is nice. And I guess she likes me, 'cause she keeps trying to take me back with her again. But . . . how come most people are so . . . so . . ."

"Distant?"

The boy nodded. "That's a good word. Distant. They don't want to talk to me or touch me or even be around me." He fingered the puckered flesh on his cheek and jaw. "Is it 'cause I'm real ugly?"

Birdsong trilled from the brush lining the roadway. The sun beamed round and cheerful overhead, lighting the fresh, unfurling tree leaves and the little sprigs of green breaking across the earth. A cool breeze scented with moist earth and new growth teased Levi's senses. A day like this should lift a man's spirits, but heaviness weighted his heart instead. Why did this boy have to remind Levi of the most painful part of his own life?

Levi shifted the reins to one hand and curled the other arm around Tommy's narrow shoulders. The boy needed to know someone was willing to touch him. "You aren't ugly, Tommy." Long-buried memories attacked, bringing with them the fresh sting of resentment. "People . . . they can be self-ish. They keep their distance to protect themselves. Because" — awareness dawned, sending a chill from Levi's scalp down his spine — "they're scared."

Tommy's head turned in Levi's direction. "Of me?"

"Well . . . sort of but not really." Levi searched for an explanation Tommy would understand. An explanation that would help justify his own initial refusal to offer Tommy shelter. "When people are afraid of something, they . . . avoid it. Right? So maybe folks are just scared they'll say the wrong thing — make you feel bad. Or maybe they don't know how to talk to somebody who can't see." Or to someone who no longer seemed grounded in reality. Another chill attacked Levi's flesh. He gave Tommy's shoulder a squeeze and then returned his hand to the reins. He finished in a weak voice, speaking as much to himself as to the confused boy on the seat beside him. "So instead of taking a chance of doing the wrong thing, they just . . . stay away."

Very slowly Tommy nodded. "I guess that makes sense." Then he snorted and folded his arms over his chest. "Ain't right, though. Seems to me that folks with scars an' such, they're the ones who really need somebody to treat 'em like there's nothin' wrong with 'em. Hard enough to *be* different without everybody treatin' you different." His stiff pose relaxed, his face shifting again as if peering into Levi's face. "How come you talk to me like I'm just a regular boy with no scars?"

Levi's hands involuntarily tightened on the reins. His throat grew tight, and when he spoke, his voice sounded raw. "I know how it feels to be treated different because of scars."

Tommy's sightless eyes grew wide. "You have scars, too?"

Levi's scars were internal rather than external, just as Far's had been, but that didn't make them any less real. "Yep."

The boy stretched out one hand and placed it on Levi's knee. He squeezed, the touch filled with compassion. "I'm sorry, Mr. Jonnson."

Tears stung Levi's eyes, and he couldn't answer. So he held tight to the reins and guided the horse the remaining distance to the church, with sunshine warming his head through his suede hat and Tommy's hand warming his knee. He drew the team to a halt as the church bell began to ring. Tommy's hand slipped away, and the boy bobbed his head in the direction of the reverberating *bong, bong.* But he made no move to leave the seat.

Levi lightly bumped the boy with his elbow. "Go ahead. Get yourself down and follow the sound. You can do it."

Tommy folded his arms across his middle. "Huh-uh."

Townsfolk in their finest garb, Bibles cradled in their arms, moved up the stone-paved walkway to the church steps. The service would start soon. Levi set the brake and took hold of Tommy's arm, giving him a little push to the edge of the seat. "Hurry up now. That bell won't ring forever."

"Not goin'." Tommy planted his feet against the floor and pressed himself against the seat back. His chin jutted — a defiant gesture that made Levi grit his teeth in aggravation.

Miss Willems had specifically requested Tommy be delivered to church each Sunday, and Levi had promised to bring him. He might not have much use for church himself, but he didn't want to go back on his word. "Now listen, Tommy —"

"They don't want me." Belligerence faded, and pleading filled its place. "Can't I just stay with you?"

While the community worshiped together, Levi had planned to drive to the poor farm to see what kind of damage the rain had caused. If water had soaked wood inside the house, Miss Willems might need additional lumber. He could easily take Tommy with him, but it would upset Miss Willems. And he didn't want to upset Miss Willems. And not because he was scared to face her wrath. Even all riled up, she was harmless as a kitten.

He reminded the boy, "Miss Willems is expecting you."

Tommy's chin quivered. "Please, Mr. Jonnson? I don't wanna go in there where the preacher talks about how God wants us all to love each other but people don't pay me any mind."

The lament too closely echoed Levi's deeply held hurt. He wouldn't force Tommy to sit in the church pew and be ignored by self-righteous hypocrites. He drew in a breath. "All right then. You can stay with me." Remorse pinched. He hoped he could find the words to explain his decision to Miss Willems, because she'd surely ask why he hadn't brought to Tommy to service.

" 'And we know that all things work together for good to them that love God, to them who are the called according to his purpose.' "

Cora listened as the minister read a verse from chapter 8 of Romans. Her heart gave a hopeful leap, and she allowed her mind to return to the conversation she'd shared with Miss Willems yesterday evening. The mercantile owners — people who'd been robbed of forming their own family — needed a helper. Miss Willems had told Cora to take the job if she wanted it. At first Cora had resisted. How could she work side by side with a woman whose womb couldn't hold a child while her own belly swelled? It would be cruel — like mocking the childless woman.

But the verse from the Bible sent Cora's thoughts skittering in a new direction. Maybe . . . just maybe . . . her carrying this child could be good after all. Mr. and Mrs. Creeger sat on a bench across the aisle, Bibles open in their laps and faces turned attentively to the preacher. They were fine people — Miss Willems held them in high esteem. Surely they were the kind of people the preacher meant when he said "them who are the called." They wanted a baby. And Cora carried a baby she didn't want.

Maybe God was going to let her help the Creegers with more than just clerking.

Satisfied that the canvas someone had

nailed around the doorway between the damaged kitchen and the poor farm's dining room had offered sufficient protection from the rain, Levi headed across the grounds to the barn. When they'd arrived at the poor farm, Levi had instructed Tommy to go in the barn and stay there while he checked the house. Tommy had eagerly entered the large rock structure, saying he'd get in the pen with the goats, so Levi clomped immediately to the goat pen in the far corner of the barn. But Tommy wasn't there.

Levi turned a slow circle, searching for signs of the boy. "Tommy?"

"Over here."

The voice came from the stall where Levi had piled the lengths of lumber. Levi chuckled in mild self-deprecation. He'd been so lost in thought he'd walked right past Tommy. He headed back to the front of the barn and rounded the slatted wall defining the stall. "There you are. I thought —" Levi froze, disbelief bringing him to a stop.

Tommy was kneeling beside a scattered tumble of splintered boards. The boy patted one board, his palm moving back and forth across its battered length. "The wood, it's all messed up. I reckon the men won't be able to use these to fix the house." A grin twitched at his cheeks. "I guess that means it'll be a while yet before Miss Willems can fix the poor farm house."

CHAPTER 26

Levi drove from the poor farm to the Beasley Boardinghouse with regret resting heavily on his shoulders. The loss of the lumber hurt. Such a waste . . . But as much as it bothered him to see those boards destroyed, he was more concerned about how Miss Willems might be destroyed by the news. She'd poured her very soul into that poor farm. Whoever hacked the wood to pieces might as well have taken an ax to the woman's heart.

"You stay here," he told Tommy when he drew the horse to a stop in front of the boardinghouse. He couldn't help being a bit miffed by the boy's reaction to the destruction. Didn't Tommy care about anyone but himself? Somehow he needed to help the boy understand that thinking only of himself was a selfish way to live. *That'll be a bit like the pot calling the kettle black, don't you think?* With a jolt, Levi shoved the internal taunt aside and hurried up the dirt pathway to the porch.

The boardinghouse owner answered Levi's knock on the front door. She blinked at him blearily. Her dress was rumpled, her knot of gray hair askew, and she yawned widely behind her hand. Obviously he'd disturbed her Sunday afternoon nap. "Can I help you?"

Levi snatched off his hat and held it in both hands. "I'd like to speak to Miss Willems, please."

A slight frown creased the woman's face. "She ain't here. Always spends Sunday afternoons with the poor farm folk. Last week they all went to Tina Claussen's place, on Washington Street. Dunno where they went today, though."

Levi fiddled with his hat. "When will she be back?"

"Somewhere around four so she an' Cora can prepare supper for my boarders." Her gaze narrowed. "But she'll be workin' then. No time for visitin'."

Which meant he needed to locate her before she returned to duty. He slipped his hat into place. "Thank you, ma'am."

She closed the door without a word.

Levi returned to the wagon and swung himself into the seat. He took up the reins but sat with them draped over his palms, unmoving. What should he do? He could return to the mill and come back tomorrow morning, but Wes would stumble upon that damaged lumber when he went out to feed the animals. No doubt the man would go straight to Miss Willems. Levi needed to be the one to tell her — he'd find a way to gently share what had happened rather than just blurt it out. But how would he find her? She could have been invited to lunch by any number of parishioners.

His stomach rumbled. He and Tommy needed to eat. Brambleville's only café wasn't open on Sunday, but they could go to the hotel dining room. Hopefully he had enough in his pocket to pay for two dinners. He tugged the reins, urging the horse to turn the wagon around.

Tommy grabbed the seat with both hands and looked back and forth. "Where we goin'?"

"To get something to eat."

"Oh." The boy aimed his face away from Levi and fell silent.

Levi gritted his teeth. They might both end up with indigestion, but while they ate, he'd talk to Tommy about putting other people's needs ahead of his own. He couldn't let the boy grow up to be self-centered and reclusive — Levi's chest tightened — like him. Only a couple of wagons were parked outside the hotel, leaving Levi plenty of room. He called, "Whoa," and his horse snorted as they came to a stop. Levi set the brake, hopped down, and said, "Let's go, Tommy."

Tommy eased his way to the edge of the wagon and took hold of the side. Slowly, as stiff as an old man, he lifted one leg over and found the wagon wheel with his foot. Levi stepped back, close enough to catch the boy if he fell but far enough away to give him space. Tommy's feet met the ground, and he heaved a sigh of relief.

Levi took Tommy's elbow and guided him onto the boardwalk. Even before they reached the door, the aromas of fried chicken, biscuits, and apple pie greeted them. Tommy sniffed the air, and Levi's stomach rolled over in eagerness. He gave Tommy's arm a little tug and sped his feet.

The dining room waited to the left of the wide hallway, its glass french doors open in invitation. From the sound of things, a sizable crowd was taking advantage of the hotel's cooking today. Levi hoped there'd be room for him and the boy. They stepped from the stained-oak hallway onto a thick red carpet covered in green ribbon swirls and large cream-colored roses. Levi had always liked the feel of carpet beneath his feet — almost as nice as a thick covering of sawdust.

Round tables draped with white cloths crowded the room, and — as Levi had suspected — folks filled nearly every chair. He paused and glanced around, seeking an empty table. To his relief two were available. He urged Tommy toward the closest one.

The hotel owner's daughters, Birdie and Virgie — a pair of stout young women who'd had the misfortune of inheriting their father's oversize nose and broad chin — bustled from table to table, refilling coffee cups or delivering plates of food. He caught Birdie's eye, and she hurried over as he and Tommy slid into chairs.

"Good afternoon." She swiped at her glistening brow with the back of her hand. "Do you need to see a menu, or would you like to order the special? Fried chicken with fixin's today."

Levi plopped his hat on the table next to his silverware. "Is the Sunday special still thirty-five cents a plate?"

"Yep. Or forty cents with pie."

Levi patted his pocket, imagining the coins inside. The cinnamon essence of the apple pie drifting from a nearby table enticed him, but he needed to be sensible. "Two specials, no pie."

She hurried off.

Tommy sat with his head low and his shoulders raised, a familiar pose when surrounded by people. Levi was ready to tap his arm and instruct him to sit up straight instead of hiding like a prairie dog in its burrow, but the boy suddenly bolted upright, his gaze bouncing around. He groped and found Levi's arm.

"Mr. Jonnson, I hear —"

Before the boy could complete the sentence, the swish of skirts alerted Levi to someone's approach. He turned slightly and found himself looking at the round silver watch that always hung against the bodice of Miss Willems's green muslin dress.

When Levi Jonnson entered the hotel dining room with Tommy in tow, Christina could hardly believe her eyes. She'd been certain some catastrophe had kept the man from venturing into town. Perhaps the rain had flooded his roadway, or maybe he'd had some sort of emergency in his mill. What other explanation could there be for his breaking his promise to bring Tommy to church? Now, seeing them share a round table as if coming to the hotel to eat were an everyday occurrence, anger stirred.

The man leaped to his feet. "Miss Willems."

She aimed a frown at Mr. Jonnson while placing her hand on Tommy's shoulder. "I see you're surprised to find me here. Had Mr. and Mrs. Creeger not invited the poor farm residents to join them for a celebratory dinner today, you would have escaped my notice completely."

"Actually, I'm glad you're here." Mr. Jonnson met her gaze. Something akin to sympathy glimmered in his eyes.

A prickling disquiet nudged her irritation aside. Beneath her palm Tommy shivered as if he were planted in a snowbank. She turned a worried gaze on the boy. "Tommy, are you ill?"

"He's fine." A hint of impatience colored the man's tone. He held his hand toward the double doors leading to the hallway. "Could we step outside for a moment? I need to talk to you."

One of the servers approached the table, balancing white plates piled high with crisp fried chicken, boiled potatoes, green peas, and buttery biscuits. She sent Mr. Jonnson a puzzled look. "You gonna eat?"

"Yes. Thank you, Birdie." Mr. Jonnson took the plates and set them on the table, one in front of Tommy and one in front of his empty chair. "Tommy, go ahead and eat. I'll be right back." Then he commandeered Christina's elbow and guided her to the hallway.

Her face flamed at his familiarity. The moment they cleared the doors, she pulled loose of his grip, but the imprint of his warm, strong hand lingered, sending odd tingles up and down her spine. She peeked into the dining room, certain everyone would be staring at them. But they all seemed focused on their meals. Relieved, she straightened her skirts and folded her arms over her waist in a protective gesture. "All right. I'm listening. Why did you not bring Tommy to service this morning if he's fine?"

He ran his hand through his hair, leaving the thick, wheat-colored strands standing in appealing ridges. "He didn't want to go. And I decided not to force him."

"*You* decided —"

"Miss Willems, there's something more important I need to tell you."

Christina shook her head. "There's nothing more important than Tommy's spiritual development. I thought you understood —"

"Miss Willems!" Although he held his

voice to a low volume, his tone became stern.

Christina clamped her lips closed.

He finger-combed his hair once more, his gaze dropping to the floor for a moment. "I'm sorry. I don't mean to snap at you, but . . ." Raising his head, he looked directly into her eyes. The compassion she'd glimpsed earlier returned. "Tommy and I rode out to the poor farm this morning instead of going to services. I wanted to look at the house — see if the rain had caused any further damage."

Christina's heart fluttered in her chest. "And had it?"

"No. The canvas someone hung —"

"Wes," she inserted.

"It kept most of the rain out. But there was . . . something else."

Fingers of trepidation tiptoed up her spine. "W-what else?"

Mr. Jonnson pulled in a deep breath and released it. "Miss Willems, someone took an ax to the lumber I brought out to rebuild the walls."

Christina's head whirled. She reached for the doorjamb and missed. If Mr. Jonnson hadn't caught her, she might have collapsed. He quickly put his arm around her waist and led her to a pair of chairs tucked in an alcove off the entry. She sank down, grateful for the sturdy seat beneath her. Placing her head in her hand, she moaned, "I can't believe someone would do such a thing."

Mr. Jonnson eased into the second chair. "I wouldn't have either if I hadn't seen it. The wood is a mess, completely unusable for building walls."

She looked at the man, his image blurring through a spurt of tears. "Is that why Tommy is upset? Did you tell him about it?"

"He found the wood first. But he —" He drew in a deep breath, and when he spoke again, great tenderness colored his tone. "Miss Willems, he seemed more pleased than upset. He said if the lumber couldn't be used, it would take longer for the men from town to repair the house. Then he could stay with me longer."

He couldn't have hurt her more if he'd lifted an ax and brought it down on her head. Tommy didn't want to return to the poor farm. To her care. Tears filled her eyes, then lost their moorings on her lashes and spilled down her cheeks in a warm torrent. Abashed, she covered her face with her hands. She almost missed his quiet question.

"You don't think Tommy was the one who

swung the ax, do you?"

Protectiveness welled. She wiped away her tears and met his gaze. "Absolutely not. Tommy isn't strong enough to wreak such damage. And even if he were strong enough and saw this as his means of . . . of staying with you, I can't imagine him being deliberately destructive." She lowered her head again, battling another wave of tears.

"I'm awfully sorry, Miss Willems. I know this is hard for you." The man's voice — soft, kind, understanding — cut through her fog of pain. "Remember he's just a boy. A confused boy who feels accepted and needed with me."

Though sweetly uttered, his comment did nothing to soothe her pierced soul. Tommy hadn't felt accepted and needed by her?

He went on in that same tender tone. "I promised you enough lumber to fix your walls, and I'll make sure you get it. It'll take me a while longer now. I have to wait for my shipment of logs to arrive and then cut them. But you'll have it."

Of course she wanted the lumber. She couldn't replace the kitchen without it. But even more than the lumber, she wanted Tommy's devotion again. She'd cared for him for two years, and during that time she'd grown to love him as if he were her own son. Within the span of a few weeks, he'd transferred his affection from Christina to the mill owner. How would she regain it?

"I'll have a talk with Tommy. I'll make sure" — he hunkered forward as if his stomach pained him — "he understands his staying with me is temporary. As soon as the poor farm house is repaired, he'll go back. I won't allow any argument."

A glimmer of hope wriggled its way through Christina's breast. Yes, as soon as they were back under the roof of the poor farm, things would return to normal. Tommy was simply reacting to all the changes thrust upon him recently. He'd found a sense of security with Mr. Jonnson, and he didn't want to lose it. Who could blame the boy? He needed a father figure, and Mr. Jonnson was strong and able and — she gulped, recognition dawning — worthy of admiration. His acceptance of Tommy, his willingness to provide lumber at no cost, even his determination to return Tommy to her care when she knew he'd grown fond of the boy endeared him to her.

She sat gazing into his handsome face, seeking a way to thank him. But words wouldn't form. She drew in a shuddering breath, bringing her tears under control.

"Your dinner is growing cold."

He blinked twice, frowning slightly. Then his expression cleared, and he nodded. "And you need to return to your celebration." He tipped his head, giving him a boyish appearance that set her heart fluttering in a strange and somehow pleasing manner. "What are you celebrating?"

"Mr. and Mrs. Creeger's anniversary," her voice squeaked out. She cleared her throat. "Their fourteenth."

He smiled. "That's nice."

"Yes." She jerked to her feet, wiping her cheeks to remove any vestiges of tears. "They're probably wondering where I am."

"Let me escort you."

"No." She backed away, suddenly very uneasy in his all-too-appealing presence. "I . . . I can find my own way."

Disappointment seemed to flicker in his eyes for a moment, but then he nodded. "I understand."

Did he? A new burst of heat seared her cheeks. She turned and fled.

CHAPTER 27

Tommy tipped his head, listening. The slight creak of rocking wood joined the gentle burble of the river. They'd reached the mill. In moments Mr. Jonnson would stop the wagon. He'd tell Tommy to climb down and go into the house. And he'd have to go in, because where else could he go?

His jaw ached from clenching his teeth so hard. He'd hated sitting there alone eating his chicken. He'd hated listening to all those voices from people at other tables and knowing none of them were talking to him. Then Mr. Jonnson hadn't even apologized for leaving him by himself. And Miss Willems hadn't bothered to say good-bye. And worst of all, Mr. Jonnson was angry with him. *Angry.* With *him.* Tommy's stomach hurt.

"Whoa . . ." Reins squeaked, and metal fittings from the horse's rigging clanked. The wagon creaked to a stop. The *ahem* of a clearing throat sounded next to Tommy's ear, and then Mr. Jonnson spoke again. "All right, Tommy. Head inside. I'll be there as soon as I unhitch the horse and put the wagon away."

Tommy unfolded himself from the seat by inches. He'd sat so still and stiff on the ride from town his muscles didn't want to co-operate. With jerky movements he managed to climb down from the seat.

"Maybe six steps to the porch. You can find the door from there."

Tommy gritted his teeth and balled his hands into fists. He wished he could see where to go without having to rely on Mr. Jonnson's instructions. He didn't want to listen to the man. Didn't want to need him. Not now. But he wouldn't be able to find his way on his own. So he did what Mr. Jonnson said, but he dragged his feet rather than lifting them. On the sixth shuffling step, his toes bumped the edge of the porch stair. Hands stretched in front of him, he felt his way to the door and let himself inside.

Out of Mr. Jonnson's sight, he walked without shuffling to the sofa and sat. Pressed his palms together between his knees. Stared straight ahead into the black noth-ing. And planned what he would say as soon as Mr. Jonnson came through the door. *I thought you were my friend. I thought you liked me as much as I like you. I thought you understood me. But you're not my friend. You're a hypocrite, too.* The thought of calling Mr. Jonnson such an ugly word stung, but he wouldn't take it back. Mr. Jonnson was a hypocrite, acting like he cared about Tommy but then telling him he was all wrong.

Tommy remembered the man's words, spoken in a nice voice but still scalding him with shame. *"You need to think about Miss Willems's feelings, Tommy. Think how much it will hurt her to put off rebuilding the kitchen so she can go home again. I'm disappointed in you for being so selfish."*

Mr. Jonnson had been disappointed in Tommy for leaving the Tatums and trying to get to the mill again. Now he was disappointed in him for wanting to stay at the mill. Why couldn't Mr. Jonnson support Tommy's desire to be with him? Why couldn't Mr. Jonnson understand how Tommy felt?

Miss Willems didn't need him. He was just a burden for her, same as he'd been for Pa. Here at the mill, fending for himself and learning to do something useful, he'd finally felt like he mattered. Why should he want to go back to the poor farm even if it meant it would make Miss Willems happy? Didn't Tommy's happiness count for anything? Mr. Jonnson wanted to ignore Tommy's needs. It hurt, being misunderstood and ignored. It hurt having Mr. Jonnson disappointed in him. And he didn't like feeling hurt. He wished he could just not care at all.

Mr. Jonnson wouldn't go to church because of the hypocrites. So Tommy wouldn't stay with a hypocrite either. Just yesterday Mr. Jonnson had told him it wouldn't be long before he'd be able to start working on that chair seat because his weaving was getting better all the time. As soon as he'd mastered caning, he'd leave. He'd go to a big city where there were factories, where they made furniture, and he'd show the boss how he could cane. And he'd get a job and take care of himself.

In the back of Tommy's mind, worry niggled. How would he take care of himself? Would the people in the city run ropes everywhere for him to follow? How would he even find a factory? He pushed all the questions aside. He'd find a way to make it work. Because he sure wasn't going to stay with a hypocrite. He wouldn't stay with Miss Willems either. If he went back to the poor farm, he'd be treated like a baby again.

And he might even get threatened again. His body broke out in goose flesh, and he pushed the memory deep down where it couldn't escape. He had to get to a big city. He had to get away.

Suppressed tears created a sharp sting in his nose, and he sniffed hard. He wouldn't cry. Babies cried. And he was no baby — he was a man. A man who could make it just fine all on his own.

Boots clomped on the porch. Hinges complained, and a *click* signaled the door had closed. Then footsteps approached. A soft movement of air let Tommy know Mr. Jonnson had passed in front of him, and he scooted closer to the armrest when the sofa sank beneath Mr. Jonnson's weight. A hand — a strong hand, with fingers that gripped but didn't bruise — landed on Tommy's shoulder.

Tommy lifted his chin and clenched his fists, grabbing hold of all his gumption. "Mr. Jonnson, I got something to say to you."

Cora held her skirt above her ankles as she walked to the boardinghouse with Miss Willems. Although they used the wooden walkways rather than walking in the street, the wood was warped in places and held puddles of rainwater. Cora didn't want to soil the hem of her brown serge skirt — the nicest skirt she'd ever owned. She'd had to move the button on the waistband a good inch in order to fasten it this morning. By next Sunday she might not be able to wear it at all. She couldn't deny a rush of sorrow at the thought. In this brown serge she felt pretty. Respectable. Emmet Wade would probably tell her she looked like a lady.

But she knew better.

She sighed, watching her brown lace-up shoes to avoid stepping directly into a puddle as she moved along. Maybe it was time to put this skirt in the wardrobe. It wasn't a work skirt, after all. Starting tomorrow, she'd be clerking all day at the Creeger Mercantile, and her calico dress would better suit such a position.

Excitement danced in her belly. Having lunch with the Creegers — watching how they smiled at each other, touching each other's hands all soft and tender — had sealed her decision. She liked them. They were good people. All they needed was a baby to make their family complete. And Cora would provide them with one. Just like the preacher had said, all things worked out for good.

At least most things. It would be hard to

leave Miss Willems. Especially knowing the woman would have to take care of Mrs. Beasley's boarders all by herself. But pretty soon Miss Willems would be back out at the poor farm again, and Cora's leaving would make room for some other person who needed a place to stay. So it'd all be for the best eventually. She soothed herself with the thought.

They turned onto the dirt pathway leading to the boardinghouse's back door. Just before stepping inside, Cora touched Miss Willems's arm. "Ma'am, I . . ."

Miss Willems paused and looked at Cora. Her eyes seemed sad. They'd been that way since she'd talked with Mr. Jonnson at the hotel. What had the man said to upset her so? Funny how Miss Willems reacted to Levi Jonnson. Sometimes after she'd seen him, she'd be all quiet and almost fluttery. Sometimes spitting mad. Other times — like now — she was troubled. In Cora's experience a woman's emotions got tangled up when she cared for a fellow. But Miss Willems surely hadn't gotten herself attached to the mill owner, had she?

"Cora, we need to go in. What did you want?"

Miss Willems's question pulled Cora out of her musings. "I'm sorry. I just wanted to let you know, I'm . . ." Was she doing the right thing? What would happen when the Creegers discovered her secret? She wouldn't be able to hide behind aprons and shawls much longer. Would they cast her out of the store? Maybe she should just stay with Miss Willems. Or maybe she should leave altogether before these people she admired learned of her downfall. She gulped.

Suddenly Miss Willems offered a nod. A sad smile appeared on her face. "You're taking the job at the mercantile, aren't you?"

Cora hung her head. She had to take it. She had to find a good home for the babe growing inside of her. "Yes'm."

"When do they wish for you to start?"

"They said if I wanted to, I could come over tonight and get settled — start workin' in the morning." Cora could hardly believe her good fortune. A job and a little room all to herself. Ma would be so surprised.

"Well, I won't lie and say I won't miss you." Miss Willems's voice trembled a bit, but when Cora peeked at her, her eyes were dry. "Even so, I'll not hold you back. It's a fine offer, and the Creegers are good people."

Cora nodded. The Creegers would give her baby the best home. She just knew it.

"Yes'm."

"You should be proud, Cora, taking a job and providing for yourself. Not many women your age would possess the strength and courage to be self-sufficient."

Warmth flooded Cora's face. Oh, such feelings washed through her at Miss Willems's praise. Her tongue felt too clumsy to speak, so she just smiled her thanks.

Miss Willems smiled, too. A less-sad smile. Then she embraced Cora. And for once Cora didn't stiffen up. "After supper I'll let Mrs. Beasley know you won't be working here any longer, and then I'll help you take your things to the Creegers. Does that sound fine?"

A lump formed in Cora's throat. It was fine and dandy for her. But poor Miss Willems, left here alone . . . She stood within the circle of Miss Willems's arms and blinked back tears. "Yes'm. Thank you."

The woman released her and stepped back. "It's all settled, then." She turned to the door, her movements brisk. "Supper, and then we'll send you out on your new adventure."

Levi clamped his hands over his knees and held tight. The temptation to take hold of the boy and shake the obstinacy out of him became more difficult to resist by the minute. After Tommy had blurted out his intention to take himself far away from Brambleville, the poor farm, and the mill, he'd sat as silent and unmoving as if he were carved of stone. Levi had repeated the same question multiple times, but Tommy refused to explain why he was so adamant about not returning to the poor farm and to Miss Willems.

He waited, listening to the steady *tick, tick* of the mantel clock counting the minutes. Two minutes. Three. Then four. The muscles in his arms twitched. If he'd pulled such a stubborn act as a boy, his father would have taken the razor strop to him. Part of him wondered if a few whacks across the boy's backside would loosen his tongue, but he knew he'd never find the wherewithal to actually do it. Maybe he was a little like Miss Willems after all.

He slid his hand along the sofa and touched Tommy's arm. The boy jerked, but he didn't speak. "Tommy, whether you answer me or not, it doesn't change anything. You can't go off to a big city by yourself. Not until you're grown up. You'll have to go back to the poor farm."

The muscles in the boy's jaw tightened, but he kept his face aimed straight ahead rather than turning toward Levi.

Levi went on, using his gentlest voice. "You being here . . . was just for a while." As he spoke, he examined Tommy's profile. No reaction. What would it take to get through to the boy? He blew out a noisy breath, shaking his head. "Listen, Tommy, I know it's hard for you to be different. I understand why you'd want to settle in one place, a place where you feel secure and maybe where you don't have to worry about people staring at you or ignoring you. But you can't spend your life hiding. You —"

Tommy leaped up so abruptly Levi fell backward. The boy swung to face him, his lips twisting into a snarl. "You don't know nothin'. You don't understand."

Levi rose. "Then explain it to me, Tommy. Help me understand."

"No!" Tommy whirled and took off at a trot, plowing straight into Levi's rocking chair. The chair teetered, and Tommy went with it. Levi grabbed his arm, but Tommy shook loose. "Don't help me! Just . . . lemme alone!" He pushed himself upright. Sobs racking his shoulders, he stretched out both hands and stumbled across the room to the front door. He pawed along the doorframe until he located the porcelain knob, then yanked the door open. One foot inside and one foot on the porch, he gulped great breaths of air until his crying ceased.

Gazing outward, he spoke in a cold, emotionless tone that pierced Levi to the center of his being. "You acted like my friend, but you're just like all the others. I used to love you, Mr. Jonnson. But not anymore. I hate you." He shuffled to the edge of the porch, sank down next to a square post, and pressed his forehead to the wood.

Levi eased back onto the sofa and stared through the open doorway at the boy's lonely, dejected pose. He didn't know how to help Tommy any more than he'd known how to help his father when he'd escaped into a bubble of self-pity. And in that moment he hated himself.

CHAPTER 28

Was she foolish to love her new job? The worrisome question had toyed at the back of Cora's mind off and on all day, all week long, and even woke her at night to tease her with misgivings. As much as she might like to, she couldn't work at the Creeger Mercantile forever. When this baby was born, she'd have to leave. So maybe she should try harder not to like stocking the shelves just so, cutting dress goods into rippling lengths, measuring flour and sugar and good-smelling cinnamon into brown bags. Maybe she should eat by herself in her small but cheerful room instead of sitting down with Mr. and Mrs. Creeger — or Pa and Ma Creeger, as they'd laughingly told her to call them — for their evening meal.

She could hardly believe it when she found out the Creegers were a year older than Ma. Ma had been just seventeen when she'd birthed Cora, so being a year older than Ma meant they were thirty-six. Cora'd come to think that being thirty was old. Ma sure seemed old, with her round shoulders, long lines dragging down both sides of her mouth, and thin hair always hanging in her face. But the Creegers didn't seem old to Cora. Not at all.

Oh, little fan lines showed at the corner of Pa Creeger's eyes, and Ma Creeger's chin wasn't quite as firm as it might've been in previous years. But they both moved sprightly and laughed loudly. She never saw either of them lean against a wall or a table and sigh as if life was weighting them down. In spite of the babies they'd lost, the same way Ma had lost babies after bringing Cora into the world, the Creegers still wore joy. Ma only wore bitter sorrow. Maybe, Cora mused, joy kept a person looking young.

And they'd be even more joyful when she put this baby growing inside her into their empty arms.

Knowing her time with them would be short, Cora tried hard to keep her distance. Every morning she told her reflection in the little mirror above her washstand, "Now remember, don't be so friendly with 'em. Just gonna get yourself hurt in the end." But every day, even before noontime rolled around, she'd be laughing and talking, teasing with Pa Creeger and letting Ma Creeger catch her in a hug. Cora had never liked anybody as much as she liked the mercantile owners, and a part of her couldn't wait to tell them she had something very special to give them. But another part of her dreaded the day, because it meant she'd have to move on.

On Saturday at the end of her first week as the mercantile assistant, she slipped on her faded pink calico dress. She pushed the top three buttons through their holes, but the last three — the ones that should march across her belly — wouldn't reach no matter how much she tugged at the fabric. Thankfully her full-bibbed apron covered her front. She tied the strings loosely, hoping the draping fabric would hide the growing mound beneath. Then she trotted down the narrow stairs to the mercantile floor.

Ma Creeger was already there, tacking little handwritten placards to the shelves underneath the day's special items. She smiled when Cora pattered into the room. "You're just in time to unlock the door, Cora. Already shoppers are lined up on the porch waiting to come in. Looks like it'll be a busy day!"

That suited Cora just fine. She'd never

been afraid of hard work, and keeping busy meant she didn't have time to think. She dashed to the door and twisted the lock. The moment she opened the door, women-folk with baskets over their arms and young-sters in tow spilled through the doorway. Just as Cora had wanted, the early morning hours passed quickly. She stayed busy filling orders, bustling to the storeroom to bring out more sweet potatoes or canned peaches, and carrying crates of goods to waiting wagons.

Between tasks she munched salted peanuts. She'd never been overly fond of peanuts, but for some reason she craved salty foods, and the bin of peanuts proved to be a temptation she couldn't resist. She had her hand in the bin for the fourth time that morning when Pa Creeger called, "Cora! Miss Willems just came through the door. Do you want to see what she needs?"

Guilt immediately smote Cora. She'd been enjoying her new job and nice place to live so much she hadn't even thought about Miss Willems all week. She brushed her palms down the front of her apron, removing the salt from her fingers, and darted around the corner. "Miss Willems!"

"Cora . . ." Miss Willems opened her arms. Cora's legs turned stiff as she moved forward to receive the hug. She pulled back after only a few seconds, keenly aware of her blossoming belly. She stared into Miss Willems's tired face, and another rush of guilt brought the sting of tears. The woman appeared to have aged in the past six days. "How . . . how're you doin'?"

"I'm fine." She spoke in a cheery voice, but the dark circles under her eyes told a different story. "Busy, of course, but . . ." She lifted her hand and touched Cora's cheek — a light, motherly touch. "You look good. Your face is filling out, and you have some color in your cheeks. The Creegers are treating you well?"

Cora twisted her hands together. "Yes, ma'am, they surely are." Better than she deserved. But then, so had Miss Willems. She blurted, "I miss you." Truthfully, she'd forgotten all about her friend working alone at the boardinghouse, but she'd never say so.

Miss Willems smiled. "That's good to hear. I miss you, too, but I'm very happy for you."

Cora wondered if Miss Willems might be fibbing a bit, too, because the smile didn't reach her eyes. She gnawed her lower lip, seeking some means of encouraging the woman. Before she could find anything, though, Miss Willems took a step back. She glanced around the store, seeming to count the customers.

"I won't keep you from your duties, but it's so nice to see you, Cora."

"But don'tcha need something?" Cora, embarrassed by her blunt question, laughed self-consciously and recited the greeting Ma Creeger used with customers. "I mean, may I help you with somethin'?"

Miss Willems patted Cora's arm. "Not this time. Go ahead and see to the other customers. I came to see Mr. Creeger."

Cora watched Miss Willems move across the pine-planked floor to Pa Creeger. Although she took brisk strides, her shoulders were bent as if she carried a load on her back. When she reached him, she took something from her dress pocket and held it out. Light glinted on silver. What was Miss Willems doing with the etched pocket watch she always wore on a chain around her neck? Cora had often admired that watch. The design on the cover was pretty, and Miss Willems kept it polished so it shined like a full moon in a cloudless sky.

Together, Miss Willems and Pa Creeger moved to the counter, and Pa Creeger took out his cashbox. The two began what appeared to be an intense conversation. Curious, Cora eased up to the counter and began sorting suspenders by color. She tipped sideways and listened in.

". . . from Mama to Papa for Christmas in 1863. She'd received a small inheritance from her grandfather and wanted to give Papa something that would last." Miss Willems laughed softly — the saddest laugh Cora had ever heard. "He carried it in his pocket every day. He was always so proud that Abraham Lincoln had one just like it."

Pa Creeger took the silver-cased watch from Miss Willems's hands and turned it this way and that. "No doubt the Waltham Company knows how to put together a quality watch," he said. "And even though the William Ellery wasn't one of their top watches, it's still a good one." He snapped the cover and peered at the face. "Keeps perfect time. Reckon that's why most of the railroad men carry 'em."

"Yes." Miss Willems sounded so forlorn, Cora's heart ached. "I hate to part with it, but I . . . I find myself more in need of funds than a timepiece. I realize you aren't a purchaser, but I thought perhaps . . ."

Cora gulped. All those letters Miss Willems had been sending to the mission board hadn't done any good at all. They weren't going to give her money to fix the house. Miss Willems shouldn't have to sell something so dear to her. Cora held her breath, caught between hope and fear that Pa Creeger would buy it.

Pa Creeger worked his jaw back and forth, cradling the William Ellery watch in his palm. "You're right, Miss Willems, that I've not done any buyin' of used items to resell in the store. I'm not real certain I can even give you what your mama must've paid for it. But . . ." He puffed out his cheeks, holding in a big breath. After several seconds he blew out the air in a noisy rush. "I could do ten dollars. How's that?"

Cora's heart pounded like a tom-tom and seemed to beat out the message *Don't do it! Don't do it!*

Miss Willems lowered her head and closed her eyes. Was she praying? Would God tell her to keep the watch her mama'd given her papa? The woman sighed and lifted her gaze to Pa Creeger. "I'll take it. Thank you very much."

Pa Creeger pressed a crumpled bill into Miss Willems's hand. He placed the watch in the cashbox and closed the lid with a snap. "Can I help you with anything else?"

Miss Willems stared at the box. Her chin quivered. "No, thank you, Mr. Creeger."

He pushed the box to the far corner of

the counter and bustled off to see to other customers. Cora stood, hands gripping a pair of blue-and-green-striped suspenders, and watched Miss Willems. Agony ebbed from the woman, and Cora ached to do something to help. But what? She didn't have ten dollars to offer. And she didn't have any words of wisdom to share either. So she just mourned the loss along with the heartbroken woman until a customer walked between the two of them and tapped Cora's arm.

"Miss, I need a quarter pound of pepper and a pound of salt."

Cora nodded briskly, setting the suspenders aside. "Yes, ma'am." She scurried behind the counter and bent down to retrieve two brown paper sacks. When she rose, she glanced toward the spot where Miss Willems had been standing. She was gone. For a moment Cora froze, sadness squeezing her chest so tight it hurt to breathe.

The customer tapped the counter. "Miss? Hurry, please. I have other errands to run."

Cora gave a jolt. "Yes, ma'am. You said . . . quarter pound of pepper and . . ."

The woman sighed. "A pound of salt."

"Yes, ma'am." Cora filled the order, measuring carefully and rolling down the tops of the bags neatly as Ma Creeger had shown her. But when she opened the cash-box to drop the customer's money inside, her gaze fell on the silver William Ellery watch that Miss Willems's father had been given for Christmas in 1863. And she burst into tears.

Christina battled tears. Oh, how it pained her to part with Papa's watch! The timepiece had been his pride and joy — the only extravagant item he owned. But how else would she raise money to purchase train tickets for herself and the twins? How else would she pay for plaster and paint to finish the walls of the poor farm kitchen? The mission board had ignored her repeated requests for funds. She couldn't depend on anyone else to offer financial support. Besides, it was her fault that Louisa, Rose, Wes, Tommy, Joe, and Florie were all displaced. Somehow she had to repair the damage she'd done, and she knew no other option than to sell the watch.

"Miss Willems! Miss Willems!"

The excited shout brought Christina to a halt. She turned and spotted Wes running toward her in his awkward lope. His round face shone with joy. He'd be even happier when she told him she now had the funds to repair the house. She greeted him with a smile. "I have good news."

"Me, too!" He nearly danced in place, his big hands repeatedly clasping and unclasping. "I been workin' at the livery to earn my keep. An' Mr. Taylor, he says I've done a right fine job."

"Oh, Wes, I'm so proud of you." She meant it. Wes worked hard and deserved praise.

"An' ya know what? He wants to keep me on! Says he's gettin' older, can use a good, strong pair o' hands around the place. His brother passed on to glory awhile back an' left him a little house. He says I can live in it. A job an' my own little house! Ain't it a wonder, Miss Willems?"

Christina stared at him in shock. "You won't be returning to the poor farm?"

Wes's countenance dimmed. "Well, no, ma'am."

By biting down on her lower lip, Christina held back a bevy of selfish questions. Who would push the plow? harvest the crops? feed the stock? She'd come to depend on Wes — perhaps too much.

He went on, wringing his hands in a fretful manner. "But don't you worry. I'll keep goin' out an' takin' care o' the poor farm critters until you all move back out there." His brow furrowed. "Miss Willems, ain'tcha happy for me?"

She couldn't bear to dash cold water on his excitement. She forced a smile. "Of course I am, Wes. I'm just surprised is all. I'm very happy for you. Truly I am."

He beamed again. "Thank you, Miss Willems." He began moving backward, almost skipping, his feet were so light. "Gotta get back to work now, but I wanted you to know. Bye!" He turned and loped off.

Christina watched until he turned the corner. She fingered the bill in her pocket. So, Wes wouldn't live at the poor farm any longer. She needn't mourn over him. It was a fine thing for him to be able to take care of himself — something Papa would have encouraged and celebrated, were he still alive. And soon she'd be so busy with the twins, Tommy, Rose, and Louisa, she'd hardly notice Wes was gone.

Her head low, she aimed her feet toward the boardinghouse again. As she moved past the butcher shop, Louisa stepped onto the boardwalk, a broom in hand. Her face lit when she spotted Christina. She set the broom aside and held out her arms. Christina moved eagerly into the embrace, sorely in need of comfort. When they parted, Christina held up the bill Mr. Creeger had given her. "Look, Louisa. I have ticket money now."

Louisa's faded eyes grew round as dinner plates. "Oh my, that's a small fortune! Where'd you get it?"

Christina forced a smile and closed her fist around the money the way she wished to hold Papa's watch. "The Lord provided."

Louisa released a chortle of joy. She stuck her head inside the shop and bellowed, "Rose! Come here!"

Moments later Rose joined them, her face wreathed in worry. "What's the matter?"

"Nothing's the matter. Christina has travel money. She's going after the twins."

Rose raised her hands and crowed, "Hallelujah!" Then she sobered. "But the house isn't ready. Where will you put them?"

"Back with the Spencers." Christina slid her fist holding the ten dollar bill into her pocket. "They indicated a willingness to provide a temporary home for Joe and Florie. And with this money I can purchase plaster. Mr. Creeger said he'd go to the house in the evenings and plaster the kitchen as soon as the townsmen have the outside walls rebuilt."

Rose clapped her hands. "Oh, glory! It won't be long now, and we'll all be together again."

Christina cautioned, "We'll have to wait for lumber, of course. Mr. Jonnson indicated he wouldn't have more wood to spare until his new shipment of logs arrives. That could be the end of April." The waiting was torturous, but Christina had little choice. As Papa used to say, beggars couldn't be choosers. She'd have to bide her time at the boardinghouse until the lumber was available.

The pair of elderly women nodded soberly. Rose took Christina's hand. "I'm not trying to be pushy — I know you're a grown woman and capable of making your own decisions — but I don't feel too comfortable about you traveling all the way to Topeka by yourself."

Louisa gave a somber nod. "I agree. A woman traveling alone? Why, it's deemed unseemly."

The word *unseemly* pierced Christina. She pushed aside the recollection of someone else accusing her of being unseemly. "Regardless, I have little choice." Who would travel with her? For reasons beyond her understanding, Levi Jonnson's face appeared in her memory as if requesting him to accompany her would be more proper than traveling alone. She must be overly tired to entertain such a ridiculous thought.

Rose pursed her lips, clearly disapproving.

"When do you intend to go?"

Christina gave an uncertain shrug. "I need to make arrangements with Mrs. Beasley to find a replacement. I don't imagine she'll be in much of a rush to do so. She seems perfectly content allowing me to handle the cooking and cleanup chores."

Louisa let out a gasp and grabbed Christina's arms. "I'll do it!"

Christina stared at the older woman. "Are you sure? It's a great deal of work."

"Why, of course. I helped Cora those days you were ill, so I know what to do, and I don't mind a bit. It'll make me feel as though I'm helping you bring those youngsters home again."

Christina threw her arms around Loiusa. "Thank you!" If Mrs. Beasley agreed, Christina could leave for Topeka on Monday's train and be back with the children by Tuesday night.

Rose sidled up to Christina. "Honey, as much as I want to see those curly-haired scamps brought home, I still don't like the idea of you going all the way to Topeka on your own. All sorts of ills can befall a woman traveling alone."

Christina smiled — her first genuine smile in days. How the woman's concern warmed her. "I'll be fine, Rose. Truly I will."

Rose drew back her shoulders and peered down her narrow nose at Christina. "Yes you will. Because, my dear, I'm going, too!"

CHAPTER 29

Levi rubbed a final application of linseed oil into the top of the finished buffet. The grain of the oak glowed like polished brass. Even though he'd chosen not to add embellishments such as engravings or decorative carvings, the buffet was beautiful — a real work of art. Any woman would be proud to store her finest dishes behind its raised panel doors. His hand stilled in its task, and he released a disgruntled huff. No woman would be using this buffet. It would go in the corner of his dining area to hold his simple tin plates.

Why was he thinking of women? Another derisive snort left his lips. Not women. One woman — Miss Willems. He couldn't seem to erase her from his mind. And he knew why.

He angled his head to watch Tommy for a few moments. The boy sat cross-legged on the floor in the area Levi had cleared for him, fingers twisting the shredded lengths of canvas into a woven square. Every day, all day, for the past week the boy had dropped into that same spot and had performed the same task. When he reached the end of the lengths, he unraveled them and started again. Over and over and over . . .

He practiced with the same diligence Levi had witnessed on previous weeks, but over the past days — since last Sunday — he'd shown no delight in his work. He never smiled. He made no cheerful exclamations. No eager queries — "Mr. Jonnson, come look! Is it better this time?" — begged Levi to offer a word of praise. Tommy had retreated into a bubble of solitude that couldn't be penetrated. Each day Levi's concern for the boy grew.

He dipped his rag in the bowl of oil and returned to rubbing the buffet. Should he take Tommy to town and leave him with Miss Willems? Maybe she'd be able to break through the barriers the boy had built around himself. A feeling of failure swept over Levi, bending him forward. He pressed his palm to his forehead, fighting the urge to rail in fury at his helplessness. Why had he opened himself up to this boy? Once again he'd been forced to watch someone who mattered to him descend into a pit of melancholy.

A sigh — deep and burdened — came from behind him. He shifted to peer at Tommy, who'd bowed over his lap and buried his face in his arms. The boy's shoulders shook in silent sobs. Levi had witnessed similar soundless outpourings of grief over the past days, but despite repeatedly asking Tommy to share the reason for his sorrow, the boy hadn't spoken a word of explanation.

So this time, even though Levi longed to offer comfort, he remained rooted in place, his lips clamped tight, and waited for the tears to run their course. While he waited, he made the decision to return Tommy to town. To Miss Willems's care. He couldn't do anything more for Tommy than he could for Far all those years ago. And once Tommy was no longer under his roof — out of sight and hearing — he'd be able to go back to his solitary existence without having to worry about anyone but himself.

And he'd be happy. He *would.*

Christina scurried out the back door Sunday morning, her Bible in hand, as the church bells rang their invitation. Late . . . She disliked being late for service, but doing all the cleanup on her own took much longer than it had when she and Cora shared the responsibilities. Still, she wouldn't bring Cora back to the boardinghouse even if she could. Clearly the young woman was flourishing in her new position with the Creegers as her mentors.

Jealousy coupled with regret stabbed, but she resolutely pushed the unwelcome emotions aside. Soon she'd be too busy to miss the residents who'd found other places to live. The mission board would allow her to return to the poor farm as its director. She refused to entertain any other idea. And in time new people would move in and rely on her for shelter and encouragement. As she'd learned over her years of serving with her father, there was always someone in need.

A striped lizard dashed from the rocks beside the path and nearly ran across her toes. Christina released a little shriek of surprise. At once a familiar voice called, "Are you all right?"

She whirled to find Mr. Jonnson's wagon rolling toward her. Tommy sat beside the man on the seat. Elation and apprehension struck with equal force. She hadn't seen either of them since last Sunday, when Mr. Jonnson had told her about Tommy's reaction to the damaged wood. Although she'd intended to drive the poor farm wagon to the mill and discuss the situation with both of them, Mrs. Beasley hadn't allowed her the time to do so.

Two quick strides brought her to the edge of the street, where Mr. Jonnson drew the wagon to a stop. "I'm fine," she said in response to his question. "A lizard startled me, and —" The brim of her borrowed bonnet shielded the sun from her eyes as she peered upward at the pair of somber faces. "I believe I should ask you the same thing. Are you all right?"

Tommy stared straight ahead as if caught in a trance. Mr. Jonnson rested his elbows on his knees and sighed. "To be honest, Miss Willems, we're not. Can you climb up on the seat? I need to talk to you."

Christina looked toward town where the church's steeple poked above the greening treetops and beckoned to her. She hadn't missed a Sunday service for anything other than illness for as long as she could remember. What would Papa think? She turned to Mr. Jonnson, prepared to ask him to wait until the service was over, but something in his expression — a desperation — brought a different response. "Of course."

He gave Tommy a little nudge. "Climb in the back, Tommy, so Miss Willems can come up." Tommy, his lips set in a grim line, did as Mr. Jonnson had asked while the man hopped out of the wagon and trotted around the back to offer Miss Willems his hand. She found herself trembling as she placed her palm in his. From worry about whatever he wanted to discuss with her or a reaction to his nearness? She couldn't be sure. She only knew the unfamiliar fluttery sensation within her breast left her breathless.

As soon as she'd settled herself on the seat, he climbed up behind her. She tucked her skirts back as he stepped over her feet and plopped down next to her. The seat bounced, and she grabbed the edge to keep from tipping against him. He offered a brief, apologetic look, then released the brake and took up the reins.

They rolled slowly toward the church, and Mr. Jonnson cleared his throat. "Miss Willems, I think it best if Tommy comes back to town to stay with you."

She shot a look into the back, where Tommy sat with his arms folded over his chest. His gaze seemed aimed at the wagon's bed. As she watched, he blinked, his thick eyelashes sweeping up and down so slowly his eyelids appeared weighted. Something was dreadfully wrong with the boy.

"Early next week I'll start retrieving logs from the mouth of the Kansas River, and I won't be able to take him with me. Nor can I leave him alone."

Mr. Jonnson did nothing to soften his voice, which meant Tommy had heard everything. Yet he reacted not a bit. Christina's worry increased with every word from Mr. Jonnson's lips and every creak of the wagon wheels on the dirt street.

"Besides, he's . . . not happy with me." For the first time the man faltered. He gave a sharp yank on the reins, stopping the wagon a block short of the church. "He won't talk. Hardly eats."

Tommy's chin began to quiver. The boy set his jaw, and the quivering stopped.

Mr. Jonnson went on. "I don't know what to do for him." He swallowed and looked into the back, where sunlight glistened on Tommy's ruffled hair. "You take him before . . ." Lowering his head, he ran his hand over his face in slow, jerky increments as if he were erasing something unpleasant. Then he sighed. "Just take him."

Christina leaned across the seat's back and placed her hand on Tommy's head. The boy gave a start, his shoulders stiffening, and then he scooted out of her reach. She pulled back her hand as abruptly as if he'd slapped her. With effort she maintained an even tone. "Tommy, I know you heard Mr.

Jonnson say you aren't happy with him. Is that correct?"

Tommy's lips twitched briefly.

"You were happy before." The boy had done everything in his power to make his way to Mr. Jonnson's mill. "What's changed, Tommy?"

Catching his lower lip between his teeth, Tommy angled his face away from Christina.

Mr. Jonnson touched Christina's arm and shifted sideways in the seat, pinning her with a haunted look. "He says he hates me." He grimaced. "And I believe him."

Christina jerked her attention back to Tommy. His emotionless appearance baffled her as much as it worried her. What had happened to bring about such a change? She wouldn't hear it from Tommy — at least not in Mr. Jonnson's presence. Perhaps when she got him alone, he'd find the courage to share whatever troubled him.

But she couldn't take him now. She'd already purchased train tickets — one for her, one for Rose — for tomorrow's early departure to Topeka. Mrs. Beasley had made it clear Tommy couldn't stay at the boardinghouse, even though Christina was certain Louisa would be willing to look after him for a few days. No one else had been willing to harbor the boy.

"Mr. Jonnson, of course I want to take Tommy if he's unhappy with you, but —"

"Not goin' with you, Miss Willems."

At the sullen outburst Christina and Mr. Jonnson exchanged a startled look. In unison they peered at Tommy.

The boy raised his chin high, anger emanating from his trembling frame. "Won't stay with you neither, so no sense in takin' me."

A rumbling chuckle intruded from nearby. Mr. Jonnson looked past Christina's shoulder, a frown marring his brow. Christina turned, and her breath caught in her throat. What was *he* doing here?

She gripped her Bible with both hands in an attempt to garner strength. "Can we assist you with something, Mr. Dresden?"

From the wagon bed Tommy emitted a sharp gasp.

Before Christina could respond to it, Hamilton Dresden sauntered to the edge of the wagon and peeked into the back. He waggled his brows. "Well, looky there. I thought that was Tommy's voice I heard." Another chuckle rolled. "How you doin', boy?"

Tommy sat upright, eyes wide and palms planted on the worn planks of the bed. His head bobbed this way and that as if seeking an escape route.

"He's fine." Christina answered for Tommy.

"Oh, I can see that. I can see that he's right as rain." Dresden inched his way around the wagon as he talked. Tommy inched in the opposite direction at the same time. "What'samatter with you, boy? Cat got your tongue?" He laughed.

Mr. Jonnson stood. "I don't know who you are, but you're obviously upsetting Tommy. I'd like you to leave."

Ham aimed a cocky grin at the mill owner and held his hands wide. "Why, now, mister, I ain't intendin' to upset the boy. Just bein' friendly. An' this here's a public street. I reckon I got as much right as anybody to be standin' on it."

Mr. Jonnson balled his hands into fists.

Christina caught hold of one of his fists. With her eyes she begged him not to start a fracas. She knew all too well how unpredictable Ham could be, and she didn't want Tommy caught in the middle of a ruckus. To her relief Mr. Jonnson seemed to recognize her silent plea, because he eased back onto the seat. But he kept his steely gaze pinned on the man.

Ham laughed again, lowering his hands to

rest on the wagon's high edge. His eyes aimed at Christina, he addressed Tommy. "These folks don't seem to cotton to me, Tommy-boy, so I reckon I'll just mosey on for now. I'm stayin' in the Brambleville Hotel for a while, bidin' my time between business deals."

Christina wanted to ask with which business he had become associated, but she feared it might be something unscrupulous, so she held her question inside.

"Maybe we'll see each oth. . ." He paused, scratched his chin, and released another chuckle. "Well, better find a different way o' saying that. Hmm. How 'bout 'maybe our paths'll cross sometime soon, an' we'll have us a chance to talk an' get all caught up'? Would you like that, Tommy-boy?"

Tommy scuttled on his toes and hands like a crab to the front of the wagon, where he cowered against the back of the seat. His breath came in little puffs, his face white. When she put her hand on his shoulder, this time he didn't pull away.

"Mr. Dresden, I think it best if you move on." Mr. Jonnson spoke firmly.

Ham gave a slow nod, his grin intact. "Why, sure, mister. Got better things to do than lallygag here on the street with you folks anyhow." He tipped his hat. "Bye now,

Miss Willems. You, too, Tommy. Have your-selves a good day, ya hear?"

He kicked up dust with his shoes as he ambled around the wagon and headed toward the center of town.

As soon as he was far enough away to be out of earshot, Christina squeezed Tommy's shoulder. "Are you all right? I'm sorry he frightened you so." She didn't care for Hamilton Dresden either — the man made her skin crawl. But Tommy's fear seemed extreme. Did the boy sense some kind of evil in the man?

Tommy panted, his chest rising and fall-ing. "Wanna go back to the mill."

Christina gave a start. "But I thought —"

"Wanna go back to the mill." He pawed the air until he found Mr. Jonnson's hand, which rested on the seat back. "Take me there now, Mr. Jonnson."

"Tommy, I —"

"Take me back!" The boy's voice rose with panic. "I can find my way around the mill — all I gotta do is follow the ropes. You can go get your logs an' not fuss over me. I'll stay outta your way, I promise."

Christina stroked Tommy's hair, cringing when the boy jerked away from her gentle touch. "Tommy, won't you please tell us what has you so upset?"

Tommy hunkered down, his head bouncing here and there as if seeking something no one else could see. "No. Don't wanna talk. Just wanna go to the mill. Take me back!"

Mr. Jonnson looked at her, silent questions filling the air between them. She gazed back, captured by the depth of emotion in his eyes. As much as she longed to keep the boy in town where she could explore his unexpected fear-stimulated rebellion, she now wondered if it was better to distance him from Ham Dresden. Tommy harbored an irrational but very real aversion to the man. But she wouldn't tell Mr. Jonnson what to do. She'd trust him to make the best decision for Tommy and for himself.

With his gaze locked on hers, he drew a slow breath and turned his face slightly toward Tommy. Even then, his eyes bored into hers as if reluctant to release her from his sights. "All right, Tommy. We'll go back to the mill."

CHAPTER 30

Cora took another subtle peek over her shoulder as the congregation settled into the benches following the hymn singing. Time for the sermon to start, and still no sign of Miss Willems. An image of the woman's heartbroken appearance after she'd sold her papa's watch haunted Cora. Her own pa had disappeared when Ma was carrying her fourth child, and he hadn't left anything of value behind. But if Cora had something from her pa as special as that watch, she wouldn't want to give it up. Might even make her sick to do it. Her heart twisted. Maybe Miss Willems was too sorrowful even to get out of bed.

Worrisome ideas kept her from listening to the sermon. She gazed at the squares of stained glass forming a frame around the clear, rectangular pane on her left. The rippled panes in red, yellow, green, and blue were so bold and pretty compared to her dark thoughts. Was Miss Willems sick? Was she too tired to come to church, working all by herself for that persnickety Mrs. Beasley? Had she given up all hope because the mission board wouldn't help her get the poor farm going again?

The final thought scared her the most. She tried to remember the last time she'd heard Miss Willems pray. Really pray, like she and God were close friends. But the last prayers Cora could recall were ones said over their vittles — mindless prayers lacking feeling. Cora didn't know how it felt to be close to God, but she'd envied Miss Willems's strong faith. What must it be like to be so certain that God was there, that He cared, and that He'd help folks who asked Him to? But things sure didn't seem to be going right for Miss Willems, so maybe God wasn't really there after all. Maybe Miss Willems had figured it out and had given up on church, the way Mr. Jonnson had.

Beneath the buttons of her new blue-checked dress, purchased from the ready-made rack with her entire first week's pay, Cora's heart gave a painful lurch. God surely had no use for people like her and Emmet Wade — the ones who'd done things that went against His holy Word — but He ought to be proud of someone like Miss

Willems. She'd spent her whole life taking care of folks in need. So why didn't God help her?

Tears threatened. Seemed like lately she could cry at 'most anything. Tears always sat there behind her eyes, ready to spill. She sniffed hard to keep from giving in. Crying wouldn't fix nothing. Never had. All the crying she did when she missed her first monthly hadn't made the next one come. So she wouldn't cry. But she'd sure try to think of some way to make Miss Willems feel better, to help her somehow. After all she'd done for Cora, she owed her.

Turning her attention to the front of the church in a pretense of concentration, she began to plan.

Monday morning Christina thanked Louisa for her willingness to assume her duties, lifted the little valise that one of Mrs. Beasley's boarders had lent her, and headed for the train station. The March morning smelled of dew and grass — delightful aromas. Long shadows painted the ground, and she found herself trying to plant the soles of her shoes on the splashes of sunlight filtering through gaps in the trees. A childish game, perhaps, but it gave her heart a small lift. She'd often seen the twins leap from one patch of sunlight to another like a pair of errant toads. She couldn't wait to bring them back and witness their joyful antics again.

Rose already waited at the Atchison, Topeka, and Santa Fe Railway station, pacing back and forth beneath the overhang where passenger benches sat in a straight row. She rushed at Christina. "Here you are! I came far too early, but I couldn't wait. Oh, such an adventure we're taking!" She leaned close, her eyes sparkling. "I've never ridden a train before. Sixty-two years old and finally riding a train!" She laughed, and Christina found herself laughing with her. How wonderful to have a reason to laugh! The laughter refreshed her.

She'd lain awake last night, worrying about Tommy. She hated to leave town with the boy so distraught, but once she'd returned with the twins, she would ask Louisa to handle one extra day at the boarding-house so she could drive out to the mill and spend time with Tommy. Somehow she'd pry from him the reason for his unsettling behavior, and then she'd enlist Mr. Jonnson's assistance in correcting the problem. She gave a little start. When had she begun depending on Mr. Jonnson for support? She couldn't pinpoint a time, yet it felt perfectly natural to expect his collaboration.

"Have you got the tickets?" Rose held out her hand expectantly.

Christina cast aside her reflections of Mr. Jonnson with a reluctance that puzzled her and fished the squares of stiff paper from her bag. Rose snatched one and pressed it to her skinny chest, her smile bright. Although Christina had initially cringed about spending money for two tickets instead of one, happiness now filled her breast. Rose's absolute delight was worth much more than a $1.40 railroad ticket.

"Shall we sit over here and wait for the train?" Christina pointed to the row of individual seats joined to create long benches. "It's due in at seven forty-five for an eight o'clock departure, so we have —" Automatically she reached for her watch. Sadness struck when her hand clutched only air. She finished lamely, ". . . a bit of time to relax."

Rose nodded in reply, the graying bun on the back of her head bouncing with the movement. She took Christina's arm and guided her to the seats. They perched side by side with their bags in their laps, but after only a few seconds, Rose stood and began pacing. Christina wished she possessed as much energy as the older woman. Tiredness brought on by the worries of the past weeks had robbed her of her usual vim. But once she'd righted the wrong she'd committed against the poor farm residents by reestablishing a place for them to live, this great burden would lift, and she'd finally be restored. She clung to that hope.

"It's coming!" Rose's excited cry brought Christina to her feet as AT&SF Locomotive 645 approached with a rumble that vibrated the ground. She joined Rose and watched the shiny black engine chug toward town, steam billowing and mighty crankshafts pumping. The screech of the brakes nearly pierced her eardrums, and Rose laughed when Christina covered her ears. Then she threw her arm around Christina's shoulders and bellowed, "Let's board!"

The porter accepted their tickets and offered the use of a small wooden stepstool. Rose moved with a sprightliness that left Christina feeling as if their ages had been reversed. The older woman slid onto a green velvet cushioned bench in the center of the car, placed her small travel bag at her feet, and pressed her nose to the window. Christina dropped beside Rose and leaned her head on the backrest.

Were it not for the five stops between

Brambleville and Topeka, the train's amazing forty-mile-per-hour speed would have delivered them to their destination by nine thirty that morning. But the ticket master had warned her that each stop added another fifteen minutes to the journey. They would reach Topeka at ten forty-five instead. Sufficient time for a lengthy nap. She wanted to be well rested when she reclaimed Joe and Florie.

"Rose?"

Rose flicked a smiling glance over her shoulder. "Yes?"

"I'm quite weary. I intend to sleep. Do you mind?"

"Not at all." She gave Christina's knee a brisk pat. "You just rest easy. I'll keep an eye on the countryside and wake you when we get to Topeka."

With a grateful sigh Christina closed her eyes. But despite her efforts sleep proved elusive. The rocking of the train jarred her head back and forth. Additionally, the porter's bellowed announcements of upcoming stations, the shrieking application of brakes followed by shuddering stops, and the noisy activity of passengers boarding or disembarking provided constant intrusion. By the time they reached the Topeka station, Christina couldn't wait to alight from the car and find a quiet place to gather her senses.

But the bustling station proved far from quiet. Christina took Rose's arm, and they weaved their way across the tile floor until they emerged on the opposite side of the enormous brick-and-mortar building.

On the sidewalk Rose swiped her hand over her brow and let out a wheezing "phew." Her gaze seemed to rove across the arched window frames and along the row of spindled posts supporting the roof of a full-length porch. "Mercy, at least half of Brambleville's businesses could fit inside this station." She shook her head. "I'm more relieved than ever that I thought to come with you. A city of this size is downright overwhelming!"

Christina agreed. Her stomach churned in nervous apprehension. She withdrew the paper on which she'd recorded the address for the Kansas Children's Home. Should she summon a cab to transport them to 614 Kansas Avenue? As she pondered the best course of action, Rose suddenly grabbed the paper from Christina's hand.

"Why, look there! Kansas Avenue is just ahead." She swung her head right and left, one hand above her eyes, and surveyed the area. "Looks to me like once we land on that street, we need to go south. Let's go!"

Christina had little choice but to trot alongside the eager woman. When had Rose taken charge of this excursion? She cringed as Rose pulled her into the street, where carriages and wagons rattled over cobblestone. Somehow they made it to the other side unscathed, and Christina started to ask Rose to please exercise caution. But Rose gave her no time to speak. Her hand gripped firmly around Christina's elbow, she propelled her along at a brisk pace, eagerly taking in the towering brick buildings.

"Oh, what would it be like to live in a city like this! Look at the shops! Anything a person could ever want, it's ready and available." Rose babbled, her words jumping out between breaths. "I've never been one to hunger for riches, but it would certainly pleasure me to be able to —" She stopped abruptly, nearly pulling Christina's arm from its socket. She released Christina to point excitedly at a wooden placard attached to the side of a three-story, brown brick building. "This is it!"

A flowing script announced *Kansas Children's Home Society, President: Rosswell L. Cofran.* Christina's stomach lurched in nervous excitement. "This is it," she repeated in a much more subdued tone than Rose's.

Rose giggled — a girlish sound. "Let's go in. I can hardly wait to wrap my arms around those two urchins!"

Once again Christina found herself being dragged along by Rose. But she didn't mind. She shared Rose's desire to be re-united with Joe and Florie. They stepped into a deep, narrow entryway. Painted white plaster walls reflected the sunlight pouring in through a pair of tall, uncovered windows. A railed stairway on their right led to the other levels, and a wall with wide double doors stood closed on their left. The mumble of voices carried from behind the doors.

A large wooden desk faced the front door. A woman in a blue dress, starched apron, and ruffled mobcap sat behind the desk, scribbling in a ledger. Rose pointed to the woman, and Christina nodded. Christina's elbow still caught in Rose's grip, they crossed the polished dark wood floors and placed their bags near their feet.

The woman looked up, a smile on her round face. "Hello. May I help you?"

Rose opened her mouth, but Christina placed her hand over Rose's in a silent request to allow her to speak. "Yes. I understand two children — Joe and Florie Alexander — were delivered to the children's home two weeks ago by Mr. Silas Regehr."

The woman began flipping pages in the ledger. "Alexander . . . Alexander . . ." Her face lit, and she jammed her finger against an entry penned in black ink. "Yes. You're correct. Mr. Regehr transferred Joseph and Florence Alexander, whom he stated had been orphaned, into our care." She bounced a curious look from Christina to Rose. "Are you relatives of the children?"

"No. I'm Christina Willems. My father and I served as directors for the Brambleville Asylum for the Poor." Christina reached for her watch, needing a connection with Papa. Its absence again took her by surprise, and she stammered out her next words. "Th-the children were left in our care more than a year ago."

"That's right," Rose added, leaning slightly toward the woman. "Miss Willems took excellent care of Joe and Florie. Just because the poor farm house is now —"

Christina gave Rose's hand a gentle squeeze. "Mr. Regehr was not authorized to relocate them. So I've come to take them back to Brambleville."

A frown appeared on the woman's face. She stood. "Our understanding, Miss

388

Willems, is the Brambleville Asylum is under the directorship of the Kansas Mission Board and is being disbanded."

Rose's shoulders squared. "What utter nonsense!" She turned a disbelieving gaze on Christina. "That's not true, is it, Christina?"

Christina swallowed, seeking an honest yet reassuring reply. "The poor farm house sustained some damage from a fire and is in the process of undergoing repairs as we speak." She stretched the truth, but surely the promise of lumber and the funds to purchase plaster counted as progress. "Granted, it isn't ready for us to occupy as yet, but I have placement arranged for Joe and Florie until which time we are able to move back into our home. So" — she drew a breath, angled her head, and fixed a firm look on the children's home worker — "I would greatly appreciate you retrieving the children and their belongings so we might be on our way."

The woman pursed her lips. For a long moment she frowned at Christina, and Christina sensed she was forming a fierce argument. But then, without saying a word, she left her station and disappeared behind a door. Minutes later she returned, followed by a second woman wearing a utilitarian navy skirt, a crisp white blouse, and an air of authority. The woman in the mobcap took her seat behind the desk again. The other advanced upon Christina with her hand extended.

As Christina took her hand, the woman said, "I'm Miss Wallenstein, director of the Kansas Children's Home Society. Judith tells me you are Miss Willems from Brambleville."

Christina offered a polite nod and withdrew her hand from the woman's dry grasp. "That's correct. I've come to collect Joe . . . er, Joseph and Florence Alexander."

Miss Wallenstein locked her hands behind her back and peered at Christina through the round lenses of her spectacles. "Are you related to the children?"

"No, ma'am."

"They have been orphaned?"

Christina quickly shared the same explanation she'd given Judith. "But they are my responsibility, so if you'd kindly —"

The children's home director shook her head. "I'm terribly sorry, Miss Willems, but I'm inclined to agree with the gentleman who brought the children to our facility. A poor farm is not an appropriate placement for young children." Her face registered a brief, sympathetic look before she added,

"Besides which, we've already made arrangements with a Kansas City couple to adopt the twins."

CHAPTER 31

Christina sank against the edge of the sturdy desk. Rose hovered close, patting her shoulder. Christina had never appreciated the woman's presence more. Her mind whirled. "But I . . . I've come all the way from Brambleville for them. I sold my father's watch . . ." Her babbling made no sense. The children's home director would call for a doctor if she didn't gain control of herself. Forcing a calm tone, she formed a question. "When will the children go to their new home?"

"As a matter of fact, the Dunnigans plan to arrive late this afternoon on the five o'clock train."

So soon . . . Christina swallowed. "Could we at least have a little time with the twins so we might tell them good-bye?"

"Of course, Miss Willems." Genuine sympathy showed in the director's eyes. She touched Christina's hand. "What if I excuse the children from their lessons this afternoon and allow them to spend those hours with you?"

Christina forced herself to stand. Her legs trembled, but she remained upright. She must be strong for Rose and for the twins. "Yes, please."

"That'd be real fine," Rose said. Tears glittered in the woman's eyes. "We're going to miss those golden-haired scamps. They were like grandchildren to Louisa and me. I sure hoped . . ." She covered her quivering lips with her fingers.

Miss Wallenstein addressed Judith. "Inform Mr. Rudd that Joseph and Florence will not be in classes this afternoon." The woman gave a quick nod in reply and scurried off. Miss Wallenstein guided Christina and Rose to a bench in front of one of the windows. "Judith will be down shortly. You may wait here."

Christina sat, but Rose stood, gazing out the window at the busy street. Tears rolled silently down her cheeks, and her downcast pose pierced Christina. How quickly the woman's countenance had changed from this morning's ebullience.

Miss Wallenstein turned toward the door from which she'd emerged earlier, but halfway across the floor she stopped and faced Christina again. "Miss Willems, I realize this is a shock for you, but aren't you happy for Joseph and Florence? The Dunnigans are a wealthy couple who will give the children every advantage."

Rose shot a sour look over her shoulder. "Wealth isn't everything."

"Of course it isn't," the director countered calmly. "In addition to possessing a fine home, they are Christian people who will be kind and loving parents."

Rose faced the window again, heaving a sigh.

"I am very grateful they chose the twins." Miss Wallenstein focused her attention on Christina. "So often people come to the children's home seeking babies or toddlers. As a matter of fact, adopting a baby was the Dunnigans' original intention. But Mrs. Dunnigan met Joseph and Florence right here in this foyer. They were battling over a rag doll, which, I was given to understand, Joseph intended to shoot from a slingshot onto the roof next door —"

Rose emitted a soft snort, and despite herself Christina couldn't stifle a smile. The twins hadn't changed a bit.

"And Mrs. Dunnigan intervened. Both she and her husband were quite taken with the mischievous pair, and after a brief exchange they decided to make them their own." The director tipped her head, a hint of warning coloring her expression. "This truly is a fine opportunity for Joseph and Florence. As much as you will miss them, I trust you will express only enthusiasm about their new home and parents."

Christina admitted a deep-seated joy for the children's good fortune, yet it would pierce her to bid them a permanent good-bye. How she'd grown to love the children while they'd resided beneath her roof. She forced a bittersweet smile to her face. "Yes, Miss Wallenstein. Of course. Both Rose and I are delighted for the twins."

Cora took a bite of the thick ham sandwich. A salty taste flooded her mouth. She couldn't resist murmuring, "Mmmm . . ."

Ma Creeger smiled in reply, and Pa Creeger waggled his brows, chomping down on his sandwich. Cora hunched her shoulders and giggled, happier than she could ever remember being. Across the little table tucked in the corner of the storeroom, her employers — her friends — shared a short bench. They had to crunch so close together they might have been two peas in a pod, but it didn't seem to bother them any.

She liked sitting here all together in the

middle of the day. They always ate their evening meal together at the Creegers' house on the other side of the alley behind the mercantile. But that was after the store closed. Usually for lunch they each ate alone, leaving the other two free to wait on customers. But today'd been quiet. Not one soul had come in all morning, so Ma Creeger had said, "Let's have a picnic." And that's just exactly what they did. They spread a checked cloth on the table where they usually sorted deliveries, unwrapped the sandwiches Ma Creeger had made that morning, and commenced to eat the simple fare.

Nobody said much while they ate. Cora discovered that suited her, too. When Cora's mother got all quiet, it was because she was too mad or too moody to talk. Those silences at home had always left Cora feeling fidgety and nervous inside. But being quiet with the Creegers was peaceful. Comfortable. Homey. This baby inside her sure would be lucky, growing up with people like Jay and Mary Ann Creeger.

As if in response to her thoughts, the child within her rolled and nudged — a stronger movement than ever before. Startled, Cora sat upright and dropped the remaining portion of her sandwich. It hit the edge of her tin plate, fell apart, and tumbled toward the floor. Cora tried to catch the ham, but she only managed to bat it. The pieces of bread landed beside her, but the piece of ham flew over by Pa Creeger's foot.

Horrified, Cora jumped up. "I'm sorry! I'm so sorry! I didn't mean to waste it! Honest, I didn't!"

Ma Creeger bustled around the table and patted Cora's shoulder while Pa Creeger bent to pick up the mess. Tears coursed down Cora's face — embarrassed tears but also regretful tears. Food came dear. How could she have been so clumsy and wasteful? She sobbed so hard she barely heard Ma Creeger's words.

"Cora . . . Cora!" Ma Creeger gave Cora's arm a little shake, then cupped her cheeks and looked directly into her face. "Cora, calm yourself."

She took several shuddering gulps that brought her crying under control.

Ma Creeger smiled, stroking Cora's cheeks. "My, my, you've shed some tears of late." She leaned close and whispered, "It's just part of being female. Happens to me, too."

Heat flooded Cora's face. Ma Creeger knew? She *knew*?

The woman straightened and gave Cora's

face one more loving pat. "But all that crying over a little bit of bread and ham doesn't make much sense, does it?"

The brass bell above the mercantile door clanged. "Finally a customer!" Pa Creeger dropped the remains of Cora's sandwich into the waste bin and gave her an impish grin. "If you're still hungry, go help yourself to a handful of peanuts." Chuckling, he headed for the sales area.

Cora watched Ma Creeger return to her bench and reach for what was left of her sandwich. *"It's just part of being female."* Her heart boomed like the biggest drum in a marching band. Had the woman been letting Cora know she understood and wasn't mad? "M-Ma Creeger?"

"Yes, Cora?"

Cora's mouth went dry, and she licked her lips, seeking courage. "You . . . Did you . . ." Before she could make the question come out of her mouth, Pa Creeger let out a shout.

"Mary Ann!"

She'd never heard Pa Creeger use that tone before. Ma Creeger headed for the doorway, and Cora trailed close behind. He stood at the counter, the open cashbox in front of him and his hands on his hips. The customer stood on the other side of the counter, her eyes wide.

Ma Creeger hurried to her husband's side. "What is it, Jay?"

"We need to summon the sheriff." He gestured to the box, his brows forming a V. "I went to make change for Mrs. Fulton, and look what I found. Our cashbox is empty. Every penny from last week's sales is gone, and so is that silver William Ellery watch I bought from Miss Willems."

Christina felt dowdy in her simple button-up, green muslin frock next to Mrs. Dunnigan's peach silk walking suit. But the woman smiled warmly and enclosed Christina's hand between the palms of her tight-fitting ivory gloves when Miss Wallenstein introduced her. "So you're the Miss Willems that Joseph and Florence told us all about on our first visit. I'm so pleased we've had the opportunity to meet."

Christina had specifically requested a private moment with the Dunnigans to give her an opportunity to question their motives in taking the twins. Too many people preyed upon orphaned children, using them as servants rather than loving them. She'd been prepared to distrust, even to dislike, the people who were stealing the children from her, yet such warmth and friendliness shone in the woman's eyes Christina felt herself drawn to her. "Thank you."

Miss Wallenstein lifted a hand to garner attention. "The children are in the play yard with Miss Willems's companion, Mrs. McLain. I'll go retrieve them."

Mr. Dunnigan stepped forward. In his brown tweed trousers and matching vest and jacket, he looked every bit the sophisticated businessman. Christina eyed him carefully. Would he be too stern and formal with Joe and Florie? But then he smiled, which lifted the corners of his neatly trimmed mustache and gave him a mischievous appearance. "We're very eager to take the children home today."

Mrs. Dunnigan released a light laugh. "We spent a delightful weekend equipping the children's rooms with clothes and a mountain of toys and books."

Mr. Dunnigan leaned forward in a conspiratorial manner, his eyes twinkling. "I suspect young Joseph will be particularly enthralled by the tin windup train. It travels on an oval track and even makes a *toot-toot* sound. I found it quite entertaining."

Mrs. Dunnigan gave her husband's chin a teasing pinch. "We'll have to secure a governess quickly to keep the children occupied, or you might give up work completely and wile away your day in the playroom with them!"

He waggled his brows in teasing reply.

Rose, holding the twins' hands, rounded the corner. The pair released Rose and dashed to Christina. She bent down to receive their hugs as Rose turned a haughty look on the Dunnigans. "Did I hear you say you're hiring a governess to see to the children's care?"

"Why, yes." Mr. Dunnigan smiled indulgently at the twins. "Parmelia and I are quite involved in philanthropic activities around the city, taking us out of the home frequently for evening events. Additionally, my business requires travel, which would leave Parmelia home alone with the children. Therefore it seems sensible to hire an individual who will be available when one or both of us must be away."

"Not," Mrs. Dunnigan inserted, "to take full responsibility for their upbringing, please understand. As their mother" — pride and joy flooded her features — "I fully intend to provide the majority of their care. But both Maxwell and I feel more comfortable knowing there will be a person of whom we approve seeing to the children's well-being in our absence."

Christina tucked her arms around the

twins, savoring each moment with them as their separation neared. "So you haven't yet hired someone?"

"Maxwell placed an advertisement in yesterday's newspaper." Mrs. Dunnigan gazed longingly at the children, who pressed their cheeks to Christina's ribs. "We expect to find a suitable governess within a week or two."

With the same exuberance she'd exhibited on their train ride, Rose stepped forward and flashed a bold smile. "Mr. and Mrs. Dunnigan, there's no need to look any further for a governess. Hire me."

Chapter 32

"Rose!" Christina could scarcely believe her ears. "Did you just —" Rose whirled around to face her, a triumphant look on her face. "Yes I did. And doesn't it make perfect sense?" She scooted close to Christina and placed a hand on Joe's tousled head. "I know the children. They know me. I love them." Tears filled her eyes as she gazed down first at Joe and then Florie. Without a word the pair separated themselves from Christina and burrowed against Rose's full skirt. "And with all the troubles at the poor farm, it just might be I'll need a different home soon."

Rose's comment pained Christina, but she had no real defense. She stood stupidly while Rose went on, oblivious to the incredulous stares of Maxwell and Parmelia Dunnigan.

"If I take the position as governess, I'll get to be with Joe and Florie. They'll feel more secure, having me close as they settle into their new home, and you'll feel more secure, knowing they're being cared for. And everyone will be happy." She bent down and planted a kiss on each child's head, then beamed at Christina.

Mr. Dunnigan cleared his throat. "Mrs. McLain . . ."

Rose gave a start and turned her attention to the man. "Yes?"

He slipped his thumbs into the little slanted pockets on his vest and set his feet wide. "Do you have previous experience as a governess?"

Rose blinked twice. "Well, I reckon not."

"Do you have experience raising children?"

Rose's skinny shoulders squared. "I certainly do. Raised two fine boys, Peter and Paul. But" — sadness crept across her features — "neither one came home after the War between the States."

Christina placed a comforting hand on Rose's shoulder.

Rose sniffed, then lifted her chin. "But I helped with the children who showed up at the poor farm. Joe and Florie, of course, as well as Laura, Francis, and Tommy." Her eyes narrowed in a challenging manner. "Do you need to know anything else?"

"May I ask" — he cleared his throat again, a hint of pink entering his cheeks — "your age?"

Rose pursed her lips. "I don't consider it a gentlemanly question, but I'll answer anyway just to set your mind at ease. I turned sixty-two this past December." To Christina's abject horror, Rose waggled a finger at the man as if he were a misbehaving boy. "But don't think for a minute that makes me too old to be a governess. I've got more than enough vigor to keep up with these two scalawags."

Christina quivered in embarrassment. She loved Rose, and often she'd found herself amused by the woman's lack of inhibition. But in that moment she wished to clamp her hand over Rose's mouth and prevent her from saying anything else that might offend Joe and Florie's new parents.

But Mr. Dunnigan laughed — loudly, boisterously. His eyes twinkled merrily as he grinned at his wife. "Well, what do you think, Parmelia? Should we pursue hiring Mrs. McLain as the governess for our children?"

Mrs. Dunnigan tipped her head, the tiny diamond studs in her earlobes catching the light. "Employing an individual who is familiar with the children might hasten their settling in with us."

Rose flashed a bright smile of success in Christina's direction before fixing a businesslike look on Mr. Dunnigan. "I'd be pleased to consider the position. But of course it'd be nice to know where I'd be staying and how much it pays before I give my final answer."

Mr. Dunnigan laughed again. "Then I suppose we should show you." He slipped his arm around his wife's waist. "Parmelia, you stay here with the children while I visit a telegraph office. I shall alert the staff to ready a guest room for Mrs. McLain."

He turned slightly toward the door, but Mrs. Dunnigan stopped him with a gloved hand on his chest. "Please have them ready *two* rooms, Maxwell. I think perhaps spending a few days with the children at our home would assure Miss Willems they'll be well cared for." Understanding sympathy shone in her eyes as she faced Christina. "Am I correct, Miss Willems?"

Cora chased dust off the shelves behind the counter with a feather duster and listened as Louisa visited with Pa Creeger. Since Monday's awful discovery of the empty money box, Pa Creeger had sent Cora home with Ma Creeger each evening, and he'd stayed in her little room over the store. If the thief returned, he wanted to be ready. The whole town was abuzz about the theft, with people speculating on who could've done such a spiteful thing. Cora wanted to know, too. She kept her ears tuned for any clue that might help the Creegers solve the mystery.

"Seeing as how telegrams cost money, I can understand why Miss Willems would send such a short one." Louisa sounded more dismayed than angry. "But I'd just like to know why she and Rose have been delayed."

Ma Creeger arranged new button cards on a pegged rack. "How are you getting along over at the boardinghouse?"

"As well as can be expected, working for the likes of Imogene Beasley. Mercy, but that woman is a tyrant!"

Cora cringed as she flicked the stiff feathers between little boxes of medicinal cures. Tyrant, indeed! Louisa was probably counting the hours until Miss Willems returned and took over those duties again.

"But I told her," Louisa went on, a hint of smug defiance in her tone, "a body can only move so fast, and her boarders won't starve to death if supper lands on the table a few minutes past six. I told her if she wants things done just so, she can either lend a hand or do them herself. That took the wind out of her sails. She hasn't pestered me nearly as much since."

Cora and Ma Creeger exchanged a quick smile. Cora wished she could've been there to see Mrs. Beasley's face when Louisa stood up to her. Ma Creeger said, "Did Christina's telegram say when she and Rose would come back to Brambleville? Jay said several men intend to do some work at the poor farm Saturday. They don't have enough lumber to do the walls since so much of it got battered by the ax, but they hope to protect the house in case we get more rain. I'm sure Christina would like to oversee their efforts."

Cora finished dusting and tucked the duster beneath the counter next to the cash-box, which Pa Creeger now kept out of sight of customers. She moved to the end of the counter to help Ma Creeger.

Louisa sighed. "Not a hint of when she might return. It just said, 'Delayed. Visiting Kansas City with twins.' Visiting! As if she has money for such a treat."

Ma Creeger shrugged. "I'm sure she'll share the entire adventure with you when she comes home. And if it isn't by Saturday, then she'll have a nice surprise waiting, with some of the repairs already done at the poor farm."

"I suppose that's true . . ." Louisa fingered a card with four mother-of-pearl buttons. Her gaze drifted to the button beneath Cora's chin. "Why, look here, these match your dress just right, Cora. I admired your new dress at church last Sunday. Did you buy it here in the store?"

Cora smoothed her hands over her hips, pride filling her. "Yes, ma'am. Found it on the dress rack and paid for it with my clerkin' money." It felt mighty good to be able to see to her own needs.

Louisa gave Cora a lingering look-over. "You chose a good color. The blue makes your cheeks seem pinker. You've always been so pale and thin." Her gaze seemed to settle on Cora's midsection. A light chuckle left her throat. "Of course, here of late you've been filling out some." Louisa reached out as if to give her stomach a light pat. "Mrs. Creeger must feed you —"

Cora jerked backward so fast her head spun. She caught hold of the edge of the counter to keep herself from falling flat.

"Why, Cora!" Ma Creeger took a step toward her, concern lining her face.

Cora braced herself for the questions that were sure to come. But before Ma Creeger said anything, the mercantile bell announced an arriving customer.

Louisa eased toward the door, sending Cora a puzzled look. "I'd better get back to the boardinghouse. It'll be time to start the evening meal soon. So . . ." She moved past the man who'd shown up on the boardinghouse back stoop awhile back. He tipped his hat, but Louisa didn't pay him any mind as she scurried out the door. The man shrugged and ambled to the counter.

"Howdy, ma'am. I'm Ham— Hamilton Dresden." He plopped his hat on the wooden top and rested his elbows on either side of it, idly grinning at Ma Creeger. "Can you fetch the owner for me?"

"That's me." Ma Creeger smiled, but Cora noticed she wasn't as friendly as usual. Either she was uncomfortable around the man, or she was still thinking about why Cora had jumped away from Louisa's touch. Shame burned through her swollen belly. Louisa had skedaddled in such a hurry. Would everyone run from her when they learned the truth? She eased behind the apple barrel.

"You sure?" Dresden raised one eyebrow. "Don't know of many businesses owned by a lady." He barked out a laugh.

Ma Creeger wiped her hands on her

apron. "My husband and I own the mercantile together. But if you'd rather talk to him . . ."

"I'd like to talk to you both if you don't mind." He glanced around the store. "He here?"

Ma Creeger looked at Cora. "Cora, would you call Jay from the storage shed, please?"

Cora hated to leave Ma Creeger alone with Hamilton Dresden. Miss Willems didn't like him, and he gave her a funny feeling. But she couldn't refuse. She gave a quick nod and trotted as quick as she could to the backyard where Pa Creeger was arranging a new shipment of plows and harrows in the shed. He whacked the dust from his britches as he followed Cora. When they entered the back door, Cora heard Ma Creeger exclaim, "What are you doing with that?"

A concerned look crossed Pa Creeger's face. He zinged past Cora, and she broke into an awkward run behind him. They burst onto the store floor, and Pa Creeger went straight to his wife. "What's the matter, Mary Ann?"

Panting, Cora reached the end of the counter as Ma Creeger pointed to a silver disk cradled in Dresden's hand. "Jay, look what he's got."

Cora leaned forward slightly. The man held a watch — with etchings exactly like the one Miss Willems had. It even had a tiny nick near the clasp, the same as hers.

Dresden chuckled. "You folks act like you've never seen a watch before. I took it out to check the time — wanted to make sure I wouldn't be late for an important meeting at the hotel. Soon as I brung it out, the lady here got all excited."

Pa Creeger extended his hand, and Dresden amiably plopped the watch into his palm. Pa Creeger turned the watch this way and that, then rubbed his thumb on the nick. He frowned at the man. "Is this your watch?"

"Has been since this past Sunday." Dresden reached across the counter and plucked the watch from Pa Creeger's hand. "Used to belong to Miss Christina Willems. You folks know her? She an' her pa ran the poor farm." He shook his head, poking out his lips in a sad pout. "Such a sad, sad thing — what happened out there. But much as it pains me to say so, I'm not surprised."

Cora nearly danced in place, nervousness making her edgy. Wes had told her this man wasn't to be trusted. Miss Willems had seemed downright scared of him. She wanted to warn the Creegers not to listen to him, but she couldn't find the words.

Ma Creeger shifted closer to her husband. "Surprised about what?"

He acted shocked by the question. "Why, that fire of course. Something was bound to happen by and by, seein' as how the place didn't have no man in charge." He touched his lips with his fingertips and ducked his head in a humble manner. "No offense to you, dear lady, but womenfolk . . . Well, lemme just say there's a reason God plucked out one o' Adam's ribs to make the first lady. It was His way of showin' that a woman needs a man's arm tucked around her. Miss Willems, she wouldn't let any man give her help. I tried — heaven knows how I tried." His eyes beseeched the couple to believe him. "But she wanted to do it all by herself in her own way. An' look what it got her . . . a fire-burned house."

"That doesn't explain how you came to have her watch," Pa Creeger said.

Cora silently cheered. Pa Creeger was too smart to be taken in by this fellow. She held her breath, waiting for Dresden to answer.

"Well . . ." He rubbed his chin, pushing his whiskery skin back and forth. "I come by it when she sold it."

Pa Creeger's frown deepened. "To you?"

The man released a throaty chuckle.

"How else would I come by it?"

An uneasy feeling scampered up Cora's spine. Miss Willems wasn't at church Sunday. And the sheriff said the cashbox probably got emptied on Sunday. How many letters had the woman sent requesting money, only to be told no again and again? Had she finally lost patience and done something . . . Cora shook her head hard, dispelling the unwelcome thoughts. Of course Miss Willems wouldn't steal!

Dresden continued. "She's probably tryin' to get money in hand to make a new start somewheres else since the mission board's told her she can't live at the poor farm no more."

Ma Creeger grabbed for her husband's hand. "That isn't true! Why, several townsmen are planning to work on the house the day after tomorrow. The owner of Jonnson Millworks is donating the lumber. All the work is at Christina's request. Why would she go to such trouble if she didn't intend to live there?"

Cora couldn't stay silent. "That's right, mister. Miss Willems wouldn't try so hard to fix up the place if it wasn't gonna be her home."

Dresden angled his head to the side and shrugged with the opposite shoulder. "I can't rightly say what she's thinkin'. She's a hard one to figure. But I reckon you can ask her when she comes to the mercantile next. You, um, seen her lately?"

Pa Creeger frowned. "She's out of town."

"That so?"

Cora blurted, "She went to Topeka on Monday to get Joe and Florie so we can all go home." But then what was she doing in Kansas City? Cora's stomach twisted into knots. She wished Miss Willems was here to explain everything.

Dresden quirked one eyebrow. "Mm-hmm . . . Topeka. That's what — less'n a half-day's journey? An' she left on Monday, you say?" He held his hands wide. The silver watch caught the light and sent a shaft of white across the room. "Then why ain't she back?"

Ma Creeger took on a fierce look. "Mr. Dresden, I don't like what you're implying. Why, Christina Willems is a fine young woman who serves her Lord."

Pa Creeger marched from behind the counter. "I agree with my wife. I think it best if you leave."

Dresden chuckled. He slipped the watch into his pocket and picked up his hat. "All right. If that's what you want, I'll go. But throwin' me out the door don't change nothin'. She's still gone, seemingly with enough money for a lengthy time away. You reason it all out your own selves."

"We will." Pa Creeger ushered Dresden out the door and closed it behind him. He stood for a moment, staring out the glass. Then with an abrupt motion he turned the lock. Ma Creeger bustled up behind him and touched his arm. He held it out, and she snugged herself against his ribs, tucked up close, the way Dresden said women should be. Pa Creeger sighed. "Mary Ann, how do you suppose he got that watch?"

Ma Creeger rested her cheek on his shoulder. "I can't believe it was from Christina. We need to see the sheriff."

Cora gulped, relief flowing over her. With them focused on the watch and how Dresden had gotten it, they weren't thinking about her and Louisa's hand reaching for her swollen belly.

CHAPTER 33

Saturday morning Tommy inched his way to the edge of the porch. His seeking hands found a post, and he sank down, leaning his shoulder against the sturdy wood and stretching out his legs. The air was cool, still a little dewy, but heat from the sun soaked through his britches to his legs underneath. A bird sang from somewhere nearby. Wind whispered in the trees. The river added its song. The morning sounded beautiful.

Behind him the door latch clicked, and then boots clomped across the porch — Mr. Jonnson. He stopped, so close his pant leg brushed against Tommy's arm. Tommy hugged the post.

A sigh, then the man spoke. "Are you sure you don't want to come with me? You've been alone quite a bit already this week."

He'd sometimes been lonely, staying in the house by himself while Mr. Jonnson traveled upriver to retrieve logs for cutting.

But being lonely was better than letting himself get attached to Mr. Jonnson again. Getting attached meant getting hurt all over again. He'd protect himself from now on. "I'm fine."

"Well . . ." A slight creaking sound told Tommy the man had shifted in place on the porch boards — a sign he wasn't certain what he should do.

"Just go on." Tommy grabbed the porch post and pulled himself upright hand over hand. "I'll use the rope and go to the mill — do some caning." He jutted his chin. "I won't bother nothin' I shouldn't."

A hand descended on Tommy's shoulder. The touch was gentle yet firm. "I trust you, Tommy." Mr. Jonnson spoke kindly, but Tommy also heard some sadness in his tone. There'd been sadness in his voice a lot lately. Guilt tried to take hold, but Tommy refused the emotion. Mr. Jonnson might say he trusted Tommy, but he wouldn't if he knew the secret Tommy carried. And he didn't dare tell, or something worse than a kitchen fire would happen.

Tommy pulled away from the man's hand. "Then go. Leave me be."

The bird kept singing. The wind kept whispering. The river kept flowing. But on the porch silence fell. Tommy sensed Mr.

Jonnson staring hard at him. Maybe with his hands on his hips. Maybe with anger on his face. Or maybe more sadness. Tommy tipped his head this way and that way, wanting to see. But all the wanting in the world didn't change the darkness.

Finally Mr. Jonnson cleared his throat. "All right. I shouldn't be gone as long today. I'll be back before noon for sure so we can have lunch together."

As much as Tommy wanted to stay mad, he was pleased he wouldn't have to sit at the table and eat a cold sandwich all alone. Even so, he set his lips in a firm line and didn't answer.

Clomp, clomp, clomp . . . Mr. Jonnson left the porch. Minutes later horses' hoofs and wagon wheels crunching across hard ground signaled his departure. Tommy listened until he couldn't hear the wagon any longer. Then he eased himself back to his perch, curled his arm around the porch post, and stared into nothingness.

Levi drew the horses to a stop outside the mercantile. The list in his pocket wasn't as long as some weeks, but this time it contained items he wouldn't ordinarily buy. Licorice whips. A boy-sized hat. And a harmonica. He'd caught Tommy humming while he worked. Maybe the boy would enjoy creating music on one of the pocket-size instruments. Bribes, every last one of them, but he'd run out of other ideas. Before he returned to the mill, he'd stop by the boardinghouse and talk to Miss Willems about Tommy.

As he'd noted on previous Saturdays, the mercantile buzzed with activity. Mr. and Mrs. Creeger and Cora were all helping other customers, so he snagged an empty crate from the supply near the storeroom door and ambled up and down the aisles, seeing to his own needs. Snippets of conversation reached his ears as he added items to the crate.

". . . still hasn't come back. Think maybe she was the one who . . ."

". . . out there working on those walls, but I have to wonder why since . . ."

". . . lived at the poor farm for a while, so I reckon he'd know better'n most how . . ."

Levi had never been one to listen to gossip. Living out away from town, he didn't have the opportunity to turn an ear to it. But mostly, having been hurt by gossip in the past, he'd made it a point not to involve himself in speculating about others' lives. Today, however, the nervous whispers and half-fearful musings stirred his curiosity.

When he plunked his crate on the counter and Mr. Creeger approached to tally things up, Levi found himself asking, "What's all this prattle?"

The mercantile owner scowled. "Oh, you know how folks get to chewing on a topic, and one thing leads to another. I don't care how it looks. I don't believe for a minute Miss Willems stole back her watch and emptied my cashbox."

Levi jolted as if poleaxed. "What?"

Mr. Creeger began removing items from the crate and stacking them on the counter. He set them down with solid *thump*s, as if expelling irritation. "To accuse a good Christian woman like Miss Willems . . . Just because she decided to go to Kansas City, that's no reason to —"

Levi shook his head hard, confusion making his ears ring. "I don't follow anything you're saying. What about Miss Willems emptying your cashbox? And what's she doing in Kansas City?"

Understanding registered on the man's face. "I'm sorry. I forgot you live out away from the town's tittle-tattle." He released a little *humph*. "Makes you a lucky man, to my way of thinking." He pushed the crate aside. "Last weekend, most likely while we were all in church, somebody came into the mercantile and helped himself to the contents of my cashbox. He took every dollar I'd made the week before and a silver William Ellery watch I'd bought from Miss Willems. Then on Monday, Miss Willems boarded a train for Topeka. She told everybody she was going to retrieve the twins who'd lived out at the poor farm with her, but she hasn't come back yet. Folks are speculating she skedaddled to start a new life somewhere else."

Levi tried to absorb everything Mr. Creeger had said. As he put the pieces together, fury writhed through his gut. Miss Willems wouldn't steal — he knew that from the very depth of his being. He didn't know why she'd stayed away so long, but she loved the poor farm and its residents too much to walk away from them without an explanation. He glanced around the store, examining the faces of people who'd lived beside Miss Willems for years. How could they turn on her so easily? He gritted his teeth.

Mr. Creeger continued, his voice taking on a hard edge. "Add to that, Mr. Hamilton Dresden is marching all over town, flashing that watch and speaking ill of Miss Willems, and you've got a mess that won't be settled until Miss Willems comes back and sets everything straight."

Levi whirled back to face the mercantile owner. "You said Hamilton Dresden has Miss Willems's watch?"

Mr. Creeger nodded.

"Then it seems pretty plain to me he's your thief."

The man held out his hands in a helpless gesture. "I said as much to the sheriff. But until he talks to Miss Willems and can get both sides of the story and disprove what Dresden's saying, he can't arrest the man. He did tell Dresden not to leave town just yet." He shook his head sadly. "If only Miss Willems would come back and explain where she's been. Until she does, the rumors will keep flying. My wife's half sick over it all."

Levi gnawed the inside of his cheek. Unpleasant memories crowded his mind. He couldn't let Miss Willems be hurt the way he'd been hurt. The scars inflicted by thoughtless tongues never completely heal. The protectiveness he felt toward the woman took him by surprise. Why did he care so much? He couldn't explain it. He only knew the feelings were real and strong and sure. He slapped the counter so hard his palm stung. "She didn't do it."

"You don't have to convince me," Mr. Creeger said. He returned to tallying Levi's purchases. "But if you've got some kind of evidence to support her, you might want to share it with the sheriff. He intends to have a long talk with her as soon as she gets back."

Levi blew out a breath. "Mr. Creeger, do you mind if I leave these things here for a little while? I . . . I need to run another errand."

"Why, sure. No problem at all." The man hefted Levi's crate off the counter and set it on the floor. "Take as much time as you need. It'll be here when you return."

"Thanks." Levi spun and charged out onto the boardwalk. Fool people. Fool, gullible people believing the likes of Hamilton Dresden over a fine woman like Miss Christina Willems. By the time he finished with the sheriff, the town would be singing another tune.

The house always felt confining when Tommy was alone, so he'd followed the rope to the mill and spent the first hour of the morning twisting the lengths of canvas into the same pattern as the chair's seat had. He couldn't be completely sure it matched. The smooth cane and the rough canvas had such different textures. But he thought it was close. The overlapped bumps and tiny

424

square open places felt the same. He'd have to ask Mr. Jonnson to be sure, though.

Defeat bowed his shoulders. He missed Mr. Jonnson. He missed talking with him. Laughing with him. Feeling at home with him. But all that good feeling had washed away when Mr. Jonnson claimed he was disappointed in Tommy. Which meant the man didn't know him after all.

His stomach rumbled. He'd skipped breakfast, too restless to sit at the table and eat a bowl of mush with Mr. Jonnson. But the leftovers were probably still on the stove. It didn't taste as good cold, but he knew better than to try to light the stove. If Mr. Jonnson had left the jug of sorghum on the table, Tommy could stir some into the pot and flavor the cold mush. At least it would satisfy his hunger.

Hands outstretched, he felt his way to the wide doorway and groped for the rope. His fingers swept across the bristly fibers, and he caught hold. He scuffed toward the house, his heels dragging and stirring up dust that tickled his nose. Caught up listening to his own feet, he almost missed the sound of horse hoofs clop-clopping. He stopped, lifting his head and keying in on the sound.

The clops, slow and steady, grew louder.

Drew near. One horse, not two. And no wagon wheels crunched. So it wasn't Mr. Jonnson coming back. Probably someone wanting to buy lumber. Tommy gripped the rope and waited until the horse and its rider stopped. Then he called out, "Mr. Jonnson's not here right now. He went into town."

"Already know that, Tommy-boy."

Goose flesh broke out across his arms. Not again!

Dresden's throaty chuckle rolled. "Your ears don't ever hear wrongly, do they?"

A saddle squeaked, and a quick *thump, thump* spoke of boots hitting the ground. Tommy clutched the rope with both hands, his heart pounding, as footsteps neared. Then two fists grabbed his shirt front and yanked him to his toes. The odor of stale cigar smoke filled his nose. "You an' me's gonna have us a talk, boy. An' those sharp ears o' yours are gonna listen real good to what I say."

Chapter 34

"Mr. Dunnigan, I appreciate your taking the time to escort me back to Brambleville." Christina placed both hands against the green velvet seat to hold herself upright as the train rocked along the track. The man sat opposite her, his hat on the brass rack above his head swaying with the motion of the car. "But I regret how it must inconvenience you."

Maxwell Dunnigan smiled and linked his hands over his stomach. "I assure you, Miss Willems, after all you've done for my wife and me this past week — ascertaining the children are settling well into their new home — we owe you a tremendous debt of gratitude."

Christina lowered her head. She'd never confess how much it hurt to leave the children and Rose behind. Yet days of being a guest of the Dunnigans proved to her how fortunate the twins were. The Dunnigans' beautiful home in one of Kansas City's most prestigious housing districts offered every amenity, and the children's rooms were bright, cheerful places for both play and rest. Maxwell and Parmelia Dunnigan were warm, kindhearted people. She couldn't have handpicked a more loving couple or a better home for Joe and Florie if she'd searched a dozen years.

Last night, as she'd visited with Rose in the lovely cranberry-and-beige room across the hall from the children's rooms, Rose had said, "Hasn't God smiled upon the twins and me, giving us such a wondrous place to live? It's a gift, Christina — a true gift." Christina determined to focus on how Rose and the children were being gifted rather than her own heartache at bidding them farewell.

Lifting her face, she offered Mr. Dunnigan a weak smile. "You and Mrs. Dunnigan have more than paid your debt by providing me with two new dresses." Parmelia Dunnigan had taken Christina and Rose shopping, insisting a lengthy stay required a more extensive wardrobe. She smoothed her hand across the silk skirt of saffron yellow. The fabric shimmered, tones of deeper ocher emerging and disappearing with her touch. Christina had never owned such a high-quality frock. "Not to mention your willingness to explain to Louisa why Rose chose to remain in Kansas City. She certainly won't scold you, although I know she'll miss Rose terribly."

Christina could still scarcely believe Rose had chosen staying with the twins over returning to Louisa. The two women were so devoted to each other, having lived together since their husbands had been killed more than four years ago when lightning struck the ground near them. But Rose insisted that Louisa would be free to explore new options — perhaps even a new relationship — if she didn't feel obligated to provide companionship for her.

Mr. Dunnigan threw back his head and laughed. "Oh, that Mrs. McLain. She adds an element of lightheartedness to the household, which will benefit all of us, I'm sure. Being new at parenting, Parmelia and I might attempt to be too strict and stodgy with the children. Mrs. McLain's interaction with them — her mild reproofs as well as her demonstrativeness — has been a wonderful example for us to follow. I believe she is going to be the mortar binding us together as a family."

"Perhaps you're right." Christina gazed out the window and watched the passing countryside. Every mile brought her closer to Brambleville. Within her breast two opposite desires warred. Eagerness to resume her position at the poor farm, to be needed again, battled against a reluctance to look at the rooms previously occupied by Alice and her children, Wes, the Schwartzes, the twins, Cora, and Rose. Those spaces would be glaringly empty. How would she bear it? She'd been gone less than a week, but so much had changed. It seemed as though years had passed.

Mr. Dunnigan folded his hands in his lap. "Miss Willems, tell me about where Joe and Florie had been living. I'd like to understand more about their life before they came to Topeka."

Christina swallowed the lump of sadness rising in the back of her throat and honored the man's request. Talking about the beautiful house and grounds of the Brambleville Asylum for the Poor — as well as her father, the other residents, and their family-like manner of sharing the duties — increased her fervor to return. Reluctance slipped away, despite knowing how different it would be with so many of her former charges now in other places. But new people would arrive, new opportunities to serve would open. A sheen of perspiration cooled her brow. Once she was needed again, she would be fine.

When she finished, Mr. Dunnigan leaned forward and rested his elbows on his knees. "I admire you, Miss Willems. You've dedicated your life to assisting others. I find it quite commendable."

Embarrassment brought a rush of heat to Christina's face. "To be honest, it's all I know, Mr. Dunnigan. My parents set an excellent example of service for me to follow. I . . . I am aimless without a means of ministry." Fear gripped her. If she wasn't able to convince the mission board to reinstate her as a director, what would she do? Where would she go?

His brows came together briefly in a mild scowl. "Mrs. McLain intimated you'd encountered some difficulties recently, which led to the twins being transferred to Topeka. Please don't consider me forward, but I'd like to know what those difficulties are. Maybe there's something I can do."

"Well, I don't know what you want me to do." Sheriff Garner plopped into his squeaky barrel-shaped chair and squinted at Levi. "Nobody saw the thief. So right now everything's speculation."

Levi leaned one hand on the edge of the

431

desk. He'd spent nearly an hour hunting for the sheriff, building up a full head of steam as he searched. Now that he had the man cornered, nothing he said seemed to impact him at all. "But Hamilton Dresden has the watch in hand. How could he have it if he didn't take it?"

"Could've bought it from Miss Willems, same way Creeger did."

"But Miss Willems didn't have it anymore!"

"We don't know that, do we?" The sheriff rocked in his chair, the steady *squeak, squeak* of loose joints echoing against the rock walls. "According to the minister, Miss Willems wasn't in church Sunday morning like she usually is."

Levi huffed out a mighty breath. "Because she'd been sitting on a wagon seat, talking with me!"

"You already told me so." The sheriff spoke patiently, but his eyes showed frustration. "But you also said you couldn't account for her whereabouts late mornin' or afternoon."

As the sheriff continued, Levi clamped his teeth together so hard his jaw ached.

"According to Louisa McLain, Miss Willems claimed she'd only be gone a day or two. But instead she's stayed away nearly a week with only a half-hearted explanation as to where she is or what she's doing. You and I both know travel takes money. Oh, now, Creeger said he paid her ten dollars for that watch, but a person would use up ten dollars pretty quick paying for train fare, meals, and a hotel room — especially for two people, since she toted off one of the poor farm ladies with her. So where'd Miss Willems get the money for a long trip? Nobody can answer that question for me."

Levi threw his arms wide. "Miss Willems could tell you."

"Except Miss Willems isn't here, is she?" The sheriff rose and faced off with Levi. "Listen, Jonnson, don't it seem at least a little likely? The house where she was livin' got damaged, and she needed money so she could start a new life somewhere else. Her pa's watch didn't fetch enough from Creeger, so she sneaked into the mercantile — a six-year-old could've busted the flimsy lock on the store's back door — and took the timepiece along with Creeger's money, then sold the watch to Dresden for more money before skedaddling."

Indignation filled Levi's chest. "You can't honestly think Miss Willems would do such a thing. A woman who's spent her whole life taking care of other people suddenly turns selfish enough to steal from friends?"

Sheriff Garner shrugged. "Desperation can change a person. I've heard plenty of whispers about how her attempts to get that poor farm running again have all failed. She's got no family holding her here, so why wouldn't she just pack up and go? It makes sense, doesn't it?"

Levi had seen her with Tommy, with Cora and Wes, with the other poor farm residents. *They* were her family. He growled, "It doesn't make sense to me."

"Doesn't have to make sense to you. You're not the law." The sheriff rounded the desk and moved to the door. He opened it, a clear invitation for Levi to depart. "As I said earlier, it's all speculation right now even though circumstantially things don't look too good for Miss Willems. But I won't be filing any charges until I've had a chance to speak to her. Assuming, of course, she ever shows her face in Brambleville again."

Levi bit his tongue to hold back words of fury. She'd be back. She wouldn't abandon Tommy and the others. And he'd cheer when she proved the sheriff and the entire town wrong.

Tommy hunkered beneath the window with his knees pulled tight under his chin. He'd folded his arms across his chest. Sweat poured down his forehead and stung his eyes. Even so, he shivered uncontrollably. Would Dresden come back? Threaten him some more? *"Just do as I tell you, boy, an' nobody'll get hurt."* The man's voice rang in his head, blocking out all other sound. He didn't believe Dresden. Not for a minute. Anybody who'd lie to blame somebody else for his wrongs wouldn't mind lying about hurting people either. He'd be back. And next time he might not just talk.

When would Mr. Jonnson come home? Tommy's anger with the man fled in light of his fear. He didn't want to be alone. For all he knew, Dresden was sneaking around outside right now. More of his vile words paraded through Tommy's memory.

"Cross me, Tommy-boy, an' I'll burn down the mill. I didn't mean to start that fire at the poor farm. Lantern just slipped outta my hand. But fires — they cause a lot o' damage. Won't bother me none to start one out here. That what you want, boy?"

Tommy covered his ears with both hands, pulling into an even tighter ball. But Dresden's voice wouldn't go away.

"The mercantile owner's gonna want this back. An' you're gonna give it to him. But make sure you tell folks that Miss Willems

gave you this money to keep for her." In Tommy's pocket a wad of bills burned like a fire. *"And don't you tell nobody I was here. You hear me, Tommy-boy? You hear me?"*

"Do you hear me?"

Tommy jerked, a live voice chasing the one in his head into hiding. He pressed his palms to the floor and looked around, frantic. "Who — who's there?"

A hand touched his shoulder, and Tommy screeched in alarm. He scrambled sideways, but strong hands curled around his ribs and hoisted him to his feet. He flailed, hollering, but the hands held firm.

"Tommy, what ails you? It's me!"

The voice penetrated his fog of fear. He stopped fighting, his breath coming in heaves. "M-Mr. Jonnson?"

"That's right." The hands let go of his ribs and moved to his upper arms, holding him steady. "I didn't mean to scare you. I thought you were asleep."

"I . . . I . . ." Tommy gulped twice. *"Don't you tell nobody I was here. I'll burn down the mill."* "I must've dozed off. Dreamin'."

A soft chuckle rumbled. So different from Dresden's. "Must've been a bad dream. You wanna talk about it?"

"No!" Tommy wriggled loose from Mr. Jonnson's hold and stumbled forward,

436

hands pawing the air. He located the back of a chair, pulled it away from the table, and slid into the seat. Leaning on the table, he willed his rapidly beating heart to calm.

"I'm sorry I was gone so long." Mr. Jonnson moved around the room, and little bumps and thumps accompanied him — putting his purchases away. "I ran an extra errand. It took longer than I expected." A light slam told Tommy he'd closed the cupboard. "I bet you're ready for some lunch."

Tommy wasn't hungry. He'd had the hunger scared right out of him. But he nodded anyway.

"Well, here. Munch on this while I put some sandwiches together."

Something brushed his palm — fragrant licorice. Tommy's favorite candy. "Th-thanks." He held the string in his fist, but he didn't lift it to his mouth.

"I got you something else, too, but I'll wait 'til after lunch to give it to you."

"A-all right."

A long silence fell. Tommy twitched in the chair, gripping the licorice, listening for any sound or scent that might tell him Dresden lurked outside somewhere.

"Tommy?" Mr. Jonnson's voice boomed next to Tommy's ear. Then his hand brushed across Tommy's forehead. "You're white as a sheet. And your hair's wet. You're not sick, are you?"

Tommy licked his dry lips. He had to act normal. If Dresden was watching — if Dresden was listening — and Tommy let slip anything he'd said, he'd make good on his threats. "No, sir." His voice squeaked. He cleared his throat and tried again. "No. I'm fine."

"Well then, eat your candy while I fix lunch. It won't be long."

Tommy chomped off a bite, but he found no pleasure in the sharp taste. He chewed. Swallowed. Busy sounds came from the work station, which faced the corner of the kitchen. Tommy took a chance that Mr. Jonnson wouldn't see and shoved the licorice deep into his pants pocket. His fingers encountered the bills Dresden had given him, and he started to shake.

Within seconds Mr. Jonnson was at his side again, placing his hand on Tommy's head. "No fever, but you sure aren't acting like yourself."

Tommy pushed Mr. Jonnson's hand away from his head and stood. He squared his shoulders and stuck out his chin, determined to bring his trembling under control. "I'm fine, I told you. Just groggy from . . .

from fallin' asleep like I did." He tipped his head. Was Dresden hearing him? He raised his voice. "Nothing's wrong."

The clock across the room ticked the seconds, but no other sound intruded. Tommy released a light sigh of relief. Surely Dresden had gone. He wouldn't risk being caught by Mr. Jonnson. He was safe now. Safe.

He said, "Except I'm hungry."

Mr. Jonnson laughed. A short, not-too-sure laugh. "All right. We'll have us our sandwiches. And then —"

"Then tomorrow I wanna go to church," he blurted out. He needed to talk to somebody. Cora. Or maybe Wes. Somebody who could keep a secret. And they'd be at church.

"I thought you didn't want anything more to do with church." Mr. Jonnson sounded plenty confused.

Tommy scrambled for a sound reason to go. "Well, but you, um, you told me people don't come close to me 'cause they're scared."

"Yes, I told you that."

Would Mr. Jonnson figure out Tommy's strange behavior was caused by a mighty fear? He hurried on. "So I shouldn't hold it against them, right? Miss Willems wants me to go, so . . ." He ran out of reasons.

Once more Mr. Jonnson's hand found Tommy's head. He tousled Tommy's hair — the gesture so kind and loving, tears spurted into Tommy's eyes. He sniffed hard.

"All right, Tommy. I'll take you to town tomorrow."

Relief sagged his knees, and he sank back into the chair. "Good. Good. Thanks." Tomorrow he'd get Cora's or Wes's advice. Together they'd figure out what to do about Dresden. There wasn't any reason to be scared anymore. So why did his hands keep shaking?

Chapter 35

The train rumbled into the Brambleville station early afternoon. The moment the conductor gave permission to disembark, Christina reached for her bag, but Mr. Dunnigan took it as well as his own small valise. She smiled her thanks and preceded him from the passenger car to the boardwalk.

Beneath the cloudless sky, he placed the bags on the walkway and removed his gold watch from his vest pocket. A flick of his thumb opened the cover, and he gave the face a quick look before clicking it closed and returning it to the little pocket. Watching his simple motions, Christina experienced a deep ache in her breast. How many times had she seen Papa check the time in the very same way? Loneliness for her father, and for his watch, welled in her breast.

She swallowed a wave of sadness and forced a cheery tone. "Do you want to arrange for your return trip while we're here?"

Mr. Dunnigan stooped to lift the bags again. "I prefer to get settled in the hotel first. I'm uncertain as yet when I'll return to Kansas City."

Christina sent him a curious look. "You have business in Brambleville?"

A secretive smile toyed beneath his mustache. "Perhaps."

She longed to question him, but eagerness to see how Louisa had fared in her absence overrode curiosity. "Very well. The hotel is this way."

As they walked toward the hotel, Saturday shoppers paused with crates or packages in hand to stare at Christina. Her face flamed. She could well imagine what they must be thinking — Miss Christina Willems being squired down Main Street by an unfamiliar gentleman. The gossip wheels would spin madly until she had an opportunity to explain Mr. Dunnigan's presence in town. She smiled and nodded greetings, feigning an ease she didn't feel, and her discomfort rose with each blank stare or frenzied whisper.

At the hotel entry Mr. Dunnigan returned Christina's bag to her. "I see a livery farther up the street. Do they rent conveyances?"

Christina nodded. "They have a nice four-seat buggy often used to transport grieving folks to the cemetery east of town."

To her surprise he laughed. "Ah. Well, I'm sure it's quite nice. But I was thinking more along the lines of a sturdier vehicle. A buckboard or something similar to a good Missouri Springfield wagon."

"You'd be more than welcome to make use of the poor farm wagon," Christina offered. "Our wagon and horses are at the livery. Wes, a young man who resided at the poor farm, is employed there. If you tell him I sent you, he'll hitch the horses for you and will probably even offer to drive you wherever you'd like to go." Curiosity rose above propriety. "What is it you wish to explore?"

"Spoken in true female fashion." He laughed lightly, his eyes twinkling. "You remind me of Parmelia, always wanting to know what I'm up to. But being left out of an occasional secret does not harm, and it might eliminate disappointment should things not work the way one plans." His cryptic reply confused Christina further. "I'll go in and get settled now. But as soon as I've secured a room and put my bag away, I'll be ready to visit Mrs. McLain's sister-in-law. Where will I find you?"

"I stay at the Beasley Boardinghouse, on

the corner of Main and Maple."

He nodded. "Very well — Main and Maple. Until later, then. Thank you again for your kind assistance."

"You're welcome. Good day, Mr. Dunnigan." She waited until he entered the hotel. Then she turned to hurry to the boarding-house. Louisa would surely be relieved to be set free from her duties in Mrs. Beasley's kitchen. She'd only taken two steps when someone blocked her pathway. She let out a little cry of surprise, then broke into a relieved smile. "Sheriff Garner . . . Good afternoon."

"Good afternoon, Miss Willems. Been watching for you." His somber expression chased away her momentary relief.

"For me?" Her pulse scampered into a frenzied beat. Had something happened to one of the poor farm residents in her absence? She shouldn't have stayed away so long! "What's wrong?"

"Plenty." He took her elbow. "Come with me."

Her bag fell from her hand. "But —"

Mr. Dunnigan strode up on her other side, his expression stern. "What's the meaning of this?"

The sheriff scowled at Mr. Dunnigan. "This don't concern you, mister, so step

444

aside and let me do my duty."

Mr. Dunnigan bristled. "And is your 'duty' accosting women on the streets?"

Sheriff Garner's face turned nearly purple. "My duty's questioning possible thieves, and that's just what I'm fixing to do."

Christina's jaw dropped. "Thievery?"

Mr. Dunnigan held out one hand toward the sheriff. "See here, sir. I —"

The sheriff pointed at Mr. Dunnigan. "Mister, I told you to step aside." He began herding Christina in the direction of his office.

Christina looked helplessly over her shoulder at Mr. Dunnigan.

He moved to the edge of the boardwalk, uncertainty on his face. Then he picked up her discarded bag and disappeared into the hotel. Fear rose in Christina's breast. What would happen to her now?

As Levi approached the churchyard Sunday morning, a tingle of awareness rolled across his scalp. Something was awry. People stood in little clusters, all talking excitedly in hushed tones. Tommy must have sensed it, too, because he sat up straight and bobbed his head as if testing the air.

The boy groped for the brim of the brown suede hat Levi had purchased and tugged it low on his brow. Then he hunched his shoulders, slouching forward and burying his chin in the open collar of his jacket. Tommy's odd behavior increased Levi's feelings of impending doom. Something had the boy spooked, but he'd fallen into another sullen silence and refused to talk. Levi hoped some of his poor farm friends might be able to get through to him.

He tugged the reins to halt the horses, then propped his foot against the brake to keep the wagon from rolling forward. "All right, Tommy. Here we are, so —"

"You comin', too?"

The abrupt question took Levi by surprise. Tommy knew Levi didn't attend service, so why would he ask such a thing? "I'll wait for you at the livery, same as always."

Tommy popped out of his hiding pose and shook his head wildly. "Huh-uh. You come, too."

Levi's stomach clenched. Clearly the boy was troubled. He wanted to help Tommy, but sit side by side with the same kind of folks who'd ridiculed his family, rejected his father, and held him and Mor accountable for Far's death? "Tommy, I —"

"Mr. Jonnson!" Mrs. Creeger, with Cora in tow, scurried to the side of the wagon.

"Oh, I'm so glad to see you." She peered up at him the way a drowning man would view a rescuing hand — concern and relief mingling together.

Levi gestured to the groups gathered on the grassy churchyard. "What's got everyone so excited?"

Her lips pursed. "Shameful, isn't it? Jay took one look and went to fetch the reverend to talk sense into them. They're all blathering about the sheriff arresting Miss Willems."

Tommy let out a frightened gasp, and Levi jammed the brake's lock into place with an angry thrust. Forcing a calm tone for Tommy's sake, he looked at Cora. "Take Tommy, will you?" He waited until the young woman caught Tommy's hands and helped him down from the seat. Then he hopped down and moved close to Mrs. Creeger. "Tell me everything." Cora led Tommy to the shade of the towering maples growing at the edge of the churchyard, away from the wagon and from the busybody groups. It wouldn't do the boy any good to hear what folks were saying — that Miss Willems showed up in a fancy gown and paraded up Main Street with some dandy like she owned the town. Cora wanted to defend Miss Willems, but fear held her silent. Once these folks discovered her sin, they would surely turn on her the same way they were now turning on Miss Willems.

Beside her, Tommy crossed his arms over his chest and shivered. Cora put her arm around him. "You doin' all right, Tommy?"

He shook his head. He wore a new hat — one just like Mr. Jonnson's. He looked handsome in it and very grown up. But he sounded like a little boy, whispering so soft Cora had to strain to hear him. "Gotta talk to you. About somethin' real important."

She leaned down, putting her ear close to his mouth. "What is it? Go ahead an' tell me."

Instead of speaking, Tommy slowly pushed his hand into his britches pocket. When he pulled it out, he held a clump of rumpled bills. One fell from his fingers and fluttered to the grass at their feet.

Cora's jaw dropped, and she quickly snatched up the bill. "Tommy!" In her surprise she forgot to keep her voice soft. "Where'd you get this money?"

Tommy clutched the wad of bills to his chest and rocked nervously in place. "Shh!"

But it was too late. Some folks close by had already turned to stare. Another ripple spread across the grounds, and more people turned their heads, looking at Cora and

Tommy. She wrapped her arms around him, shielding him and the money with her body.

A man separated himself from one small group and ambled toward Cora. She recognized Hamilton Dresden even though he'd gotten a fresh haircut and wore a different suit — a gray pinstripe in the latest style. But his leering grin hadn't changed. She gritted her teeth.

"What'cha got there, boy?" Dresden asked.

Tommy burrowed his face into the curve of Cora's shoulder. She tightened her grip on him. "Leave him be, Hamilton Dresden. Tommy's no concern of yours."

As if he were a politician making a speech, Dresden swept his arm around, indicating the crowd that was surging toward them. "These fine folks might think otherwise." He reached for Tommy's shoulder. "C'mere, boy. Show these people what you got there."

Levi Jonnson strode across the grounds and pushed Dresden's hand aside. "Leave the boy alone."

Dresden backed up, hands upraised. "Easy now. Not lookin' for a tussle. Just tryin' to get at the truth."

"You wouldn't recognize the truth if you tripped over it."

Cora secretly cheered Mr. Jonnson's bold

statement. But Dresden only smiled in an insolent way and slipped his watch — Miss Willems's silver watch — from his pocket and flicked the case open, closed, open, closed. He said in a sly tone, "I ain't the one tryin' to hide somethin'." He nodded in Tommy's direction. "Why don'tcha see what the boy's got there if you're so interested in the truth?"

The muscles in Mr. Jonnson's jaw clenched, but he turned his back on Dresden. Very gently he took hold of Tommy's arm. "Tommy?"

Tommy's whole body turned stiff. Cora instinctively pulled him tighter against her. Somehow Tommy's fear — Tommy's secret — got tangled with her own. She cried, "Can't you just leave us be?"

Mr. Jonnson's eyes looked sad, but he shook his head. "I need to see. Tommy . . ."

Tommy's tears formed a wet splotch on Cora's dress. Ma Creeger scurried over and put her arm around Cora's waist. She whispered in Cora's ear, "Let go, Cora. It'll be all right. Just let go."

Let go . . . Let go . . . Cora lost all strength. Her arms dropped away from Tommy, and Mr. Jonnson turned the boy to face him. He caught Tommy's hands and pulled them from his chest. Green bills stuck out of

Tommy's fingers like clumps of weeds at the edge of the road.

A gasp rolled across the churchyard. Dresden leaned close, his grin triumphant. "Now ask him where he got that money, Jonnson, since you're so set on knowin'." Dresden poked Tommy on the shoulder, and his voice turned hard. "Tell 'im, boy. Tell 'im."

CHAPTER 36

Tommy's breath came in short little spurts. He felt dizzy. Mr. Jonnson's hand on his arm kept him from falling, but it also kept him from escaping. He wanted to escape. He didn't want to say what Mr. Dresden had told him to say. But the man stood right there. Tommy smelled the cigar smoke that always clung to his clothes, the same odor he'd smelled the night the poor farm burned. He'd wanted to get help from Cora, but she'd gone and hollered out, and now everybody waited. He sensed them surrounding him the way he'd once seen a pack of wild dogs surround a lame lamb. Then, he'd cried out of sympathy for the poor creature. Now, the tears rolling warm down his cheeks were for himself.

"I . . . The money — it . . ." *"I'll burn down the mill."* Tommy shrank against Mr. Jonnson.

Dresden spoke again. "That's the money

took from the mercantile. Am I right, boy?"

Tommy bit his lip and managed to nod in a jerky manner.

Mutters and gasps filled Tommy's ears. Firm, familiar hands gripped his shoulders. Mr. Jonnson's warm breath, scented from this morning's pancakes and maple syrup, brushed his face. "Are you sure the money's from the mercantile, Tommy?"

Tommy pulled in a shuddering breath. He told the truth. "Yes, sir."

"Take the boy to the sheriff." Dresden's booming voice carried over all the other angry murmurs.

Suddenly a new voice intruded. "Folks, come inside the church now." Reverend Huntley, Tommy realized. Would the people listen to the minister, or would they rather listen to Dresden? If they'd go inside the church, like Reverend Huntley asked — if they'd stop thinking bad things about Miss Willems — then maybe they weren't really hypocrites after all. Tommy needed to believe something good existed somewhere. He held his breath, waiting, hoping.

It seemed hours passed, but then feet shuffled. Voices still murmured, but the murmurs grew softer. Soles of shoes pat-patted on steps — the steps leading to the church. Mr. Jonnson let go of Tommy's shoulders, but he curled his hand lightly around Tommy's neck instead. Tommy stayed still, holding the money Mr. Dresden had given him and waiting until all the noises from the crowd's leave-taking faded away.

He sniffed the air, searching for a whiff of cigar smoke. Had Dresden gone inside, too?

"Tommy . . ."

Over the past weeks there'd been plenty of times Tommy thought Mr. Jonnson sounded sad. But he'd never sounded sadder than he did just then. "Y-yes, sir?"

"We'd better take that money to the sheriff."

Someone cackled. Chills broke across Tommy's body. Dresden was still there. The man spoke. "That's exactly what you oughta do, Jonnson. Hand it over to the sheriff. Let the boy tell where it came from. He'll do what's right. Won'tcha, boy?"

Tommy stiffened, hugging the money tight to his chest.

Mr. Jonnson gave Tommy a little push. "Come on."

Tommy stumbled alongside Mr. Jonnson with Mr. Dresden's cackling laugh following them. Mr. Jonnson boosted him into the wagon, then climbed up, too, the seat shifting under his weight. Not until the wagon had rolled forward a good distance did Tommy find the courage to ask the question tormenting him.

"Mr. Jonnson, if the mercantile people get their money back, will the sheriff let Miss Willems go?"

"Well, Tommy, that's not quite the way things work." Mr. Jonnson's voice sounded tight, like something was stuck in his throat. "You see, when people do something wrong — like stealing — they have to be punished for it."

Tommy's heart thudded so hard he worried Mr. Jonnson would hear it. "Punished . . . how?"

"They usually have to go to jail, Tommy."

Miss Willems in jail? How could he say what Dresden wanted him to if it meant Miss Willems might go to jail? But if he didn't say what Dresden had told him, the man would burn down Mr. Jonnson's mill. Tommy swallowed.

"Whoa . . ." The wagon stopped. The brake was set. A hand clamped over Tommy's knee. Firm. Comforting. Steadying. "Here we are."

Tommy swallowed again, but the sour taste in his mouth — the taste of fear and sorrow — didn't go away.

"Let's go talk to the sheriff, Tommy. Then

—" Mr. Jonnson's voice caught in a funny way. The same way Tommy's did when he was trying not to cry.

Mr. Jonnson helped Tommy down, then took his elbow and led him onto the boardwalk. As Tommy moved slowly beside Mr. Jonnson, he suddenly realized why the man was so sad. He believed Miss Willems had stolen the money. Why was everything so mixed up?

Reverend Huntley preached a fiery sermon. Cora found herself shivering as he pounded his Bible and worked his way through the Ten Commandments. She'd never seen the man so overwrought. Even though she didn't want to listen — he scared her with his stern frown and thundering voice — she couldn't turn her attention elsewhere.

"These aren't my words, brothers and sisters. These are given to us by God Almighty Himself, and He says, 'Thou shalt not bear false witness against thy neighbour.' Lies! Idle gossip! Speculation! God is a God of truth, and He calls us to defend and promote truth." His eyes roved across the congregation. Cora released a little gasp as his gaze found her.

"Promote truth . . ." Did he know? Oblivious to the minister's continuing admonish-

ments, she leaped up and scrambled over the Creegers' feet. Ma Creeger reached for her, but Cora pushed her hands away and stumbled up the side aisle and out onto the grassy churchyard. Her chest heaving, she slung her arms around the trunk of the same maple that had shaded Tommy and her earlier and gave vent to the deep fear and sorrow and guilt weighting her down.

"Cora, Cora . . ." Ma Creeger's tender voice carried over the sounds of Cora's anguish. She took hold of Cora's shoulders and pulled her into an embrace. Stroking Cora's hair, she soothed, "Shh, now, shh. Everything's going to be all right. You'll see. The truth'll come out, as truth always will. And everything will be fine."

Cora shook her head, hiccups jolting her shoulders. Once the truth came out, her life would be ruined. "N-no it won't. It won't ever be fine again."

"Of course it will. All these rumors about Miss Willems —"

Cora jerked free. "Miss Willems?"

Ma Creeger's brow crunched into a confused frown. "Why, yes. Isn't that what's got you all upset — what people have been saying about Miss Willems?"

Cora's tears continued to roll down her cheeks as she let out a wild laugh. "I wasn't cryin' about Miss Willems. I was cryin' 'cause —" *"Promote truth."* Cora cupped her swollen belly, hidden by the full layers of her blue-striped skirt. She gulped twice, gathering strength, and then blurted, "I was cryin' over me, Ma Creeger. 'Cause I went an' got myself in a family way, an' I don't know what to do."

She held her breath, waiting for Ma Creeger to purse her face in distaste. To rail at Cora for her stupidity and shamefulness, the way Ma had. To storm away and not look back. But instead a soft look — a look of such deep tenderness it brought a new rush of tears — crossed Ma Creeger's face. She opened her arms, and Cora fell against her, weeping anew.

Somehow Ma Creeger managed to hold on to Cora and walk at the same time, because the next thing she knew, Ma Creeger was settling her into one of the rocking chairs at the mercantile. She fetched a handful of new cotton handkerchiefs from the little box on the shelf and pressed them into Cora's hand. Then she sat in the other rocker, put one hand on Cora's knee, and waited until Cora ran out of tears. It took a good long while. Cora hadn't known a person could hold so many tears.

When she'd finally run dry and cleaned

up her face by using three of the handkerchiefs — it seemed a shame to sully such
bright, crisp squares of white — Cora wadded the sodden cotton in her lap and
sighed. Head low, she rasped, "I'm sorry,
Ma Creeger, for not telling you the truth
sooner. An' I'll understand if you send me
away. But would'ja . . ." — she braved a
quick glance at the woman's face —
"would'ja wait 'til after I have my babe?
'Cause I wanna give it to you an' Pa Creeger. For you to raise."

Ma Creeger slipped out of the rocker and
knelt before Cora. She cupped Cora's chin
in her hand and lifted her face. Cora's sore
eyes stung with new tears at what she saw
in Ma Creeger's eyes. Something she'd
never seen aimed at her before. Love. "A
child is a gift. You're growing life inside your
womb, Cora." She spoke so soft and sweet
that Cora's chest ached. "Do you really
want to give it away?"

Cora gripped the mound where life blos-
somed. Something pushed against her palm
— a little hand or a foot? Longing washed
through her to nurture this babe, to raise it
with the love she'd always wanted from her
own mother. She cried, "But I have to!"

"Why?"

" 'Cause I don't know how to be a ma.

An' I got nobody to help me."

Ma Creeger gave Cora's cheek a gentle pat and then took her hand. "Of course you do. God will help you."

Cora hung her head. "God doesn't want nothin' to do with the likes of me."

"Why?"

Cora gawked at the woman. "You know what I done! I laid with a man, an' we weren't wed. Now I'm carryin' a babe who's gonna grow up bein' called every kind o' bad name. I shamed my ma, an' I made a mess of my life an' this poor little baby's life, too. I can't fix none of that!"

Ma Creeger smiled. "You still haven't answered my question, Cora. Why wouldn't God want anything to do with you?"

Cora pushed out of the chair and paced back and forth, frustration making her restless. "I'm dirty, don'tcha see? When the preacher talks about sinners, he might as well be pointin' right at me!"

Ma Creeger rose and followed Cora. "When the preacher talks about sinners, he's talking about every person sitting on a bench in the church. He's even talking about himself." She plucked a Bible from the shelf of books and flipped through several pages. Then she turned it toward Cora. "Look here. See what it says in

460

Romans, the third chapter? 'As it is written, There is none righteous, no, not one.' We're all sinners — every last person ever born."

"Not you."

"Of course I am."

"Not as bad as me."

"Of course I am."

"But you" — Cora gulped — "you didn't do . . . what I done."

Ma Creeger let out a soft chuckle. "Maybe not, but in God's eyes sin is sin. My getting impatient with a customer, or repeating a word of gossip, or turning my back on a person in need — none of those things honors God. That makes them sins."

Cora raised her chin. "None o' those're as bad as mine . . ."

A tender smile crossed Ma Creeger's face. "What you have to understand, Cora, is what it says here in verse twenty-three: 'For all have sinned, and come short of the glory of God.' *All.* Every last one of us is in need of a Savior. And when we accept Jesus as our Savior — when we ask Him to take away our sins — He throws that sin so far away it can never be found again. Then when He looks at us, He doesn't see the ugly stain of the things we've done wrong. He sees His child — holy and spotless and blameless."

Cora hugged herself. If only it were true! "I'll never be blameless. Not as long as folks know I had a baby without bein' wed. As far as folks are concerned, I ain't worth nothin'."

Ma Creeger set the Bible aside and stood staring at it, her shoulders slumped forward as if someone had piled bricks on her back. "Unfortunately, some people will treat you unkindly because of what you did. Some people like to make themselves feel better by pointing at others who've made mistakes. Some people forget how God forgives and try to sit in judgment. As long as we're living among people, there'll be unpleasantness, because people aren't perfect."

She straightened and faced Cora. "But you can't let people's behavior convince you you're not worth anything. That's wrong. You're worth so much that God sent His very Son into this world to die on a cross — the most shameful way a person could die — and take on every sin committed by every man and woman born before, during, and after Jesus's time here on earth. That means your sins, too. But He can't take them unless you're willing to let go of them." Ma Creeger took Cora's hands. Tears glittered in her eyes. "Are you willing, Cora?"

Cora filled her lungs with a shaky breath.

"Will askin' Jesus to take on my sins make this baby go away?"

Very slowly Ma Creeger shook her head. "No. Sin carries consequences, and the choice you made to lie with a man can't be erased. But the shameful way you feel? He can send that far away, Cora, and He'll remember it no more."

Cora so much wanted to be free of the burden of shame. It sat like a boulder on her heart. Could Jesus really take it away and leave her all fresh and clean as if she'd never let Emmet Wade touch her? She wanted to know. She reached for Ma Creeger's hands. "I wanna try. Will you tell me how?"

CHAPTER 37

After keeping Christina holed up in the little cell at the back of his office for two days — he wouldn't risk having her leave town again while he investigated her claims of innocence — Sheriff Garner let her go. But even as she stepped onto the boardwalk, he cautioned, "We still have to get this mess ironed out. I might not have enough evidence to bring in a judge yet, but that doesn't mean I won't. I've told Dresden to stay put in town until I have a chance to get to the truth, and I'm telling you the same thing." His brows descended, giving him an ominous appearance. "Running will look pretty suspicious, so don't leave town again."

She brushed the cobwebs from the skirt of the beautiful saffron silk dress Mrs. Dunnigan had given her and lifted her chin. "I have no reason to run, Sheriff, as I've done nothing wrong."

He gave a mirthless chuckle, shaking his head. "So says that fancy schmancy lawyer who demanded I either show solid proof or let you go."

Christina's heart skipped a beat. Not once had she been allowed a visitor. The sheriff claimed he couldn't have her concocting tales with somebody. Who would have hired a lawyer to speak on her behalf? She started to ask, but the sheriff sighed and continued.

"To be frank, Miss Willems, I'd rather think you didn't steal that money and watch from the Creegers. Your pa had a good reputation, and I don't want to see it tarnished. But I just can't ignore all the strange coincidences. A poor farm burned, money missing, you gone from town for a long time, and —" He stopped abruptly, leaving Christina wondering what he'd intended to say. He finished gruffly, "I gotta investigate. It's my job."

Christina's chest tightened in protest, but respect for his position held her silent.

He waved his hand as if dismissing her. "Well, do as I say, then. I'll get to the truth eventually." He closed the door behind her.

She stood on the boardwalk, blinking against the bright sunlight and breathing in great drafts of the fresh air. Even though the breeze stirred dust, the scent was heavenly after her days of breathing the stale air in the damp, closed cell. Ah, freedom . . . She would never take it lightly again.

Lifting the hem of her rumpled, dirty skirt, she crossed the street and went directly to the boardinghouse. Just as she'd always done, she followed the rock pathway to the back door and reached for the door handle. But after her lengthy time away, she suddenly felt self-conscious about walking in without notice. So she tapped lightly on the glass with her knuckles.

Within seconds the door swung wide, and Louisa stood in the opening and gaped at her. "Why, Christina! What . . . When . . ."

Christina stepped forward and embraced the woman, tears stinging. "The sheriff let me go. He said he didn't have enough evidence to hold me."

"Well, of course he didn't." Louisa patted Christina's back and then released her to close the door. The patchwork cat padded across the floor and wound itself around Christina's ankles, purring loudly. Louisa flapped her hands at the animal. "You little pest, skedaddle before you trip her! Here . . ." The cat darted for the pantry, and Louisa guided Christina to the worktable. She pulled out a chair and gave Christina a little push. "You just sit right there and let me pour you a cup of tea. After your ordeal you can surely use one."

She bustled to the stove and shifted the teakettle to the back burner, jabbering on as she prepared a cup with tea leaves. "The sheriff made me show him that beautiful dress from your satchel, but I told him just what the man from Kansas City — Mr. Dunnigan — told me." Raising one brow, she nodded at Christina. "Right nice of his wife to buy it for you. Did she buy the one you're wearing, too?"

Christina smoothed the skirt. "Yes. The Dunnigans are kind people. They'll be wonderful parents for Joe and Florie."

Leaving the cup behind, Louisa hurried to the table and sank into the opposite chair. "I could scarce believe it when he said he and his missus were adopting the twins. When they could've adopted a baby! Why, with Joe and Florie as big as they are already, I never would've thought it possible. They sure are a pair of lucky ones."

A soft smile formed on Christina's face. "Indeed, they are."

"But that Rose!" Louisa let out an unlady-like snort. "How could she go and do this to me without saying a word? After all our years together!"

Christina took Louisa's hand and gave her

a comforting squeeze. "She loves the twins, but it doesn't mean she loves you any less. I suppose she just felt the twins needed her more."

"I suppose . . ." Louisa sighed, gave Christina's hand a pat, and then returned to the stove to pour hot water into the waiting cup. "Her taking on the position as governess for Joe and Florie helped me make a decision." Slowly she turned toward Christina, a slight grimace on her face. "Mrs. Beasley asked me to stay on permanent-like and do the cooking for her boarders, and I . . . I want to do it."

Christina drew back, stunned. "You *want* to work here?"

Louisa shrugged and fiddled with the teacup's curled handle. "Maybe it seems silly, but I like being in charge of a kitchen again. Deciding what to cook. Seeing folks' smiles when they enjoy what I've prepared. At first Mrs. Beasley near drove me to leap off a cliff. She can sure be snappish! But once I lost my patience and snapped back at her, she settled right down and now is as meek as a lamb."

Christina wondered if Louisa might be stretching the truth. Mrs. Beasley meek? But a more important question came to mind. "Are we to work together here, then?"

Louisa's thin face turned bold red. "I didn't want to be the one to tell you. I'd hoped Mrs. Beasley would talk to you first, but . . ." She lifted the cup meant for Christina and took a gulp. "All the talk going around town has got Mrs. Beasley in a real dither. She's scared she'll lose boarders if she lets you stay, what with Hamilton Dresden telling everybody how it was likely your carelessness that got the poor farm house burned."

Guilt raised its ugly head again. Was Ham right about the fire?

"And then folks got to wondering if you stole the money from the mercantile since it came up missing at the same time you left town." Louisa took another slurp of the tea, then clunked the cup onto the dry sink. "If only you'd come back right away, Christina, instead of staying gone so long without an explanation. You and that money disappearing at the same time, then you coming back with brand-new clothes." Louisa glanced from Christina's neckline to the hem. "Expensive clothes . . . I don't believe one word anybody's saying, but I can see why people are asking questions."

For long seconds Louisa gazed to the side, working her lips between her teeth. At last she sighed and pinned a sorry look on

Christina. "I believe you stayed away to help get the twins settled. I believe the Dunnigans bought you these fine clothes. But there's one thing I don't understand."

Christina tipped her head, tiredness draining the remaining strength from her body. "What's that?"

"Why Tommy claimed he got the stolen money from you."

Christina's heart skipped a beat. Tommy had accused her of thievery? No wonder the sheriff had questioned her. Her chest ached so badly she could hardly draw a breath.

Louisa went on, her brow furrowed with confusion. "Why would he say such a thing?"

"I . . . I don't know." Deeply stung, Christina rose. "I should gather my things and go . . ." Where? She had nowhere to go.

Louisa scuttled toward her, wadding her apron skirt in her hands. "I'm so sorry, Christina. You and your father have been so kind to Rose and me. I don't want to think poorly of you. But it . . . it all just looks so bad for you."

"Were the situation reversed, I suppose I might question your innocence as well." Despite her best efforts to stifle it, bitterness marked her tone. She entered the little sleeping room she'd shared with Cora. Louisa scrounged an empty burlap sack. Dust and a few dried onion stems lay in its bottom, but Christina shook it out as best she could and then placed her belongings in it. Tossing it over her shoulder like a pack, she headed for the back door.

Just before she stepped through, Louisa enveloped Christina in a hug. "I'm sorry for all the troubles following you of late. You'll be in my prayers."

Christina gave Louisa's bony shoulder a few pats. "Thank you, Louisa." She pulled loose and made her way to the street. But once she reached the corner, she stopped and looked up and down the block. Where should she go? She had money left from selling her watch, so she could pay for a hotel room for a few days. But then how would she pay for plaster and materials to repair the poor farm house?

After dropping her pack, she sank down and sat on the dusty edge of the raised boardwalk. *You'll be in my prayers,* " Louisa had said. She buried her face in her hands and battled tears. She hoped Louisa was praying right now for a home to make itself available, or she might end up sleeping in an alley or a barn somewhere.

"Excuse me, miss."

Christina gave a start. A middle-aged man

wearing a mink-brown three-piece suit and a satin top hat stood on the boardwalk beside her. From her hunkered position, he appeared at least eight feet tall. She bolted upright, but he still towered over her — an imposing figure with a midnight-black goatee and thick, arched brows above piercing eyes so dark they seemed ebony.

He peered down at her. "Might you provide me some assistance? I need to locate the Beasley Boardinghouse."

Christina gathered her wits. Salesmen traveling through the area often preferred to stay at Mrs. Beasley's rather than the hotel. She pointed down the block. "Of course. The boardinghouse is on the opposite corner — the white two-story home with green trim. You can't miss it."

"Thank you. I was given to understand that Miss Christina Willems resides at the boardinghouse. Can you confirm if this is accurate information?"

She blinked in surprise. "I —" Her voice cracked. She swallowed. "I'm Miss Christina Willems."

A smile broke across his face. "Miss Willems! Delighted to make your acquaintance."

Confusion clouded her brain. Who was this man, and what did he want with her?

She stood staring at him in stunned silence, her hands clasped in front of her.

He said cheerily, "Of course the circumstances could be better, but the Good Book tells us, 'As thy days, so shall thy strength be.' The two of us will simply lean on His very adequate strength and trust that we will emerge triumphant, yes?"

Christina shook her head hard. "I'm so sorry, but . . . who are you?"

An apology glimmered in his dark eyes. "I've befuddled you." He held out his hand. "Miss Willems, I am Mr. Benjamin Paul Edgar from Edgar, Edgar, and Lofton, Attorneys-at-Law in Kansas City, but I much prefer being addressed as Ben. I'm here at Maxwell Dunnigan's request to ensure your previously pristine reputation is restored."

Frustration tied Levi's stomach into knots. Where was Miss Willems? Louisa said she'd taken her belongings and left the boardinghouse. Cora at the mercantile said she hadn't seen her. Neither had Wes. The only other place he knew to look was at the poor farm, so instead of retrieving the load of logs surely waiting upriver, he aimed his team for the poor farm. The irony didn't escape him. He, who'd sworn off involving himself in anyone else's life, ever, was rumbling across the countryside in search of a woman.

Tommy sat beside him on the wagon seat, blowing sour notes through his harmonica. At least the boy had seemed to cast off his worry when the sheriff admitted he'd been forced to release Miss Willems from the jail. Levi envied his lack of concern. But Tommy didn't know Miss Willems had all but disappeared. And Levi wouldn't tell him. He'd let the boy enjoy a light heart for as long as it would last.

Suddenly Tommy jerked the harmonica from his lips. He twisted his head left and then right. "Why ain't we goin' back to your place?"

"What makes you think we're not?"

"I oughta be smellin' the cedar trees that grow along the river. Besides that, wind's still blowin' in my face instead of hittin' me on the back, so we didn't turn around."

Levi couldn't suppress a grin. The boy had a better grip on his surroundings than some sighted people he knew. "Well, you're right. I decided to drive out to the poor farm."

"Oh." Tommy placed the harmonica to his mouth again and blew. A warbling melody escaped. After a few more discordant blasts, he slipped the instrument into his shirt pocket. "What'cha gonna do out there?"

Levi sought a truthful answer that wouldn't reveal his anxiety. "Look around a bit."

The boy folded his arms over his chest, and wariness marked his features. Over the past couple of days, Tommy had once again become Levi's constant companion. If Levi went to the mill, Tommy went to the mill. If Levi got into the wagon to retrieve logs, Tommy rode along. He'd even found the boy waiting outside the outhouse for him. Although Tommy still wore defensiveness like a shield, he'd nonetheless dropped the desire to be left alone. Levi puzzled over the change, but he didn't question it. He didn't want Tommy retreating into solitude again.

Funny how attached he'd grown to the boy. Maybe Tommy wasn't the only one changing. The thought took him by surprise.

They topped the rise leading to the poor farm, and Levi squinted ahead. A movement caught his attention — the outhouse door swinging open. His heart leaped with hope. She was there! But instead of Miss Willems stepping from the small building, a slight-built man emerged. Levi leaned forward a bit, examining the man from his straw hat to his boots. He'd never seen the stranger before. Had squatters decided to take up residence out here?

Levi flicked the reins. "Get up!" The horses broke into a trot, and Tommy gripped the seat as they bounced across the rough ground and Levi drew the wagon to a halt behind the huge barn. "Stay put," Levi told Tommy. Then he hopped down and strode to meet the man halfway between the outhouse and the farmhouse. The man grinned as Levi approached, but the grin faded when Levi barked, "Who are you, and what are you doing out here?"

Instead of answering, the man cupped his hands and bellowed, "Grover!"

A second man — as big boned as the first man was wiry, wearing work pants and a shirt with its sleeves rolled up to expose his trunk-sized forearms — stomped from behind the house. Levi braced himself. Two against one wouldn't be easy, but he'd take them both on if necessary.

As soon as the second man joined his buddy, the first one looked at Levi. "I'm Tucker. This is Grover. We're rebuildin' this house. Who are you, and what're you doin' here?"

CHAPTER 38

Christina paced the small hotel room paid for by Mr. Dunnigan. Mr. Benjamin Paul Edgar — or Ben, as she tried to remember to call him — sat on a ladder-back chair he'd carried in from his room across the hall and watched her. He'd draped his jacket over the chair's back and loosened his tie. In his casual pose — one arm looped over the chair's top rung and his ankle propped on his knee — he looked more like a man enjoying a break on a park bench than a lawyer determined to prove her innocent of robbery charges. She wished she could feel as relaxed as he appeared.

"Miss Willems, you'll wear a path in the carpet if you don't cease your endless marching to and fro." His wry comment, accompanied by a teasing grin, did nothing to put her at ease.

Crossing her arms over her chest, she turned and retraced her steps. "I can't help it. Why would someone be so cruel as to steal from the Creegers, then give the money to Tommy and tell him it was from me?" There could be no other explanation for Tommy making such a claim. She'd never believe Tommy would deliberately try to hurt her, and he wouldn't lie. So someone had to have misled him.

Without shifting his position Ben threw out a question. "Can you suggest a likely party?"

She stopped. She couldn't shake the notion that Hamilton Dresden played a significant role in this situation. But should she accuse him? She knew far too well the pain of being held accountable for a wrong of which she was innocent. "I . . . I'm not sure."

"Please sit down," Ben said, gesturing toward the end of the bed.

Christina released another heavy sigh and did as he asked.

"Now, let me tell you what I've discovered over the past couple of days while the sheriff had you behind lock and key. Perhaps something will open up a new possibility in your mind." He raised one hand and ticked off his findings by extending one finger at a time. "First of all, the money taken from the mercantile was not recovered in its entirety. The boy Tommy had a significant portion of it, but close to another twenty dollars is still missing. Second, the watch Creeger purchased from you is now in the possession of a man who openly brandishes it about town."

"Yes, the sheriff told me. Ham Dresden has my father's watch. But when I asked how Ham got it, the sheriff only said I should stop playing games and confess." She threw her hands wide. "Confess to what?"

"Dresden claims you made it available to him for a price."

"But I did no such thing!"

Ben offered an unconcerned nod. "And of course that will all come out in court." He raised another finger. "Third, there has been been sabotage at the poor farm — the deliberate destruction of donated lumber."

But that had nothing to do with the thefts. Or did it? Confused, she remained silent.

"All right then. One more point." He flicked the fourth finger upward and fixed Christina with a steady look. "Most of the rumors circulating about town concerning your probable guilt seem to originate with one person — Mr. Hamilton Dresden. Do you know why he would be so determined to sully your name?"

Christina swallowed and chose her words

carefully. "Ham Dresden resided briefly at the poor farm. He behaved inappropriately toward one of the other residents, and I had to ask him to leave. He . . . he didn't take it well. So I'm sure he holds a grudge against me." The man's scathing remarks rang through Christina's mind. She cringed.

Ben stroked his goatee as he considered this, a gesture Christina had already witnessed several times in their short time together. "Would resentment develop into revenge, do you think?"

Christina couldn't suppress a short laugh. "To be perfectly honest, I think he's too lazy to invent a plan of revenge." Sadness settled around her heart. "My guess is he seized the opportunity to expound upon what others were saying in order to inflict pain on me."

"Well, then, what we have here is a puzzle." Ben rose and snagged his jacket with one finger, then tossed it over his back. He stroked the length of his goatee with two fingers. "But puzzles always have a solution, and they're usually more obvious than we'd expect."

He strode to the doorway, which they'd left open for the sake of propriety. Pausing, he gave Christina a reassuring smile. "Enjoy a few days of leisure, Miss Willems. Mr.

Dunnigan has arranged for your meals to be delivered to the room. If you require anything — books, writing materials, additional clothing — just tell one of the employees. They've been instructed to check on you hourly and meet your needs. But" — he turned stern — "do not, for any reason, leave the hotel. We chose this room for its location. There is no possible means of sneaking out unseen. We must have means to verify your whereabouts at all times so you can't be held accountable for any further illicit activities. Do you understand?"

"I understand."

"Good." His smile returned. "Now it's time for me to go solve our puzzle. Good day, Miss Willems."

The door latch clicked behind him. Christina stared at the closed door, then let her gaze drift across the rosebud wallpaper, tall bureau, washstand, and colorful quilt. Although the room was much more comfortable and cheery than the cell at the sheriff's office, she was no less a prisoner here than she'd been there.

Levi ran his hand over the newly plastered walls. Smooth as silk. He had to admit, the men seemed to be telling the truth. They'd

481

done too fine a job to be anything but skilled builders. And they'd done just as well on the outside. The roof still lacked shingles, but the fire-damaged joists and sheathing had all been replaced. The walls wore four-inch cedar lap boards over one-by-twelve framing of crisp white pine. Tongue-and-groove boards formed the soffit, and they'd added a decorative molding where the soffit met the siding. Levi whistled through his teeth. No expense had been spared in reconstructing the damaged areas.

"So whaddaya think, mister? Will the owner be satisfied?" The shorter man, Tucker, smirked at Levi.

Levi stepped back and gave a nod. "More than pleased, I'd say. I didn't realize the mission board had the funds to do the repairs." Miss Willems wouldn't need his donated lumber after all. The realization brought an unexpected disappointment.

"Mission board?" Tucker scratched his head. Outside the open door Grover carted off scraps of leftover lumber. "We weren't hired by any mission board. Man from over in Kansas City — name of Dunnigan — bought the place lock, stock, an' barrel an' sent us over to work the very same day. Pulled us off a job there in the city an' said he'd pay double if we could have it all done in less than a week. So we've been busy as a pair o' beavers over here. Even sleepin' in the barn so we don't have to leave the grounds. 'Course, some big fella — comes out every day to tend the critters in the barn — near run us off 'til he saw what we was doin'. Then he seemed pleased as can be an' didn't give us no more trouble."

Levi listened with half an ear. Did Miss Willems know the poor farm had been sold? Maybe that's why he couldn't find her. Maybe she'd left town since she no longer had a place to live. If so, he'd never see her again. And what would become of Tommy?

Pushing aside his worrisome thoughts, Levi said, "Dunnigan will be very happy with your repairs. Any idea what he plans to do with the place? Seems odd for a fellow who lives so far away in a big city to be interested in a house in a little town like Brambleville."

"Mister, we don't ask nosy questions. We just do our job." Tucker inched toward the door. "I gotta get back to work. We still need to paint inside an' out an' get those shingles on the roof. Dunnigan'll be sendin' somebody out to inspect the place on Saturday, an' if we ain't finished, we don't get our double pay."

Levi watched the man head out the door.

Lock, stock, and barrel, the man had said. That must mean the house, its furnishings, and the outbuildings, too, leaving Miss Willems with nothing.

Even though he had no reason to stay any longer, desire to familiarize himself with the place she'd called home overwhelmed him. Hands in his pockets, Levi wandered the house, counting sleeping rooms as he went. Seven in all — one on the ground floor behind the kitchen, and six on the second floor. Decorative spandrels, a spindled staircase, and elaborately carved door and window trims seemed ostentatious for a poor farm, but all the space made the house a perfect place to shelter several people. He knew of no other house in or near Brambleville that would work as well for a poor farm.

So if she hadn't already left, she'd have to leave soon. A band wrapped itself around his chest and squeezed, making it hard to breathe. He didn't want to lose her. Tommy needed her. *He* needed her.

"Hey, mister?"

Tucker's voice pulled Levi from his sad ponderings. He trotted down the stairs and met the man at the base. "What?"

"We just found something kind of curious. You know anything about the people who lived here . . . how they made a living?"

Levi shrugged. "The house has been used as a poor farm. As far as I know, the woman in charge relied on the mission board to help with expenses."

"So she wouldn't have lots of money pigeonholed away somewhere?"

The fine hairs on the back of Levi's neck stood up. "I don't think so."

"Come look at this." Tucker led Levi to the backyard, where Grover crouched beside the house. As Levi and Tucker approached, the man stood, revealing a gap in the stone foundation. Tucker pointed. "Grover here bumped the foundation with his ladder, an' one o' the stones moved. Shook us up a little bit, you know. We don't wanna be creatin' more work. Then we got to lookin', an' that stone was held in place with nothin' more'n mud. The cement mortar'd all been scraped away. Grover kicked at it a little bit, an' it fell clean underneath the house. When he reached in to pull it back out, this what he found."

Grover, a dumbfounded look on his face, thrust out his beefy hand. He clutched a stack of bills bound by a strip of brown paper. Levi took the stack. All fifties, crisp and new looking. He probably held a thousand dollars. He gaped first at the money and then at the pair of men.

Tucker nodded. "Uh-huh, that's exactly what we thought. And there's more, too. Grover said three or four bundles for sure. A fortune right there under the kitchen." He shook his head. "Me 'n Grover, we ain't never seen that much in one place. I'll be right honest with ya — I come close to sayin', 'Let's just grab this an' skedaddle.' But my mama raised me better'n that, God rest her soul. So we ain't gonna take it. But seems plain foolish to leave money in such a place. Why not use a bank?"

Grover gazed solemnly at the stack. "The only reason I can think why a person wouldn't use a bank is if he didn't want anyone to know he had so much money."

Levi nodded thoughtfully. The money had been well hidden. Someone wanted to keep it a secret. He marveled that the fire hadn't burned it to a crisp. The house's firm stone foundation had protected the treasure. But whose treasure? The question begged an answer.

Tucker tapped his finger on the thick stack. "Whaddaya think we should do with it?"

Levi chewed the inside of his cheek. If he took the money into town, the sheriff would probably think it belonged to Miss Willems. That could be true, but Levi was more inclined to believe she had no knowledge of the stash. Otherwise why would she have sold her watch? Whoever put it there probably thought it was secure, and he might come back for it. If he found it missing, he'd go straight after Miss Willems. Taking it could only cause problems.

He shoved it back into Grover's hands. "I think we should leave it where you found it. Try to get that rock back in the hole. I agree it looks mighty odd to keep money under the house this way, but sometimes rich folks are eccentric. Maybe the people who built the house hid that money there and then forgot about it."

Tucker's eyes grew round. "Would you forget about that much money?"

Levi chuckled. "No. But then I've never been rich."

Grover knelt and plunged his hand through the opening. He grunted as he worked to bring the rock back into place. Tucker stood watching, his tongue caught in the corner of his lips as if hungering for something.

After several minutes Grover managed to wedge the rock back into its spot. His fingertips were bleeding, and he wiped them on his dusty pant legs as he straightened.

"Well, that's that, then." Tucker seemed disappointed. Levi understood. Holding it had spurred ideas of all the things he could do with such an amount. But it wasn't his. It now belonged to the new owner, who'd purchased the property lock, stock, and barrel. The man sighed. "Guess we'll just forget we saw it."

Grover stared at the rock, which sat loosely in the opening. "Kinda hard to forget a thing like that."

"Don't forget," Levi said. "You'll want to tell Dunnigan about it. And . . ." Concern pricked. If these two men had located the secret stash, someone else might stumble upon it, too. He gave the pair a serious look. "Keep an eye on it. You see anybody nosing around here, chase them off."

Tucker looked right and left, his body tense. "Whew. Knowin' it's there makes me edgy. How many times does a fella come upon a real fortune? Almost feel like one o' them leprechauns that found a pot o' gold." He danced a little jig.

Grover guffawed and smacked Tucker on the back.

Levi shook his head, grinning at the pair. "Just be sure to let Dunnigan know it's there. He can decide what to do with it."

"You betcha, mister. Bye now."

Tucker and Grover returned to work, and Levi headed for his wagon. He'd spent enough time out here. Wasted time, since Miss Willems wasn't here and never would be. Sadness bowed his head, and he scuffed up clumps of grass as he crossed the grounds. He rounded the barn and lifted his gaze to apologize to Tommy for taking so long. But to his shock the seat was empty. Tommy was gone.

CHAPTER 39

Cora hummed as she swept the walkway in front of the mercantile. Only another hour until closing. She could hardly wait. Not because she was tired of working, but because she'd get to sit down with Ma and Pa Creeger for some Bible reading and prayer. After she'd told Jesus she wanted Him to take away her sins, Ma Creeger said she'd need to grow in her faith. The best way to do that, she'd claimed, was to study His Word.

Dust and bits of dried grass deposited by people's feet scooted from the broom's straws. Cora chased every bit of grime clear into the street as she pondered her newly discovered delight in studying. She'd never been much of a scholar. Book learning was something to be borne rather than enjoyed, but learning from the Bible was different. Exciting. Pa Creeger taught so patiently, explaining the portions she found hard to understand, and she could ask as many questions as she wanted without him ever getting aggravated.

She paused, considering how Pa and Ma Creeger would be the best parents ever for a child. But they'd both said no. They insisted Cora would regret giving up her child. She put one hand to her lower spine and arched backward, easing a stitch that caught at her side. Maybe they were right, but —

"Cora . . ."

The single word held condemnation and startled Cora out of her daydreams. She turned to find Mrs. Tatum on the edge of the boardwalk, staring straight at Cora's belly. Instinctively, Cora dropped the broom and folded her arms over her swollen middle.

The woman's astounded gaze lifted and bored into Cora's face. "You're with child!" Her voice quivered with indignation.

Ma Creeger had warned Cora that folks might start noticing. Pa and Ma Creeger had both been praying for Cora to be strong if anyone was unkind. But even though they'd prayed and she'd braced herself, this first arrow plunged deep.

She trembled, but she held herself erect. "Yes, ma'am. I am."

Mrs. Tatum came closer. "Do the Cree-gers know?"

"Yes'm."

"And they still allow you to . . . to serve decent folks?"

A familiar ball of shame began rolling in Cora's chest. Ma Creeger had said Jesus took the shame away and she shouldn't let people give it back to her. She swallowed and answered bravely. "Yes'm. I made a mistake. An' I'm gonna have to" — she searched for Ma Creeger's exact words — "bear the consequences, but I don't hafta hang my head in shame 'cause Jesus forgave me."

Mrs. Tatum's mouth dropped open so wide she looked like a big old bass gasping for air. If things hadn't been so tense, Cora might've laughed. Mrs. Tatum finally found her voice. "I'm appalled. Completely ap-palled!" She barged past Cora into the mercantile, slamming the screen door against the wall and making the cowbell clang angrily. "Mr. Creeger! Mrs. Creeger!" Her screech was even more raucous than the bell.

Cora snatched up the broom and scurried in after the woman. She clutched the broom in both fists, ready to give Mrs. Tatum a good whack if she said anything hurtful to

Ma or Pa Creeger.

Ma Creeger rounded the counter as Pa Creeger hurried in from the storeroom. Mrs. Tatum charged up to them, placed her fists on her hips, and let loose. "This girl you've hired to serve customers is an abomination to every Christian woman who comes through your door! How can you possibly allow her to stay here, knowing she's a . . . a —"

"Sinner saved by grace?" Ma Creeger cut in. She put her arm around Cora's shoulders. Cora took strength from the woman's comforting touch.

"She's a sinner, all right, and her sin is ever before her!" Mrs. Tatum waved her hands toward Cora's stomach and then covered her eyes with both palms. "Why, it's offensive to me even to rest my eyes on the evidence of her wrongdoing!"

"Then don't look," Pa Creeger said, a hint of impishness in his expression.

Mrs. Tatum lowered her hands and exposed a wide-eyed look of shock. "Wh-what did you say?"

"Don't look at her," Pa Creeger repeated in the same dry tone. "If it offends you, turn your eyes somewhere else. But" — he scratched his chin, rolling his gaze toward the ceiling — "I reckon you'll be hard-pressed to find a direction that doesn't expose somebody's wrongdoing, seeing as how every last one of us is walking around in imperfection."

Mrs. Tatum's round eyes narrowed to slits. "Are you insinuating —"

"I'm saying the Bible I read tells me, 'There is none righteous, no, not one.' That includes Cora, my wife here, me, and even you."

Cora thought Mrs. Tatum might burst, her face turned so red. She held her breath, waiting for the explosion.

"Of all the impertinent statements! Don't you dare preach to me when you stand there deliberately supporting a wanton girl!"

A wanton girl . . ." Cora's ma had said the same thing. Shame reached for a hold on Cora's heart. She sent a silent prayer heavenward. *Don't let me grab onto it, God.*

Ma Creeger released Cora and stepped forward. "Mrs. Tatum, when Jesus came upon a crowd accusing a woman of immoral behavior, He said something worth considering. Do you remember what He said?"

Mrs. Tatum's chin quivered. She balled her hands into fists and glared at Ma Creeger, but she didn't answer.

Ma Creeger went on quietly, gently, the same way she talked to Cora. "He said, 'He that is without sin among you, let him first cast a stone at her.' Now, I'm not going to cast any stones here, but I think we'd all be wise to examine our own lives before we go pointing out the wrongs other folks've done."

The banker's wife raised one hand and pointed at Ma Creeger. Cora gripped her broom, ready to swing away if needed. The woman spoke between gritted teeth. "You've clearly made your choice, and now I'm making mine. I will not do one more penny's worth of business here until *she*" — she jammed her finger in Cora's direction — "is sent elsewhere." Then she whirled and stormed out, leaving the bell once again clanging in her wake.

Cora twisted the broom handle the way she wanted to wring Mrs. Tatum's neck. "What're we gonna do?"

Pa Creeger looked at Ma Creeger. She looked back. In unison they shrugged. Pa Creeger said, "I'm going to go finish unloading those bags of pinto beans."

Ma Creeger said, "I'm going to finish dusting. Cora, did you get the walk all swept? Yes? Well, then perhaps you could straighten the cloth bolts. Someone left them all askew."

Cora gawked at the pair of them. "But"

— she waved the broom toward the door —
"you heard Miz Tatum. She ain't gonna
shop here anymore! An' she'll probably go
around tellin' others to stay away, too!
Don't that worry you?"

Pa Creeger crossed to Cora and gave her
shoulder a squeeze. "Cora, standing up for
what's right sometimes brings trouble. But
God promises to be with us in times of
trouble. So instead of worrying about what
Mrs. Tatum and her ilk might do, I'm going
to keep doing what God's called me to —
running an honest business and ministering
to those in need."

Tears stung Cora's eyes. "But ministerin'
to me is gonna cost you so dear. Maybe I
oughta —"

"Absolutely not!" Ma Creeger scurried
over and took Cora's face in her hands.
"You aren't going to skulk away somewhere
and hide. We love you, Cora, and we want
you with us."

Cora sniffed hard and rubbed her nose. "I
— I love you, too. Both of you. But I feel
bad, causin' you trouble." She sighed.
"Seems like there's an awful lot wrong right
now, what with the poor farm house gettin'
burned, an' somebody stealin' from you,
an' Miss Willems bein' accused of doin'
wrong. I'm glad God's with us, 'cause we've

got plenty of troubles in need of fixin'."
Shaking her head, she added, "Sure hope
nothin' else bad happens 'cause —"

The door burst open, the cowbell clanging. Cora turned, expecting to find Mrs.
Tatum followed by a mob of angry support-
ers. Instead, Mr. Jonnson strode across the
floor with a worried look on his face. "Creeger, I need your help."

Pa Creeger separated himself from Cora
and his wife and moved toward Mr.
Jonnson. "What is it?"

"Tommy Kilgore — the blind boy who
stays with me . . ." The man gritted his
teeth. "He's wandered off, and I can't find
him."

Why'd he let Dresden sneak up on him that
way? Tommy berated himself. If he hadn't
been facing the wind, he'd have smelled
Dresden's cigar smoke. If he hadn't been
playing on his harmonica, he'd have heard
the man's feet on the grass. But he hadn't
paid attention, and Dresden had managed
to sneak up on him.

His lips still stung from being pressed so
hard against his teeth. Dresden had held his
mouth closed until Tommy promised not to
holler. How could he risk yelling with the
man threatening to take his gun and shoot

anybody who came running to help? So he'd kept quiet and let Dresden drag him off . . . somewhere. Tommy couldn't be sure where he now sat. Maybe a cellar, considering they'd used a ladder to get down into it. The moldy smell and dampness reminded him of a place underground. It was quiet, too, like a cellar, but it didn't seem to be the one under the poor farm kitchen because he couldn't detect the odors of apples or onions or sauerkraut. This place only smelled old and neglected.

"Sorry to do this to you, Tommy-boy." Dresden's voice echoed as if it came from far away. "But I can't have you losin' your senses an' spewin' everything you know to that snoopy lawyer before I've had a chance to get out of town. 'Sides, I needed everybody away from that house. If they're all out ahuntin' you, they won't be payin' me any mind." He laughed, and the sound bounced around Tommy's ears.

Tommy twisted his head, willing his ears or nose to capture something that would help him understand where he was so he could get out. "Where you goin'?"

Another laugh rolled, and it seemed to come from above Tommy's head. "None o' your affair, Tommy-boy. But you can bet it'll be far away."

Scraping noises came from overhead. Was he taking the ladder? Panic struck. "But wait! What about me? You can't just . . . just leave me!"

"Oh, now, Tommy-boy, you'll be all right." Dresden sounded impatient. "I'm gonna write a note an' put it where your friend Mr. Jonnson'll find it. He'll come get you out."

Tommy dug his fingers into the slimy dirt supporting his weight and angled his head upward. "How do I know you ain't lyin'? You been lyin' about everything else."

A grunt exploded. "I'm a lot o' things, but I ain't a murderer. Not gonna face no hangman's noose, not even for five thousand dollars."

Tommy gulped. "F-five thousand dollars? Where you gonna get five thousand dollars?"

"Didn't I say none o' this is your business?" Dresden's tone moved from impatient to angry. "Now you just sit still like a good boy an' wait for somebody to find you. Long as you sit tight, no harm'll come to you. Bye now, Tommy-boy." A muffled *thud* reverberated from above, and the air turned still and dead.

"Mr. Dresden!" Tommy scrambled to his feet, clawing the area in front of him. His hands collided with the ladder. He grabbed hold and clambered upward as quickly as he could. His head connected with something hard, and the jolt knocked him down a couple of rungs. His head ringing, he hung on the ladder for a few seconds until he gathered his senses again. Then he inched his way back up, slower this time, and explored with his hand. Splinters poked into his flesh, but he ran his hand as far as it would go in every direction. Wood planks stretched from side to side. No opening anywhere.

"Mr. Dresden, come back! Come back!" He banged on the ceiling with his fist. Dizziness struck, and he slid down the ladder. On the ground he stumbled forward, hands outstretched, until he connected with a wall. He patted it with both palms. Rough, curved, damp. Stones, he realized. Grunting with pure fright, Tommy inched his way along the wall, seeking a door. But it felt the same all the way around.

Around . . . His heart fluttered, and cold sweat broke out across his entire body. A circular stone wall. Damp. Closed in. Dresden had put him in an old well. And no matter what the man had said, he wouldn't let anybody know where Tommy was.

Panic rose from the center of his chest and

exploded in frantic, hopeless actions. He clawed at the damp wall, screaming for help from Mr. Dresden, from God, from anybody. Eventually exhausted, he collapsed onto the moist-smelling floor. Sobs heaved from his dry throat. Dresden had sealed him in. Nobody would hear him. This well would be his coffin.

CHAPTER 40

Levi listened to Cora's musings as he flicked the reins, urging his horses to hurry the wagon back to the poor farm. The young woman had insisted on riding with him while the Creegers rounded up more searchers, and despite misgivings he'd succumbed to her pleas. He regretted it now. She hadn't stopped talking since they'd left the mercantile. He'd already considered every possibility she named, but he recalled his mor needing to sort things out aloud, so he let her talk without interrupting.

"He probably wanted to go to the outhouse an' just got lost tryin' to find his way back to the wagon." Cora swayed with the motion of the wagon, her hands cupped loosely around her belly. A belly which, Levi tried not to notice, formed a swelling mound beneath the pale green calico skirt of her dress. "Or he decided to visit the goats in the barn. Tommy's always been crazy about them goats — pettin' 'em like he can't get enough. He could've followed his nose to the barn, an' maybe he curled up somewhere for a nap an' didn't hear you callin' for him."

As loud as Levi, Tucker, and Grover had bellowed, they could've roused the dead. If Tommy was within shouting distance, he'd have heard. But Cora seemed to need assurance, so he flashed her a tense smile. "Maybe you're right. You can look there as soon as we get to the poor farm."

"I will."

Wagons bearing townsfolk followed Levi's cloud of dust. If Tommy was hollering for help, they'd never hear him over the racket made by rattling rigging, thundering hoofs, and crunching wheels. But once they reached the poor farm, they'd all set off on foot. They'd surely hear him then. *Let us find him.*

Levi jolted. Had he just petitioned God for help?

"Mr. Jonnson?" Cora shifted slightly, seeming to memorize his profile. "All my yappin' about this or that happenin' — it's just for show. To be truthful with you, I'm really scared Tommy might not've wandered off by accident. I'm scared he might've took off on purpose an' doesn't wanna be found."

Levi frowned. "Why would he do that?"

"He was scared of somethin' at the poor farm."

"Of what?"

She lifted her shoulders in a helpless shrug. "I dunno. But remember that time me an' him went out there with you an' Miss Willems? You was gonna look an' see how much wood was needed to fix the place."

He remembered his nostrils filling with Miss Willems's scent — floral, fresh — as they sat together on this wagon seat. He remembered the grace of her slender form as she moved from room to room. He remembered the sunlight shimmering on her stained-cherry-wood brown hair. He remembered the gratitude in her soft blue eyes when he'd said he'd provide the lumber. He swallowed hard. "I remember."

"Tommy was scared that day. He hunkered up close to me an' shivered."

Levi thought back. "It was cooler then," he said.

Cora shook her head hard. "Huh-uh. They wasn't cold shivers, Mr. Jonnson. That boy was scared o' somethin'. An' I'm wonderin' if you takin' him out there got him all worked up again an' he just decided to light out."

Levi didn't know what to say, so he fell silent and stared straight ahead. Cora stopped talking and sat smoothing her hands over her mounded stomach again and again while biting her lower lip.

The wagon rolled onto the poor farm property, and Tucker and Grover ran out to meet it. Tucker, panting, grabbed the edge of the seat. "No sign of him yet."

Grover shook his head, clicking his tongue on his teeth. "For a young un, he must have good strong legs. We've covered every direction stretching a good half mile. Don't know how he could've gone farther'n that."

" 'Less he's put himself in a hidey-hole o' some sort," Tucker added, brow crinkling, "an' we just ain't seein' it."

Levi leaped down and then reached for Cora. She took his hands at once and allowed him to help her down. When her footing was secure, he turned to the men. "Since you know where you've already hunted, I'm going to let you direct the townspeople who're coming out to help."

Tucker looked toward the approaching wagons. "Whoo-ee! Half the town's comin', it seems!"

"With them all searching, you two can get back to work on the house so you can make your deadline. You've already spent enough time looking for Tommy."

Tucker dropped his jaw. "Mister, I don't know what you take me for, but I got two young uns myself. No job's more important than findin' that boy. Right, Grover?"

Grover nodded his great head. "Right. We'll keep lookin' with you all. The paintin' an' such can wait."

Levi swallowed a lump of gratitude. He'd never witnessed such unselfishness. Except maybe from Miss Willems. He nodded. "All right then. Let's —"

"Mr. Jonnson?" Cora touched his arm. Tears shone in her eyes. "Before you start huntin' again, I . . . I'd like to pray."

Before Miss Willems arrived on his doorstep with Tommy in tow, Levi would have scoffed at the notion. Yet at that moment he wanted nothing more than to beg God to lead them to Tommy. But after his long time away from the Almighty, he didn't know how to begin.

"I ain't never prayed out loud in front o' anybody before — me an' God, we just recently got acquainted." Cora released a self-conscious laugh. "But I'm gonna try." She bowed her head. Tucker and Grover whipped off their hats and followed suit. Levi removed his hat and held it to his pounding heart as Cora began in a faltering voice. "Dear God, Tommy's lost."

I'm lost, too. Levi's body involuntarily jolted. Had he really admitted that?

"We don't know where he is, an' we're real worried about him."

A fierce ache filled Levi's chest, stealing his breath.

"He's probably scared an' waitin' for someone to come along. Would You please help us find him?"

Yes, God. Please. Please . . . Would God even listen to Levi after being ignored for so many years?

"An' whatever was ailin' him when we was here last, fix it, an' help him not to be scared no more. Keep him safe 'til we find him. Amen." She opened her eyes and turned a troubled look on Levi. "Do you think I was too bossy with God?"

Levi gave her arm a gentle squeeze. "I think you prayed just right, Cora. Now, why don't you go sit on the bench in the shade over there" — he pointed to the spot near the barn — "and keep watch in case Tommy manages to find his way back here." If his suspicions were correct, she shouldn't be wandering all over the countryside. She made a face, but then she nodded and headed for the bench. Levi turned to Tucker. "I'm setting off north. Tommy's

507

smart enough to know the wind at his back will lead him toward my place."

Men began pouring out of wagons and moving toward the house. Tucker and Grover would direct them. So Levi grabbed his lantern from the back of the wagon — who knew how long he'd be searching — pocketed a tin of matches, and set off with a determined stride. Cora's prayer became his. *Keep him safe 'til we find him . . .* He couldn't lose another person he loved.

With nothing to do and the walls closing in on her, Christina had stretched out on the bed for a nap. But the church bell's clang had startled her awake. The bell announced Sunday service, the noon hour, and emergencies. She'd reached for her watch, then shaken her head, frustrated with herself for her inability to break the habit. Besides, she hadn't needed a timepiece to know it was neither Sunday nor noon. Which meant something was wrong. And her promise to Ben to remain in her room had hindered her from going downstairs and making inquiries.

So for the past hour she'd paced, pausing occasionally to peer out the window in hopes of capturing a clue. Wagons bearing men had rattled south out of town. None

508

had yet returned. She pondered the little she knew. The men had all departed in the same direction as the poor farm property. But of course at least three farmers lived in that direction, too, so she wouldn't allow herself to draw conclusions so quickly. The number of men leaving indicated it must be a sizable emergency. Another fire? Perhaps a fence down and cattle escaping? Desire for information sent her to the door, but as her hand closed on the knob, she remembered her promise. She'd keep her word.

Nibbling her thumbnail, she paced the room again. Creaking floorboards in the hallway signaled someone's approach. Christina dashed to the door and swung it open. Ben stood outside. The serious look on his face immediately stirred her concern. "What is it?"

"Miss Willems, I'm sorry to tell you this, but the little blind boy, Tommy, wandered away today."

Christina sank onto the edge of the bed, her thoughts whirling. The wagons had gone south. The mill was north. Realization dawned. "Was he at the poor farm?"

Ben nodded.

"But why?"

"Apparently he and the mill owner drove out there. I'm uncertain of their purpose.

But while Mr. Jonnson was otherwise occupied, Tommy disappeared." Sympathy showed in his dark eyes. "The sheriff and many of the town's men, as well as the men who've been working to repair the house, are out searching. I'm sure they'll find him."

Christina pressed her fist to her lips. "Oh, I want to go help . . ." Then she frowned, something he'd said capturing her attention. "Men working to repair the house? What men?"

Streaks of red crept up his cheeks. "It was meant to be a surprise, but I've blundered. I suppose it would be cruel to stay silent now." He grabbed the chair and seated himself, placing his hat on his knee. "Clearing your name is only part of my purpose for being in Brambleville. My secondary purpose was securing the poor farm property for Mr. Dunnigan. He's been seeking an appropriate property for a, er, pet project for some time. And after your description, he went out to view the house and grounds himself. He asked me to contact the mission board and arrange for purchase the same day."

Christina's chest ached so badly she feared her heart had stopped beating. The poor farm sold? "I . . . I don't understand. Why would Mr. Dunnigan be interested in buying an old house that served as a poor farm?" And why would he purchase her house when she'd told him how much it meant to her? His betrayal stung like a slap.

A crooked smile quirked Ben's lips. "Mr. Dunnigan is an astute businessman, and he knows a good investment property when he sees one." He rose. "And that is all I'm at liberty to divulge."

Christina jumped up, extending her hands to the lawyer. "I know you said I shouldn't leave the room until the issue concerning the theft is solved, but I can't stay here knowing Tommy is lost somewhere. Please, won't you take me out to the poor farm? If I'm with you, no one can suspect I'm doing anything illegal."

Ben pursed his lips, seeming to ponder her request.

"Please. I won't be able to rest until he's found."

He released a heavy breath and nodded. "Very well. We'll go to the livery and ask to borrow a buggy. I'll take you out and hunt with you."

Christina grabbed his arm, so relieved she nearly hugged him. "Thank you."

He settled his hat over his dark hair and escorted her down the stairs. The desk clerk stared as they passed through the lobby, but

Christina didn't care. Let people stare. Let them whisper. It didn't matter anymore. The poor farm was sold. Her residents — Louisa, Rose, Alice and her children, the twins, Cora, Wes, the Schwartzes — had all found their own places to work and live without her assistance.

She still had Tommy. Dear, sightless Tommy. But no home to which she could take him. Tears threatened, but she couldn't think of herself now. She needed to focus on finding Tommy, on bringing him back to safety.

Ben made arrangements to borrow the buggy often used for funerals. The last time Christina had ridden in it, she and Wes had transported Mr. Regehr and Mr. Breneman to the poor farm to examine the damage. Little more than a month ago. How could one's life turn upside down in such a short time? She'd lost so much — her home, her residents, her purpose, her reputation, her closeness with her heavenly Father. And all she'd gained in return was a deep affection for a man who wanted to remain stubbornly aloof from the world. At least Papa wasn't there to witness her plunge into failure. She found a small measure of comfort in having spared her father this heartache.

Ahead on the right a ramshackle house,

long since abandoned, caught Christina's attention. She grabbed Ben's arm, encouraging him to pull back on the reins. She waited until the buggy rolled to a stop. Then she pointed. "Do you suppose anyone has checked inside there?"

Ben wrinkled his nose. "It seems a rather gloomy place for a child to seek refuge."

"But Tommy can't see. He'd only know it was shelter." She edged herself over the seat. "I'm going to look inside."

Ben wrapped the reins around the brake handle and climbed out after her. "Miss Willems, please wait. The roof doesn't look secure to me. Allow me to explore instead."

Christina sighed but agreed. She waited just outside the broken door, squinting through the shadows at Ben, who moved gingerly through the single room, pushing aside broken crates and a rusty bedframe. After only a few minutes, he emerged covered in cobwebs.

Sweeping the strings of white from his hair and shoulders, he sneezed. "No one's been in there in a very long time. I suggest we continue on."

Christina's shoulders sagged. "I so hoped . . ."

He took her arm and spoke kindly. "Come now. We've only begun to search. Don't lose heart already."

She smiled her thanks and turned toward the buggy. As she did, a strange sound met her ears. Ben must have heard it, too, because he stopped and looked around, a puzzled expression on his face.

"What was that?" Christina asked.

They stood still as fence posts, listening. The sound came again — an odd, warbling whistle. Ben frowned. "Perhaps a bird?"

"I've never heard birdsong like that before." Christina turned a slow circle, seeking the source of the strange noise. "Could it be wind in the trees?"

Ben shrugged. "I suppose that's possible. Wind through a knothole or other small space could create a whistle."

Christina shook her head. "Well, we can't stand here trying to determine what's making a whistling sound. We need to find Tommy."

Ben took her arm and hurried her across the uneven, grassy ground.

CHAPTER 41

Cora leaned against the cool barn wall. The rough stone pulled hair loose from her bun. She tucked in the strands as best she could and resituated herself more comfortably. Wagons and horses crowded the yard, but the people had all scattered. From a distance voices called for Tommy.

"I want to help," she muttered as the breeze tossed another strand of hair across her face. She considered setting out, but Mr. Jonnson had said Tommy might turn up here. Someone should be at the farm to welcome him. So she anchored the tangled strand of hair behind her ear and scanned the landscape, hoping for a glimpse of a slender, blond-haired boy.

"God, where is he?" Asking the question out loud reminded her she could pray while she waited. Hands pressed against her swollen belly, she closed her eyes and addressed the Father, who Pa and Ma Creeger said was always available to her. She prayed for Tommy. For the people out hunting for him. For Pa and Ma Creeger's store. For Miss Willems. And then she prayed for her baby. "It's gonna need a family, God. I'd like Pa an' Ma Creeger to raise it, but they said no. Reckon You already know that, seein' how You know everything. Well, You know this baby's gonna need more'n I can give it, so would You please send a lovin' family for my baby? Thank You. Amen."

She opened her eyes and spotted something duck behind the house — low, at the same level as the thick clumps of grass growing along the foundation. What had she seen? A small critter — a dog or a raccoon? Or could it have been a boot? Maybe Tommy's boot?

Hope filled her breast. She leaped up, nearly stumbling in her excitement. One hand supporting her stomach, the other holding her bun in place, she ran as quickly as she could around the corner of the house. Someone knelt, all bent forward, in the trampled grass by the wall. Although all she could see was the soles of two brown boots and someone's britches-covered hindquarters, she knew instantly this wasn't Tommy. All her breath whooshed out in a rush of disappointment.

The man jerked, planting one foot on the ground and angling his upper body to look in her direction.

Cora drew back. Why was Hamilton Dresden prowling out here?

He pushed to his feet, his gaze moving back and forth. "Where'd you come from, girl?"

"I been out by the barn, watchin' for Tommy. He's lost."

The scowl he'd been wearing suddenly melted into an expression of deep concern. "I know. I . . . I was lookin', too." He kicked at something in the grass with one foot and then strode forward, grabbing her arm. "But he ain't here. So let's go."

Cora had no choice except to scuttle along beside him. His firm grip pushed her toward the corner of the house, but curiosity made her glance over her shoulder. Shock flooded her. Digging in her feet, she wrenched her arm free and hurried back to the spot where he'd been kneeling.

He pounded after her. "You come back here, girl!"

Cora skittered out of his reach. She bent over and grabbed what had caught her eye. Holding the thick stack of paper money in both hands, she gawked at Dresden. "Where'd you get this?"

He swung at it, but his fingers caught air as she pulled it back. He glowered at her, clenching and unclenching his dirty fists. "Girl, if you know what's good for you, you'll hand that over."

Cora edged backward, holding the fat wad of bills against her thundering heart. "Where'd you come by so much money?"

"Never you mind!" Dresden advanced on her, fury sparking in his narrowed eyes. "Just give it to me!"

Cora shook her head. The pins from her bun came loose, and her hair blew across her face as she continued working her way slowly, inch by inch, backward over the ground. "You stole it, didn't you?" Hair caught in her eyelashes and stuck to her lips. She tossed her head, sending the tangled strands over her shoulder, and threw out another accusation. "You must've robbed a bank or a stagecoach. Tell the truth — you stole this money!"

"I worked for it!"

Her back collided with something hard and immovable — the wall of the wash house. A satisfied smirk tipped up the corners of his lips. Cora's mouth went dry as fear wrapped its tentacles around her. His menacing advance changed to a cocky saunter. She was trapped, and he knew it.

She glanced left and right, seeking an escape route. If only one of the searchers would return to the house!

Drawing on her only defense — gumption — she tried to hold him at bay. "You're a liar. I know a ne'er-do-well when I see one. Betcha you ain't done a lick o' work in your whole life. So how would you earn so much money?"

A growl emerged from his gritted teeth as he lunged forward and planted his palms against the wall on either side of her shoulders. He leaned close, his rancid breath smacking Cora in the face. "Not that it oughta matter to you any, girl, but I'll tell you how I come by that money. I *made* it." When she jolted in surprise, he grinned. "That's right. Printed it myself in the basement of an old warehouse. I'd sneaked in there just wantin' to get warm, but imagine my surprise when I found counterfeiting equipment all set up an' ready for use. Nobody was around, so I spent the night makin' enough money to keep myself in fine form for a good long while.

"Stayed there two days, sneakin' in an' out and spendin' a few bills just to make sure they'd pass for real. Figured on makin' a lot more, but that third night some fellas — seedy ones, if you get my meanin' —

found me. Chased me off." A regret-filled sigh heaved from his chest, assaulting Cora's nostrils with a foul odor. She turned her face sharply away, and he grunted out a laugh. " 'Course, I had full pockets when I ran, so it didn't bother me too much."

Cora trembled within the barricade of his arms, but he seemed talkative. The longer he talked, the longer he'd wait to hurt her. So she asked, "If you had plenty o' money, why'd you come here?"

He laughed as if she was the dumbest person he'd ever met. "How could I stay around the city, knowin' them men would be after me? I came here to hide out for a while. Figure where to go next. Stashed my money under the house." He snorted. "But then Miss High-an'-Mighty Willems sent me off, spoutin' Bible verses at me about he who does not work does not eat an' siccin' that dull-witted Wes on me. Makin' me feel like *nothin'*."

To her surprise sympathy welled. Cora understood feeling like nothing. And she'd done some wrong things to try to make herself feel important. Maybe Hamilton Dresden just needed a Ma and Pa Creeger in his life to show him he didn't have to be a nothing anymore. She started to say so, but he went on.

"Oh, I left like she said I should, but I had to come back for my money. Had me a little fun after that fire, watchin' her squirm an' wonder where she was gonna end up layin' her head, same as she done to me. Played a few tricks, too. But I'm through with all that now." His tone turned matter-of-fact. "I'll get my money, an' I'll take myself on the train to a big city an' live like a king. But first I gotta take care of you."

Cora gasped. She dropped the bundle of money to cup her hands over her belly, where the babe stirred. If he killed her, this baby would die, too. God wouldn't let that happen, would He? "Wh-whaddaya gonna do with me?"

He grabbed a handful of her loose-flying hair. She let out a screech of pain, and he barked, "Hush!" Keeping a firm grip on her hair, he bent both of them over and snatched up the money she'd dropped. He shoved it into his pocket, and then he herded her toward the house, where he'd managed to remove one stone from the foundation. His fingers tore at her hair, hurting her, but she gritted her teeth and remained quiet even when he jerked her down to the ground beside him and knelt on her skirt. "Don't you move, girl." Too frightened to do otherwise, she remained on her hands and knees and sent up plea after plea to the heavens for deliverance.

His reaching under the house resulted in four more stacks of paper money. Counterfeit money, Cora now knew. He'd surely kill her. He couldn't risk her telling anybody about what he'd done. Oddly, instead of wild panic, an unexplained peace settled over Cora. If he killed her, she and her babe would go up to heaven, up to God. She didn't want to die — everything within her longed for escape and a chance to keep living — but the fear melted away. God was with her. She felt Him from the top of her head to the soles of her feet. Without conscious thought she smiled.

Dresden filled his pockets with the money and rose, yanking Cora up with him. "C'mon now. I got someplace special for you." He gave her a vicious shove toward the corner of the house, chuckling. "Reckon there'll be enough room for you. Tommy don't take up much space."

She whirled to face him, her jaw dropping.

An evil grin creased his whiskered face as he nodded. "Uh-huh. Somethin' else I get to hold over the holier-'n-thou Miss Willems. Now you an' me are gonna —"

A man in a three-piece suit, holding a

short length of wood over his head like a club, burst around the corner. Yelling like a medieval warrior, he charged at Dresden and brought the wood down on the man's head. Dresden's mouth fell open. His eyes rolled back. And then he crumpled on the ground with his arms flung outward. The man — the lawyer from town, Cora realized — stood over Dresden for a few seconds, the board still gripped in his hands. When Dresden didn't move, he tossed the piece of wood aside and grabbed Cora's shoulders.

Aiming a glance past Cora's head, he called, "It's safe now, Miss Willems!" Then he dipped his knees and peered into Cora's face. "Are you all right, miss? We've been watching, waiting for the chance to intervene."

"I — He — You —" Cora stared at the tall lawyer, so many emotions rolling through her she couldn't form words.

He gave her a little shake. "Speak to me, miss. Did he hurt you?"

Miss Willems scurried over, her white face wreathed in worry. "Oh, Cora, we saw him accost you. Are you —"

With a cry of despair, Cora broke free of the lawyer's hands. She dropped to her knees next to Dresden and grabbed his shirt front with both fists. "Wake up! Do you hear me? Wake up!" She shook him, but his head only lolled to the side, his slack mouth releasing a dribble of drool.

Miss Willems knelt beside Cora and touched her back, real soft with just her fingertips, like she was afraid Cora had something catching. "Cora?"

Cora spun on her friend. Tears clouded her eyes, making Miss Willems's puzzled face blur. "He was gonna take me to Tommy." She flung an accusing look at the lawyer. "But you killed him, an' now we'll never know what he did with Tommy!"

Tommy blew another lungful of air through the harmonica's mouthpiece. A single note rolled through the well. All the hollering he'd done when Dresden took off had left him hoarse. His throat wouldn't make anything more than a raspy whisper. For a while he'd cried. But that'd hurt his throat, too. So he'd sat in silence with his legs stretched out in front of him and his back against the curved wall. But the quiet made him edgy. So he'd begun filling the space with melodies of his own making. Some of his tunes weren't too pretty, but at least they gave him company.

He wished he had his jacket. When he and Mr. Jonnson'd set out in the morning, it'd been warm enough that he hadn't needed it. But down here, underground, it felt chilly. Would it be cold like this in a grave? He didn't much like the thought, so he pushed it aside. He drew up his knees and fit his elbows between them. Huddling up that way warmed him. Cupping the harmonica to his lips again, he played one long note after another. He took his time, exploring each little hole with his tongue before sending a stream of air through.

Had Mr. Jonnson found the message Dresden promised to write? Not that Tommy really believed Dresden would leave one, but he had to hold on to hope no matter how useless. Miss Willems always said faith that wasn't tested wasn't real faith at all. He'd never quite understood it before, but now it made sense. If a person only believed the easy things, it didn't take much effort. Believing the things that were more unlikely — such as Dresden really writing a note for Mr. Jonnson — required some deep-down belief.

Tommy blew air slowly through the harmonica and listened to the warbling tone. His faith was wobbly, just like the note, but it was still there. He'd keep playing — he'd keep believing — until he didn't have another breath left in him.

CHAPTER 42

Christina placed a rag, dripping wet with cold water from the well, over the knot on Hamilton Dresden's head. The man hadn't stirred when she, Ben, and Cora had carried him into the house and stretched him out on the parlor sofa. For the hour she'd sat beside him watching for signs of waking, he'd lain as still as a corpse. But he was breathing. The moment he opened his eyes, she'd make him tell her where he'd hidden Tommy even if she had to give him a dozen more knots on the head.

A hysterical giggle built in her throat. No doubt the result of weeks of stress and worry. In her mind's eye she saw Benjamin Paul Edgar, attorney-at-law, barreling at Dresden while letting loose a cry fierce enough to frighten an Apache war chief. She never would have guessed the tall man capable of such undignified behavior. She stifled her humor, though, as she gazed upon Ham's white, motionless face. Ben had certainly saved Cora, but his enthusiasm may have cost Ham his life. If Ham died, would Ben face charges of murder?

Yet another worry to add to a list already stretching far too long.

Releasing a sigh, Christina rose and crossed to the window. For more than a dozen years, she'd admired this view. Whether coated with snow, dotted with autumn leaves, or blooming with wildflowers, the rolling landscape meeting a seemingly endless sky had always inspired a sense of wonder in her. She and Papa had marveled at breathtaking sunsets, laughingly imagined cows or ducks in the clouds, and watched sheet lightning fill the sky and raindrops fall in a shimmering curtain. Wonderful memories, each and every one.

But today the landscape seemed tainted. Somewhere out there Tommy was lost, the victim of Hamilton Dresden's strange revenge. Christina turned slowly and stared at the man, thinking of everything Cora had told her. She admitted something about him had made her uneasy, but his bold trickery — using counterfeit equipment, misleading people into casting blame on an innocent person, hiding a helpless boy in a secret location — surpassed anything she would have expected. What made a man choose such harmful pathways?

Papa would probably quote the eighteenth verse from the seventh chapter of Romans to answer her question. The scripture crept through her memory, delivered in Papa's patient, wise tone — *"For I know that in me . . . dwelleth no good thing: for to will is present with me; but how to perform that which is good I find not."* Papa believed there was good in every person, but one's sin nature too often took control.

In a burst of frustration, Christina threw open the window. She propped her palms against the sill, leaned out, and aimed her face at the sky. "Why did You allow Ham to tell lies about me? Why didn't You protect Tommy?" Although addressed to God, the angry outburst couldn't really be called a prayer. Prayer, her father had taught her, was offered in reverence, submission, and expectancy. But the words pouring from her lips held only disdain. "You're supposed to be all-powerful — able to move mountains! So why didn't You keep that fire from starting? Why did You separate me from the people who matter to me? Why did You take my home, my ministry, my very heart?"

My home . . . *my* ministry . . . *my* heart . . . The words she shouted to God reverberated inside her head, awakening her to a humbling realization. In all the years she'd served with Papa, she'd never once heard him refer to his work as his own. All he possessed — all he held dear — was a gift bestowed by his Father God. When, at the tender age of eight, Christina had acknowledged Jesus as her personal Savior, Papa had embraced her and whispered through his tears, "You're His now, my darling daughter, for all eternity."

Another of Papa's favorite scriptures winged through her memory — *"Whatsoever ye do, do all to the glory of God."* She dropped to her knees and rested her forehead on the windowsill as bitter tears rolled down her face. "Dear God, forgive me. This service, this ministry of caring for the destitute, wasn't for Your glory. I've been doing it for me. So I would feel important . . . and needed." The breeze drifted across her head, tender as a father stroking his child's hair. "I'm sorry, God. I'm sorry I ceased to trust You. I'm sorry I blamed You for choices made by sinful men. I'm sorry for serving myself rather than You. Help me change, Father. Guide me. I . . . I trust You to meet my needs in whatever way You deem best."

Oh, such joy in placing herself in her

Father's hands and trusting He would keep His promise never to leave her or forsake her. She continued to weep and pray for several minutes, allowing her tears to wash away the deep resentment of the past weeks. When she finally rose, shaky yet refreshed, she added a final plea. "Dear Lord, please let the men find Tommy before it's too late."

Dusk had fallen. Although Levi could light a lantern and continue searching, he turned his feet in the direction of the poor farm. By now Mrs. Creeger probably had sandwiches waiting for them. The men could eat, rest a bit, compare the territory they'd covered, and then set out in new places.

His feet hurt, his back ached, and his throat was dry from calling Tommy's name. But nothing pained him more than his heart. If Cora was right about Tommy being scared of something — and he suspected she was, based on the way Tommy had stayed close to him over the last couple of days — then Tommy hadn't trusted him enough to divulge the source of his fear. And if fear had sent the boy off on his own and he met with harm, Levi would carry the guilt to his grave, the same way he carried guilt over Far.

A groan wrenched from his soul, and he

slowed his pace. Mor's voice from long ago eased through his mind, speaking not to him but to Far. *"Axel, where is your faith? You know our God has mighty strength. Lean on Him, Axel, instead of yourself. Give Him this burden you carry and find freedom."*

Far hadn't let go, and eventually the burden of unforgiveness and resentment had killed him. Guilt and bitterness would not kill Levi's body — this he knew — but it was a horrible thing to bear. It slowly devoured his soul.

Ahead, other men moved across the shadowy landscape and milled on the poor farm grass. Levi pushed aside his dismal thoughts and broke into a trot. Mrs. Creeger handed out sandwiches, fruit, and tin cups for water. As the men ate, they talked, sharing the areas they'd explored and their findings. The findings were all the same — no one had seen any sign of Tommy.

Levi drained a second cup of water, the cool liquid soothing his sore throat, and set the cup aside. He tucked a sandwich into his pocket — Tommy would be hungry when they found him — and then turned to the gathered crowd. He opened his mouth to call for their attention, but he found himself speechless for a moment.

So many men. Young men. Old men. Tired

yet determined men. They'd all set aside their own duties and responsibilities to help seek one small, blind boy. Why now? In past months these same people had refused to harbor Tommy. They'd cast accusations at Miss Willems. Yet here they all were, ready to work together to bring Tommy back to safety. And he was working alongside them. A part of them.

Levi's eyes began to sting. If one of them had offered a place of refuge to Tommy, he would never have brought the boy into his house or into his heart. If the townsfolk hadn't turned on Miss Willems, he might never have recognized how much he cared for her. If Tommy hadn't gotten lost, Levi wouldn't have found his way into the center of this community. All the wrongs had guided him to one important right. He could never live off on his own again. He'd discovered the joy of reaching out, of being included.

He wanted to explore these strange and wondrous realizations stirring to life in his chest, but first they had to find Tommy. He cleared his throat and raised one hand. The murmurs ceased, and all faces turned toward him.

"We need to figure out where to look next — maybe take the wagons this time so we can go farther. Since it's getting dark, let's go in groups of two or three. It'll be safer." Men nodded in agreement and began pairing up. Levi called out the various directions, and men stepped up to claim the areas.

One man from the back of the group waved his hand. "Jonnson, there's an abandoned farmstead northwest o' here — an old house, barn, an' some outbuildings about to fall in. My brother an' me will check it."

The lawyer who'd been in town the past several days put his empty cup in the crate near Levi's feet and turned to the man. "I believe that's the same farmstead I explored earlier today. I saw no evidence that anyone had been on the property in quite some time."

"So there's no need to explore the farmstead? Is that what you're saying?"

"That's correct." The lawyer released a low chuckle. "Unless you'd like to satisfy my curiosity about a melody wafting from the trees. A very peculiar sound — haunting almost."

One of the men snorted. "We got no ghosts in Brambleville."

The lawyer — tall and lean with a black beard and top hat that made him look like

Abraham Lincoln — shrugged. "I doubt a ghost would warble like a songbird."

Warble? Levi's pulse stuttered. "What exactly did you hear?"

The tall man stroked his goatee. "Shouldn't we be searching for the boy rather than discussing mysterious melodies?"

Levi grabbed his arm. "What did you hear?"

"Very well." The lawyer gently extracted his arm from Levi's grip. "I heard a trembling note. And then another in a different pitch. Soft, yet distinct, and seemingly carrying from far away."

Levi let out a whoop. "That was no ghost — that was Tommy's harmonica!"

Mr. Creeger dashed forward. "Are you sure?" The crowd waited, all eyes pinned on Levi.

For a moment Levi's certainty wavered. "Just in case I'm wrong, go ahead and spread out like we'd planned. But I'll take Tall Abe here and go to that farmstead."

The men nodded in agreement and headed for the wagons. Levi put his hand on the lawyer's back and gave a gentle push. "My wagon's over there. Let's go."

CHAPTER 43

Cora leaned on the wall and watched Miss Willems lay a fresh wet cloth on Ham Dresden's head. Instead of putting it there and moving away, she stayed on her knees beside the man and held the cloth in place. There was a tenderness on Miss Willems's face — a tenderness Cora couldn't understand.

Almost uncomfortable witnessing the gentle ministrations, Cora turned her gaze to Ma Creeger, who knelt in the middle of the parlor floor, her head bent and hands clasped in prayer. She'd been praying for nearly half an hour already. Dresden was an admitted thief and kidnapper, but she was praying for him to wake up and be all right.

Cora eased herself down the wall until she sat on the floor. She crisscrossed her legs and rested her palms in the nest made by her skirt. Automatically, her hands formed a loose sling for the child growing inside of her. Puzzled, she looked from Ma Creeger to Miss Willems. How could they be kind to someone who'd wronged them so?

As she sat watching the two women who'd treated her kindly give the same attention to Hamilton Dresden, tears sprang into her eyes. Understanding dawned. They weren't loving with their own love. They were loving with God's love, which was so much bigger than a person could hold. That's why they could embrace her — broken, sin-battered, unlovely her — instead of pushing her aside.

"I wanna be like them, God . . ." Cora whispered the prayer while warm tears dribbled down her cheeks. "I wanna love with Your love instead o' mine. I'm gonna need it to raise up this baby the right way." She drew in a sharp breath, something else becoming clear. She'd prayed for God to give this baby a family to love it, and He'd already answered. He'd brought her to Brambleville, to Miss Willems and to the Creegers, who treated her like their own. This baby would have an aunt in Miss Willems and grandparents in Ma and Pa Creeger. And if she kept watching these two women, learning from them and copying them, she'd know how to be a loving mama to her baby.

Lowering her head, Cora allowed the tears

to flow. Tears of deep gratitude. God *did* love her. Even in her sinfulness He'd provided for her. She had a family to call her own.

Levi swung out of the wagon, and the lawyer leaped out after him. "C'mon, Abe," Levi said.

The man cleared his throat. "The name is Benjamin Paul Edgar, thank you."

Levi would shake his hand and get formally acquainted later. Right now they had a job to do. Lanterns in hand, they headed in opposite directions between broken-down buildings and across the thick grass laid flat by the spring winds. They met at a cross point, Lawyer Abe's long shadow stretching past Levi's as if racing to a finish line. Levi only hoped Tommy waited at the end of that line.

"Do you hear it?" Levi strained to hear over the night sounds — an owl's mournful hoot, wind, and their feet tromping on grass.

"No." The man sounded disappointed. "But the wind was stronger then. Maybe it was only a wind noise and that's why we aren't hearing it now."

Levi resisted the man's reasoning. He so wanted to believe the sound was made by Tommy's harmonica. He raised his voice and bellowed, "Tommy! Tommy! Are you here?"

Lawyer Abe took up the cry, too. "Tommy! Tommy!"

Although Levi wanted to break into a run, cover lots of ground, he forced himself to maintain a slow pace. A quieter movement. Side by side he and Lawyer Abe eased in a circle around the abandoned property. Stopping now and then to holler Tommy's name. Creeping forward a few more feet, lanterns high, eyes searching. More calls.

Nothing.

Levi lowered his lantern, his spirits falling with the beam of light. It was useless. If it had been Tommy's harmonica, the boy had moved on by now. Levi had let his hopes carry him away. Just as Mor's hope for Far's recovery had been futile, so was Levi's fragile belief that Tommy would be waiting at the old farm.

Lawyer Abe tromped a little farther, then stopped, turning back to send Levi a puzzled look. "What's the matter?"

"He's not here. We might as well give up."

The tall man shook his head. "We haven't explored the entire grounds. Let's make sure before we turn back."

"But —"

And then it came. A single note — weak,

trembling, but clearly not from a bird or even the wind. Levi stumbled forward two steps, swinging the lantern first left, then right, his pulse beating so hard his head ached. "Tommy! Tommy! Play some more!"

Another note — this one lower in pitch and even weaker than the first — reached Levi's ears.

Lawyer Abe pointed. "Over there!" Excitement quavered in his voice.

They bolted forward, lantern light leading the way, one long note after another pulling them the way a horse pulls a plow. Then Levi saw it — a round, warped, wood-planked cover perhaps six feet in diameter. He handed the lantern to the lawyer and dashed ahead. He tripped over something in the grass and fell hard with his hands landing next to the cover. Hope burst through Levi's chest, bringing the sting of tears. "Tommy! Tommy!" He pried at the edge of the wood with his fingertips.

The lawyer set the lanterns down and knelt beside Levi as he thrust the cover aside. Lying on his belly, Levi peered into the opening. "Tommy?" A black void met his eyes. No answer rose from the darkness. He turned to Abe. "Give me a lantern." The man pressed a handle into Levi's waiting hand, and Levi held it over the opening.

The dim light flowed across a rickety ladder to a small shape pressed against the rock wall. Levi squinted, his heart pattering with hope. Was it . . .

Joy exploded through him. Yes, there at the bottom, Tommy huddled with the harmonica gripped in his fists, his dirty face aimed upward. His lips moved, but no sound emerged. Fear seemed to pulse from the boy.

"Tommy, it's me — Mr. Jonnson."

Delight broke across Tommy's face. He reached with both hands. Tears carved clean paths down his cheeks, and his wide-open eyes beseeched Levi. But he still spoke not a word.

"Grab the ladder, Tommy, and come on up."

The boy took hold of the ladder's frame and slowly, as if every step carried him through thick molasses, he pulled himself upward. Levi held his breath, counting the steps, and the moment Tommy was within reach, he caught the boy under his armpits and pulled him the final distance. On his knees he swept Tommy into his embrace.

The boy clung, repeatedly rasping in a coarse whisper, "You came. You came. He told you."

Levi buried his face in the boy's moist

neck, thankfulness washing through him in waves. Yes, God had to have led them here. "Yes, He told me, Tommy. You're safe now." He held the boy for several more minutes, stroking his hair, kissing his temple. "I've got you. You're safe. You're safe." *"I've got you. You're safe."* The words reverberated through Levi's mind, and an image of God's guiding hands holding fast even when Levi couldn't see Him formed in his head.

Still gripping the boy, Levi struggled to his feet. Tommy wrapped his arms and legs around Levi's frame, resting his head on Levi's shoulder. Levi imagined God's arms enfolding them both. He turned to Abe, whose smile beamed as brightly as the light glowing from the lantern in his hand. "Get my gun from the wagon and fire up a shot — let the others know we've found him. Then I'm going to take Tommy home."

Abe held the lanterns well in front of them, lighting their way as they headed for the wagon. "Although I'm not well acquainted with firearms, I shall gladly alert the men. But afterward I'll need you to transport me to the poor farm so I can retrieve Miss Willems. I left her there caring for Hamilton Dresden."

At the mention of Dresden, Tommy's arms put a stranglehold on Levi's neck. Levi was forced to stop and loosen the boy's grip. "What is it, Tommy?"

Tommy burrowed deeper into Levi's shoulder. "Dresden, he . . ." — his words scraped out — "put me in the well."

Levi clung to Tommy, offering security with his own strong hold. "Why would he do that to you?"

" 'Cause I know . . . what he done." Tommy went limp in Levi's arms.

"We'll get to the bottom of this later," Levi said, setting off again for the waiting wagon in a determined stride. "This boy needs water and rest."

"The poor farm's closest."

And according to the lawyer, Miss Willems was there. Levi wouldn't argue.

A single rifle shot carried on the night air. Christina lifted her head toward the open window and let out a gasp.

Mary Ann Creeger reached across the short expanse of worn carpet and gripped Christina's arm. "They've found him." Her words washed out on a note of relief.

Yes, the shot indicated Tommy had been found. But unharmed? They wouldn't know until the men returned. She pressed both palms to her chest and winged up a hopeful prayer. *Let him be all right, Lord, please.*

Cora had fallen asleep in a chair, so Christina roused her and asked her to keep watch at Dresden's side while she and Mary Ann hurried into the yard. Moonlight spilled across the ground, illuminating the searchers, who came from every direction. Christina scanned each arrival, her heart beating an eager *thrum.* But none of the men on foot or in a wagon carried Tommy to her.

Yet another wagon rumbled toward the poor farm, its horses frothing. Christina squinted at the pair of forms on the seat, lit by the lanterns swinging from hooks on the wagon's sides. Her heart caught in her throat. One of the men cradled Tommy! With a strangled gasp she staggered forward over the uneven ground, her hands reaching. As the wagon rolled onto the yard, she recognized the man holding the reins and the one holding Tommy. Her gaze jumped past Ben to Levi, and the flutter in her chest became wings of delight. Of course he'd found Tommy. It was only right that the man she loved would return the boy — the boy who owned a significant portion of her heart — to her waiting embrace.

Men crowded behind her, excited voices filling the air, as she held out her arms for Tommy. Levi lowered him to her, and she nearly collapsed beneath his weight. But another pair of arms reached to assist her — Mr. Creeger, with tears in his eyes.

"Let me take him. I won't let him fall."

Christina swallowed and released the boy, feeling a great weight lifting not only from her arms but from her heart as she trusted him to bear this burden for her. Mr. Jonnson alighted, and without a second's hesitation Christina turned and threw herself into his arms.

CHAPTER 44

Levi held Miss Willems the way he'd held Tommy. Close to his heart, his cheek pressed to her hair. He drank in her scent, amazed at how she completely filled his senses. She belonged right there, nestled in his embrace. His heart bounced inside his chest like a bell's clapper. He didn't want to let her go.

But as quickly as she'd fallen against him, she wriggled loose. In the moonlight her cheeks bore bright patches of scarlet. She touched her lips with trembling fingertips, and without thought Levi's gaze dropped to their rosy fullness. Her blush deepened, and she lowered her head.

"Forgive me." Her voice released on a whisper. "I was just so thankful I . . . I lost myself for a moment."

Odd how her loss was his gain.

Lifting her chin, she met his gaze. Her eyes shimmered with unshed tears. "Thank you, Levi, for finding Tommy."

She'd called him Levi. She hadn't quite collected herself yet. "I found more than Tommy, Christina." He sampled her name and deemed its delivery sweet. "I found my place in Brambleville."

Her head tipped in puzzlement, and her lips parted as if to question his statement, but someone screeched her name. Christina stepped away from him, toward Cora, who raced across the yard in an awkward gait with her skirts in her fists.

"Miss Willems, he's rousin'! Hamilton Dresden — he just now opened his eyes!"

The lawyer leaped down from the wagon, captured Christina's elbow, and propelled her toward the house. The men swarmed after the pair, creating a barrier between Christina and Levi. He hesitated — should he leave? Tommy was safe now with Christina. Good ol' Abe would dig to the bottom of Dresden's activities. Levi wasn't needed any longer.

The surging crowd suddenly came to a muttering halt. From within the throng, Christina's voice lifted. "Levi? Levi Jonnson, are you coming?"

Levi grinned and broke into a trot. He'd stay.

■ ■ ■ ■

Christina walked Ben to the poor farm's
front door. The tall man yawned, then
smiled sheepishly. "Forgive me. I'm not accustomed to this kind of activity." His grin
widened. "But I wouldn't have missed the
excitement for the finest desk job in the
world."

Even though Christina had heard Dresden's confession with her own ears, she still
found it amazing how much harm one man
could cause. Although at first he'd resisted
admitting any wrongdoing, when con-
fronted by Cora and then by Tommy and
finally informed, very tartly, by Mary Ann
Creeger that Christina had sat by his side
and tended his wound, he'd turned into a
blubbering mess and spilled every foul deed
perpetrated in the name of revenge.

Ben continued, "The sheriff won't have
any reason to continue holding you accountable for either the fire at the poor farm
or the theft at the mercantile." In the soft
glow from a lamp on the windowsill, she
observed his wink, the daring gesture changing his austere appearance to that of an
ornery lad. "I suspect an apology will be
forthcoming. And if it isn't received

promptly, I shall have no qualms about encouraging its delivery."

Christina shook her head. "Being out from under this cloud of suspicion is apology enough." Although the sheriff had arrived at the poor farm well after Ham's outpouring, a good dozen of the town's men had witnessed the disclosures. Word would spread, the truth finally revealed. She recalled Hamilton Dresden's broken appearance when the sheriff had escorted him to a wagon for transport to the town's jail. Sympathy twined through her chest. What a miserable man he must be to create such chaos for others. Lifting her face to Ben, she asked, "What about the counterfeit money? Will he face charges for printing it?"

Ben stroked his goatee, his expression serious. "I imagine so. He spent a few of the bills when he knew they weren't legitimate. He'll have to answer for that. But the Kansas City authorities might decrease his sentence if he helps them capture the ones who set up the counterfeiting equipment in the first place."

Christina sighed. "I hope he'll be willing to cooperate."

A grin twitched at his cheek. "If he isn't, perhaps another clop on the head might knock some sense into him."

Christina couldn't stifle a laugh, but she clapped her hand over her mouth, muffling the sound. Tommy and Cora slept, and she didn't want to wake them.

Ben hesitated in the doorway. "Shall I ride out tomorrow and retrieve you?"

From the shadows at the foot of the stairway, Levi Jonnson materialized. He stepped beside Christina and addressed Ben. "I'll make sure Christina gets back to town. My wagon's still here."

Heat flooded Christina's face when Ben's grin turned knowing. He tipped his hat, gave a dapper bow, and departed, leaving Christina standing very close to Levi at the doorway. The lamp glow lit his profile, the blond whiskers on his cheeks picking up the light. Tousled hair, grizzled cheeks, tired eyes . . . and still so handsome Christina's stomach fluttered in response. For long seconds they stood looking at each other, with Jay and Mary Ann Creeger's soft voices carrying from the newly rebuilt kitchen and Tommy's occasional snuffle competing with the gentle croak of a bullfrog somewhere outside.

Levi cleared his throat, and Christina jumped. He apologized, and she released a light giggle, the sound so girlish it startled her. "It's all right. I suppose I'm a little jumpy from the long day of worry."

His brows furrowed, genuine concern showing in his green-blue eyes. "You're tired. I should leave and let you rest."

Yes, she was tired, but she knew she wouldn't be able to sleep. The evening's revelations — not only Dresden's confession, but her own to God concerning why she'd followed in her parents' footsteps — still stood out strongly in her mind. And Levi had said something that bore examination. She said, "I don't want you to go. Not yet."

His lips quirked into an odd little smile.

That silly rush of heat returned. She ducked her head. "I . . . I hoped we might . . . talk."

He held his hand toward the front porch, and she stepped outside. The night air was cool but not overly so. Even so, Levi tugged off his jacket and draped it over her shoulders. The duck fabric was warm from his body, infused with the musky smell of his skin. Another wash of warmth flooded her cheeks. But she wouldn't remove it.

She led him through the patch of lamplight that fell from the window to the corner of the porch where a white painted swing hung on tarnished chains. A cricket began chirping a cheerful song as they settled into the seat together. Stars winked blue and white in a black velvet sky, like many eyes keeping watch. The breeze tossed coils of Christina's hair across her shoulders. To her amazement, Levi reached out and lifted one strand, seeming to examine its texture between his fingers, then tucked it gently behind her ear. The tender gesture brought the sting of tears to her eyes. She whispered, "Thank you."

His hand lingered near her ear, his finger-tips brushing the delicate spot on her jaw line. Did he feel the pounding of her pulse? Discombobulated by the unfamiliar feelings coursing through her, she blurted, "What did you mean when you said you'd found your place in Brambleville?"

He lowered his hand, placing it over his thigh as if holding himself in the swing. He cast a sidelong look in her direction, his eyebrows lifting. "That question requires a lengthy answer. Are you sure you want to explore it?"

At that moment she wanted to explore everything about him. She nodded.

"All right." Levi pulled in a long breath, his shoulders squaring. Then he shifted on the seat, placing his arm along the back. He didn't touch her, but he didn't need to in order to alert her senses. She nearly sizzled, having him so near. And when he began to speak in a soft, serious voice that held both pain and peace, she found herself mesmerized.

"I've held on to a burden — a burden of unforgiveness — for many years, and it kept me from trusting people. I told Tommy that folks kept their distance from him because they weren't sure what to say to him — that being uncomfortable with his blindness and his scars kept them quiet. I encouraged him not to blame them for their ignorance. But not once did I stop to offer the people who turned their backs on my far — my father — the same understanding."

Christina braved a question. "What happened to your father?"

A sad smile crossed his face. "Far was a furniture maker — a true craftsman. His designs were unique, different from anything else available, and people clamored to purchase his fine tables, desks, and wardrobes. He couldn't keep up with orders, so he brought in a partner. The partner, without my father's knowledge, took Far's designs and showed them to a man who owned a furniture factory. That man stole the designs, purchased patents so no one else — not even my father — could use them, and then simplified them for his workers to churn out the pieces in great numbers and at a much-reduced cost."

The unfairness pierced Christina. "So your father's business was ruined?"

Levi nodded, his head low. "He felt he'd lost everything. He sank into a deep melancholy and refused to come out no matter how much Mor begged and prayed. She tried to get Far into a hospital where they treated illnesses of the mind, but we had no money, so they refused him admittance. Townspeople held their distance from our family, some fearful and others disdainful of my father's odd behavior. Far died two years later, a broken, bitter man. And I've carried his bitterness with me, blaming the townspeople for their unkindnesses toward us, blaming his partner for cheating him, blaming God for not healing my father. I refused to forgive, and I refused to trust. And the one I hurt the most by holding myself away from everyone was myself."

Christina gazed at him in silence. So much pain he carried. She dared to brush his arm with her fingerstips. "I'm so sorry, Levi."

He turned to look deep into her eyes, startling her with the intensity of his gaze. "I am, too, for the years I've wasted, hiding away, thinking I could be happy completely on my own. I was wrong, Christina — so very wrong."

Something in his eyes ignited a warmth deep in her soul. She held her breath, wondering what he might say next.

His voice turned husky, thick, as if he battled a fierce emotion. "I might have gone on that way my entire life if you hadn't come knocking on my door in the middle of the night and forcing an eleven-year-old boy into my keeping. But you did, and now everything's changed." He took her hands, his grip strong yet gentle. "I never wanted to be like my father, yet I've become him, trapping myself in solitude. I'm tired of being alone. I'm tired of running from the God I loved and trusted as a boy. I'm tired of carrying the burden of bitterness. I realized tonight when Tommy lifted his hands to me in complete trust — me, who he has never seen — that it's time for me to lean trustingly into the hands of the One who might be unseen but is always watching me."

Tears pricked Christina's eyes. The sincerity in his face, the fervency of his tone, the sure pressure of his fingers on hers communicated so beautifully his desire to return to a right relationship with God. She clung to his hands, unable to speak, but hoping he read joy in the smile she offered.

The cricket ceased its chatter. The lamp

flickered and then went out, leaving the two of them in deep, shadowy silence. The moon slipped lower in the sky, its white face fading as the black changed to a smudged gray. In the east, pink fingers of dawn crept upward, announcing the impending arrival of the sun.

Levi pointed to the wisp of lavender illuminated by the first rosy beams. "Look, Christina. A new day is dawning."

Christina absorbed the sight, her heart lifting. Papa's voice rose from her memory, and she found herself repeating his oft-delivered words of promise. "No matter how dark the night, God's mercies are new every morning. Great is His faithfulness."

Levi's hand slipped from the back of the swing to Christina's shoulder. He drew her against him, his chin resting lightly against her temple. Together, they watched the sky change until the sun eased above the horizon. And when its bright beams had chased away the vestiges of night, Levi rose and held out his hand.

"Come, Christina. I'll take you and Tommy to town. The sheriff said he needed you to stop by the office and confirm Dresden's confession."

Christina took his hand, allowing him to draw her to her feet. But she didn't move toward the house. Not yet. She met his gaze. "And . . . then what?"

"And then . . ." His fingers tightened on hers. Determination squared his jaw. "I must return to my mill." He lifted her hand, placed it in the bend of his elbow, and guided her into the house.

CHAPTER 45

As Ben had predicted, Sheriff Garner apologized to Christina for the confusion. Withdrawing Christina's watch from a drawer in his desk, he said with a hint of contrition, "I got this back from Dresden, but I've gotta take it to the Creegers. They bought it from you, you know."

Christina nodded. She stood on the boardwalk and watched the sheriff until he disappeared into the mercantile. Part of her wished she could follow the man and offer to buy back Papa's watch, but she needed the little money in her pocket for her new start. Now that the poor farm house was no longer hers, she must seek a place to live. She'd promised Ben not to leave town until he'd received a letter from Mr. Dunnigan, which he'd been instructed to share with Christina. Until then, he would cover her hotel bill. Although tempted to decline their charity, she swallowed her pride and offered appreciation instead. The old adage " 'Tis easier to give than to receive" certainly rang true after spending her life observing her parents giving to anyone in need. How odd to be the one in need, yet how peaceful to rely on God to meet her needs.

She set off for the hotel, tiredness slowing her pace. Had she really sat up all night talking with Levi Jonnson? If Mr. Regehr knew, he'd call her unseemly, and this time he'd be right. Although she'd done nothing untoward — except lean against his shoulder and let him hold her hand — her feelings for him delved more deeply than her actions indicated. As she'd sat on the swing with him, listening to him share his darkest hurts and then profess his desire to stop hiding, she'd longed for him to draw her into his embrace, to declare he wanted to build a future with her, to press his lips to hers in tender possession.

But despite the sweet embrace they'd shared, igniting hope within her breast, upon reaching town he'd merely deposited her at the sheriff's office, offered a quiet and somewhat regretful farewell, and departed with Tommy in tow. Tears threatened. What of all his fine words proclaiming a desire to change? Hadn't he meant them after all? Or perhaps he wanted to change but not with her. The thought hurt.

She entered the hotel, offered a smile and a hello to the clerk in response to his greeting, then climbed the stairs to her room. Once she was inside her little sanctuary, the long night of worry and no sleep stole her remaining energy. Still fully clothed, she stretched out on the bed, closed her eyes, and allowed exhaustion to carry her away.

Levi paused in carving a rose petal into the fragrant piece of cedar and glanced at Tommy. The boy hummed as he twisted the ends of two lengths of reed across each other. A smile grew on his face of its own volition. How good to see Tommy's cheerful countenance restored.

Such a time of healing the two of them had shared the past few days. The boy had asked forgiveness for keeping silent about smelling Dresden's cigar when Francis accompanied him to the outhouse the night the poor farm caught fire. He'd wept, his face pressed to Levi's chest, and lamented how much trouble could have been avoided if he'd told instead of allowing fear to keep him quiet. Levi had assured the boy he shouldn't carry regret and said, "From now on we'll trust each other, yes?" And with a shuddering sob, Tommy had agreed.

With the release of regret, peacefulness descended. Levi sent up a quick, grateful prayer for the lessons learned and then set aside his tools. He strode across the floor and put his hand on Tommy's shoulder. Levi examined the frame and woven pattern formed by thin strips of reed. He shook his head, awed. Tommy's nimble fingers, keen sense of touch, and abundance of determination had brought success.

"You did it, Tommy. It's perfect."

The boy beamed upward, his head bobbing in excitement. "It is?"

"It is. I'm so proud of you."

"I can do the chair now?"

Levi ruffled the boy's hair. He needed a haircut. But then, so did Levi. They'd both get one so they'd look spit-shined and presentable when he delivered his gift to Christina. "You know what, Tommy? You already did."

Tommy's mouth fell open.

Levi chuckled. "That frame I made for you to practice with the reeds will fit the opening in the seat. So now all I have to do is pry out the old one and put the new one in its place."

Tommy jumped up and pounded the air with both fists. "I did it!" His flailing brought one hand against Levi's arm. He gripped Levi's shirt. "Can we show Miss Willems? Huh? I want her to see what I done." Then his excitement faded. "But she might still be mad at me . . . for telling that lie about her to the sheriff."

"She won't be mad," Levi said, certainty squaring his shoulders.

Tommy's expression didn't clear. "You sure? 'Cause of me, she got put in jail. She oughta be powerful mad."

Levi slung his arm around Tommy's shoulders and pulled him close, emotion clogging his throat. "She won't be mad, Tommy. She loves you too much not to forgive you."

Tommy blinked, his cheek pressed to Levi's chest. "Even after all I done?"

"She'll never stop loving you, Tommy." Levi's heart swelled. Christina loved the boy the way God loved Levi. Tommy just needed to accept its offering.

Tommy snuffled and pulled loose. "Then I wanna show her. Can we go?"

The desire to see Christina nearly turned Levi's chest inside out. But he couldn't go yet. Not until he had his own project finished. A man needed more than a few flowery words when he asked a woman to become his life partner. And he wasn't ready yet. He pulled Tommy into another hug. "Soon, Tommy."

The boy wriggled in Levi's light embrace. "When? Tomorrow?"

Levi looked at his workbench. He'd spent the last three days ignoring everything except this special project. Just like Tommy, he wanted his work to be perfect. A load of logs still waited on the riverbank. More logs were piled in the yard, ready for cutting. But he wouldn't touch any of it until he'd finished this gift.

Apparently Tommy grew tired of waiting for an answer. He tugged at Levi's shirt and demanded, "When? Tomorrow? Saturday? Sunday?"

Levi considered the amount of work remaining. He could have it done by Saturday, but wouldn't it be better to wait until Sunday? The Lord's day, when they would gather for worship. He'd go in his best suit, meet her in the churchyard with his gift in his hands. Then after he'd made his intentions known and she'd accepted — she would accept, wouldn't she? — they'd enter the church together for worship.

Anticipating the moment gave him tremors.

"Mr. Jonnson!" Tommy's patience had worn out.

Levi laughed and pulled Tommy backward against his hip in a mock wrestling hold. "I hear you, I hear you. You can show her Sunday, all right? Now, scoot over there" — he landed a light pat on the boy's backside — "and clean up your mess. Can't leave those little pieces of reed all over my nice clean floor."

Laughing, Tommy returned to his corner of the mill, dropped to his knees, and did as Levi had requested. Levi turned back to his own work. He touched the partially completed rose, and his chest expanded. Sunday . . . Three more days. He hoped his heart could wait that long.

Saturday morning, as Christina stood at the washstand in her hotel room fastening her hair into its usual twist, a light tap sounded on the door. At once hope rose in her chest — could it be Levi and Tommy? She'd missed them terribly these past days. Jamming the last tortoiseshell comb into place, she scurried to the door and opened it. Her hopes immediately plummeted. Ben stood in the hallway, his hands locked behind his back and a bright smile on his narrow face.

He took one look at her, and his smile drooped. "You look as though you lost your best friend."

He had no idea how astute he was. She sighed. "I'm terribly sorry. I was expecting someone else."

"Ah." Ben nodded, his expression wise. "Well, perhaps the next visitor will be the one to put the sparkle in your eyes again. In the meantime" — he withdrew one hand from behind his back and held out a long, thick envelope — "this can keep you company."

The promised letter . . . Christina took it, curiosity rising. Although she'd repeatedly asked Ben what business Mr. Dunnigan needed to complete with her, he'd remained aggravatingly vague. She fingered it, eager to tear it open. "Are you to read it with me?"

He held up both hands, his smile wide. "My work here is done. As a matter of fact," — he pulled a watch from his pocket and clicked open the case — "my train will leave in less than thirty minutes. So now is when I tell you good-bye, Miss Christina Willems." He captured her hand, slipping something into her palm as he leaned forward and kissed her knuckles. He straightened and offered a teasing wink. "Serving you has been a distinct pleasure. I wish you much success in your future endeavors." Then without offering her a chance to reply, he released her hand, turned, and briskly strode to the stairway.

Christina turned her hand over, and joy

exploded in a gasp. Papa's watch! He'd regained it for her! She hugged it to her chest, its steady *tick, tick* matching the tempo of her heartbeat. She closed her eyes, savoring the wonder of reunion. Then, wanting to offer a thank-you, she scampered after Ben. But she'd waited too long. His long legs had already carried him away. Slowly she returned to her room, cradling the watch in one palm and holding the letter in the other.

Settling herself on the foot of the bed, she returned Papa's watch to its chain and hung it around her neck. Its weight rested comfortably against her bodice. She closed her eyes for a moment, savoring the reunion, and then finally slipped her finger beneath the flap of the envelope. She removed the contents and unfolded the letter. A single thin slip of paper slid from her grip and landed, facedown, on the floor. She'd retrieve it later. The typewritten words on the pages in her hand begged her attention.

Dear Miss Willems,
By now you must realize the poor farm house, outbuildings, and surrounding land have a new owner, namely myself. You must also wonder why I would go to such lengths to procure such a prop-

erty and keep it secret. Well, now is the time for my secrets to be unveiled, and I trust when you have completed the reading of this missive, you will forgive me for my rather clandestine arrangements.

You see, Miss Willems, although I enjoy wealth and the honor of high society, that was not always the case. My early life was quite dismal, being born to a woman in very poor health and to a man who was a common laborer. When I was but a toddler, my mother passed away, and my father could not care for me. So I was given over to an orphanage. Being very young and charmingly handsome (so I was told),

Christina giggled aloud. What a proclamation!

I was adopted fairly quickly by the Dunnigan family, who, although already parenting two children of their own, never treated me as an outsider. I was quite loved, and upon the death of my adoptive father, I received an equal inheritance.

Just as your parents impressed upon you the importance of benevolence, I was raised with the same expectation.

My father's most oft-quoted admonition was "To whom much is given, much is expected." Therefore, I have sought to honor him by sharing my wealth. For years I've harbored a very personal desire to do something specifically for children who are left without the tender care of parents. The crossing of our pathways finally allowed me the opportunity to see my long-held aspiration to completion.

In speaking with the director of the mission board, Mr. Regehr, I realized the property would be dispensed with. Thus, knowing you would be displaced regardless of who purchased it, I chose to act hastily and secure it not only for me but for you as well. Have I completely befuddled you by now, Miss Willems?

A smile pulled at her lips, and she shook her head, imagining the man's impish smirk as he tapped out the question. Bending back over the page, she continued reading.

The house will no longer serve as a poor farm but as a refuge for orphaned children. I would like to make available to you the position of headmistress if you're so inclined to accept it. If not, I shall proceed with securing another able woman or perhaps a couple to assume leadership. (Initially, I assumed you would leap at this opportunity, but I have since learned from Ben Edgar that perhaps another opportunity, one involving matrimony, might be forthcoming.)

Christina slapped the pages to her chest, heat filling her face. Why had Ben told Mr. Dunnigan such a preposterous thing! But then again, was it preposterous? Oh, how her heart yearned to hear words of love from Levi's lips. But she couldn't dwell on unrequited longings. This offer of Mr. Dunnigan's was solid, tapped in black ink on white parchment. She'd received nothing remotely close to a promise from Levi.

Pushing aside the melancholy wiggling its way through her middle, she opened the letter once more and read it through to the end.

And so, Miss Willems, when the work is completed and I have a staff available, the doors will be opened to the Dunnigan Orphans' Asylum. I pray you understand now my interest in the house and my need to keep quiet my dealings until all was approved. I have taken the liberty of enclosing a money order in the sum of fifty dollars to serve as your first month's salary as headmistress.

Stunned, Christina lifted the piece of paper from the floor. Just as Mr. Dunnigan had indicated, it was a money order made out in her name. Fifty dollars! He would pay her this amount each month? She'd never dreamed of receiving such an extravagant salary. She lay the money order on the bed and returned to the letter.

Should you choose not to take the position, please accept the money as a token of my appreciation for your wonderful care of my dear son and daughter and use it to fund your new beginning.
I remain your faithful servant,
Mr. Maxwell Dunnigan

Below his flamboyant signature, a postscript written in bold and somewhat sloppy penmanship filled the bottom of the page.

P.S. I have taken yet one more liberty and inquired of the Kansas City School for the Blind about an availability for Tommy. They assure me they can enroll him for the coming year. It would delight me to cover his expenses there, should you decide to have him attend. I believe the school would do an excellent job of teaching him the greatest level of independence. When you reply concerning the position as headmistress, you may tell me your desire concerning Tommy's education.

Such a giving man was Mr. Maxwell Dunnigan. He'd certainly taken his father's admonition to heart. Christina reeled, considering everything he'd done thus far and all he wanted to do. He'd made fine offers, and accepting them would ensure a home for her and a bright future for Tommy. What should she do?

In response to her inner pondering, she recalled her father's sage counsel. She slipped to her knees beside the bed, folded her hands, closed her eyes, and petitioned her heavenly Father for guidance.

Chapter 46

The church bell beckoned Christina as she walked toward the building for morning service. Already people milled in the yard, putting their heads together and visiting while waiting to go inside. In past weeks their chatter had held notes of condemnation and distrust. Her feet slowed in their brisk pace, the memory of the hurt inflicted by her fellow townsmen rising up to torment her. Should she escape back to the hotel? But the peace she'd discovered yesterday evening during prayer crept over her once more, offering strength. She had no reason to hide. No matter what others chose to do, she would worship the God who had welcomed her back into fellowship.

Her chin high, she clutched her Bible in the crook of her arm and marched forward, nodding a greeting to any who turned her way. When she reached the stone pathway leading to the church's porch, a subtle hush fell across the waiting folks. All heads turned in one direction. A few dropped their jaws in surprise. She came to a halt, unease sending a prickle across her scalp. But they weren't gaping at her.

Curious, Christina looked in the same direction, and her heart leaped like a nimble deer. Levi Jonnson, his tawny blond hair combed back from his forehead in a smooth sweep, set the brake on his wagon. He stood, revealing his attire, and Christina was captured by the sight. Without deliberate thought she examined him by increments, beginning with the dark trousers, which set off his long, muscular thighs. A dove-gray jacket fit his torso the way skin fit a potato and emphasized the breadth of his shoulders. Beneath his clean-shaven chin, a black floppy bow tie nestled within the folds of his crisp white collar.

Her limbs went weak. This cultured, handsome gentleman? *This* was Levi?

But then she received a glimpse of the mill owner as he placed his hand on the edge of the seat and gave a lithe leap that brought the soles of his polished black boots to the ground. He glanced down his length, swatting at his legs to dispel dust, and when he raised his head again, his gaze met hers. A soft smile formed on his handsome face.

Looking upon his perfect appearance, she became aware of a strand of hair tugged loose by the Kansas breeze. She lifted her hand and fussily pushed the waving lock behind her ear. His eyes seemed to follow her gesture, and a knowing expression crept across his face. Was he thinking of their time on the swing when he'd tucked her hair into place?

She'd never been as aware of another person as she was of Levi Jonnson in that moment. Everything else — the townspeople, the endless wind releasing her hair from its spot once more, even the resounding toll of the church bell — faded away until it seemed all that existed in the world was Levi and her. What was happening to her?

Levi suddenly turned and strode to the back of the wagon. Christina tipped her head in his direction, unwilling to lose sight of him. He reached into its bed, the fabric of his suit jacket going taut across his back, and he lifted something out — something rectangular, wooden, and richly stained. Then he turned toward her, cradling in his wide hands a beautifully crafted box with carved feet resembling an eagle's claws.

New murmurs broke out behind her,

reminding her of the presence of the parishioners, but she kept her gaze riveted on Levi. He walked slowly toward her, dust rising with each step. She wanted to move forward, to meet him partway, but her quivering legs seemed incapable of carrying her. So she stood still on the boardwalk, her breath releasing in tiny puffs and her chest rising and falling with such quickening she feared she might swoon.

He stepped onto the boardwalk and stopped directly in front of her. His eyes glittered, the gold and green flecks prominent in his irises of blue. Not a word left his lips, but his eyes spoke volumes. Christina became lost in the sweet message flowing from his fervent gaze. His arms lifted slowly, holding the box toward her, and his chin gave a subtle bob, as if inviting her to see what he held.

She accepted the silent invitation. Carving decorated the top of the box — delicate swirls and intricate roses. And in the center, carefully formed letters proclaimed a scripture from the Song of Solomon.

> Rise up, my love, my fair one,
> and come away.
> For, lo, the winter is past.

Her hand flew upward, her fingertips covering her trembling lips. Her gaze bounced from the beautiful carving to Levi's handsome face. In a voice so tender it raised a rush of tears in her eyes, he said, "Christina, I love you. I've moved beyond the bitter cold and am ready for a new beginning. Will you partner with me in a fresh start? Will you become my wife?"

Christina drew in a deep breath, basking in the wonder of the moment — of this man declaring his love to her. She opened her mouth, words of acceptance on her tongue, when Tommy suddenly sat up in the wagon bed and grabbed the tall side.

"Hurry up an' answer, Miss Willems, 'cause I got somethin' to show you, too!"

Laughter exploded behind Christina — loud and intrusive. And she couldn't resist joining in. Levi's grin spread across his face, and then he tucked the box under one arm and swept her into a hug with the other, lifting her onto her toes. Her arms around his neck, she exclaimed in his ear, "Yes! Yes, Levi! Yes!"

And finally his lips found hers, the kiss firm and warm and possessive. Christina never wanted it to end, but fortunately Levi exhibited greater restraint. He lowered her feet to the boardwalk, his arm remaining loosely around her waist, and brushed a kiss across her forehead. Nose to nose, he whispered, "You'd better go see what Tommy has, and then we need to head inside before Reverend Huntley thinks the entire town has deserted him."

September 1890

Christina leaned her temple against Levi's shoulder. The porch-swing chains creaked softly, adding harmony to the gentle whisper of wind through the thick bushes growing alongside the porch. The remnants of their celebration — strips of colorful crepe paper, flower petals, and food scraps — decorated the still-green yard. She supposed they should clean it all up up before night fell, but reluctance to leave her cozy spot at her husband's side kept her curled on the swing.

Levi's chest rose, and his breath whisked out on a sigh. She shifted her head slightly to peer into his face. Pure contentment showed in the slight upturning of his lips and lazy droop of his eyelids. She raised up and placed a kiss on the underside of his jaw just because she could. Her *husband . . .* Was there any sweeter word?

He tightened his arm around her shoulders as the breeze picked up. "Reverend Huntley did a fine job today."

She nodded although she couldn't recall a thing the man had said except, *"I now declare you husband and wife."*

"Mary Ann and Louisa outdid themselves with that feast." He slapped his belly. "I've never seen so much food."

Had there been food? She'd been so busy feasting her eyes on the man to whom she'd pledged her life all hunger had fled.

"And that little one of Cora's . . . Cutest baby ever, I'd wager."

Two-month-old Mary Christina was beautiful, she concurred as she nestled her cheek into the curve of Levi's neck. But she expected their own baby, should the Lord bless them someday, would outshine any other.

"It sure was good of the Dunnigans to come." Levi stroked Christina's upper arm through her lace sleeve. The warmth of his broad palm raised tremors of awareness from her scalp to her toes. "But don't you think Rose did an awful lot of crying for someone who was supposed to be happy for us?"

Christina gave a start. "Did Rose cry?"

His eyebrows shot skyward. "She cried through the whole ceremony."

"She did?"

"Yes."

"Oh." Christina brought up her legs and tucked her slipper-covered heels against the edge of the seat. "I suppose I didn't notice."

Levi chuckled, his belly vibrating against her side. "She probably didn't cry as much as you will tomorrow, though, when it's time to tell Tommy good-bye."

"I won't be the only one crying," she predicted.

"You're probably right," Levi said.

As difficult as it would be for both of them to send Tommy to Kansas City tomorrow with the Dunnigans, they knew they'd made the right choice. Tommy was far too bright to be denied the best education available, and he'd receive it at the Kansas City School for the Blind. Christina marveled anew at Mr. Dunnigan's benevolence.

She wriggled more securely into Levi's embrace as a night owl called from a distant tree and shadows lengthened across the ground. They fell into a peaceful silence, enjoying the quiet after the boisterous afternoon. Christina appreciated the support of the town, coming out to the poor farm — the Dunnigan Orphans' Asylum, she corrected herself — to celebrate Levi's and her nuptials. Within weeks the rooms would begin to fill with children in need of care. Private, quiet moments like this would become a thing of the past.

She allowed her eyes to close. She breathed in, enjoying the scents of her wedding day. Musky earth, crisp breeze, a hint of wood smoke from the bonfire where they'd danced to Tommy's harmonica. And, best of all, the woodsy, rich smell that clung to Levi's skin. Even though he'd sold his mill, he continued to carry the scents of pine and cedar and oak. His woodworking tools waited in the barn, along with a supply of cut lumber, which he would use to craft one-of-a-kind pieces of furniture, just as Far had done before him.

At first she'd resisted his decision to let the mill go, but then, in prayer, God had reminded her of the significance of his choice. No more would he hold himself away from others, living in solitude, but he would willingly share his life with fatherless children. Such a change God had wrought in Levi's heart . . .

"Christina?"

She sighed. How she loved the sound of her name uttered in his deep, tender tone. "Yes?"

His arms slipped around her middle, his chin against her cheek. "Are you ready to turn in?"

So many bits and pieces of her day had

already slipped away, but Christina knew she'd never forget the coming minutes — when she and Levi would join in the most intimate of ways. The words Levi had carved into the handcrafted cedar box whispered through her heart.

She stood and held her hands to him. She quoted, her voice husky, " 'Rise up, my love, my fair one, and come away.' "

He took her hands, a tender smile blooming across his face. He rose, his shadow stretching across the porch floor to encompass hers. And then, hand in hand, they entered the house together.

ACKNOWLEDGMENTS

Mom and Daddy, when you took out a loan to fund the printing of my first book in 2002, did you have any idea I'd one day celebrate the release of my thirtieth novel? You probably did, because you've always believed in me more than I believed in myself. Thank you for your confidence. I love you both muchly.

Don, bless your heart, you take on so much responsibility to allow me the time to write. Thanks for cleaning, cooking, doing laundry, and giving your military-brand encouragement: "Get in there and write!"

Jay and Mary Creeger, your names fit perfectly in this story of new beginnings. God bless you both as you continue to journey with Him.

FSBC choir members, your prayers and support are so important. Thank you for willingly offering both just when I need it.

CritGroup14, what would I do without you

ladies? I would flounder. Thanks for always being there.

Tamela, I appreciate you as an agent, but more than that I appreciate you as an advocate of Christian fiction. Thank you for being such an integral part of my writing ministry.

Shannon and the wonderful team at Water-Brook, it's been a delight to become acquainted with my new publishing family. Thank you for making me feel so at home.

Finally, and most important, abundant gratitude to *God* for Your gentle guidance, Your ever-presence, and for carving new pathways when my road seems to reach a dead end. You complete me. May any praise or glory be reflected directly back to You.

DISCUSSION QUESTIONS

1. For years Christina found her sense of worth and purpose in taking care of the residents of the Brambleville Asylum for the Poor. When the house burned and her people were scattered, she lost not only her home and companions but her own feelings of value. Has your sense of worth ever been shattered? How did you rebuild it?

2. Levi turned his back on faith when people who claimed to be Christians hurt him. Do we have higher expectations for those who proclaim Christ as Lord? Is it fair for us to judge Christians and non-Christians differently? If so, why? If not, why not?

3. Levi chose to handle his hurt by separating himself from others rather than risking being hurt again. When someone you

trust hurts you, how can you resolve the situation without suffering a rift in the relationship?

4. Cora was raised by someone who was emotionally distant; therefore, when she was offered affection, she found the attention so gratifying she allowed it to go beyond what was appropriate. By what yardstick can we measure friendship so that the people we choose as companions build us up rather than break us down? If you are a parent, what are you doing to make sure your children are loved and accepted so they won't feel the need to search for affection from others who might not have their best interests at heart?

5. Christina experienced frustration, confusion, and anger when Tommy preferred Levi's caretaking to her own. How did Tommy grow and change when Levi expected him to take on responsibility for himself? Was Levi kind or unkind to put such high expectations on a boy who couldn't see? How can we determine what are fair expectations for the people with disabilities in our lives?

6. Christina was accused of a crime because

of circumstantial situations. She was reluctant to accuse Hamilton Dresden, despite her suppositions, because she knew how it felt to be wrongfully accused. Have you ever been falsely accused? Did you seek to exonerate yourself or allow time to expose the truth? Which path is more biblical, if either?

7. Christina, Levi, Cora, and Tommy were all impacted by people in their pasts. The things they heard from those they loved continued to influence their present lives. Some of those influences were positive, and others were negative. Who are the people in your life that have influenced you? Has their impact been more positive or negative? How do we overcome the negative voices that live in our heads? How do we apply the positive ones?

8. Maxwell Dunnigan honored his adopted father's kindness by "paying it forward." What kindnesses have you received that you could share with others?

ABOUT THE AUTHOR

Kim Vogel Sawyer is a best-selling author highly acclaimed for her gentle stories of hope. More than one million copies of her books are currently in print with awards including the ACFW Carol Award, the Inspirational Readers Choice Award, and the Gayle Wilson Award of Excellence. Kim lives in central Kansas, where she and her retired military husband, Don, run a bed-and-breakfast inn with the help of their feline companions. She savors time with her daughters and grandchildren.